THE DEBT COLLECTOR

RACHEL ANN HUBERT

To everyone who has ever had to set the things they enjoy on the back burner
in the name of necessity:

It's time to do the things that make you happy again.

And to Morgan. For everything.

CHAPTER 1

Evening had fallen, and I was already running late. I hurried past a mess of ivy-covered stone shops, their windows boarded up with roughly cut black wood from the forest to the east. I followed a path that seemed to narrow as I drew further in, carefully hurrying as I darted down a slope in the road that took me deeper into the city.

I glanced at my wrist and winced when I saw the flashing red coordinates. Not much further now.

I hung a left and slowed, scanning the empty alley. The smell of garbage littering the streets reached my nose. *Rotten food...* It smelled of decay and mold, and my stomach churned at the recognition. Those who lived this far into Thiar could afford such surplus that waste was commonplace. Expected. They, of course, rarely ventured out of the precious safety their prosperous city provided. And few of them knew the risk an empty stomach posed.

I drew my hood further down and sucked in the evening air. The homes were tightly packed, making it hard to determine where one ended and another began. Carefully, quietly, I peered at the markings beside each street-facing window. Etched symbols denoted to whom each belonged. Step by step, I slithered further in to the shadows, eyes scanning until they landed on the three interlaced R's denoting the residence of one of the old textile merchants. If only they know that his hands were dirtied by far *more* than fabric dyes.

I stared at the window, silently cursing the absence of any doors. I looked around for a way in and dipped around into the narrow passageway between home blocks. I slid in sideways and inched further as the walls hugged my front and back. The walls felt vaguely moist and the bricks were uneven, creating scattered pressure along my spine.

I slipped my hand into my chest pocket and pulled out a ball of tangled wires.

"Mion," I whispered. "Mi, find door." The metal contraption slowly unraveled itself. Wire legs sprung forth and raised metal prongs stared back at me in confirmation.

My steel companion skittered out and darted onto the walls, moving in a zigzag pattern away from me, using its hands and feet to tap along the stone as it went. I hadn't been too far off. It stopped a few meters in front of me before darting straight up. It climbed to what must have been the third level of homes, then set its body flush against the block. I peered at the path there, grimacing at the sleek, glistening edge of the towering infrastructure.

Why is it never the ground floor...

I withheld a sigh and wiggled my way deeper into the opening. There wasn't enough room to reach down into my boots for the sticky scaffolding gear I usually used in situations like these. Leaning back, I leveraged my weight against the hard rock and drew up my knees one by one, pressing their caps sturdily in front of me. Decently wedged, I continued, moving my back and then my knees as I made my way higher.

When I made it to where Mion was waiting, I clicked my tongue, and the wired body lifted itself, scurried down my arm, and nestled back into my pocket.

My palms scanned the stone. Nudging it gently, I felt a familiar static in the air trace up my fingertips. I closed my eyes and *demanded* it open. Wind encircled me, and beneath my shut eyelids, I saw a shimmery blue line leading me through the darkness. I mentally grabbed on and felt my body go weightless.

I landed in the home's doorway with careful precision, expecting the uncomfortable landing. Instinct coupled with expertise carried my path from there.

The home was modestly sized, but well adorned. Even in the night, I could see the soft glimmering of paintings in golden frames and taste the lingering spices in the air. Rosemary, thyme, garlic. My stomach growled, growing impatient.

There was only one bedroom in the home, and I followed the hallway to the back of the residence, where I knew I'd find it. When my alert had gone off a few hours ago, and a few towns away, I knew I'd find him alone. Everyone in Thiar lived alone.

I stepped into his room and saw the outline of a large man beneath strained satin sheets. His bed was suspended by four wooden beams that seemed to cave inward at the effort to keep it hovered above the floor. You could have mistaken his stillness for slumber. But I had smelled the subtle saturation of death the moment I stepped into his home.

When I reached the bed, I peered down at the full, rounded cheeks of a man resourceful enough to have made it to his late sixties, hair grayed and face stubbled. I had underestimated his size from the doorway—this was a *massive* man, stomach protruding from years of overindulgence. I snatched my bag hanging beside my hip and set it on the bed beside him. I pulled out a cork-topped vial, syringe, and delicately curved knife.

Angling the tip down, I carved my incision at the base of his throat where crumbs had gathered in the folds of his flesh. A tiny scarlet X oozed out. I wiped the blade on the pillow and set it aside. As I reached for my syringe, my right arm recoiled at the rekindled burning sensation emanating from the coordinates still risen on my skin. The pigments shifted, at first dissipating altogether and then congregating to form the numbers of a timer—a timer which had evidently run out.

Three zeros stared back at me.

*I know...*I growled.

Steadying my hand, I grabbed the syringe and plunged the full needle length into my neatly drawn X. As I drew out the translucent liquid threads, I popped open the spare vial. The syringe quickly filled with speckled silver. With its contents now filled as I withdrew it, I could feel my wrist respond in acknowledgment, and the stinging sensation subsided.

I deposited the contents of the syringe into my vial and corked it. A deep exhale escaped my lips, and I finally felt the room-filling silence around me. I *hated* silence, and was thankful for the clattering of glass in my pouch as I added this vial to the others neatly tucked away in the folded fabric I kept at the very bottom of the bag.

And this one makes three.

I threw the rest of my tools lazily back in, slinging the bag back over my shoulder. I stole one last look at the man. Arms and legs splayed. His eyes wide and glassy. Cloudiness eclipsed his irises. He almost looked shocked, as if some part of him knew that this would not be his eternal slumber.

Not yet.

I retraced my steps back to the entrance, making careful note of the objects that would be taken as soon as word spread that the once great Rafford of Thiar had passed. Ornate candlesticks, silver serving platters, gemmed goblets. This place would be picked clean. I wondered for a moment why he hadn't just sold these petty belongings to pay off his debts, why he had hoarded his wealth at such a steep cost. But my wonder was short-lived as I departed through the hidden door once more.

Outside, I appeared in the same scrunched-up position I had been prior, pressed against the stone. I lowered myself softly and darted back into the open.

A relentlessness grumble emanated from my core—it was high time for food.

I retraced my path out of the city. I trudged along on foot, the glimmering of the stars returning more and more as I departed. The path was well worn, flattened from years of passersby's making their way around for trade. There was a time, I'd been told, when these roads were better kept, and it was commonplace to travel from one town to the next. But now, most remained in the towns they were born, never bothering to venture out into the unknown. And who could blame them...

There were still reminders of the old ways if you bothered to look. Tiny spells for protection, good luck charms for bartering, or the glamoured entrance like that at Rafford's. But such things never held my attention. Most, like the glamoured door, were merely for show and awe, a status symbol, not a resource.

Regardless of preference, I had to be flexible, and I wasn't about to walk the several days' long trip to the tavern in Osta when the Crann, a series of teleportation gates, was less than an hour outside the city. The Crann still functioned through a web of ancient magic that connected the north, south, and western lands for fast transport. The eastern Crann port had burned down decades ago, and it remained that way—a rumored useless, unmoving pile of ash. And a reminder of the wilder side of magic.

Off the path up ahead was an enormous birch tree, the white reflecting the moonlight gently cascading down through the darkness. Several branches wider than my torso sprouted from its core in every direction. As I approached, I felt the crisp stillness in the air surrounding it. The smell of wintergreen filled my nose.

I set my fingertips on the curled, peeling bark, traced the carved four-pronged clover on its trunk. I clutched my bag, whispered my desired destination, and felt myself slip apart into pieces. My stomach lurched—I never could quite get used to the sensation—but as soon as I felt it, it was gone, and I was already pieced back together at what looked like an identical tree, but one far away from where the trip began.

Home.

Or at least as much of a home as I had come to know lately. A disheveled tavern faced me, surrounded by green forestry so vibrant you could still make it out in the shadows of night. Though I never tired of taking in its familiar beauty, my nagging stomach reminded me it was time for a well-overdue meal.

Though Osta used to refer to an entire village, what remained was mostly abandoned homes and trees, so as its sole standing remnant, the tavern wore its name.

I finally removed my hood as I walked through its door. I perked up at the sight of packed tables and a crowded bar. For most, night meant calm—a time for peace and slumber. But for others such as myself, making our livings through messy, less *savory* means, meant time for ale and gauche humor.

"Ah," followed by a raspy cough, "successful night?" The innkeeper was a short, plump woman who everyone called Mel. Mel was ringing a towel through her hands, hunched over a recently vacated table, wiping up what appeared to be spilled ale without so much as a turn of her head.

"It was a night." I reached into my other chest pocket, not the one with my little friend, and pulled out a silver piece. "Ale, and whatever you have today."

She glanced sideways. She snatched the silver from my hand and walked back toward the bar at the other corner of the room. As she poured my drink, I sat down at an empty booth and slouched against the wall.

There were all types of folks out tonight. Some stuck to themselves—as I intended to—while others told grossly exaggerated tales of conquest to those naïve enough to listen, and others still, caught up with old friends or acquaintances as their paths happened to cross at the tavern. Two heavyset men sat opposite of me across the room, laughing so loud and violently that their oversized knees kept slamming against the underside of their table as their bodies roared.

Mel approached, mug in one hand and a steaming bowl in the other. She sat them both down and turned away. She wasn't much for small talk. *Thank goodness.*

"And for another night's stay." I revealed a gold from my palm, setting it at the edge of the table while I greedily pulled the food and drink closer.

Calloused, aged hands took the gold. She nodded and returned to cleaning up the table she was previously at, which would no doubt still be sticky when she was done. Osta was a place where everything had a fine film of tackiness to it. Boots clung to the wood as you walked.

I didn't know what was the in the stew. But I didn't care. It was hot, and my core ached something terrible. Spoonful after spoonful, I ladled the mostly salty broth into my mouth. The occasional vegetable would fill up my stomach and get me through to tomorrow. And that was the way it was now—make it to tomorrow. There wasn't need to plan beyond that.

As my body warmed and the familiar bitterness of the ale touched my lips, I felt the heaviness of my weatherworn coat weigh down upon my shoulders. I slipped out of the layered leather, casting it beside me and kicking my muddy boots onto the seat in front of me.

Night after night, I found myself here, rarely paying for more than a couple at a time. It was always a mix of vaguely familiar and unfamiliar faces.

The face that slipped through the door was one I had not seen before.

A man in old, tattered Sheirsan regalia made his way clunkily to a vacant spot. His hair was rustled and dark, and a scar trailed from his bottom lip down beneath his chin, its puckered pink peeking through his beard. His eyes didn't seem to notice mine as he ordered two drinks in a hush and sat. I hadn't seen Sheirsan fighters in here in a long time. And the last time I did, they were rowdy.

As if on cue, a lanky, straggly older man who often frequented the bar joined him, appearing seemingly out of nowhere. They called the regular Echo, as he often repeated stories told him as his own to unknowing passers-by.

Amusing as it was to see the juxtaposition in demeanor between the small hungry eyes of Echo and the steadiness of the soldier, I tried to keep my gaze to myself. I had finished the soup much too quickly and stared at the bottom of the bowl. When I looked up, a young boy was sitting my opposite.

"Caydin." He smiled.

"Busy." I didn't have the energy for conversation, regardless of my curiosity as to why a boy his age would be in a tavern of this sort. He must have been around eleven or twelve, wispy blond hair hung over his face and periodically blocked his eyes. His face was full, healthy, and slightly flushed.

"What brings you in here?" he persisted, sitting down at the table.

My eyes narrowed. "You shouldn't speak to strangers." I could feel the slowly rising soreness in my back and legs from my maneuvering earlier. Tired joints craved an early evening to lay down and rest.

He frowned, just shy of a pout. Not to be discouraged, he changed the subject and continued, "I came in from the city just north of here. I took the main path, the one lined by juniper trees. I'm told the berries are most delicious in the spring."

I took a long drink and set the mug down roughly. I kept my left hand on my bag as he spoke. Strangers rarely brought good tidings.

Roaring laughter kept booming and distracting most of the patrons around me, but I felt unease creep along my skin. I glanced to my side and met the stranger's eyes as he paused mid-word. He held my stare for a breath and returned his focus to the man his opposite. He'd do better than to talk to the town gossip.

I realized the boy had gone silent, staring at me patiently.

"Hmm?" He waited. Had he asked me another question? Was I distracted that long? "Have you tried the juniper berries or not? I'd kill for a juniper berry pie or a—"

"This," I hissed, "is not the place for someone like you. Go home."

His eyes flickered for a moment—a trick of the light, maybe? The tan of his eyes seemed to darken, tinged a deepened shade of gold. His pupils...his pupils did something...I blinked away the thought. I needed sleep, not small talk.

"Oh?" He smiled, childish like before, but also...different. There was a sharpness added to his features. There was shadow cast from his eyes. "And what do you know about someone like *me*?"

I felt the air chill around me. I went to answer as I noticed that Echo now stood between our tables, pointing and shouting as he gave his own personal introductions. *This is what happens when you're distracted.* Staring at Echo provided me an extended peek at the stranger with him. He carried no weapons that I could see, which made determining his occupation or intent more difficult.

The hum of drunk women whispered in the back as they flirted, batting their eyelashes at wealthy fools looking to trade drinks for companionship.

The sound of muddy boots walked in and out of halls and between tables. More ale was sloshed as it was poured. And those dammed men were still laughing.

I had had about enough being around people for the night.

"And *this* one," Echo rolled his eyes, "I wouldn't bother with this one." He tossed his head in my direction and let out a nasally laugh.

It was then I noticed the hilt of a sword over his left shoulder. I could see the slightest bulge beneath his heavy, wool-coated cloak as he pivoted toward me. Sheirsa insignia, the upside-down stacked crescent moons, tattooed on the backs of his hands. There was no doubt that he had not only served the previous ruling family in some capacity, but that he had also held high rank. Though his towering size didn't concern me much, his probable fighting experience did.

I looked around for Mel. She stood with her back turned, ladling out more servings of soup. Or broth, more fittingly.

"I was just—" I faced forward again, but the boy was gone. I quickly searched the tavern but couldn't find his short, ruffled head, "—leaving..."

As I stood, so did the stranger. He stood several heads over me, shoulders broad and outfitted head to toe in black. We held each other's gaze and my hand drifted to the blade concealed at my hip. His eyes reminded me of the forestry I had walked through earlier, deep green, shaded in darkness.

"You won't stay a while?" He raised an eyebrow, slightly grinning as he fidgeted with one of the gold rings on his finger.

My face held no amusement, no kindness. Heaviness lingered on my eyelids, silently reminding me of my exhaustion.

I could feel his stare as I ignored his question and strolled past to the tucked-away steps at the back corner. I didn't look back as I turned and started up the stairs to my room.

For all its liveliness on the main floor, the rest of the tavern hardly suggested lodging. But I guessed that was almost certainly deliberate. I couldn't imagine cleaning up after scoundrels and thieves all night *and* day.

I reached the same room I had been staying in prior, down a hallway of identical unnumbered wooden doors. Each doorway was peppered with aged, chipped red paint. It seemed appropriate that the speckles always reminded me of dried blood.

I entered my room and peeked over my shoulder as I shut the door. Even once shut, I paused, resting my ear against its surface.

Nothing. Silence.

It wasn't a guarantee I wouldn't be followed, but it did allow me a moment to snatch the extra lock from my bag. I latched the metal chain already screwed into the wall beside the door, the thin metal feigning as sufficient security, but added my own larger one down near the handle. I had picked up the contraption in Alaria, using it religiously ever since. I wiggled the thin metal end into the sliver where the door clicked into its hatch, jamming it in snugly, so if opened, it would catch the door long enough to buy me some time.

The room didn't have any light. No windows. It only had a bed, which was plenty to be grateful for.

I fell asleep before I even remembered my head hitting the pillow.

My body tossed and turned in the darkness—felt encased by it. The heaviness of it felt like a wool blanket.

Tap... Tap...

My eyes stayed shut, but my senses heightened as I slipped seamlessly further out of my slumber.

A single additional *tap* resonated from outside my room. I could place its origin, but heard nothing else. I stayed perfectly still, listening. No footsteps, no breathing...I waited.

And waited.

Sleep begged me back, pulled at the edges of my tired mind.

And soon, I yielded.

CHAPTER 2

There was no sense of morning, no birds chirping or fingers of sunlight. I groaned out from beneath a single thin blanket. I knew it was time to leave.

Get. Up.

I did as I commanded, flinging my legs around to the edge of the bed, sheathed dagger still in my right hand. My breath caught as I remembered being stirred from my sleep last night. A game? A drunken joke? ...Idiots regardless. My eyes hardened, and I pulled out my bag from beside my pillow.

It was velvet, the opening pulled tightly shut by two drawstrings. Silver stitching swirled in repeated patterns over the plum felt. I tugged on the strings and checked to make sure all my belongings remained.

Three sparkling vials, wrapped up carefully between protective fabric. The cloth prevented them from clanking around too much as I walked, but it also covered their contents. I hated looking at them. A pit of unease would gather in my throat whenever I'd stare too long. The liquid sloshed around slowly, densely, collapsing again and again on top of itself. Like a sea of silver starlight, their waves intricately weaving despite the minimal vial space.

I always returned once I had three to turn in. My assignments would pause until they were delivered.

I shut the bag, stood up, and left the room. I didn't have much, spare my bag and belt, so departing was brief. As I made my way back down the stairs,

I took in the morning filth leftover from the evening before. Tables tossed sideways, chairs on their backs, dishes stacked up in the sink in the visible corner kitchen.

The groggy subdued silence stood in stark contrast to the liveliness of last night. I left, not minding ridding my nose of stale ale and sweat.

I couldn't take the Crann into the capital. It lay near the middle of the country, a couple days' trek north from here. Instead, I set out on the designated path, the trail marked by a single wooden beam with a painted moon on its side. I savored the surrounding dense tree cover.

Lush forest broke into a single winding road, endless plains of tall grasses littered both sides. The hum of the blades swayed in the warm air, a gentle song as I journeyed to Alaria.

You could smell the city before you saw it. I knew I was close when the wind carried the delicate earthy smell of the fields of chrysanthemums to me. It wasn't as sweet as the lily, or as floral as the rose, but it was elegant, and it was strong.

Family farms could be seen periodically on the horizon, but they soon disappeared as the city outskirts made their appearance. Where Thiar was uniform, business-centric, and grayscale, Alaria was chaos.

No two buildings were the same. A spectrum of colors decorated each shop as I neared the center of town. Homes and people alike took it upon themselves to accessorize to their hearts' delight. Women wore extravagant gowns to tight-fitted tunics, and men donned anything from full armor sets to nothing but loose trousers. I passed children in the streets throwing stones without supervision, and individual markets lined each of the internal streets.

It was late springtime. And there was a lightness about spring that got everyone out conversing and spending money.

The sun beamed down, uninterrupted by clouds. I twisted my neck and loosened my coat, feeling painfully out of place amongst the laughter and heat.

I continued. Shop owners and beggars glanced as I kept my focus forward. A few familiar faces would occasionally nod my way, but the rest stayed their distance.

Up ahead, I faced a tall, narrow building decorated in waves of reflective shingles. It was like staring at a million fragments of warped reflections. It was intentionally attention-grabbing. It made you stop when you saw it. It demanded the drop of jaws. These mirrors were often the talk of visitors, while purposely left off the tongues of those who lived here.

I stepped inside, away from the spirited commotion, and was met with an empty lobby. There were uncomfortable wooden benches placed in neat rows, and at the very back of the room was one of several interchangeable receptionists.

She was conventionally lovely. Rose-colored lips, caramel eyes, and hair that was pinned neatly up behind her, not a strand out of place. Her lips turned up in a predictable, rehearsed way.

"Welcome, Adelliah." Her voice was welcoming, but her stare remained lifeless. "Do you have an appointment?

Unamused, I set the pouch on her pedestal of a desk. "No."

She waited. Tilting her head ever so slightly, her painted smile didn't break. "Can I help make you an appointment?"

"You can help me get Nox out here..."

Her brow furrowed. "Without an appointment—"

"I can just wait here." I shrugged, hopping myself up to sit on the front of her desk.

Disgust flickered on her face, but was quickly washed away. Slender fingers flipped through a notepad in front of her, eyes feigning interest as she searched.

"He is completely booked today. If you come back tomorrow morning, I can—"

It was always the same fabricated, front-end professionalism. A neat and tidy mask could convince even the most apprehensive of their seemingly pure intentions.

"*Fine.*"

I snatched my bag back and slung it over my shoulder. A night without work and without somewhere to be...

A devilish grin teased the corners of my lips. I left the building and squinted up at the still high sun. It was uncomfortably warm, and beads of sweat had gathered at the nape of my neck. Eyeing the hub of assorted vendors, I spotted a familiar one just before the cobblestone overpass that separated each district in Alaria.

I approached the clothing shop with its distinctive navy awning. It had doubled in size and inventory since I last saw it...Maybe even tripled. It had to have been years since I was here last. The owner stayed busy talking to potential customers as they strolled by. Her curves were hugged by a deep teal gown, simple but eye-catching, and wrists full of golden bands on both arms.

"By the *gods,*" her friendly freckled face said, jaw dropped, "I haven't seen you in...what...since you were about yay high?" With her dark gray eyes still wide, she popped out her hip and held her hand to her waist.

I snorted despite myself. "It hasn't been *that* long." Rolling my eyes, I met her in a hug.

"I suppose I didn't have as many of these when I saw you last, though either..." She frowned, picking up some of her gray-peppered hair.

We both laughed through our embrace.

And *gods*, did it feel good to laugh.

I suppose she was right, though. I did frequent the city here and there, but my arrivals usually came at night. And by morning, I would be gone. It was easier that way. Fewer questions from the handful of faces I remembered. Because what could I possibly say if one of them asked what I'd been up to? Shame, for a fleeting moment, balled in the back of my throat. But I swallowed it away.

"I—"

She cut me off with a knowing look up and down. "Oh yes, please, you need out of those clothes."

"Something light, please." She had already turned around and rushed to the back of the shop. I wasn't sure she had even heard me, just knew immediately why I had come. Maybe my flushed forehead and reddened cheeks had said enough.

Clothes on hanging rods covered every wall, aisles of assorted gowns and neckties and every accessory you could imagine. She held up a hand from the back—a soft pink dress with frills and sparkles hung limp on a hanger. My face recoiled.

As if she saw, despite her nose being buried in a sea of clothing, she chuckled knowingly.

"*Light,* as in, can be rolled into a ball and stuffed in here when needed." I gestured pointlessly at the bag as she continued to rummage on.

She stuck her face back out, "Rolled into a ball," she looked aghast, "is not how one of my garments will be cared for."

I sighed loud enough for another patron to turn and glare. This may have been a bit more than I was hoping to get myself into. But the sweat between the black leather and my skin told me to stay quiet.

"Ah," triumph in her voice, "I got it." A beckoning hand waved me near the back where a curtain could be pulled across for privacy. "Give it a go."

I did as she said. I unclipped my belt and felt an immediate relief from the heaviness of the defenses it carried. I peeled off my clothes, setting them into a ball in the corner. I prayed she wouldn't look too closely at those. Dirt and stained blood cracked the dark surface.

I pulled the lightweight fabric through my shoulders and over my head and stepped into the airy trousers. Deep violet kissed my collar bones and framed my figure snuggly, but comfortably. I wiggled around slightly to test it. The slacks had slits on the outside of the legs, and the breeze that snuck into the tent tickled through.

"Freyah." I beamed. "This is perfect." I bowed my head in appreciation. I reached for my bag to pull out the remaining coin but she grabbed my wrist before I could.

"Absolutely not." Her voice like honey, she held my hand beside her cheek. It was only then that I noticed the fine lines creasing her forehead. Age, as she said, *was* finally catching up to her. "I know Til' and I couldn't help much back then—"

As she spoke, I pictured it. My young, famished body swam in tattered clothes, dirty bags burrowed beneath my eyes, running around in the street before her storefront.

"—let me at least help now."

Every day during my teenage years, as the sun would start to tuck beneath the horizon, I'd hear her call for Tillian. He'd wave goodbye as he was ushered away for dinner, leaving me alone and hungry, though at no fault of his own.

When Marek had not returned from the Icesone Mountains all those years ago, Freyah had waited. I'd sometimes sit outside beneath her home's one lit window and smell her cooking through the draft. I often envied Tillian, having a mother to dote on him and serve him a warm meal at night. There were times I'd even curse them, angry at all they had while I sat with nothing.

But that kitchen light would stay on far after he went to bed. In fact, I don't think I ever saw it off.

And she would sit at that kitchen table. Alone. Waiting.

I didn't see it then.

But she struggled. Just in a different way than I.

I locked eyes with her and nodded. "Thank you."

"And—" she glanced behind me at the crumpled ball of clothes, "let me wash those for you." It was not an ask. "Where are you staying tonight?"

I paused.

And she knew.

"Til' will be ecstatic when he hears." She winked and went back to the front of the shop where an older couple had drifted in.

She didn't wait for my additional outpouring of gratitude.

I refastened my belt, donned my bag, and decided to walk around the city streets a bit longer before I'd return. I had so long avoided returning during the light of day, fearing meeting the eyes of those who had known me before.

But warmth spread from my chest as I passed by unfamiliar faces far too concerned with their own happenings to so much as glance my way. Warmth, not solely from the sun's concentrated rays.

Rosy clouds wisped along the sky as the daytime drew to an end. Shops closed, and fewer footsteps rhythmically clicked against the brick-lined roads.

I hadn't wandered too far. A few blocks east, in a quieter district known for its music and artists, I had found myself lulled into a trance beneath the shade of the setting sun. It was a struggle not to fall asleep right then and there, rocked into a slumber by the flutes and drums while lying down in a bed of shaggy grass. I wasn't sure why I hadn't visited this courtyard more often when I was young.

I grumbled as I pulled myself up.

The streets had mostly emptied. I made my way down the numbered lanes, half looking at the signs and half letting the memory of the streets guide me. The shadows crept into the paths and darkened the tight corners. Early night air nipped at my exposed arms.

I paused.

My senses tingled, and I waited to hear if footsteps followed. *Nothing.*

A few more steps and I heard it, the awkwardly timed steps trying to move in tempo with my own. I continued, sliding my hand to the hilt of a dagger resting against my hip.

I could feel the clunky attempt at concealment weaken as it drew closer.

I lingered for a hair mid-step and turned around swiftly.

Two of them. I caught my breath as I inhaled. *Fuck.*

Men not much older than I startled back at my notice. I didn't recognize their greasy faces, but I knew from their demeanor and stance that they didn't mean me well. All women knew the look, had that inner voice that warned when men with sinister intentions drew close.

"What's a lovely lady like you doing out on a night like this," tiny beady eyes met mine, "*alone?*"

The shorter of the men spoke as the other slowly made his way around my side. I realized the street we stood in was narrow. And that no one else was around. I swiveled slightly so one of the walls of the adjoining buildings was behind me, preventing them from surrounding me.

He took a step forward, shrinking the space before us.

"Those eyes," he purred, "a man could get lost in eyes like those." I gripped the knife and unsheathed it. He smirked and continued, "I can't say I've ever seen eyes like those before, silver as a winter moon...Have you?" He gestured to his friend, who was now uncomfortably near to my side.

His friend shook his head, lustful eyes wide and mouth agape. His gaze met mine before shamelessly looking me up and down. Revulsion trickled down my throat.

"We only mean to—"

As he spoke, I rushed toward the silent one with the hungry eyes, barreling my blade forward. He leaned back and threw his arms up, his meaty forearm tasting my dagger instead of its intended target.

Using his surprise and unbalance, I darted, shoving my elbow up under his and jabbing again. *Miss.* I needed to land a hit if I was to leave here unscathed. I needed to be *faster.*

He snatched my wrist midair and squeezed, a soft pop escaping as the knife dropped to the ground. I pushed the pain aside and twisted my back around, trying to avoid his other hand. I glided my panicked fingers across my belt, snatching for another dagger and landing it under his bicep.

He released me, and I backed up, inching away, creating as much space as I could between the two and myself.

My back hit a chest. *A third.* My heart sank.

Arms reached forward and trapped me beneath them. This one smelled like rotten fish, his lips grazing the hair on the back of my head. I squirmed and thrashed at this foreign body so close to mine. I looked around, trying to find something to give me an edge or a distraction or a person walking by...He held me tighter, crushing my chest.

The chatty one walked up, laughing to himself as the other pulled my dagger out from his arm. He tossed it to the side as if it were a discarded toothpick and not a bloody blade.

"You won't be needing this, now, will you?" He reached for the weapon still in my hand, wrestling it out from my fingers. He paused.

No.

"Well, what is this?" He flipped my hand over, holding it palm up. I held my breath and cursed every god I could think of as the dilated pupils of recognition bloomed.

His face retracted in horror as he leered at the red smudged tattoo on my arm, still currently showing the timer down to zero. He knew.

Anger erupted over his features. The man holding me squeezed harder but drew his head back from mine as if I was the one to be leery of. As if I was the one who stank of poor decisions and warranted disgust.

"Of all the ways to make a living," he snarled, "you chose *this*?" Men hunting the streets waiting to brutalize unsuspecting women...here, casting judgment...

"I *chose* nothing." Hatred burned and fire danced in my throat.

"Bull*shit.*"

He grabbed the wrist that was already aching and pulled my fingers down, stretching the ligaments further. His clammy hand caged mine, bending it back further and further...

I stifled a scream from behind my teeth.

Movement.

A flash of someone in the distance. I went to call out to them, beg someone to come here, but the back of his hand met the side of my face with a solid *thud.*

He may have been the smallest of the bunch, but he had a surprising amount of force. Or maybe it was the hatred that hardened the back of his hand into a shield. My ears were ringing, and my vision grew hazy. A lightheaded fog settled over me. The world was turning gray. And all I had accomplished was a shallow flesh wound in one of them. I could feel my face redden at the blow and the embarrassment.

Another *thud*.

I tasted the metallic liquid gathering in my mouth.

Everything was a kaleidoscope blur as a shuffle of frenzied movement breezed from somewhere behind me.

The man holding me gasped, and his hold went limp. I immediately slumped onto my hands and knees in dulled shock. A whirlwind of rearranging erupted, the men cussing as I made out their bodies slamming into the walls around us. I tried to steady my breath and closed my eyes, the unevenness of my vision making me nauseous. I heard the pained grunts of the men escalate into screams. It almost drowned out the other noise...the low inhuman gurgle that was now slithering around in my mind as I searched for a logical explanation.

Swollen and pained, I cautiously lifted my eyelids once the world around me went silent, head still throbbing. I could feel my consciousness slipping away.

A pair of deep yellow eyes met mine, thin vertical pupils. I remembered these eyes.

Weightlessly, my mind went black.

CHAPTER 3

I awoke in a panic. Jolting up, I glanced up at the pitch-black sky. There were no stars tonight, only thick, endless clouds preventing the nighttime constellations from making their appearance. The men were nowhere to be seen.

A sigh of relief deflated me as my hand clutched my bag. I hadn't protected it during the altercation. It could have been taken, or violently tossed aside, its fragile contents bursting open...

Stupid.

The entire exchange was pitiful. And while I had spent the last few years in close quarters with dangerous men, most were dead by the time I got to them. I stood, swallowed the self-loathing, and brushed the pebbles and dirt dust off me.

My wrist throbbed. I turned it around a few times, testing it for mobility as shockwaves of pain urged me to stop. I picked up my daggers from the ground and set them back in their place. I hurried back to Freyah's, more embarrassed of the late hour than the bruise settling in beside my eye.

The streets at night appeared almost serene, if only because the garbage and homeless were shadowed away from the light. Almost indistinguishable to Sheirsan guards, if they ever bothered to look. I tried to avoid looking too closely at the occasional sleeping masses as I ran back toward the city center. Street after street, corner lamp after corner lamp. I would have recognized the path with my eyes closed. But it was the nostalgic smell that hit me in the face like a closed door that told me I had arrived. I moaned at the smell of meat, slowed my race to her doorstep, and knocked on the heavy wooden door.

Tillian opened it. Chestnut curls and striking blue eyes. He held a fork with a potato on it from excusing himself mid-dinner. His jaw hung open. He searched my face for a reaction, to gauge how I was feeling after my very apparent confrontation.

Stern eyes said *no*, I did not wish to talk about it. So, he didn't ask, instead opening the door wider to a table set for three.

Freyah looked up from a bite of food and smiled, though concern flashed in her stare. Sheepishly, I sat. They both watched me as I did, wondering the best way to ask...

"Are you—" she tried.

"I'm fine." Another grin. "I promise."

Tillian walked around behind the back of my chair, calculating. He set his hand on my shoulder, and gave it a small squeeze, as if to assess and ensure this was not a dream. I could feel the pain, the flicker of betrayal creasing his face as he surveyed me. The question building at the back of his mind—'Why hadn't you told me you were leaving?'—painting his features. But I knew he'd never come out and ask it.

With a lukewarm smile, he sat.

An uncomfortable silence befell us. I couldn't ask him how he'd been, what he'd done with his life all these years...How would I answer the inevitable return when he asked the same of me? A welling of guilt tickled my core.

Freyah, sensing the back-and-forth thoughts between us, nudged forward a bowl beside her I hadn't seen. "Here, you must be starving."

I nodded and tried to pace myself as she handed me a bowl filled with root vegetables and stewed meat. The latter was not common outside the capital. It had been months since my mouth tasted the savory saltiness of lamb.

She elbowed her son. "Get her some bread." She tilted her head to the windowsill, where browned, crusted bread lay on a wooden board.

An overwhelming warmth tickled my cheeks as my stomach filled to contentment. This was not a kindness I had been shown in quite a while. Tillian could seemingly tell as he glanced over while I funneled food into my mouth.

"Thank you," I bowed my head, "both of you, for your hospitality."

"Will you be staying long?" he asked, waiting to finish the meal still set out in front of him. He had grown so much since I'd seen him last. From loud scraggly boy running down dirty alleys beside me as we'd pocket an apple from an unsuspecting vendor, to reserved and distant.

Was I to blame for that? Had I contributed to that change?

"I—" I searched for the words.

"He's been working down at the lumber yard." Freya gestured to him and turned to me. "You remember Wosdyn?"

Big burly fellow who lived on the very edge of town. Crude, but always well-meaning.

She saw my acknowledgment and continued, "Wosdyn's been needing more men to help him with the wood." Wosdyn had to be getting older, I realized, since he'd been grayed and balding since I first met him, nearly a decade ago.

She talked for a while about Wosdyn, his mill, his workers, how a young lady had been seen leaving his home early in the mornings. She emphasized *young* and rolled her eyes. Her gossip kept the air around us light.

Eventually, she stood and cleared the table. She pointed to a room down the hall. "Your clothes are cleaned, folded, and I set them on top of a prepared cot." Her words were nonchalant, as if the hospitality was truly not a second thought. She excused herself and went to bed for the night, leaving Tillian and me alone in uneasy silence.

"I looked for you." His eyes were down, and he fiddled with his hands. "I looked for you for weeks." He ran his fingers through his hair and sighed, something like defeat slumping in his shoulders.

"It was complicated." I tried to catch his gaze as he looked back up. *It wasn't personal,* I wanted to say, *it wasn't you.*

He paused, as if wondering whether to inquire more.

"When are you leaving?" he asked again flatly, expected disappointment steadying his tone.

"Tomorrow."

He rolled his eyes, deflated, and got up to look out the window facing the darkened, empty streets. He was a few heads taller than when I saw him last, but still lanky and still easy to frustrate.

"Well, we don't have long then, I guess." He didn't turn to face me, but I heard the glimmer in his tone. "C'mon, I have to show you something."

Delight crept into my grin. He grabbed a light, navy coat hanging beside the door and tossed it to me as I stood.

"Try to keep up, will ya?" He flashed me a wicked smirk and took off out the door.

Despite the occasional throb from my sore wrist and lingering headache, I raced behind him. Winding around street corners, breezy cool air brushed the hair out of my face. My senses were on high alert, watching every shadow for a form.

Damn, was he fast.

I stayed a step behind him now, much closer than when we were kids when I'd often have to pause for breath, reassess my location and follow deflatingly once he stopped and backtracked.

Tonight, I pushed my legs further and faster. I felt the ground slant upward as our elevation grew. He didn't turn to see where I was, but I knew he could hear my steps just moments behind his. Higher and higher we soared, streets widening and knobby trees lining both sides of the road. Delicate, grayed blossoms kissed their ends and littered the ground beneath them. Floral decadence filled my nose.

As abruptly as the path opened, so too did he stop. I skidded to a halt behind him. Hopeful eyes beckoned me closer.

I stood beside him and saw in the spacious courtyard opening a black-stoned bordered pond. Reflective obsidian caught the tiniest of light coming from the corner lanterns a bit behind us. He nodded ahead but stayed as I stepped up to the water.

The surface shimmered in murky inkiness, mirroring the nighttime around it. The reservoir appeared only a couple of feet deep, but there at the bottom...

Amethyst.

Rough-edged, raw, and clustered—a floor of lavender lined the basin.

"They built this a year after you left." He strolled up beside me. "When Mum and I would argue, I'd come here." He paused, sticking his thumbs into his pockets. "It reminded me of you."

I pondered my own reflection on top of the slippery surface. Wisps of hair so dark they'd often been referred to as midnight violet hung over my face, having fallen out from my running, the rest pulled up neatly behind me.

"I'm sorry," was all I could finally muster. And I meant it.

He sat on the glossy black edge, back facing the watery glass, and shrugged. "I know."

I sat beside him and listened to the stillness around us. Wind rustled through trees, and their whisper was all that could be heard. The breeze pushed and pulled the water behind us, rippling the surface and breaking its evenness.

"They said it was in honor of the Ryvinian soldiers." He chuckled softly.

"The pond?" I raised an eyebrow.

"Mhm."

"But Ryvinians didn't even help as the kingdom—"

"I know." He shook his head. "I know."

"Then why—?"

"I think they're trying to play nice." He leaned back on his arms and stared up toward the sky as if it would open up and tell us its secrets. "It's been six years—"

Both since his father left, and since the ruling family in Sheirsa disappeared.

"—and they're still trying to piece together the fragments. And I suppose an alliance with the religious nuts beats one with the deserters." Though a statement, his voice didn't sound convinced.

I sat there pondering that quietly for a few moments.

Time passed effortlessly between us, and I felt my head grow heavy. I set it softly down as the weight grew tiresome on my neck, resting just barely on his shoulder, surrendering it to drowsiness.

We sat that way for a long while before we went back.

CHAPTER 4

The next morning started in the spare room on the cushioned mattress Freyah had set out. The sun was already billowing in. I sat up, stretching and arching the strained muscles in my back.

I gathered my belongings and savored the familiarity and comfort for a moment longer before I left the house, both hosts absent and already out starting their respective days. A small plate with a slice of bread and butter was on the kitchen table, a wordless goodbye I ate in stride as I returned to the rainbowed mirrors of Nox's.

I hurried, this time not stopping or perusing through shops and spectacles.

When I entered the obnoxiously bright building, a different but similar face sat behind the receptionist's desk. Cold eyes, warm painted smile. Perfectly pinned hair, darker than the woman's yesterday, but her eyes the same caramel.

"Adelliah." Lifeless eyes crooned. "I'll tell Nox you've arrived."

She stood, thin body wrapped snuggly in a light gray charmeuse dress that covered her from neck to toe and swayed as she walked.

I didn't bother to wait in one of the chairs that lined the hall of the lobby. I'd hoped this would be brief.

She disappeared behind the single door at the end of the room. I wiped some crumbs from my toast off my blouse and paced in a line as I waited.

As she opened the door to return, she held it ajar and wordlessly gestured for me to go back.

I passed in front of her spread arm, a harsh, clean smell radiating from her as I did—it reminded me of a doctor's office, clean to the point of sterility. She didn't follow me, shutting the door as I went into the hallway.

There was only one door at the very end. A door label beside it read: *Mr. Nox Warten* in golden cursive. I ignored the churn of unease as I entered.

His office was snug. But it was lavish. Gold-plated handles adorned the tiny apothecary-sized shelves lining the back wall from floor to ceiling. There had to be hundreds of them, squarely organized and labeled with some sort of symbols that did not suggest alphabetically or chronologically.

His desk was solid redwood, and stacks of files sat on the front corners. Between them, a conventionally handsome man in a navy suit, his face giving no tells of exactly how old he was. He bore no scars, and his perfectly white teeth mockingly shined in the light as he smiled. A rose pocket square matched a thin necktie, which he tinkered with as I sat in the leather chair his opposite.

"Back so soon this time?" He didn't bother to look up as I sat my bag on his desk.

Seemingly bored, he ran his tie through the tips of his fingers. His voice dripped in poisoned sweetness.

He looked up at me under his brows before gesturing to the bag. "Open it," he ordered, voice emotionless and face bored.

I did, carefully pulling out the three labeled vials and setting them upright between us.

"Good." He grabbed them, still seemingly uninterested, and swiveled his chair around to the wall of shelves.

He slid one drawer out, set the glass inside, and turned back around. From his desk, he opened a bottom compartment and pulled out yet another folder. Even from this distance, I could see my penned-in name on the tab.

He flipped it wide open and scribbled on the page.

"Half toward your debt." He glanced at me and then back to his paper, jotting more down. "And half for now." He passed me a small coin purse and three empty vials he retrieved from somewhere beneath the desk.

As he finished writing down notes, he swiftly shut the folder and slipped it back into his desk.

He held out his hand, expectantly.

I leaned forward and set my wrist down in his palm. His skin was soft, no callouses or roughness.

With his unoccupied hand, he reached into his coat pocket and pulled out an unnaturally vibrant-red barreled syringe. As its tip met the fading crimson tattoo on my arm, he locked eyes and pressed his thumb down evenly on the plunger.

A stinging warmth oozed to fill the tattoo, the mark itself blotting up with cherry cloudiness. I never asked how it worked, the magnetized liquid particles attaching and separating themselves in the direction of a database I could not access.

Once emptied, he removed the hollow needle. The tattoo stirred and spiraled into a filigree-covered N before breaking into nothing more than dense clouds.

Setting the emptied syringe aside, he watched the magical illustrations decorating my wrist. He held it a moment longer than usual, his fingers caressing the skin where my thumb and wrist met.

"There are so many...*faster* ways you could work to repay me," he hummed in a rasp just loud enough for me to hear.

I yanked my arm back and wiped it against my leg, as if to remove the places he'd touched.

He snickered and flashed his eyes to the door behind me.

"We're done here." He cleared his throat. "Get out."

I happily obliged.

I made my way back to his lobby. The tight high bun on the back of the receptionist's head greeted me, though she didn't bother to turn around. As I passed the empty chairs and then her desk, I heard her greet someone entering.

"Good afternoon," feigned friendliness beamed. "How can we help you?"

I tried not to glance up to see who it was. But curiosity bested me. A sickly lean woman was approaching the desk, face dirtied and lips cracked. In hand, a small freckled boy who barely came up to her hip.

Oh, please, no.

My heart tightened. I could feel their desperation, see the hunger that shook her bones with the energy it took to stand. There was a pain in the mother's quivering hands as she apprehensively approached the desk.

"I—we—" she looked around, "we need a loan. Please, we—"

I blocked it out. I shut out the noise as she proceeded to tell a story that was falling on the deaf ears of the receptionist, who was simply nodding along. I hurried past them, air leaving my chest.

The seconds it took to reach the door felt like hours, and I could feel the curious little eyes of the boy darting around the room and landing on me. Despite the obvious pangs of hunger, his stare was not yet darkened. His eyes seemed eager and questioning.

I didn't let myself pause at the door. I didn't let myself turn to warn her.

I had done so, so many times before. And they never listened. My warnings could never outweigh their immediate need.

Would I have believed me?

I left and prayed that I would never see her code flash upon my wrist.

I left town immediately, beginning my trek west. I would loop toward Thiar and then back to Osta again, waiting for my wrist to flash coordinates for my first stop. Hugging the cities on the western coast tended to yield the fastest results, thus minimizing a mad dash from afar—or at least, *for the most part.*

My departures after returning vials were usually uneventful, a continuing loop I had done so many times before, often within hours of arriving in the capital.

But this time, I had tarried, I had stayed the night, I had visited old friends.

As I walked through the woods, I wondered if leaving would have been easier if I hadn't stayed at all. If this ache for a different type of monotony—wake up, go to work, come home, and eat dinner—wouldn't be tapping on my heart, begging it, daring it to ask: *What if...what if...I could stay.*

I put it out of my mind as I set up camp a few hours outside Alaria.

I stayed on the inner edge of the Elsh forest. Throughout dusk, I gathered fallen branches from the forest floor, most rotten or roughly ripped off from a recent storm, still vaguely damp to the touch. I set them together, creating a peak with which to throw my tarp over in case the rain was to fall again.

I hurried and finally got a fire to light just as the sun fully tucked below the horizon, painting the trees a soft shade of pink and gray. I warmed my hands and stared at the dancing light, its tips flickering from the pieces of wet wood.

The fire was my only entertainment, and as I watched it, I crossed my arms over my chest, cupping my shoulders, tucking myself over the warmth. I held myself hunched over the glowing heat as the gentle pitter patter began, exemplified as it bounced off the top of my shelter.

It smelled like just a drizzle. The sky was still illuminated with breaks in the clouds to give way to the starry blanket behind, the wind pushing and pulling the clouds quickly past. As the wind grew rigid and the warmth of the fire lessened, I slipped inside the tent. Sleep came to me amidst an orchestra of rain droplets and the swaying wet heaviness of the trees high above.

The next few days came and went much the same. The welling doubt that I had allowed to creep into me when I left was soon replaced with the peaceful solitude of the woods, a bustling city in its own respect.

They say the forests are "one of the few places where *old* magic lives." I never quite knew what it meant when older men and women would chuckle to one another as Elsh or Elsarah were mentioned, or why they'd quickly shake their heads at the thought of journeying through. Different generations, maybe, or perhaps how to describe something that cannot be tamed.

As I moved past trees much older than I, I wondered how many had been here since before Alaria was established.

I was deliberate in my care not to disturb much. Keeping my fires small, my footsteps light, and bringing jerky that should last until the west as to avoid hunting here helped ensure I would not desecrate the beauty around me.

Sometimes I considered what my life would be like if I could live off in the greenery, make streams and flowers my friends and family. There was never silence here—just the ever-reminding sounds of life, be it squawking birds or chittering insects.

As I found myself daydreaming through the morning of a new day, my wrist tingled. And I knew.

Oozy redness blotched to form coordinates just north, to the coastal city of Vayne. I adjusted my trajectory and set out to my first stop, thankful I was only a half days walk to the city outskirts. I closed my eyes and conjured the outstretched map of Sheirsa—I scanned the mental image up and down, followed the crisscrossed lines for where they would intersect and my target would be. The numbers told me it would be right on the coast, on the far west of the city, which would be easy to journey to since several paths were designed to get to the water as quickly and efficiently as possible.

I tapped my fingers three times on one of the pockets of the pants Freya had gifted me, the new safekeeping for Mion, who had been slumbering on standby.

Subtle vibrations replied to my touch, as if to say: *Yes, ready to go.*

I departed, slowly making my way out of Elsh and finding the road which would take me directly into town. As I did, I felt the face of the forestry watching me, the thick trees lining the view behind formed a wall of sage and wood. It felt like eyes were observing my leave. But that stark block of outer trees did nothing more than sway in the morning breeze drifting in from the not-so-far ocean coast.

All the roads to Vayne were paved, even this far out. Though coated in a light layer of dirt, the bricks beneath were a light blue that grabbed the sunlight and reflected it back, creating an illusion that they themselves were lighting up.

I followed the path of speckled light as it took me up and down the rolling hills on the outskirts.

I arrived around midday. The high skyline was painted in blues and greens, the city a reflection of the endless ocean behind it. A testament to sea and sun, it was glaringly different than its dark, uniform sister of Thiar further south. I decided to head straight to the coast to wait out the daytime and blend in amongst others anxious for a taste of salt water sprays.

I strolled in past seafarers and traders in navy tunics. It was loud with the commotion of bargaining and friendly conversation. The noise all blended together in a mishmash of words and noises. I scanned the pleasant faces, sun-kissed skin on most, and made my way to the edge of the ocean.

There were piers as far as I could see lining the coast, several boats of varying sizes docked. Homemade shops were littered up and down, where men would drop off their largest, shimmering fish—caught just this morning—to be cut up and cooked in deep metal pans. Hanging from the tops of the stands, dried fish wrapped in twine swung in the breeze, crispy browned skin tempting hungry children that played nearby as they waited for their parents to return from a day out at sea.

Most of the boats were only large enough for a few people and, therefore, mostly for personal fishing. However, further down sat a handful of beautiful ships that could carry fleets, though they hadn't done so in a long time. Vast hulls covered in carved wooden spirals and hand-painted symbols could be seen from afar. Women of myth, some whimsical and some terrifying, stood guarding the bows of several of the largest vessels.

The oceanfront did not butt up directly against sand or shore—a tall walkway had been enacted with a railing allowing close proximity to the crashing waves themselves.

Today, the water was relatively calm.

My cracked hands gripped the railing, and I peered down below. A fine, salty mist shot toward my face after each wave made its collapsing end. I licked my lips, tasting the salt and grinning as the wind blew my mostly undone hair back.

A deep inhale filled my lungs to the brim with the cleanest air I had smelled in a long time. I clung to this feeling, savoring it. I was rarely in Vayne, but I made a note to try and return more often. The boisterous waves provided a sense of calm even amongst the busy walkways and town merchants.

"It's beautiful, isn't it?" I turned to see a woman a few years younger than myself. Tan skin, bright hazel eyes, and a navy tunic, the same design as I had seen on some of the men earlier.

I stole a glance at her, nodded, and returned my gaze to the water.

"When I was young, the men weren't in town much," she stepped up beside me, resting her hands on the rail, "and my mother and many others would watch and tend the pier."

The smaller waves ebbed against the wall, sloshing in regular cadence.

"Ya know, they say even longer ago than that, *Vayne* was the capital." Out of the corner of my eye, I saw her wink and let out a hard laugh. "Though a capital on the sea before Sheirsa was fully established seems like an awfully bad strategic location."

"Before Sheirsa?" I turned to her slightly, curiously.

"I mean, sure." She shrugged exaggeratedly. "That's what they say."

I looked at her, waiting for her to go on.

Her eyes twinkled as she saw me engage in her words. She pushed the dark blonde bangs that kept hanging over her face out of the way with the back of her hand and shook her head, short, chin-length hair a mess in the sea wind.

"My mother told me a long time ago," she took on a practiced tone as if she had retold this several times before, "long before the royal family disappeared," she waved a hand across the horizon, stopping and balling it into a fist, "and before the generations of peace they brought," she hesitated, "there were monsters that walked the land..."

She leaned toward me slightly, lowering her voice.

"—and those monsters," she paused, "were not quite beast and not quite man. But something else entirely."

I scanned her face as she spoke, dazzling eyes wrapped up in her tale and somewhere far away from this walkway.

"They say Sheirsa was built when the factions of warring people were finally done killing each other...when they decided to take up arms *together* as a final act against their common foe." Her lowered voice was now a mere whisper, "The *Alltani*." Her lips nearly grazed my ear, "The *others*."

CHAPTER 5

T illian had told me the story in passing one day—he told me about a time when the land was wild, and we were prey, and children that wandered too far from home would be snatched up by the evil unknown lurking in the shadows.

I raised a doubtful eyebrow and kept my focus on her close proximity.

"You're talking about a children's bedtime story." I smirked and shrugged, relaxing my tense shoulders but leaning close enough now that our arms touched. "And besides," I curled my lips, "it's humans that you should worry about."

My hand reached out and snatched her sneaky wrist that had been slowly withdrawing back to her side.

Her eyes widened in both shock and panic.

"Drop it," I commanded, squeezing just hard enough for the silver she had taken from my pouch to drop into my other open hand. I slipped it back into the safety of my bag.

She pulled away, but I held her there for a moment longer.

"A tip?" I met her frightened, inexperienced gaze head-on. "Stick to the tourists in the busier areas. The ones who come here to shop are the ones drunk on Vayne mead and too distracted to notice your wondering fingers."

She tugged on her arm, wiggling away from me.

At that moment, my focus shifted from her to the walkway around us, where more people had gathered as the sun rose higher into the clear, expansive sky. The warmth kissed my head and heightened the smell of the cooked fish from the dock down below. Scanning those closest, I realized nosy eyes were glued to us, women in sky blue dresses in hand with their children, snickering and speaking low beneath their breaths.

She saw it too.

And we both watched as a stocky man in crimson, Sheirsan guard attire approached us with a face that did not suggest friendly intent. Scraggly beard, hilt of a sword beside him. He smelled like boredom and sweat.

I felt her tug again, but I side-eyed her, silently relaying to follow my lead.

"Ma'am," he didn't bow but merely glanced my way, ignoring my temporary captive, "is she bothering you?"

With a widening grin, I tossed back a carefree laugh for good measure. "Oh no, not at all. We were just arguing about which figurehead was the prettiest when this one wanted to run down to get some fish."

I met her eyes and begged, *stay. Stay until he leaves.*

I released my fingers hesitantly, one by one. Confused, she awkwardly smiled in agreement though her body had been rigid since the guard walked up.

"Yeah—" she pushed the bangs back again, "I was going to race her, but—"

"This one is always up here causing problems," he interrupted. "And I haven't seen you here before. Are you *sure* she wasn't bothering you? I can take her off your hands, just say the word." His breath smelled like smoke and booze despite the midday sun.

For the first time since approaching, he stole a glance at the scrappy blonde beside me. And I immediately knew that look. Sinister intent flashed for a moment, so brief and fleeting, but churned my stomach in recognition.

"I'm sure." I straightened and let the false smile dissipate. Tilting my head to her, I added, "Let's go."

Quickly passing him and headed in the direction of the pier, I gestured up ahead. She walked beside me, letting the distance between us and the guard lengthen until he tired of watching and returned to whatever it was he was supposed to be doing.

A small voice stuttered as we made it to the delicious-smelling vendor tents, "Wh-why?"

"Never." I leaned down, only now realizing how much shorter she was than I. "Never trust people with any semblance of power. Guards, soldiers, a man with slightly more gold in his pockets than his neighbor..." Darkness shaded my sharp, silver irises, and a remembering shiver traced up my spine. "They will always want more."

She said nothing, silence her grave confirmation that she understood. We strolled aimlessly up and down the pier, not speaking much. The energetic bravado she first had, had subsided into a milder relaxation as we walked.

As the sun sank further into the sky and my skin started to redden from its rays, I heard the tiniest of grumbles. A self-conscious hand moved to her stomach as if to muffle it, and her clean skin made me wonder how she had found herself pickpocketing. Beneath the daylight glow, she bit at her chapped lips, nervously picking away at the skin with her teeth.

I approached the nearest fish vendor, and she waited back amongst the crowd. Glancing back toward her, the purpled bags under her eyes seemed impervious to the mellow, beckoning warmth around us. Even I could feel an afternoon heaviness weighing on me, the chirping of birds a sweet song to the lullaby of waves behind it.

I held up a finger to the wide man in a burlap apron taking orders. With thankfully no small talk, we exchanged silver for a hurriedly wrapped sun-dried fish.

We found a shady spot a bit higher from the coast and sat. A breeze passed, heightening the shade's welcome coolness.

I opened the parchment and split the fish open, pulling the feathery meat from inside and passing it to her. Her hunger left no desire to argue or debate the offer, and her body slacked back as she ate, eventually laying completely down in the grass as she shoveled more into her mouth.

I licked my greasy fingers clean as we quickly devoured the fish, picking every last morsel from its soft, hidden bones.

I rested comfortably, leaning back on my arms. Her eyes closed and a sigh fluttered from her lips. I tried to piece together the answers to the questions I would not ask. A worn tag on her chest had what appeared to be hand-sewn black lettering: Kori.

Despite the relative closeness in age, her face lacked the hardness of my own. Flushed, filled-out cheeks bore no residual bruising like mine. But there was still pain in the edges of her lips when she smiled.

With nothing better to do, I waited out the rest of the afternoon beneath the shadow of the coastal buildings. Kori evidently had nowhere to be either, as she remained beside me until nightfall.

I had almost forgotten I was here for business. My wrist, of course, had not let me, though.

I stared at her in her half-sleepy state and wondered where she would go now that night had fallen. The sensitive tingling up my arm urged me to put it out of mind, but I couldn't. Luckily for both of us, she soon startled upright as she realized how late it had gotten.

"I have to get back," she stammered, "but thank you." She glanced down at her feet after she stood, fiddling with a ring she wore around her thumb. "And I'm sorry again about your coin, I—"

I held up a hand to stop her. Many hungry nights had plagued me in Alaria, from as far back as I could remember. And desperation is what got me where I was now, after all.

"Go straight home and keep an eye out for that guard."

She flipped up a hood from her tunic and darted away into the shadows.

I looked at my wrist and calculated that my destination was only a few blocks away. There were no guards meandering about, at least not here, but I made a note to scan the empty streets for any signs of them as I snuck further from the coast and deeper into the homes that lined it.

Vayne at night was almost more lovely than it was in the daytime. Lanterns danced with flickering blue fire, suspended into a revolving ball that highlighted the brick buildings up and down the streets. Most of the brick was painted in dizzying arrays of colors and abstract portraits, some commissioned by the city and some a weekend project of someone who happened upon paint and a brush. Varying degrees of skill were evident, but all were lovely.

The second block in from the coast had shorter homes, square, uniform boxes except for their colorful outward displays. I reached into my pocket, pulled out the tangled ball of wires, and softly tapped on the round, metal core. Unraveling legs and detangled wires formed my spindly friend. Mion zig-zagged from my open palm down to my wrist, lowering its body and reading what the crimson order said.

I peered down the block and saw no one. There was such calm in this city, so alien from the others—even the other coastal ones, and the people so much warmer and seemingly carefree. Maybe Vayne really was the old capital…Their bravado was similar to those in Alaria, just without the casual layer of condescension.

Mion gave a soft chirp and scurried down my arm and body, carefully hugging the edge of the homes and darting up ahead.

I clutched my bag and I did the same, minimizing my shadow and staying away from the illumination of the lantern-lined road. As the ball of wiry legs reached the intersection of two roads, it paused, as if it too were trying to stay hidden. I waited behind and then followed once it continued on the path up ahead.

The home it stopped in front of had no lights on. Mi rounded the corner to a side entrance where a screen door awaited me. As if knowing it had done a good job, the ball of wires spun itself around with a chipper wiggle as it wove its legs in and out of one another. I clicked my tongue against the back of my teeth, and just as quickly as it had appeared, the ball of wires skittered back to my side and up into my pocket.

An appreciative grin painted my face as I reached for the door handle, surprised to find it unlocked.

Maybe the people here were a little *too* trusting. Or maybe whoever lived here knew Nox would be here to collect once their time was up.

I turned the knob and silently let myself in.

As I entered the home, I scanned the possessions and décor to see if the debtor lived alone or with others. The home was anything but luxurious, a few seats set around a table, a stack of dirty dishes overflowing the sink, and the subtle smell of recently discarded food. I wondered then, as I often did, what this person's cause of death would be. I numbly assumed sickness as the unkept house suggested no energy for tidying.

I found my answer behind the sole door on the left opposite a bare-bones bathroom that I didn't dare peek into. The elderly body of what appeared to be a bedridden woman lay under blankets and surrounded by white prayer candles. More dirty dishes, half-eaten food, and prayer pamphlets encircled the bed like a shrine.

The eyes were always open.

At first, it had unnerved me. I remembered telling Nox I couldn't do this, couldn't collect as their eyes watched me take what little they had left to possess. But Nox...he wasn't open to negotiating. And he'd callously remind me that this fate would also befall me if I didn't shut up and get the job done.

So that's what I did, until it became second nature—being so close to the dead.

I set my bag down and, with surgical precision, went to begin the extraction. The woman's lips were white, and her hair was nothing more than wispy strands. Delicately, always delicately as to avoid bubbles, I positioned my syringe at the base of my X and withdrew the shimmering fluid. As I deposited it into one of my restocked vials, the stinging tattoo on my skin subsided, clearing to little more than what could be confused for a rash. I sighed, subconsciously holding my breath until the process was complete.

And then I left unceremoniously.

Slipping back into the street, I felt extra out of place in this seaside town of vibrancy, a heavy burden weighing in my bag. There was now a discomfort amongst the happily flickering illumination, and I decided to head out of town to return to the forest alone.

As I had turned and made it only a block or two further, I felt a surprising burning return.

I glanced down, and sure enough, the red had warped into a coordinate a mere walk away from where I had just collected. I stared incredulously.

This had never happened before—an alarm going off one right after another. The burning intensified, suggesting urgency, and I caught myself staring at the swirling, thickening pigment in partial disbelief that maybe it would soon dissipate. Maybe it was a mistake or confusion at the closeness of where I'd just been?

My hand twitched as the pain spread, causing my fingers to spasm.

I heard you, I hissed at the mark, cursing at what would now be an even longer night. I usually could mentally reset after an extraction, come to my senses a bit, and shake off the lingering sight of death. But not tonight.

Begrudgingly I turned back, rerouting to the next block over from where I had just been.

I quickened my pace, hurrying to the relative area the coordinates suggested.

Mi, I need you again.

I pulled Mion out, and it repeated its process—scanning the tattoo that was practically screaming at me with its intensity. I steadied my breath and focused as it climbed down to the ground. *Rushing leads to mistakes,* I reminded myself as I followed the path up to a home nearly identical to the last.

Mi located the side door again, darting around quickly and lowering itself with far less pizzazz. *I know,* I thought to it in agreement. Tucking my navigator safely into my pocket, I stopped to peek down the street. There was still no one out. Not a soul could be found wandering the dreamy, sapphire ambiance.

A similar screen door faced me, except this one was slightly off its hinges, crooked, leaning down so it wouldn't fit neatly in the frame. I slid between it and the main door, wondering if this one would be unlocked too. As I glanced down, a tight knot formed in my chest—the main door was open. The entrance to the home was beckoning in the vacant space that shouldn't have been there. I drew a deep breath, long and controlled, as I steadied a blade into my hand.

My limbs felt heavy as I hesitated to enter, mind racing with reasons why the door could be cracked open. Maybe a relative had hastily departed once their loved one had passed, and in that carelessness, not shut it completely? Though unusual, it made sense, and a slight relaxation loosened the stiff grip I had on the dagger's hilt.

I opened the door the rest of the way, pressing my shoulder into it as I leaned in.

Nausea gripped me as the coppery air filled my nostrils.

Blood.

There was blood everywhere.

CHAPTER 6

I immediately dropped to my knees, my body feeling heavy and numb. Red sprayed the walls in dramatic upsweeps and saturated the floor. Like a dark, churning ocean of thick death, it puddled before my knees as I stared horrified into its center. Despite my best efforts, I turned around and retched, my body now shaking at the sight.

I rocked for a moment, cradling my knees as I stared at nothing in particular. I commanded myself to get it together, to pull the reeling pieces into one and leave this place. The shadows in the home felt insufficient to cover myself in darkness, as if the blood demanded its presence, and the blackness obliged.

I knew I was wasting time. I could feel the valuable seconds slipping away as the chances of being seen here rose. I had heard no screams from down the road, but I hadn't really been listening for them...

A second, more pressing concern jolted me from my immobilization. I white-knuckled my blade and sucked in air, avoiding the slouched-over hump in the corner of the room, the source of this splattered mess. Rapidly, while still crouched low, I scanned the room, trying to see if there were footsteps or signs that whoever had done this still remained in the home. The kitchen was a disaster—bunched-up cloths used to presumably wash off lingering evidence of what had occurred in a heap, crimson tainting their color and wetting the delicate fabric so that they stuck and clung to one another.

Shakily, I forced my legs to straighten. This home had more doors than the last, three down the hall. I cursed and made my way down, side-eyeing the first, which, based on the previous layout, would be the bathroom. This door was slightly cracked, and I tipped my foot into the open wedge to silently pry it further. Dulled, bloodied footprints were before the sink, tiny droplets by the faucet, but that was it. Towels once hung up lay on the floor, and the shower curtain had been dragged off its pole.

I approached the second door, which was opposite this one, except it was shut. *I hate this.* The minerally smell still clogged my nose and made every breath I took an unavoidable reminder of what lay in the living room still needing to be collected. I opened the door and thankfully saw nothing out of place. An unimposing bed that rested directly on the floor, some books beside it, and a half-melted candle on a small table right inside the room. There were no closets, no giant curtains to hide behind...two down, one to go.

My heartbeat thumped in my ear, the staccato rhythm somehow both grounding me here and distracting my focus. I tried my best to ignore it, but doing so only seemed to make it worse, like a bug bite you're trying so desperately not to touch in fear once you finally give in, you'll scratch it into a bloodied mess. The drumming felt like that, begging me to scratch, to give in to its demands for attention, to meet its needs for acknowledgment—but I couldn't. I knew the second I did that I would be the same mess I was in when I entered, overcome by panic and unable to act.

And I needed to act. Faster.

I reached the third door that faced the end of the hall. It was shut. As I reached to open it, the handle refused my plea and merely wiggled back and forth against my hand. I tried to turn it again, but it refused. *Locked.*

Don't like that...

I weighed the pros of trying to pry it open, but with the night slipping away, I hurried back to the main room to see what was left of whoever this was. Every step I took felt wrong, my mind telling me I should walk right past into the clean air and never look back at what was crumpled in the corner. I fought that instinctive voice and swallowed back my churning nausea.

My steps felt sticky as I drew closer. I lowered myself to the mass, and in a silent command I had never used before, ordered my mind to creep backward and separate itself from the actions I was about to do. I grabbed a handkerchief from my bag and, with it, pressed the head back so that the person was leaning back instead of slumped over. His neck snapped back from the weight of the lifeless head, exposing a deep wound beneath the chin. Only trickles pooled out of the gash, most of it having previously been emptied onto his lap and surroundings. His beard was a wet mess, as was his exposed chest.

There was no gray, no aged lines running through his skin—his chest was defined and broad, and as I glanced at his hands, I could see the tears slicing their backs. The tips of his fingers had additional remnants of his fight, with nails peeled back and bloodied gunk beneath them. Surprised or not, he had definitely tried to avoid this fate. But I saw no weapons laying around him, only the evidence of those used against him, which were nowhere to be found.

A deep breath, and I looked closer in shock. Beneath the deep laceration was a mark nearly undetectable beneath the red collar of blood. At the very base of his neck, between his collar bones, was a tiny, precise X.

The hairs on my arms rose, and I shook my head in disbelief. There was no way. There were no other debt collectors as far as I knew. But as I looked at the seemingly careless mess all around me, at the gratuitous amounts of blood painting the walls and drenching his body, I couldn't help but feel like it was all a bit...excessive. And for a moment, I wondered if it wasn't all for show. If once the body was found, the attention would be so focused on the dramatic gore, and the split beneath his chin, that they'd never bother to look at what else was hidden beneath it. They would miss what else was taken.

The throbbing in my wrist subsided, though, as if close proximity for long enough was satisfactory for the system Nox had devised to move on to the next. Or maybe it had stopped as soon as I had entered the house? Amidst the panic, I hardly remembered to even check my tattoo.

I knew, regardless, that there would be nothing left for me to extract. The sunken tips of his skin next to the X were bloodied from his wound, most likely making a clean extraction impossible if there were any remnants uncollected.

The walls of the house felt smaller, the closeness of this home leaned in upon me. I was ready to leave. But what would Nox say when I come back empty-handed? Would he already know what happened?

I glanced around nervously, scanning for anything out of place that could be hidden beneath the bloody display. I gave one last look at the body, grimacing as I carefully lifted each of his arms, inspecting for subtle signs of any additional trauma. On the side furthest from me, where the body had leaned slightly more when he was slumped over, the mess was even worse—denser, caked on. In the crook of his side, a deeper blackness peered up from the skin, puckered but blurry beneath the cloudiness of his spillage.

I bit my lip, hard, as I tried to wipe away the many colors of the pooling liquid. But my already soaked handkerchief was as good as done, the hand-sized square stained and merely moving the puddle around instead of soaking it up. The ball in my throat had loosened slightly, my body responding to my commands with less hesitation.

Darting up to the kitchen, I started opening the top drawers in rapid succession, jarring *taps* as each extended fully. The third one had what I was searching for—a coarse dish towel—that I hurried back with to rub off the build-up on his side.

But as I did, something jarring caught my peripheral. I froze, the wobble in my knees returning ever so slightly, the drum of my pulse teasing my ears and pounding against my skull.

The door at the end of the hall was open.

The room that I had tried to search through, but had failed to turn the locked knob, was now cracked about a foot.

Something deeply haunting bubbled up within me, animalistic instinct coursing through my veins as I leveled my back against the walls of the main room to hide from sight. The first dagger I had drawn lay lazily beside the corpse, set down when I began examining the body, the slight glimmer from its blade a quiet mockery for my oversight.

I grabbed another from my belt.

The moonlight slipping in through the windows felt dense, thick beams of translucent light floated around, out of place in this tenseness. It shimmered and made only silhouettes, darkness layered upon darkness. I clung to it, prayed it would cover me as I inched toward the opening of the hallways and waited, listening.

But I heard no steps. And I heard no breathing.

The seconds that passed dragged, felt endless as I waited for the occupant to move or otherwise make a run to exit the home. This whole endeavor was proving significantly longer than intended, with higher stakes and no reward. I shut out the thought of Nox's reaction if I replayed it to him like this—me waiting, reacting, lingering.

I steadied my free hand on my chest, regulating the up and down of my frenzied breath. When I was young, and I had to charge myself into anything ranging from nerve-wracking to terrifying, I told myself it was best not to think about it—the more you did, the less likely you were to do it. Instead, I'd count to three, and whatever it was, I'd do it immediately without hesitation, whether it was kissing a neighborhood boy or jamming a syringe into a corpse.

One...

Two...

I sucked in air.

Three.

I spun my body into the hallway entrance, facing the looming search into the rooms once more. But instead of using one of the available spaces to wait out and hide, my fellow occupant stood brazenly a few steps before me, midway down.

His shoulders looked lax, his arms dangling beside him with no visible weapons in hand. He wore gray leathers so utterly generic it gave no indication of where he was from. And he was expressionless. No worry creased his brow, no smile pulled at the thin lips. Only calculating patience emanated from him, and in the soft, moon-speckled shade around us, his eyes returned my gaze kindled with amber radiance.

The pause was a wedge of stillness between us. He didn't move, only held my stare.

I searched through all the questions that flurried around in my head. Because despite the different outwardly appearance, I recognized those golden eyes, even if they were now framed in a more chiseled face topped with snow-colored, slicked-back locks.

"Why?" It edged out my other pertinent question—*who*—but...one at a time.

He cocked his head to the left in a quick flicker.

I gestured widely with my arm to the room behind me. "Did you do this?" He slowly shook his head once.

Growing exasperated by the night that should have ended hours ago, I considered his stance. Even with the additional time to scan his person, I could not find evidence of any weapons hiding on him. I could run up on him, maybe knock him down and threaten his departure with my blades. But the prospect of having to potentially leave an additional body to be discovered here roiled my aching core, calling my bluff as I considered all my options.

I stepped toward him. "Then *why* are you here?" I held my blade outward and kept my stance an aggressive facade.

With no acknowledgment of the threatening dagger, his look went from at me to behind me, as if my head had simply vanished and he was peering at the spattered wall behind me.

"I came for him," he said simply, his tone softer than I expected, almost velvety as the words slipped out of his mouth. "And he was already disposed of." The only semblance of emotion flashed for just a second before it was gone—I couldn't place it, but it was something dark, something sinister.

His eyes widened then, and he cocked his head ever so slightly.

"Two guards," pupils darted back and forth as if processing, "approaching from the south." The darting disks stopped, and flatly, he added, "We have ten minutes."

"*We* don't—"

His fast gate cut me off as he sped mere inches beside me into the room, a warm breeze of air passing my arm between us as he did. He analyzed the room as if committing it to memory, craning his neck around in awkward circles and turning around slightly. *Ten minutes, ten minutes...*

I ignored him and hurried beside the body, resting on my knees as I leaned over to continue what I was searching for before the...interruption. I had replaced the towel with the dagger when attempting to search the house, but I now swapped them back, sheathing my weapon and pulling out the cloth. Finding that crease at the body's waist, I dabbed at it carefully before sweeping it back and forth, mopping up the excess until the surface beneath was exposed.

A blotchy, sky-colored rash coiled in a circular pattern along his ribs. Half the size of my palm, it resembled no tattoo ink I was familiar with—in fact, as I rubbed at it to test its permanence, it did not lay on top of the skin but seemed part of it, as if the air and seas had created a birthmark all their own.

"Six minutes," he stated, fixated on the door.

I scrambled at my options on what to return to Nox. He would scoff at a vial of blood, and it wouldn't help me piece together who may have done this. With little remaining options, I shook my head as I rummaged for my curved blade.

Grimacing, I slid it beneath the skin around the mark—carefully peeling in a neat circle around the swirl. The skin cut cleanly, the edge slicing effortlessly until the ends met. I could feel the stranger turn to watch me as I lifted the skin and set it gently on another spare tissue I found at the bottom of the bag. I folded the tissue, twice, pushing down the queasiness as I then rolled it into one of the larger glass containers I had.

"Three minutes," he warned, no inflection of concern.

There was no time to argue or ask more questions—I could do that later. I approached the door and felt him follow. I slid it open, and he passed immediately in front of me, ear-length white hair carrying the subtle smell of wet earthiness, like soil in the forest after it rains.

Wordlessly we departed into a night that was somehow so much heavier than before.

CHAPTER 7

I let him lead the way. Or at least that's what I told myself as he raced off down the first side street. He proceeded to weave in and out of crisscrossing back alleys, following a particular path that I couldn't make sense of. His speed was mesmerizing, a white flash of light as he darted around corners and led us further away from the guards that would have now reached the scene.

Confirming that thought, a wailing siren started to sound out of the lanterns adorning each crossroad. Lights flickered on in more homes as the sound grew louder and woke the unsuspecting. I realized our path was leading us toward the outskirts of the city—the speckled roads that lead in and out replaced the stone, and the homes grew further apart.

And then he stopped.

Abruptly on his heels, he immediately paused. I tried to do the same but clumsily faltered, tripping forward but catching myself before needing to land on my hands. He didn't look at my misstep, he was focused on the road ahead, turning around again, peering down the roads on either side of us.

"Guards from outside the city are approaching ahead."

I saw only darkness down the path, the city lights spaced out more here than from the town center, but his unwavering tone told me not to question it.

"People are leaving their homes to search," he added.

Were murders so rare here on the coast? Was this such a new excitement that it caused droves of people to investigate, hoping to gather a crumb of gossip? Dead bodies could sometimes be found in the alleys of Alaria, especially in the poorer districts. But even I had stopped glancing whenever they'd appear in the streets...And I suppose anything could become mundane with enough exposure...

Lifeless clouded orbs appeared in my head, numbly confirming the thought.

It wasn't panic, per se, that rippled across his back as he stood beside me. Something more instinctual, rawer, shivered up his spine as he calculated our way out. The picture of the first rabbit I ever caught popped into my mind, shrill screaming erupting from its mouth, its twisted foot shattered in a trap I had poorly set—struggling to escape, tugging on the wound, and damaging it worse in an attempt to flee.

I remembered the thud of the rock Tillian had brought to end its pain on my behalf...because I wouldn't do it, couldn't do it, despite its pained thrashing.

"We could climb onto one of the homes and wait it out until morning?" I suggested, calculating the height of buildings and observing their plated roofs.

A single shake of his head. "Maybe if these homes were closer together and we could travel to the forest on top...But here, we'd be stuck. And they will keep searching through the night." His features hardened. "They won't stop until they have someone to blame."

"I don't...Why?" Incredulous, I threw my arms down. "Why all of this for one man?"

I was either unfamiliar with the seriousness Vayne handled all their murder cases, or whoever had been butchered was someone important.

The man didn't answer, but his nostrils flared slightly, taking in the night air. Glancing in my direction finally, his face painted in apprehension, he scanned me, searching for something I wasn't sure of.

"The men from outside will reach this spot in five minutes," quick intake of air, "the ones from inside will spread outward and be here in ten."

With his accuracy up until now, I said nothing in return. I didn't bother to inquire how he knew because it posed little importance. Maybe once we made it out of the city, then I would ask.

With a scarred, dry hand, he slipped his fingers through his hair and played with one of the strands. "I see only one possible option." The words were low, still soft, but felt forced out of his mouth—it was not an option he wanted to suggest.

Stepping back from him slightly, I waited. The silence of night had been desecrated by the hollering alarms, the worried stomping steps up and down the road, the voices of people overlapping into a disjointed symphony. He continued to play with the piece of hair behind his ear, twirling it between his fingers—the skin on the knuckles so cracked and tender it looked like a strong breeze could break the withered surface.

A deep swallow preceded his reply, light glimmering from his golden gaze as he opened his mouth.

"I, I could—"

"Ay!" A familiar booming voice hollered from behind us. "Come on, get in here!"

Down the end of the alley beside us, Kori leaned, hanging halfway out a doorway, her hand waving wildly in the air, motioning us toward her. The stranger and I shared a wordless glance before running down to where she was.

She held the door open as she moved us both inside, peering up and down the street before shutting it behind us with a solid thud—this door was heavier than the other screen-wood door combos in the heart of town. She fiddled with the locks behind it—a metal string one up top, two sliding levers beneath, and the center turn piece in the knob itself.

For a moment, no one said anything. This place, her home presumably, was incredibly small, evidently large enough for just one full-time occupier—it was a single room, spare a rounded dark shower curtain for what I imagined was considered the bathroom behind it.

A matted cot in the corner furthest from us, some stacked dishes beside it, and a table with four chairs in the center. I imagined with the size of this space, she wasn't having company over all that often, but the importance seemed to be on this single table, the only real furnishing she cared enough to prioritize in this place.

She patted the top of one of the chairs and smiled, flushed, round cheeks filling the space with warmth. We sat as she knelt beside the dishes and pulled out three mugs, slipping the handles between her fingers, followed by a glass bottle about halfway full of sloshing liquid. *Maybe she did have company often then...*

She set the mugs down one at a time and poured the bubbling drink to a quarter fullness for each cup.

"I don't have a whole lot left." She shook the bottle. "And it's the *cheap* stuff, but it looks like you two could use it." Her laugh was playful, light.

As I reached for mine, I froze self-consciously at my red-stained hands, my right one discolored well past the second knuckle. Kori tossed me a rag, shrugging, adding a: "It's clean, I promise," with a wink as she did.

I found myself smiling with her—it was nearly impossible not to, even as I solemnly wiped off my hands. She slouched into the seat between us, taking a long sip from her own glass, before leaning forward and setting her chin in her hands. She didn't ask directly why I was out running in the streets at night with this unusual-looking man, but patiently waiting for a tale, she raised an eyebrow which asked on her behalf.

I didn't really know where to begin, or how much to say. I searched for the right words, quickly drinking through most of the mead.

"I don't think I ever even got your name. You could start there." She offered a wide grin, glancing to her other side, where the man stared, seemingly lost in the reflection on the drink.

"Thank you." He meant it as he gestured to the glass, though he had not taken a sip. "I am Zymir."

Caught back by his answering first, she bowed her head. "Welcome, Zymir." She impishly batted her eyelashes. He didn't notice her playfulness, or if he did, he didn't show it.

I laughed beside myself, their stark juxtaposition too hilarious not to. The weight of the evening lessened from my shoulders slightly. Or maybe it was the exhaustion. Or the mead.

"Adelliah," I followed, the sweet honey on my lips loosening my guard.

I could feel her acknowledgment, and his. I watched as he finally brought the mug up to drink, watched meticulously as his hands wrapped around the mug, no semblance of the sores or flaky skin I noticed prior. Meeting my stare, I knew he saw my observation.

Sensing the relative awkwardness that fell around the table, Kori tapped on the table impatiently, jokingly, still waiting for her story.

"So, how do you two know each other?" she offered as a start, presumably because it was a much safer question than *why were you running down the streets during an official alarm and why were your hands covered in blood?*

I considered how to answer for a moment. His face was back to staring into his drink.

"Family friend." I waved off her question with a sly smile. He stole a glance from beneath his eyelids curiously. "Met up for a drink, and—"

I spun a grandiose story about meeting up near the slummier side of Vayne at Kearey's, a bar where fishermen and women of the night donned their best going-out outfits and drank from nightfall to morning. I had actually been there on a handful of occasions a while back for a bite and a strong drink when everywhere else was closed. I weaved in some details of the interior—the ridiculous fake shark the length of two men that hung behind the bar, and the wooden half fish, half woman that stood greeting you as you entered—into my fabricated retelling of our night of burned, fried fish bites and catching up.

I explained we were just leaving as we heard the alarms, and confused and unaccustomed, we were simply trying to figure out if they meant a high tide or a storm was rolling in.

She watched my retelling, smiling at times, throwing her hands up at the mention of the burned food, nodding along. And though Zymir offered no details, he too watched as I told the story, as if caught up in it as well.

I ended the story with her offering us shelter, tying her in as our lucky savior, rescuing the idiots who couldn't figure out if they needed to get to high ground or bunker down below. She nearly spit out her drink at that, rolling her eyes dramatically at *savior*.

We were all silent for a bit after. I held onto my empty cup, wishing there were more, side-eyeing my companion's still full one beside me, contemplating asking for some of his but thinking better of it.

"I still think mine from earlier was better," she said finally, shrugging and pouring the last of the bottle into both our mugs.

"Your what was better?" I sipped the mead slower this time, savoring it.

For the first time since arriving, her voice grew serious as she tilted her chair backward, balancing on the back legs and swaying up and down with her foot hooked under the lip of the table.

"My tale." She took a big gulp, set the drink down, and leveled the chair. "My lie."

I was inclined to disagree, but decided it was best not to voice that.

"You could start by telling me what that is?" She squinted at my arm, and without following her stare, I knew she was looking at the cloudy, crimson tattoo.

The familiar heaviness returned to my shoulders. It felt so unfair—here was this almost ordinary moment, people sharing tales and drinking around a table, a scene I so deeply wished was nothing more than that, ruined by a dark reality I wore on my skin, unable to hide from for long before it always, inevitably reminded me why the mundane was a luxury I couldn't afford.

My naivety disgusted me.

And I reminded myself that this was *nothing* akin to normalcy, the entire circumstances of this encounter the result of what some would call the most unforgivable of violations—stealing the souls of the dead: The very reason I found myself just an hour before carving off a peculiar birthmark from the side of a stranger whose life was brutally ripped away prematurely. In a chain of ghastly offenses committed against that slumped-over man, who most likely walked and laughed and shared stories just as we were now, I was there at the end, ready to take what little he possessed if someone had not beat me to it. I would tell her the what and the why, and I would find myself immediately back on that street, hiding from those guards until I could reach the forest edge.

She reached a hand outward toward mine, which had begun trembling unbeknownst to me, and squeezed.

With an eerie knowing, as if I had said the words aloud, she said in barely more than a whisper, "You can tell me, I won't...I won't judge you, I mean," she searched for the words, "you saw earlier, I've done what I need to, to..."

To survive.

She let her sentence hang unfinished. I ripped myself out of my self-pity-ing spiral and blinked back the emotion building behind my eyes, donning instead the cool, familiar calmness I deflected to as a base. Zymir had only watched the exchange, his blank face giving no tells as to what he could be thinking.

I was thankful when he filled the lingering silence.

"I was following a trail for Osyren." Her hazel eyes waited patiently for an explanation. "I followed it to his home and found someone had slit his throat."

We both waited for some sort of additional context, but he didn't offer any until she gestured for him to continue.

"He was a hunter for the kingdom." Again, no real explanation. He looked almost equally confused at our blank faces.

"He killed a friend of mine," he tried a third time, "so I searched for him. But someone ended his life before I could." An almost feline hiss pursed his lips as he added, "And gave him far more mercy than I would have."

"Mercy?" Wide-eyed, all I could see was the gratuitous amounts of blood, the defensive cuts littering the backs of his hands.

He cocked his head to the side, a reaction that was already growing to annoy me. His face was aflame with some sort of disdain, and I could practi-cally see the cogs turning as he merely stared back, providing nothing more, deciding this was sufficient and relaxing his features to nothingness once more.

The hush fell, and I picked at the skin on the inside of my thumb.

I poured the rest of the second glass down my throat and set it down, shaking my head dismissively as I began, my turn for the truth at last.

CHAPTER 8

"My employer provides loans," I debated how much to reveal and tried to keep to the barest of facts, moving my hands expressively as I explained, "and people have loan terms." I swallowed, trying to coat my already dry throat despite the sweet lingering taste of the mead that had wet it only moments prior.

"This," I flipped up my wrist and tried to don the most detached look I could despite the internal grimace I had every time I looked at it, "tells me when someone has passed away without fulfilling the terms of their loan."

Kori nodded slowly, mouth slightly agape as she feigned understanding.

"Anyway, I was trying to leave town, and it went off a second time, so I followed the coordinates," I paused, making eye contact and adding, "—it, it'll show coordinates when a debtor has died, so I know where to go—and anyway, I got there and saw..." And my mind went black for a moment, concealing what I had tried to stop thinking about.

"Osyren with his throat slit," the blank, angular face said coolly.

"*That*," I shot him a harsh look, "and when I went to, um," *dammit,* "collect on the loan, I noticed someone had already removed the soul, the energy—I don't know—and then Zymir here popped out of a hallway, and we ran, and now we're here." I shrugged and sighed dramatically.

A ripple of interest cascaded through his features.

"What?" he asked, intensity brewing behind those shimmery eyes.

"What?"

"How could you tell his soul was taken?"

"There was a small incision at the base of his neck, it...it was hard to see because of all the blood, but...it matches the type of cut I have to make when I'm extracting."

Kori said nothing, but the gentle press of her lips together suggested she was still processing, patiently sorting through my words, trying to make sense of what she was just told.

"And how does it know when someone dies?" Kori's voice was soft as she tilted her head toward my wrist, but she faltered on the words as if not knowing the best way to phrase her inquiry.

"I don't know."

"And how does the whole thing work? Do they work as ghosts or something to repay their loans?"

"I...I don't know." But I wished I did.

She continued through a bombardment of questions I had no answers for. I was only ever told what I needed to know, but nothing more. I had only dared to ask similar questions when I first started working for Nox, shortly after that very first day shivering from hunger in thinly cased bones, and his severe unyielding reply was simply: *Better to not know. Better to do the job and not ask.* His condescension implied he was doing me a favor. And I never broached the topic again.

I wasn't sure how much time had passed since we first ran into the safety of Kori's home. But the weight of the day clung heavily to my eyelids, and I yawned abruptly as I provided what must've been my tenth "I don't know."

She yawned in response and chuckled. She pulled out her chair and went to the back wall where storage shelves lined the space near the ceiling. Hopping up slightly, she caught the edge of the folded blankets and sent them falling down.

She handed one to each of us and sheepishly glanced all around.

"Wherever you can find room," she offered.

None of us had discussed what the plan would be for tomorrow once the sun finally rose and the guards had slowed their hunt—they'd be careful to not cause much panic when the daytime brought eager merchants and travelers looking to spend excess coin. We couldn't go back into the darkness. That much was clear. We both took a blanket and veered for opposite corners, the man propped up against the wall, awkwardly holding the blanket off himself to the side.

I curled against my own wall, thankful the entire room could be seen from where I lay.

The petite frame of our host was the last standing near the table, waiting for us to position ourselves before leaning over the nearly fully melted candle, her shadows casting up against the walls before she blew out the flame and beckoned us to rest. I set my head down, and sleep found me faster than I expected.

I was swimming. Swimming beneath a cloudy red sea, a seemingly endless array of falling waves above my head. My arms out before me, I swam through the thickness, the scarlet fluid kissing my skin as I explored deeper and deeper into its depths, away from the light twinkling down above.

Singing. Humming. A light whisper filled the void all around me, a silky, feminine voice called out to no one in particular.

Like a ship passing overhead, a black cloud darkened the water, and my arms and legs glided through the haziness, suspended weightlessly in a swirling array of sparkling wetness. The water stiffened, cracked, jarring itself roughly against my senses before spiraling around in a deep funnel.

Around and around and around I went, limply flung from side to side as the funnel sucked me down to the ocean floor. I gasped and clawed and fought as I was dragged further. My head hurled around its axis, and the inkiness rushed to fill my nose and mouth. The light dimmed to nothing. My back hit roughness. Blindly, I reached out, fingers gripping the jagged, sandy ground, the indents of stones and shells pressing into my palms as I balled my hands into frustrated fists.

The enormity of the ocean pressed against my chest, leveling me to the earth. I went to speak, but my throat was thoroughly coated in blackness.

A sweet voice danced in my ears, humming cheerfully: *What have you done...*

What have you done...

Light bolted down from above in a blue-violet downpour.

My throat unlocked, and I was screaming, the sound jutting violently into my ears. Screaming and gurgling erupted as the air escaped my lips and the liquid flowed in to replace it. My gaze tried to focus on what the lightning strike had illuminated: The suspended body above my own.

The dead man's face was inches from my own, his eyes carved out in sutured cavities, and the gash under his chin hung wide open—exposed muscle and vocal cords on grisly display. His limbs were rigid, pulled taut away from his body.

I was screaming and screaming. His mouth hung wide open as if he was screaming with me. The sweet voice giggled playfully in my head, bounding around my skull.

What

Have

You

Done

Her beautiful voice pained inside me, the volume causing my head to feel like it was being split in two from the inside. Building pressure rippled down into my core, and I tried to arch my back to relieve the sheer force, but I stayed glued down, thrashing against the invisible chains that held me.

Slowly his jaw was pulled even lower, a dislocating crack sounding as it kept widening above my face. Another giggle and a surge of blackness gushed out his mouth, an endless, inky waterfall dampening my vision as a cold like I had never felt before numbed me beneath the cascade.

Wake up, it commanded.

Wake up, it sang.

Wake up, and a painful jolt shot through my body, causing my mind to tumble over itself.

Was I still screaming, or was he?

Was I held against the ocean floor, or was I the one suspended, arms and legs flailed, dangling loosely from invisible threads?

Wake up.

And I did.

I gasped, shooting straight up from my slumber. Facing me, wide-eyed and curious, Kori stood peering over my blanket, as if she had already woken, while Zymir still sat exactly where he was prior, gaze unmoving.

I was drenched in sweat. The small half window on the wall furthest from me had the barest of coral-colored light shining in, the sun making its arrival just beyond the horizon. Steadying my breath, I stared at my knees, embarrassment dangerously close to reddening my cheeks. I inhaled, held the air in, and exhaled. Again and again.

The sunlight bounced off the angles of Zymir's face, his light hair nearly luminescent in its path.

"You were speaking in your sleep," he said, looking down from his nose.

With cold, clammy hands, I unstuck the damp hair from behind my neck, quickly pulling out the tie that had nearly come out on its own, balled up at the nape. I proceeded to reposition it high behind the back of my head, wrapping it in a tight bun, only a few strands in the front hanging beside my temples that wouldn't reach.

Kori placed a glass of water in my hands. I hadn't even noticed her pour one, too busy staring at a speck of dirt on the wall beneath the window. I said nothing but got up and folded the blanket. I glanced at the table and noticed the man's cup still untouched from last night—without thinking, I quickly replaced it with the one in my hand and poured it down my throat, lukewarm sweetness hitting my empty stomach. A rumble warned me I'd probably regret that later, but I didn't care.

"Okay..." she softly said, mostly to herself.

Another deep inhale, hold, and exhale, and I rethought. I slammed the water too. I'd need it for the long trek back through the Elsh forest.

As if hearing the thought, she rummaged for a bag near her makeshift bed and readily slung it over her back, a too eager grin painted on her delicate features. They both seemed to hesitate, as if this early morning light was as good as mine to choose how to best utilize. And considering I wanted to do anything other than talk about the nightmare that was still raw in my mind, I accepted the lead with a shrug.

"I need to go back to Alaria," I said as I held the doorknob, braced for whatever the streets of Vayne held. I took the relative silence behind the door as a promising sign. I couldn't hear the alarms from last night, or the hurried shuffle of passersby.

They both took a step toward the door, Kori's a bit more chipper as she moved right behind me.

"You two don't need to come." I hesitated. "I have to go to Alaria and tell Nox what happened. See if he's heard anything about another debt collector. Tell him I missed the second alarm…" dread swirled around in my gut, but I pushed it down. "See what my orders are."

I watched Zymir's ears twitch at the name, processing, and I cursed for using it so blatantly. Still smiling, Kori brushed off the statement, bouncing from foot to foot as if all that energy packed into such a small body needed to be released by constant fidgeting.

She waved a hand all around, gesturing to the clutter all around. Her chin was held high, but the grin she wore didn't continue to her eyes this time as she added, "I have nothing better to do."

Her tone was playful, but there was a finality to her words that I didn't pry into.

Zymir observed her as she spoke and fiddled around. He then stated simply, "I have to find who killed Osyren."

I didn't want to help him on a fool's trip for vengeance. There was no time for that, and his fight was not my own—I had plenty of other issues back in Alaria to deal with. But he, too, looked like he wouldn't be swayed as he kept his glance even and controlled.

"It is in both our best interests to figure out who got to that swine before me. I will help you find whoever killed Osyren," icy, calculated words, "if you promise that he's mine after."

A picture of the bloodied, suspended man from my dream flashed before my eyes. No more killing, no more blood…I didn't want any other faces lingering around in my head. But with his eerie, perfect stillness and knack for calculating the approach of guards, I weighed the potential pros of making such a promise with someone I had only just met. Paths crossed by sinister circumstances often ended poorly. I knew that. My options, though, with little else to go on, were limited, and my skills lay not in tracking.

"Fine. Help me find him, and he's all yours."

I knew as I said it that doing so would be a condition to avoid Nox's rage for botching the job—he would accept nothing less than full compliance to right my wrong for not extracting his debtor's collateral.

"But first, Alaria."

He nodded, and we departed, slipping out in the daylight dew.

The streets were indeed empty. The lanterns no longer held flames and the blue-stoned walkway out of town was only a block away. We found that path and strolled, avoiding a fast dash that would draw potentially nosy eyes. Rosy, vivid hues led our journey, a bit *too* bright as the sun climbed higher and we progressed to the familiar forest face.

We walked in relative silence, but what was missing in conversation was fully replaced by the songs of low-flying birds and the hum of insects in the tall grass. Strong winds carried us, pushing on our backs from the coast as if it was coaxing us out of its sight. I said nothing about my jolted wake-up earlier, and I was thankful that neither asked.

Finally, we breached the forest's edge, knobby trees densely created their own comfort from the sun's rays. They swayed in the rough wind that had decided to follow us further. An earthy, pine smell greeted us as we entered Elsh and slipped into its long shadows. Moss coated the ground and clung onto some of the branches, covering the rocks and jagged ground.

The green in her hazel eyes seemed more pronounced amongst the greenery, and they danced with delight as Kori peered up the towering trunks. Her chin nearly scraped the bark as she pressed herself against the largest of them, her stare following their lines up into the sky.

"I've never been to the forest," she admitted.

Zymir hadn't waited as she periodically stopped to rest a hand on the trees or run her fingers into the dirt. I swear he glanced at her as she spoke, though, as if to say: *Yeah, we can tell,* but his blank face gave no confirmation of his thoughts as we trudged deeper into the wooden arms of the ancient forest.

"Never?" I asked. Despite what I guessed was only a slim difference in age, the simple awe she carried through a relatively well-known path I had made at least a dozen times made the margin feel substantial.

She shook her head and shot me a devilish smirk. "My mother used to say wood sprites lived here, hiding in the trees. And that if you so much as touched one of them, one of *their* trees, they'd lull you to sleep and drag you into their trunks with them."

"Then why touch *everything?*"

The rough edge of Zymir's polished voice caught me by surprise. He didn't so much as look at her as he asked, maintaining the straight stare he had held since we entered the forest.

She responded with a slight harshness I hadn't heard from her before either, though she paired it with an off-the-cusp swing of her shoulder. "Because I don't believe in children's stories. And even if I did," she bit her lip with intrigue as she ran her fingertips along the rough bark of another tree, "I'd prefer to test them myself."

She continued despite his disinterest, "I've always lived in Vayne. The ocean waves have been my lullaby since I was young. But Vayne is a superstitious town, and both my parents never ventured far inland because of it."

"What about you?" she countered. "I imagine you've spent plenty of time here...based on your *smell.*" Her nostrils flared for dramatic effect, and I didn't know whether to grimace or laugh.

He said nothing, as if it'd cost him too much energy and time to reply. It was an uncomfortable pause that was quickly filled by a far-off cracking of a stepped-on branch snapping in two.

We all froze.

A cooler air filled the space between us, seemingly materializing out of nowhere. Another snap came from the same direction, but closer this time. I scanned, searching between trees for any signs of movement or shadows.

Golden eyes sharped, and his shoulders stiffened. I saw him reach for no weapons, but I delicately found one from my belt instinctively in my palm as Kori sidestepped between us.

A low snarl dripped from his lips. "We need to run."

Shadows moved in the distance.

"Now."

CHAPTER 9

Without hesitation, I launched forward, keeping careful watch on Kori as she ran slightly behind. Darting in and out of trees, I feared one misstep would have me tumbling over my knees—or worse, hurling straight into a tree trunk, my nose catching my fall head-on. I kept it out of my mind, following the gray blur in front of me, steering us into a seemingly random path deeper and deeper into the woods.

The ground was soft, recently wet from a springtime rain. Downed branches and fresh leaves required added circumnavigation as I leaped over several with purposeful care to avoid slipping on any smooth surfaces. I felt my legs burn as I struggled to keep up with our guide, who hadn't once bothered to glance back, as if to do so would cost us valuable seconds. I focused on that as I followed with painful urgency, telling myself that whatever would make him run like this was not something we wanted to outpace us.

But Kori struggled, her jumps and steps faintly hesitant and awkward as she tried weaving amongst the greenery. She pressed onward, but the distance between the three of us lengthened.

I slowed my pace and waited for her to catch up.

Her heavy breathing rasped, and beads of sweat topped her freckled nose. I ran beside her, slowing my legs and catching my own breath as I did. We realized at the same time that Zymir had vanished somewhere up ahead.

"I—I need—" Her face was flush.

Against my better judgment, I stopped, allowing her a moment to calm her frenzied lungs as I surveyed the area around us, intently searching for that gray tunic and rustled white hair. She leaned over on her knees, and as her heartbeat leveled, the rosiness of her cheeks seemed less because of her elevated pulse and more because of her slower pace.

A distinct shriek sounded in the distance up ahead—shrill, much higher pitched than Zymir's voice. I handed one of my daggers aside, pressing it firmly into her hand.

"Do you know how to use this?"

Worry lines creased her temples as she shook her head.

"It's a double-edged blade," I slashed the air up and then down, "meaning you can attack targets that face you and those that face away."

Her short hair bobbed as she nodded. I pulled out another blade of my own and slid it through the air, watching her as she imitated the movement.

"Downward thrust. Use it if you're approached by someone else without a weapon." As she repeated the action once more, I continued, "Now, grab the hilt, hold it up and down, *aim,* and bring the blade directly down in a slash instead of a thrust." I demonstrated and assessed her quick repeat, adding, "This is best for defense."

Another shriek, vaguely closer but followed by a hoarse grunt. Her eyes wandered up ahead, but I waved my hand to regain her focus.

"Last one—hold the weapon horizontally." I held my blade at eye level, and she stretched a limp arm out in front with hers. "Tilt the blade away from you, handle toward your body." She did as I instructed. "This will extend your reach in combat, allowing you to attack anyone approaching." I forward-slashed a few times. "The idea is to move around any sort of defensive gear they may be wearing and pierce the skin."

I watched her do all three moves, sloppily, but hoped the overview would come in handy as we waited together within the shade of the vast branches, listening for any further cries of distress.

As I went to step forward, a crunch whispered behind me. I spun on my heels, calming my breath and silencing my thoughts. I centered my concentration on the spot between two pale birch saplings where the slightest movement from a low-hanging branch told me to align my sight. My thumb trailed the hilt, applying pressure, so my hands were ready to strike.

"A dagger?" Zymir walked out unimpressed. "I can think of nothing in this forest that a dagger would do much good against."

I contemplated throwing it at him for startling us, but set it back in my belt, unamused, heart still waiting for permission to race now that the immediate demand for calm had passed. His muscled arms were lax beside him, hands wedged deep into pockets, nonchalant, if he could be such a thing.

"Where *were* you?" The color had drained from Kori's face at the prospect of an altercation, and despite the obvious exasperation in her tone, she slumped and exhaled in gratitude.

He strolled past her without answering. There were no visible wounds I could see, but as he came closer, I could smell sweat and hear the lag in his right foot, slowed just a second out of pace in his gate—lingering evidence of whatever had happened up ahead.

"What was that?" she asked again, no feigned smile or pleasantries.

When he didn't answer, her voice sharpened, and her grip around my weapon tightened.

"You left us here," she said, nearly snarling, the excess adrenaline left with nowhere else to go funneling into her shaking voice. I delicately placed a light hand on her shoulder, feeling the rapid rise and fall as she huffed.

"I'm here to find whoever is responsible for Osyren's death." Shadows darkened the amber sharpness in his stare as he faced her, thin-lipped. "And that's it—where I go and how I choose to deal with the obstacles along our course are my decisions alone. We continue our journey, that's all that matters."

Passing back my weapon and straightening out her navy shirt and leathers, she merely scoffed.

"Running from something in the woods and leaving behind two members of your party seems like a shit strategic plan to me, but what do I know?"

She swung her bag off her shoulder and set the tanned cloth on the mossy floor, muddying the bottom. Unclipping the two front latches, she dove to the bottom, nearly elbows-deep in, rummaging around as glass clattered against glass within. She withdrew a dark bottle, bit off the cork top with her teeth, and spit it back into the opened bag. She guzzled her drink, wiping her mouth with the sleeve. With an outstretched arm, she offered me the last sip, but I declined.

The sun had rested lower on the horizon now, bright yellow deepening into orange as its heat wound its fingers in between the tree's coverage. I surveyed both my walking companions. Exhaustion saturated the air.

"We should set up camp soon. One more hour east, then we'll stop for the night." Their lack of a response was as good as confirmation for me.

We walked. Zymir's hesitant leg slowly made up its speed as we continued our path, making me wonder if I had fabricated the observation. The soft bouncing of rain droplets started, ricocheting off wide glossy leaves and sliding down to periodically dampen my hair and shoulders.

Camp was set up silently. Kori gathered kindling from the forest floor as Zymir and I fashioned a shelter big enough for all of us. My tarp was already plenty wide, so we scrounged for perfectly sized sticks to lean against one another to create the frame. He secured large rocks at the corners, as the howl of the rolling winds indicated that the droplets stood a good chance of downpour later. A personal fire the size of the one I usually made just for myself was the last thing we situated—huddled onto the ground equidistant from one another, vying for any amount of warmth.

The bags under Kori's eyes darkened beneath the fire's light, and she yawned twice in rapid succession before excusing herself to the tent and curling up inside.

Dancing flames captivated me and allowed the moment to pass without any thoughts or disruptions, just mesmerizing tongues of light darting up and down. The evening welcomed us, trading the harsh sun for the twinkle of holes cut through the sky. A drone of buzzing and chirps from spring beetles filled the air behind the crackle of wood.

Traveling with others felt different.

Not wholly wrong, but not necessarily pleasant either. It was like an added layer of awareness atop every action. I wasn't just sitting by the fire. I was now conscious of seeing myself sit around the fire, the experiencer and the observer. It made my movements more particular and my words more precise. I avoided looking directly at Zymir, who sat twice as far away from the fire as I did. My body sloped over, creating a cave of its heat.

I always traveled light in more ways than one. Extra belongings or baggage or people posed an additional thought I'd have to consider before taking any action. I couldn't just run up ahead and escape a foe, I'd have to be wary of the safety of all those traveling with me. Though for some reason, that same detriment evidently was not felt universally. Why run up ahead at their risk? Zymir seemed calculating above all else, expertly timing arrivals of guards and navigating where needed—until now, his intentions had at least *seemed* in all our best interests.

But I also had no idea who he was, or his real intentions for traveling to Alaria. I wasn't even sure why he was so determined to sink a blade into whoever killed Osyren—maybe doing so would simply lessen the internal wound from the loss of his friend.

Or maybe he was just talk. Everyone's just words, after all.

We were a kingdom of words, of engrossing stories of lore and high tales of a time long ago when there were so many more unknowns and opportunities. The past was to be romanticized and never verified, since those who lived it were long gone. That old reality was now replaced by a sense of longing for anything other than the same, incessant goal of resolving hunger and surviving to do it again tomorrow. And not just the people. Even the kingdom merely survived. Thriving was for the times of war, of victory. Guards and soldiers with nothing to do had to find other ways to stay occupied, making artificial foes where they could—a hungry thief, a slighted lover, a brawl between men who had drunk too much in the attempt to blur any real sense of self.

It was an overwhelming cycle of numbness and distractions.

The rumble of thunder barreled through my mind, and a sharp strike of lighting towered down from the sky somewhere far north. The flash caused my skin to pebble in an eerie, familiar way. I ignored the glaring face in the back of my mind. I tried to forget the haunting melody from my slumber last night.

"You're still thinking about him," Zymir said it without inflection, and it was decidedly not a question. I went to ask who he meant, but his knack for tuned-in observation made that feel silly and unnecessary.

I nodded.

I could feel his darting pupils running back and forth, scanning my face for insight.

When he found none, he asked, "Why?"

I gingerly touched my wrist, running a finger over my rosy tattoo that was merely a blur in the nighttime light. I traced the bones beneath my skin, remembering the tug from my run-in with the brutes in Alaria, twisting my hand as if in thanks it was rotating properly and not delaying the use of my weapons.

"I've never seen someone murdered before." The admittance felt somehow juvenile, but I couldn't explain why.

He narrowed his brows and ran a palm through his hair, the short strands circling the tips of his fingers and gliding through without resistance.

"But," he didn't hesitate as much as scan through a directory of words to choose through for precision, "you work with the dead. Does collection not entail killing your targets?"

"Gods, no." I didn't feel like looking at him, so I kept focused on the dwindling fire that fought against the accruing rain droplets hitting its face. "They're always already dead."

"How?"

"How what?"

He shifted his seated position and drew his legs in, keeping his back still and straight. "How are they already dead if not by your hand?"

"Some from illness, old age, maybe hunger." Apprehensively I added, "There's never blood, there's never a fight...they're just...dead when I get there. They die, which triggers the alert that the loan terms have expired without being fulfilled."

He listened patiently, if a bit doubtfully. A sliver of realization peppered his face as he looked at me with a sort of softness, as if the red-painted display we had seen was replaying for him too. There was recognition there, acknowledgement that my inexperience with the grotesque nature of killing made it jarring and raw.

What have you done...

The memory whispered in my ears and pulled me into my thoughts, reminding me of the accusatory tone, the demanding inquiry of that lovely voice.

His questioning had me inclined to cross-examine him. It reignited my interest as to why he had darted out ahead so far. It made me want to ask why he'd left us to fend off whatever it was that had spurred him to bark his order to run. But as I did, I stared again at the leg he was faltering with after his disappearance. And noticed now in the flickering embers that it was damp, darkened by a deeper wetness akin to those speckled walls in Vayne.

Spotting my observation, he pushed the ankle further into the shadows, away from the fire's needy curiosity. His unease under my notice made me reconsider asking. Instead, we stayed silent amidst the evening howl of wind and prancing drops of rain. Because in that wordless motion, I knew what he wouldn't say—that whatever was up ahead of us, he had taken care of.

He had decided to take the brunt of the threat alone. Whether for efficiency or our safety or both, I wasn't sure. And in thanks, I wouldn't make him say it, even if we both knew it was true.

The next three days were much the same. Kori marveling at sloshing rivers and the peeled skin of the birch trees. Her naïve excitement was contagious, at least for me, as I found myself staring at the familiar with a newfound appreciation for their details. She and Zymir barely spoke unless it was to move past one another or when divvying up tasks to set up at nightfall. But it wasn't an awkward lack of communication between them. Zymir hardly said much at all, his focus squarely planted ahead, his head tilting and turning to best hear any unusual sounds or potential approaching feet.

We were a day out from Alaria. We could make it in the evening or spend one more night in the woods so that our arrival was in the day. Discussion was brief as to which was a better option, with Zymir unsurprisingly preferring the evening and Kori opting to see the city when the sun was high, and the shops open. As the deciding vote, I would have admittedly preferred to go with the former, sneak in and out in one night and avoid lingering longer. But I knew Nox wouldn't be at his store at night, which left no other option than to arrive as regular customers under the guise of normal business.

Zymir didn't argue when we set up camp one last time. He gathered wood for the shelter, taking the opportunity to wander out of sight for longer than needed before having to return. He returned with an armful of several unnecessarily large tree branches, carrying their weight across his forearms as if they were as light as the twigs he had been gathering on nights prior. He set them down in a huff and sat down near the bundled kindling, not yet lit but gathered into a pile ready to be.

Kori was peering down in a squat a few feet away at the base of an unremarkable tree. The curve of her back and rounded shoulders hunched all the way over reminded me of when Tillian and I would go searching for toads when we were young. We'd sneak around the outskirts of the city, hug the banks of the Irvine River. You could tell when he'd found one. He would lean over perfectly still and quiet, a break in his steady bragging about the best ways to find all the bugs and amphibians on the wet ground floor. And though I'd be behind and running to catch up to him, I knew his careful hands were waiting for the toad to choose to step into his dirtied palms before caging his fingers around and cupping it. A victorious grin accompanied the reveal as he'd stand to share his catch.

I nearly asked if that's what she had found before she waved a hand my way, beckoning me to join her.

As I approached, the smell of rot tickled my nose, and I sniffed in confusion. I paused to glance around at the varying shades of green, searching for an origin. The passing smell was fleeting, replaced just as fast with the dampness of moss and pine. She waved at me again but didn't look up.

Beneath the tree was a beautiful mess of star-shaped flowers, lavender outstretched arms around a golden center, clustered in what must've been dozens of eager, flowery faces. They surrounded the base of the tree on all sides, a collar of floral stars, extending further behind, up a slight incline and presumably beneath.

Her delicate fingers cradled one, bringing her face into its center before crinkling her nose to find no fragrance. I crouched beside her, admiring their smooth leaves and rayed petals.

"There's something wrong with them," she said softly.

I went to explain that these wildflowers didn't typically have a smell, but before I could, she explained, "These ones by the tree, they're healthy." She wiggled its stem delicately between her thumb and forefinger. "But these ones, they're—come and see."

She stood and walked toward the continued field of flowers behind the tree, up the mound, and then down through the shrubs. At the bottom of the mound, there were more, but these flowers bore no colors. The same outstretched cluster of petals were gray and lifeless, wilting over at their ends, drooping toward the earth. The centers were black, evidence of a muted lack of life. But there more of them too, some healthy and some not. The field of flowers was still growing, spreading, but it looked as if illness had struck them, and their malaise was spreading.

"Astors," Zymir said gently, having walked up silently behind us. He scanned the field, and his face sagged, a low sigh escaping his lips.

His voice grew taut. "They're called the flowers of the forest nymphs." He didn't bother to check for Kori's reaction to more lore, only solemnly combed through the flower heads with his fingers. "Did you see any nearby ponds?"

"No, I found these only because I saw the ones by the tree," she said, tucking a lock of hair behind her ear.

Zymir rubbed his temples. He walked through the listless wildflowers and followed them down a narrow path between low-leaning trees, a tunnel of woody arms forming at the bottom of the hill. We trailed behind, and the occasional waft of decay teased us further.

Without their lavender edges, the starworts were a shadow, a night sky with empty holes that once shone brightly now only displaying shades of gray. Zymir ducked low to follow the dip in the path through the tunnel, moving around the thin, woody branches. I held them up as Kori followed between us, though she needed far less breadth above her to make it through. I was careful as I held the archway up for the alternating thorns prickling out the ends.

The living tunnel broke to, sure enough, a small body of water. Or at least what used to be.

The edges of the lake were receded, remnants of blue-green algae and wispy water plants dried out on the barren ground. What remained was a retracted center of liquid a quarter of its original size. The dark, standing body of water smelled putrid, decomposition of leaves—and who knew what else—was an assault on our noses as Zymir continued to its core, seemingly unaffected spare his tensely clasped hands behind his back.

He stopped at the edge of the sludgy water. Closer, it appeared nearly black, and the smell was so intense that Kori remained back at the tunnel's mouth. But I waited beside him and heard the frustrated growl escaping his lips.

"At one time, this was called Belides Lake," his voice cracked, breaking the unreadable look on his face. "The story goes that she and the other nymphs were dancing along the water's edge when she caught the eye of another deity. To escape his pursuits, she transformed into the aster flower. They're hers."

His voice was strong but pained, and he swallowed hard as the lines between his eyes deepened in thought.

I contemplated what to ask. I knew there were many people who believed in the forest nymphs. Many retold the believed sightings, or passed on the generational stories, like the ones Kori had been told when she was young. Legends of the vast arrays of magical beings that walked the land with us were common, but no one actually saw them anymore, not *really*. Sure, a traveler here and there would come in panting from a trip where he'd tell of his narrow escape from a monster, but more often than not, the panic was rasped out on breath that lingered with the smell of alcohol and smoke.

And then there were the Ryvinians, a religious sect who not only believed the fables, but prayed to the old death deity Ryv, worshipping him in macabre admiration in fear he'd return to smite the land. But Zymir didn't wear their red hoods or circle-talon necklaces. He couldn't possibly be in their cult.

I had seen coincidences and luck, even been fortunate enough to be the recipient of it. I had seen beauty so unusual it felt beyond the grasps of normal splendor. But there was never anything further to suggest the circumstances tied back to real gods or mythical creatures. I was doubtful of his claim, to say the least.

Instead of pushback, though, I pivoted to the obvious assault on nature that gathered before us.

"What would cause the water to recede like this?" I inched out before him and his back stiffened as I went to stick a finger into the blackness.

He yanked my arm back before I could shove the tips below the surface, seriousness masking his expression.

Turning around and grabbing one of the dried aquatic leaves, he held it up by its edge and dropped it. It floated down, and as it found the watery surface, the blackness bubbled around the leaf, gurgling upward and thickly coating its back. The perimeter flaked away and caved in upon itself in a fiery rimmed ash that soon disintegrated in its entirety.

All the hairs on my body stood at attention, and a shiver ran from the base of my skull down my spine. Zymir snickered and started back toward Kori, who stood patiently next to the tunnel opening, shifting her weight back and forth between her legs and smoothing out the edges of her tunic as she waited.

"What are you not telling me?" I asked and pulled his shoulder back so that he was facing me. His body turned without resistance, and I dropped my hand instinctively. His shoulder, despite a layer of cloth atop it, felt icy to the touch, the bitterness lingering on the tips of my fingers.

"The royal family may have disappeared, but their aspirations have not." A tight lip grimace soon relaxed as he fell back to his normal blank look. "They continue to clean up Sheirsa and rid it of any creatures they fear too much to let live." He pointed to the black watery mote. "Can't have a water nymph without her lake." He pointed across at the grayed flowers. "Can't have her flowers when they suck water from the poisoned swamp they left behind."

He briskly pushed past both of us and ducked beneath the branches that led back to where we set up camp. I followed on his heels, unsatisfied by his half answer. Kori trailed behind us both, eyes darting from me to him as she tensed around the charged air. The back of his head didn't bother to rotate to us, and he didn't stop his speedy pace until he reached the camp clearing where our meager kindle lay piled up near the folded tarp that had not yet been pitched.

"Explain." I threw my body in front of his haphazardly to disrupt his determined escape, causing him to merely sidestep out of the way with zero apprehension. He started on the tent, immediately returning to the task he had abandoned when we went searching through the wildflowers.

"Zymir," I snapped, a mix between confusion and frustration wetting my forehead.

I racked my brain, trying to figure out what could turn water into the corrosive black tar we'd left behind. The limp flowers were decaying so slowly that the edges of their fields were still unaffected. The congregation spread further away in a doomed escape, unaware that their roots would soon draw from the same poisoned source. Kori's mouth hung open slightly, trying to follow the conversation or make sense of the blatant exasperation oozing from my stiff position. It was a conscious effort to not let my hand drift to the helm of a blade, but I was purposeful to keep it out beside me.

His glance casually lifted from below his eyelids as he knelt near the large branches he had collected, pulling two into his arms and jamming their ends into the softened dirt. He continued with another two, gaze unmoving as he did, not risking a single peek downward at his work and lest break the eye contact we held.

And, of course, at that moment, as the top of his lip snarled up as if ready to finally elaborate, a familiar stinging sensation buzzed below my skin. Even without looking or following his curious eyes as they darted down, I knew that the crimson tattoo was swirling around on my wrist, positioning itself for its next command.

Perfect timing.

CHAPTER 10

"**I**s that how—?" Kori ran up beside me and delicately placed my arm between her fingers, turning it around and inspecting it as the mixing colors leveled to a coordinate area I had never worked out of: the western edge of Alaria, the poorest district in the capital, as abysmally dangerous as it was utterly decrepit.

As far as interruptions went, this one was particularly shitty.

Zymir seemed to tell, the intrigue weaning from his wide eyes as he did the same mental calculation as I had. The campsite was halfway put up. All that was left was to drape the tarp over the logs and to light the fire. The sky was low on the horizon, deep oranges and pinks littered in sideswipes across the sky. The sun would be fully set within an hour, and as close as we were to the town's outskirts, I could get to my location and out by the time the stars had fully made their evening appearance.

"I can be in and out before you two even lay down," I spoke as I grabbed a stack of dried fish Kori had packed in her bag and left out on a stump absent-mindedly when she got distracted by the flowers. "Okay, well, maybe not you," I gestured to her with the flaky whitefish, taking a bite and speaking with it in my mouth as I did, "but still, in and out."

"You can't be serious." She laughed, tossing her short hair back with her as she did. "We'll come with you! We have to go into town anyway."

I froze, grimacing at the anticipated response.

"You can't, really..." I trailed off and pictured her innocent, round eyes aghast as I plunged a syringe between a corpse's collar bones. I imagined her stepping away terrified, disgust replacing the friendly smile she wore so effortlessly. "It's too dangerous. This job's in the *worst* part of the city. I need to be in and out, and I can't risk added attention."

She ignored me and packed the rest of her assorted belongings into the slacked bag on the ground, namely another empty bottle and assorted salted nuts she'd snacked on the entire journey thus far. I had no idea how she hadn't run out or gotten sick of them. Even birds didn't pick away at as many seeds and nuts as she seemed to.

"Kori," I paused her rummaging and sat a hand on her shoulder, "I mean it, you should stay here."

"She's right." Zymir's smooth but stern voice surprised me, and I tossed a suspicious look his way. In our back and forth, he had managed to throw the tarp over the wooden structure and secure it, which would mean it was ready come nightfall. "Stay here and keep watch." A flicker of his lips again pulled up at their ends. "I'll go with her."

It was as much of a smile as I had yet to see from him, as if he could hear the internal groan I made in response. The rest of his body was lax, his expression blank otherwise.

"I'm going alone." Fire dared to dance behind my words, the sincerity of my tone harsh.

"You said it yourself—the Sunset District is unsafe. If I go with you, it'll minimize unwanted interest and expedite your stop." I couldn't argue with that per se, though I searched through rationale that would allow me to. The area was incredibly unforgiving to visitors, but especially to women, and especially to women alone. But I didn't fancy myself the kind that needed to be escorted.

This burden was mine alone to bear, to collect and incrementally pay back a debt solely my own. It sat uncomfortably in my chest as I weighed his words and fought the urge to run off before needing to argue further to rid myself of the predicament altogether. He had been at the last stop, though—already seen how my fingers stayed steady as I sliced a dead man's skin off to investigate later, saw me crouched over the emptied body with blood-stained knuckles.

I didn't like it, but I sighed and accepted the logic of it.

"Do you know this precise location?" I extended my arm and waited for him to peer at the sizzling numbers fully painted now on my wrist.

Despite the distance, he didn't step closer, merely nodded in complete confidence.

With his confirmation, I pulled Mion out of my pocket and opened Kori's hand. Gently placing the tangled wires in her palm, I lowered her fingers to conceal and grasp him. Marvel dazzled her face, and she peeked in between the gaps of her hands, holding them up at eye level.

"Mion." At the sound of my voice, the tiny prongs jutted up from the center coil and waited for an instruction. "Mi, this is Kori." The left prong settled into itself slightly and rose, listening. She grinned awkwardly and stayed perfectly still, as if a bird was trapped in her grasp instead of a mess of chords. "If anything happens, if you hear anything when we're gone, tell Mion to take you to Tillian—he's a friend in town."

I could see the cloudy questions forming in her mystified look, but she simply bowed her head, keeping Mi safely in her palms as I marched begrudgingly over to Zymir.

He and I left camp immediately. A squeak of shock piped up behind us, and I knew Mi had mostly liked climbed out of her hands and onto her shoulder, where it liked to perch, or tip-toed down into her pocket for safekeeping. Our departure was speedy, our pace escalating to a run as the bottom rim of the sun kissed the treetops and sunk beneath the skyline.

The edge of the forest was closer than I thought, and the telltale signs of the Sunset District—rusted shingled homes and a breeze of rotting trash—greeted us. Deteriorating wooden panels of homes often caused the structures to collapse onto themselves, leaving planks in disarray and rusted metal work jarring out. To a degree, most families had little money in Alaria. The wealth of the city was centralized in the palace and those who kept it—soldiers, guards, nobility, priests—and those around it were subsequently tasked with tidy upkeep to extend the illusion of ever-flowing prosperity. There was a pride to Alaria's citizens even without its gold, though, a freedom to try your hand at many forms of commerce and opportunity, a bravado that only those who lived in the city of kings could claim. Even if it was foolish.

We entered the city on a dirt path. The windows of the homes were mostly broken in, shards of glass on the perimeters. A few people slept outside the homes wrapped in blankets, their faces turned away and covered. The early evening sounds were coughing and distant yelling. We passed two women, thin-framed, who huddled beside one another and whispered beneath their tattered, gray veils.

"What is Mion?" Zymir asked in a steady tone that made the starting unease creep away.

"A question for a question?" I offered, matching his pace as we continued. His chest rose and sank. "Fine."

"Honestly, I'm not quite sure." We rounded a corner where an old market stood, shut down, stands dusty and barren. "I found it in the trash one day when I was young." I chose to leave out that I had been rummaging for food. The bleakness of this part of town was flooding familiar pangs of hunger aches and chapped lips. "I wanted to see if I could detangle it, and when I did, its eyepieces shot right up, and the chords untangled themself. I think he's some sort of navigation machine."

"Interesting." He sounded sincere and turned his head to the left. The next street had one man down it about halfway, drunkenly leaning against a wall, slurring to himself with bits of food in his beard and an empty bottle clanging against the wooden door frame.

"What did you mean by the 'kingdom's aspirations?' What creatures did they fear?" I asked a bit too fast, the words spilling out of me. These weren't subjects often spoken of. It made me curious to know what else was kept in the silence.

He stepped a sliver closer to me as we passed the man, sunken bags under his eyes, a deep bruise on the top of his bald head. He rocked back and forth, repeating the word *liar* over and over, banging his head against the door at each repetition. Each thud equally unnerved me and pained my heart.

"That's two questions." We rounded another corner, deepening into the arms of the city where the homes were slightly more put together, though there were still few people out. "The first king of Sheirsa, Harolde, united generations of warring clans. Men abandoned their family banners in exchange for the crimson Sheirsan one under the promise of peace. Those stacked crescent moons represented the beginning of a new night—one where men no longer had to fear going out in the darkness."

Zymir paused and tilted his head to the house slightly ahead on our right. It was identical to the last few we passed—black wood panels, flattened roof, rounded green painted door. The ease of our approach lingered with me. No one had stopped us, spoken to us, and the few people we had passed seemed more concerned with themselves than anything else around them. I followed him around to the expected rear entrance.

I inched past him to the door. Though the sun had set, its rays were not fully replaced by moonlight, and a foggy grayness lingered in the air, just enough brightness to spur another scan down the alley between the homes. Discarded papers, broken bottle glass, something putrid and sludgy a few feet ahead—but no people. Routine hesitance aside, I found the doorknob loosely secured and wobbly, turning independent of its few absent screws. I pressed my weight against the door, and it opened without a struggle.

"I think I'm missing the part where the desire for peace is a bad thing," I whispered over my shoulder and crawled into the home's shadows. I was careful in my wording to avoid a direct question, but I only had more of them accumulating, swimming around in my thoughts, popping up one after another.

A frail, nearly colorless woman sat propped up in a torn recliner in the living room, already visible for the back door's entrance. Long, thin white hairs draped over her chest, and she wore a stained nightgown several sizes too large. Familiar blank hazy orbs signaled my destination.

I entered the bare room and knelt beside her, pulling out my tools one by one in the order in which they'd be used for fastest collection and timely departure.

"Why are you in this line of work?" He stood above me and selected his words deliberately. His expression lacked judgment—and I knew the stare of judgment—but the angles of his face seemed to cast even darker shadows than those within the room, juxtaposing the brisk light in his eyes.

Curved knife, precise crisscross incision.

A sudden realization made disgust flood into my veins. The subtlest of softness in his downward glance made me turn my head back to my work. It was *pity* in his eyes...And I would have preferred judgment to pity.

I gritted my teeth. "Different question."

He tilted his head to the side in that annoying way, and I was thankful I was too focused to reveal my irritation. I drew my syringe and went about my extraction, the pooling, shimmery liquid filing its barrel. He leaned down for a closer look, the glittery ocean reflecting on the glass of his pondering eyes. He rubbed the base of his neck with a single finger, pressing his own tanned skin in and circling it.

"What do they do with this…substance?" In the brief time since I had met him, he had never really faltered over his words. I noted the hesitation, though I didn't know what to make of it.

"I bring it to Nox," I explained as I emptied the syringe into a clean vial. I tried to ignore the bottle that contained the sample of flesh in my bag, but it felt looming and observatory. It felt like it was vying for my attention. "And he sells it."

I remembered the papers on his desk, an endless array of accounting sheets. One time when I had come to deliver vials, after that initial year when I'd return after each and every extraction to deliver a sole debtor, I cared enough to scan his penned notes when he'd left me waiting in his office with my first double return. And through the nerves and mental weight of two full vials in my bag, I saw what looked like a tally record of auctions beside names—I never wanted to see the names, I had skipped right over that—but there were debts totaled in red ink, and below, a substantially larger number in blue. The net difference continued on the far column.

"They die with an outstanding loan. People want this badly enough." I swirled the contents around in the vial. "They pay off the debt, and *then some.*"

He went to speak, but I cut him off. "What did you mean by crea-tures—what *creatures* is the kingdom after?" I secured the glass and tied my bag shut. He was fixated on the violet felt, as if he could stare straight through the fabric and find the additional answers he sought. I used to do the same. I'd stare at that liquid for hours, equal parts interest and disgust and confusion until it no longer captivated me. Because it couldn't—there wasn't time for wonder when a compounding debt pressed on to me with every extraction, every vial a singular hope for the day that my sheet would be tallied down at the bottom with a crisp black-inked zero.

"People fear what they do not understand," he began. I stood and surveyed the empty room. There were no pictures, no evidence of family, no old food on dirty plates—it was likely she laid in this chair for a while, alone, and presumably died that way.

I should have felt sadness, but didn't. I couldn't quite figure out if dying alone terrified or excited me. The prospect of those intimate last moments being reserved for me, and solely me, as opposed to under the display of mourning eyes was appealing.

But I suppose it wasn't like we got to choose.

"And before the unification of the clans, there were several entities man feared, even more than they disliked one another," a haunted look flashed, "but the thing about fear is that it cannot exist, or cannot exist for long, before evolving into hate. And fear-fueled hate is a damn good motivator to come together."

Patiently, I avoided another question, waiting instead for him to answer me more directly. But he seemed distant as he spoke, as if recalling a story or reading a fable from an old, withered book, as if the pieces had to fall into the exact right places or else risk it not coming together the way it should. We started for the back door.

"So, the creatures that used to walk the earth before humans even dreamed of ruling it came to be hunted—the sirens, the nymphs, the fae—they were all hunted. Men shared a common goal with their previous foes to make the land a safer place without the creations of Draoi." *Draoi* was not a name I had heard in a long while. As Ryv was the believed deity of death, Draoi was thought to be the deity of magic and magical beings, but he was usually only referenced when one wished to be lucky on a day of fishing or score a lucrative deal at the market.

When Zymir sensed my disbelief, his face grew serious. "Do you think your myths pull from nothing? That they weren't inspired by the actual retellings of your ancestors?"

I hushed him with a single finger. The sound of footsteps outside the back door as we approached reached my ears. I knew he could hear them too, but he continued. Slurred words slipped into the home, a clanging bottle hit the exterior at every step that drew closer.

"You would be amazed what they did when they discovered their own people possessed gifts similar to the monsters." His voice was icy, sharp. "When fear determines who is foe, anyone who poses a risk to a delicate alliance becomes an enemy."

Every muscle involuntarily went rigid, and a tendril of deep-rooted dread seized my chest, if only for a moment. An enemy...such a foreign concept in a time of peace.

The back door swung open at that moment.

Grisly beard, bruised head—the man from earlier had followed behind us. Broken bottle in one hand, a club in the other, both flickering in the moonlight as his hands shook.

CHAPTER II

"L i-ars!" he screamed, the sound coming out in a two distinct syllables as he shot the word aloud.

Neither of us could make sense of the unintelligible ramblings that followed that one distinguishable word. He blocked the exit with his arm, sinking his weight against the door frame. Heaving breaths followed, his entire body rising and falling with the effort. Wetting his lips, he coughed roughly and spit phlegm onto the ground.

"You—" He stammered in, closer.

"The, the bottle." He shook the empty thing emphatically. "They're *liars!*"

I debated whether his own imbalance would allow us to neatly maneuver around him, but with his outstretched arms, there was no way to do so without risking either of his handheld objects blocking the path. Zymir was still, patient.

I held up both my empty palms and smiled, lowering my head slightly to make direct eye contact.

Softly, but not patronizingly, I explained, "We're just leaving." Limp eyelids swelled above his eyes, and veins protruded from his neck. He held my stare despite the continued confusion he seemed to be thinking through. A bent knee pivoted slightly outward, as if he had been dragging that leg.

Carefully, I took a step toward the door.

He brought the club down across him, the weight swinging his upper body with it. His bottom lip quivered, and he rapidly shook his head. I didn't flinch as much as I cringed, wishing he'd let us path without issue. He blindly swung it back up, knocking the top against the door propped open behind him.

I could feel the time passing us by with the unforeseen interruption, and I weighed our options. I could run up to him, get him to dart forward while Zymir slipped behind him, and then distract him so I could round the turn and exit. He hadn't seen the woman behind us yet, but once he did, his gurgling cries would inevitably escalate, drawing a potential crowd. Could we draw him out into the street after us?

Level calmness spoke beside me.

"Who lied?"

I glared at him. Entertaining the stranger was not remotely on the list of options I was sorting through.

Pepper-gray, bushy eyebrows rose in response, and the hand with the club slacked.

"G-G-Gage," he hiccupped.

Zymir nodded as if invested in the answer. His pause was intentional, and the drunk took it as an invitation to continue.

"Gage, Gage and the ol' good for nothin' rat vermin he hangs with—" A mix of cuss words I wasn't often privy to spilled out in rapid succession. "They, they traded me for this useless bottle, and I tried to drink it, but it—"

The words flew now, endless, nonstop, and repetitive, his agitation over-flowed into sloppy run-ons as he emphasized that he was tricked, and they had lied to him. Statuesque and calculated, Zymir listened. I leaned the toe of my boot over and tapped the edge of his—it was time to go, and at this rate, we'd be here all night.

But he ignored me.

A booming voice shouted from somewhere behind the man. I couldn't hear the words, but the yell was followed by snide laughs. The stranger's eyes went wide, and for a moment, all incoherence slipped away, and a primal panic took over his body. He dropped the bottle, shattering it onto the ground in a splash of glass shards. And with that, he dragged his body out the door as quickly as he had entered it, uneven, clunky steps making their way down the back alley, the sound further and further away.

We both hesitated.

"Well, that was lucky," I offered unenthusiastically.

The stark contrast of Zymir's hair in the darkness made his silhouette seem all the more refined. He said nothing, an uncomfortable silence that seemed to suggest otherwise. But if he thought we still had to be concerned, he didn't voice it.

We strode out toward the door, carefully shutting it behind us as we left. As we turned to follow our path in, back out, a familiar chirp piped up from within the shadows of the home near the very edge of the wall and dirty ground. *Shit.*

Locking eyes on my metal navigator, my heart did a flip. I walked closer, but it didn't scurry up my arm. Closer still, within arm's length, and I decided to just reach down and plop it into my pocket—but Mion had other ideas. Mi zigzagged backward and paused.

Zymir's confusion radiated behind me.

"Why is it not with Kori?" I didn't look, but I would've bet he cocked his head as he asked.

Realization hit both of us squarely, and one avoided crisis siphoned right into the next. While my arm remained outstretched, Mi chittered back further. Scanning the coils of chords, annoyance flooded out, and understanding clicked into place. I stepped repeatedly behind it, Mion leading us down the back alley and toward the wider main road that went toward the center of town.

Mi picked up its pace, prancing nearly weightlessly over the tiny stones and dirt and whizzing down block after block. There were no lights guiding the path this far out—we'd hit those in roughly five or six more blocks—so we ran, minimizing the space between us and propelling us away from the heaviness of the Sunset District. Dirt turned to bricked roads, street corners blossomed into benches, and flowers lined the corners of intersections.

I knew Zymir could easily outrun me, but his pace held the rear, ensuring no one approached us from behind. It was difficult not to crane my head back to confirm he was still there, his steps so silent I kept doubting his feet touched the street at all.

The path through the city became familiar—tents of vendors I had passed and storefronts I had perused. We slowed, Mion interlacing its legs and circling its body around twice before rocketing down a street I knew without question. Headed by two pyramid-shaped bushes on either side of the opening, with an open-air jewelry booth at the north corner—Mi was leading us to Freyah's. The venom in my veins cooled, concern diminishing.

It was replaced with a different sort of worry. My yellow-eyed companion behind me, despite no weapons I had yet to see drawn, was imposing in a peculiar way—he wasn't particularly tall or broad, but it was obvious he had trained and had strength beneath the lean muscles of his arms, and there was something else. There was a subtle unease that crept into you around him that I worried Freyah and Tillian would interpret as threatening. And how did Kori even introduce herself? Would she have mentioned why we were here, what I do?

I gulped down a dry knot in my throat as we passed the neighbor's wide shuttered window.

As Mi landed outside Freyah's door, I smoothed out my top, brushing off whatever I could that accumulated on it as we ran, kicked up by our steps. Those amber eyes watched me as I did—I was sure wondering why—and then I undid my hair and repositioned it, this time gathering the loose strands and pressing them neatly down and out of my face.

I tightened my bag out of habit, sucked in the crisp night air, and positioned myself behind the door. The kitchen light was on—though it was always on—and I avoided the temptation to veer my gaze through it to gather a hint of what I was to expect. Zymir, as if sensing the nerves emanating from me, stood a decent distance behind, careful not to crowd too close.

I knocked twice.

The handle turned, and I debated what expression I should wear to minimize their bombardment of questions.

The door opened, and dazzling blue eyes made my breath stick in my chest. Tillian let the door fall the rest of the way open itself, nonchalantly returning to the kitchen counter and leaning against it with his arms propping himself up as he slouched back. Kori sat at the table, hunched over with a light blanket draped over her shoulders and a warm cup of what smelled like chamomile tea between her hands. I could feel Zymir's presence enter the home, and Tillian straightened as he did, as if he hadn't seen him behind me outside.

Zymir didn't walk further in, just barely enough to close the door behind him, polite patience and acute awareness of how strangers may perceive him.

Kori glanced up sheepishly, a forced smile pulling up her lips, but it was empty and overshadowed by fear.

Mion had apparently slipped in as well, though I hadn't noticed until it climbed up into my pocket. I *knew* Tillian noticed. The rise of his brow might as well have said, *we'll come back to that later.*

I went to Kori, setting a hand firmly on her back, and dropped down to my knees to lower to her level.

"There was something in the forest." Her tone was absolute and unwavering.

She blew on the tea, brought it up, and sipped long. I didn't want to pry or press if she wasn't ready.

"It had eyes like his," she said and looked up at Zymir, not viciously, more puzzled than sharp. "I thought you two had returned, but from where the eyes in the bushes were, came a...rustling...and then, a growl."

The room felt cold as she spoke.

"I've heard growls before." She scanned the room as if trying to confirm we believed her. "This wasn't...it...it was like nothing I had heard before. I felt like my life was in danger—and no, I didn't just run, I held onto that dagger you left me—"

I grimaced as Tillian's face landed somewhere between surprise and amusement, a gentle smirk.

"And I yelled out, I told whoever was in the bushes to leave because I was armed, and—"

By gods was she feisty. I hadn't realized she would be so quick to defend herself in a dangerous situation, mostly assumed she'd run unless cornered. I would have been leerier about providing her with off-the-cusp weapon training if I knew otherwise. I swallowed and shoved the guilt down as she spoke, telling myself I'd go deeper into those lessons next time and advise on when you should threaten an approaching enemy and when you're better off running as fast as you can in the other direction.

Her jaw slacked open as she paused, her chest rising with a deep inhale, steadying herself.

"And...it mimicked me. But not like a kid repeating what you said just in a half-assed attempt to sound like you. It...it sounded *just* like me." The mug twitched in her shaking hands. "It replied in *my* voice, and copied me: *Go away, I'm armed!* And then, she, it, laughed." She blinked fast to hold back the building water on the bottom of her eyelids.

The kitchen light flickered, perfectly timed to the rising hairs on the nape of my neck.

"And where were you two?" Tillian asked with an edge, creases of intrigue lining his forehead.

Kori's stare shot into her mug. She took another long sip to avoid the uncomfortable tone of the question posed to Zymir and me. I knew the second I hesitated to answer, his head was somersaulting with potential places we could have been and why. His gaze withheld nothing, a direct demand that I could hardly blame him for—after all, I unintentionally dragged him straight into this evening right alongside us.

I responded gently. "Can I talk to you outside?"

I could have fabricated some sort of explanation, I'm sure of it, the same way I was sure the two I was journeying with would back it up as truth. I could feel Zymir tense for just a moment, so slight I wondered if I had imagined it. Kori was scraping at a slight chip in the mug's handle as if it were the most interesting thing in the world.

The intensity of those blue eyes softened, and he ran his hand through the curls on his forehead before nodding, half begrudgingly and half in relief that whatever our conversation would hold, wasn't about to be on display to a room full of people he didn't know—that I barely knew.

Zymir moved to his right, creating space for me to leave the house with Tillian a few steps behind me. I could feel the static in the air as my friend passed closely by the snow-haired man that stood eye level with him. If Zymir could feel the awkwardness, he didn't show it.

A few days ago, not a soul knew the contract I was in with Nox. No one could cast judgment on the job I ran at night, and here I was poised to tell one of the few people that I had known since I was young that I was wrapped up in a whirlwind of escalating problems that linked back to debt collecting and climaxed at the tore-open body I found, and still saw, every time I closed my eyes at night.

We lingered in silence in front of his house before crossing the street, tense footsteps clicked beside me, waiting for my lead to determine when to stop.

I paused intentionally in front of the stone bench by the streetlamp.

I could feel his searching, wondering eyes trace the side of my face as I peered down at my boots.

"Well?" he asked, strained patience wearing thin.

"Well." I sat on the bench and patted the spot beside me. "I think you're going to want to sit down."

Words plummeted out of my mouth in rapid succession. I told him everything. Or at least, everything as it pertained to my specific circumstances. I left out why Zymir or Kori had chosen to come with, mostly because their business was their own to share, and also because I only partially understood myself. I left Zymir's presence simply at the basic principle of us both looking for the same person. I wasn't sure it would be enough to quiet the doubts buzzing around my friend's head, but it was the truth.

He didn't speak for a while, only leaned over with his forehead cupped in his hands. I wondered what the conversation back inside the house looked like, if they were worried at the time passing since we left.

Releasing his head, he sat upright and set a hand on my knee beside his.

"I still think you should have told me." A friendly squeeze and he stood, not bothering to look back but face tilted upward toward the speckled night-time sky.

"I wanted to," I said truthfully, "but I worried if you knew why I was leaving town so often, that—"

"That what?" Curls tossed as he spun his head back, slight hurt creasing his brow.

"That you would think of me differently. It's not an honest living, like working in the lumber yard. It's not something one speaks of with pride." I picked at the skin on the inside of my thumbs.

Noticing my fidgeting, he took the hand I was picking at and loosely held it for a moment to prevent my nails from scraping below the raw skin further. Warmth bubbled up into my cheeks before he quickly removed his grasp.

"Working at a lumberyard isn't the most pride-inducing job either, ya know." He glanced down at his newly calloused hands and shoved them into his pockets. "Regardless, I'm not upset at what you're doing. I just don't understand *why* you're doing it. What does he have on you? First thing tomorrow, I'm going up there and—"

"No," I cut him off wide-eyed. "Please, no; that will only make things worse."

"So what? Now I'm supposed to be content with the knowledge you're out there doing this guy's dirty work with your rag-tag group of friends back there investigating...what was it again, some chap you found with his head nearly sliced off?" Daggers, each word, fiery points hitting their intended target.

"I'm telling you so you know why I'm here, and so you don't have to wonder anymore. I'm telling you so that my *acquaintances* and I can continue with what we came here for." Sympathy whispered through my chest as he turned his head back around to avoid my gaze. "I'm not asking you to understand, Til."

A low chuckle and he started back toward the house. "Good."

Since we were young, Tillian had always been the first to anger, to let his rage ball his fists before he had thought through where he intended to land them. But he would go home, pouting and red in the face, to Freyah, who would fuss over him and stroke his hair until it inevitably subsided into hot tears. It wasn't quite envy that had me picturing that now but understanding. A warm embrace to soothe your woes was what all children should come home to. Without that, a calculating mind need only the next thought of survival to kick the emotional response deep into the back of your priorities list and subsequently bury it beneath necessity. It was no use arguing with the sharpness of his frustration. He needed time to process, which I'd gladly allot if it meant clarity on the other side.

As I trailed him back to the house a few doors down, I realized Freyah hadn't been present amongst the crowded kitchen, which was unusual for her—her life consisted primarily of her clothing shop, with any spare moments spent cooking or with her son.

"Did your mother already go to sleep?" I asked, hoping all the commotion hadn't woken her.

"She should be home now." His tone was rough. "She went out."

I knew better than to ask anything further. The finality of his words was enough to tell me that whatever *out* meant, wasn't something he cared for or cared to discuss.

Peering into the warmly lit window, I could see from our approach that he was correct. The back of her hair stood facing outward from the center of the kitchen. I rushed ahead to open the door to provide an explanation as to why only strangers sat around her table, but Tillian already had a grip on the handle and let himself in, doing so in a relaxed, casual gate that eased the ropes of worry that had momentarily gripped me.

"Adelliah," she beamed. "What a pleasant surprise!" Her cheeks were flushed, and as she drew in for a tight hug, the sweet lingering of wine wafted off her lips. Heavy bags beneath her eyes gave away any attempt to pretend she wasn't utterly exhausted, but despite their tell, her smile and bright eyes seemed to draw a comfortable sigh from everyone.

Zymir had sat across from Kori as Freyah was rummaging through her shelves for small dishes to carefully set out in front of them. She doubled back and grabbed two more, placing them at the empty seats and gesturing for us to sit as she spun around on her toes to grab a loaf of bread from the windowsill and some butter from the glass container near the sink. She hummed as she moved, a pleasant, mindless melody lightening the air as her thick waves of hair bounced with her.

"Will you and your friends be staying long?" She sliced the loaf, golden brown and adorned with oats on top. It was long and perfect for divvying up amongst company. I considered correcting her but thought better of it.

Tillian didn't bother to acknowledge his place setting at the table. He went back to leaning against the cupboards as she whirled around him. He stared at nothing in particular, eyes burning into the ground in front of him, avoiding a direct look at anyone in the room. I hated that I had brought this sudden bombardment into their evening, and I wondered if going back to the forest for what remained of the night wouldn't better suit us.

"Oh no, we're taking off tomorrow!" Kori piped up. Her dirty hands were wiped clean by what looked like a towel Freyah must have offered her, the crumpled, coarse fabric resting on her lap. She leaned comfortably in her chair, occasionally catching herself from leaning back on its legs like she had done at her own residence. She seemed enamored by this place, stopping to stare at the details in the ornate oak table and tracing the carved etchings in the corner nearest to her.

"Well, you'll have to stay here for the night then," she spoke in absolutes, endless offerings of kindness that had seemed to run in excess. "I insist."

It seemed as though Tillian thought to object or add in his input, raising his head from his downward glare and parting his lips, but a single raised hand from his mother shut them just as quickly, a tense line blocking whatever opinion he had from being voiced. Kori, however, nodded happily at her offering, the temptation of resting in the warmth of a home much more appealing than the dampness of the forest ground.

"Ladies can bunk with me, I have a few extra blankets we can throw down and use for a mattress and more pillows than I know what to do with." The maternal softness in her voice rose to a slight excitement as she reached down into a low shelf and revealed a dark brown bottle with fancy pictures of mountains on the label. "The night may be getting old, but would anyone care for a drink before you lay down? They say it helps you fall asleep faster."

Kori's petit hand lifted into the air without hesitation, and a nervous laugh brought it slightly down, awareness of her too-readiness. I had never really seen Freyah drink much. She used to scoff at people that wasted their hard-earned coin on watered-down, bitter elixirs, as she'd call it, but with her newfound welcoming nature evidently came a leisurely side open to sipping on what appeared to be a particular taste for deep red wines—at least, that was if my vision was correct, since the label on the bottle and the few other bottles I could see in the shelf all matched. And the smell as she poured herself and Kori a glass matched the scent she carried on her lips. I declined, weariness clouding my thoughts enough as is, and Zymir merely shook his head.

"And you, my handsome, silent guest." She winked, and I peeked at Tillian's dramatic eye roll, "you can get the guest room."

I was worried she was going to make the men stay together, which would have been so unbelievably uncomfortable for both of them that I would have gladly offered literally any other arrangement of bodies within the home. For only having the one spare room, though, the set-up she suggested would work perfectly. With Kori as small as she was, she and I could practically fit in one mattress set up as is.

"Thank you." He bowed his head.

Freyah's eyes lingered on him as he spoke, as if the smoothness of his voice froze the air in the room. She shook her head and cleared her throat before snagging two glasses and pouring the deep-red wine midway up. It was a generous serving. I caught her glance as she set the bottle back on the counter and sent a silent beg through the exchange.

"Let me go set up the blankets in my room for you and Kori." I could have hugged her for hearing my ask. "And I'll toss some in the spare room for—" She blushed.

"Zymir," he offered, the slightest of polite grins acknowledging her thoughtfulness. It wasn't a face I had seen him wear yet, and though fleeting, didn't seem to flatter to his features as innately as the blankness did.

Kori seemed naturally inclined to introduce herself, propelling her name without shame or concern, so it came as little surprise that it had already come up in conversation while we were gone.

The room felt vaguely off-kilter in the few moments it took her to set up the sleeping arrangements. The uneasiness between my travelers and I had only barely begun to lift in the nights prior, suspicions laxing into more quiet curiosities, but with the addition of Tillian, it seemed everyone's uncertainties were at a peak. I did not possess Kori's charm to willfully smile the woes away and smooth out the ridges amongst us, and she was too occupied with licking the wine stain off her bottom lip. I sank into the feeling, meeting the discomfort and sitting with it as I waited.

As did my counterparts. The men were in no rush to be the first to fill the silence. Zymir seemed to thrive in it, never the first to speak up when a lull entered conversation, keen to instead observe it from the outside. There were often nights after Kori fell soundly asleep where he and I would sit around the fire, no words exchanged, the crackling of embers the only sounds whispered out within the night. Freyah's son was not one who happened upon silence, though. Here, the choice stemmed from misplaced indignation.

Luckily for all of us, the pleasant sound of Freyah's voice beckoned from down the hall, indicating the rooms were ready.

I caught Kori mid-sip and raised a brow, making sure to feel out her comfort before leaving to slip into a fast-approaching slumber. A quick, sincere nod followed by a swirl of her glass told me the friendly conversation and belly-warming drink was her desired coping option after the tumultuous evening she had had.

Freyah stuck her head out just as Zymir had excused himself from the table, mechanically pushing out his chair and rising. He nodded to me, to Kori, and then to Tillian, who held his gaze a moment longer than necessary before departing to the open door on the left, the light from which was peeking out into the hall and visible from where we sat. I waited until it closed before following suit, the light from under his door cutting off as I passed, and a rattling jingle around the knob completing what I guessed was a layer of added security he fastened on the other side.

I had never seen Freyah's room, much less slept on its floor. Stained wooden beams held the four corners of her lifted bed and books stacked on the nightstand beside it. If I were to ever have my own room, I imagined it would look similar to this—neat, tasteful, the necessities laid out with each object in its precise location. A single violet candle in a rose-painted, porcelain holder stood near the worn edges of her books. I buried my legs into the cocoon of thick comforter she had folded on the far side of her bed—one of two identical setups on either side. Her room smelled of lavender, of newly washed sheets and cool jasmine. It reminded me of the vivid, colorful dresses back in her shop, gowns to be worn with perfumes and pearls. It made me wonder what life she had led before I had known her, decades prior, when she was my age, and what that life might have looked like. And what life she may have dreamed of.

As I lowered myself to lie down, I noticed on this far side of the room a thinner night table with a rounded marble top barely large enough for a single one of her books to rest on. The only thing atop it was a folded-down picture frame.

I let my imagination of what that picture may show wade through my mind before the familiar face of Osyren—not the one I found splattered open in the home, but the one suspended above me in my dream—filled its place. Eventually, amongst the nightly terror I kept tight-lipped in the deepest crevice of my thoughts, sleep finally found me. And I welcomed it with relieved surrender.

CHAPTER 12

I awoke to stillness. Soft gray filled the room, and though I hadn't heard either Kori or Freyah enter last night, I could see the turned-over mass under the blankets past my feet. I stared down my nose, blinked a few more times, and mentally tugged at my arms. But they didn't move.

Steadying the rise in my thumping heart, I inhaled, filling my lungs to max expansion, holding it, and incrementally releasing the warm breath. It was only recently that I had found myself waking, unable to move my limbs. The first night it had happened in the woods. I went to scream, but shadowy figures from my dreams held my voice captive until slumber fully slipped away and released my visions. And with it, my body could move.

Sleep paralysis felt like my mind had finally entombed me. My body was the ultimate price for the crimes my thoughts barricaded me in with. It seemed fitting that the first nightmare's lack of control and ability to move would then display itself physically. It felt deserved.

But this morning, it almost felt comfortable. Maybe it wouldn't release, and I would lay here beneath the heaviness of the blanket in the chilled morning air.

On my third exhale, a static sensation tickled through to my fingertips as I wiggled them.

I knew it was early, earlier than anyone here would be up, but not so much so that Nox wouldn't be already in his office. Appointment or not, my best bet was to catch him as soon as their door unlocked.

I pulled the comforter down and tip-toed around Kori, whose entire head was buried deep beneath her blanket, curled into a ball onto her side. Freyah slept beneath only a sheet, the collar of her floral nightgown visible and her hair ratted up half on her face and half on her pillow. The door was left partially open, enough for me to squeeze out without having to risk it squeaking.

I rubbed the corners of my eyes roughly and left the house, careful to make no noise as I passed both men's rooms. It seemed substantially easier to get this taken care of myself. Not only would Nox be immediately weary of people traveling with me, but the fewer variables I had to keep track of, the more focused and sharper I'd be in my conversation with him.

I stepped outside and stared up at the sky. There was something so limitless about mornings, something that tugged deep in my core, sparking the possibilities of what the day could hold.

It seemed right that it was raining today, though.

Overcast and gentle pitter-patter of droplets ricocheting off of the stone ground was a dawn symphony. *Limitless...*It was a child's word, really, as if opportunities were hiding around each corner with offerings full of choice and variety. It wasn't. It never had been. Not when the only choices I ever had revolved around finding food or paying off my debt.

Around each street corner was discarded glass bottles and the butts of different rolled smoked herbs tossed aside for a bird to clumsily choke down later. Maybe it was the dampness on the back of my neck or the chilly air on my lips that spurred the succession of unpleasant thoughts.

Or maybe it was because I simply didn't want to have this conversation with Nox.

My feet led me mindlessly down the path toward his colorful, reflective shop. There would be no rays of sunshine to beckon the rainbows of color from one shingle to the next. There was at least relief in that. Let the murky melancholy taint its radiance.

I passed few people up this early, in the hour before the sun would greet the sky only to be hidden beneath its heavy, clouded blanket. I passed a young couple whispering to one another and giggling into their warm cups, mist sneaking out the tops as the heat of their drinks warmed the air around them. I passed a few bearded men with sleep still lingering in their gazes, eyes cast downward en route to what I guessed would be some sort of labor-intensive job based on the hunch in their backs and the drag of their feet.

The day was painted in shades of gray that ranged from the clothes they wore to the morose ambiance to the grime gathered in the street curbs. There was a painless ache to this morning that I could not quite pinpoint. But I felt it as I found his storefront and hauled my body forward begrudgingly.

A single red light near the doorframe told me they were open, so I pushed on the door and let myself in, tapping the wetness off from my boots on the bottom ledge.

There was no cheeky receptionist to greet me in the front of the lobby. The normally overflowing table was bare, only a pen at the top and a blank paper calendar near the center. I took this as a win, be it a small one. There was no one to rattle off the same questions over and over again as I waited less than patiently to be let back. I assumed she was still brewing tea or drawing on the fake lines around her eyes, perfection etched into every careful detail.

There is a strangeness to an empty, open business—a place where people should be, but aren't. Though I suppose *no one* should really be here, at *this* particular business.

I led myself to the door of the hallway and was thankful that the knob was unlocked, darting in, and using my adrenaline to bring me directly behind

Nox's office door. The frosted glass gave no indication if he was in yet, but the slightest hint of light escaping from between the cracks surrounding the entrance made me optimistic he was.

I rattled my knuckles across its chalky exterior, the illumination of the single hallways light making his gold door label shimmer as I waited to hear if he would respond to the knock.

"*What?!*" was his means of greeting, a raspy voice thrown my way.

Wonderful, he sounds in great spirits.

"It's Adelliah," I replied, partially cringing as I did in dreaded anticipation. "I need to talk to you."

"Oh..." a pause, "Adelliah, come in," he beckoned. His tone immediately changed from sharp to curious, a sliver of relief at the edge of the words, though I wasn't sure why.

Entering the office, the first thing I noticed was the demanding smell of burnt coffee. The second, the utter uncharacteristically cluttered desk—where neatly stacked files usually lay, were instead folded sheets with ripped edges, fanned out from one side of the desk to the other. A particular pile on the right evidently slipped off, the brightness of the paper stark against the royal blue carpet, with vague outlines of the bottom of his shoes atop some, and others still, simply discarded into a balled, crumpled mess. Different seemingly random drawers on the back wall were jutting out, some opened to halfway, some hanging loosely only because the rear of the shelf caught on its top, precariously dangling.

Nox wet his lips from his chair. I barely noticed him amongst the disarray, but he sat in his usual plush chair, not a hair out of place, unlike his surroundings. His suit was light gray, as if he had known to match the apparent color theme today, and his pocket square a deep, satin purple to match his selection of bow tie. His hair always looked like wet pavement—black and damp—slicked back and reflective. I imagined it would be hard to the touch.

"Do you always greet your receptionists so kindly?" I sat in the offered chair across from him and kept my shoulders high. I crossed my legs and returned his level stare.

He blinked, debating whether it was worth the time to critique my tone.

"What do you want?" he asked instead, drinking his burnt coffee from a rounded black mug held absentmindedly in one of his hands. The assaulting smell made me nearly grimace as he did, but his face held no complaints as he drank it.

Why hadn't I gone over how I was going to word this on my stroll here? My mind was too blank from absorbing its surroundings and taking in the feel of the groggy morning to attempt to prepare for this meeting, and last night I was too overwhelmed with keeping a calm tone amongst the constantly escalating problems and introductions. I regretted that slightly now, but buried the thought and dove in.

"There was an issue at my last extraction in Vayne."

"What sort of issue?" His voice was careful, testing, as he snapped his eyes up to meet mine. He set his mug down.

I stuck my arm into my bag and rummaged minimally to find the large flask I carried. I set it on his desk, but he barely glanced at it as he waited for my answer. I set out the other two collected vials I *did* have, juxtaposing the outcomes.

"I got an alert for Vayne, collected this one." I pointed at one of the tiny vials. "And then I got another alert immediately after." A flicker ran across his brow at that.

I proceeded carefully and selectively, tiptoeing around the bloody triggers that would send my brain facing Osyren across this desk instead of Nox.

"When I arrived, I found a young man with his neck slit." I paused and considered. "There seemed to be a gratuitous amount of blood in the home, it was...excessive."

He nodded, seemingly understanding the implications.

"I attempted the extraction, of course, but—"

"But?" The ferocity of his glare made my voice catch in my throat.

"Someone beat me to it." I refused to let his presence diminish the authority in which I repeated what I saw, relaying nothing but absolute conviction of the truth of it.

"How could you tell?" He stayed calm, but I could see right beneath the surface were panicked gears turning one by one at what I was telling him.

"How do you think?" I looked unamused, felt the frustration in the marrow of my bones. I had been doing this long enough that he could afford me the endless, pointless questions and make way for the important ones.

I had never seen any semblance of fear creep into Nox's eyes—but in that moment, the fright that swallowed up all his faulty facade took with it more than just the front. It was like watching someone delicately stack glasses, glass on top of glass, a strong wind away from slightly too much wobble that would send the entirety crashing down, suddenly blunting the weight of a whole gust. The chain reaction of destruction only bringing more destruction. The look in his eyes was something like that—a realization, a gust of wind, shattering a fragile structure doomed from the start.

Don't build with glass.

A bead of sweat traced the side of his face, over his pronounced cheekbone, down his jaw.

"So, it is possible then? Do you have other collectors?"

He didn't reply, as if unable to speak. Floating downward, his gaze fell on the larger glass vial between us.

"I didn't know if you'd believe me, so I brought the only other thing that seemed out of place."

Swallowing the disgust, I opened the vial, allowing the preserved skin to slip out and unravel between the tissue. The smell made the burnt coffee smell like roses, but I tried to ignore it as I set the specimen down and fully unwrapped it. A darkness shaded his face at the sight.

"Your proximity alarm went off for this, right?" he asked after a while of tracing the swirling blue lines with his eyes.

I nodded, and he reached down into the lowest cabinet of his desk. He paused halfway down before dismissively shaking his head and looking at the mess of papers all around him, as if realizing the search would prove unnecessary. I expected rage and a tongue lashing, a heavy-handed dose of insults mixed with guilt-inducing snide remarks. I wasn't expecting this stillness, the heavy aroma of uncertainty, to fill the space between us.

"Is there anyone you can think of who could have done this?" I asked and searched the blankness in his stare for any sort of information that would shed light on why he sat so rigid and aghast.

"You can't ask me how I know this," he began, "but I'm to believe as of recently that there are other loan providers of my nature scattered throughout Sheirsa."

"Why would you be the only one to begin with?" It didn't make a lick of sense, if the capabilities were there, why others didn't seek the exploitation of those in need of an advance. This world was cruel, and people grew hungry, and for every outstretched hand asking, there was often another ready to offer necessity with strings attached.

"Because that was the arrangement."

"Arrangement with whom?"

He hesitated, as if the words were clamped tight behind his teeth, and he wanted nothing more than to release them.

"When I come back for assignments, and you refill my proximity tattoo, aren't you aware of who's next on the list? Or have a general idea?" Grim circumstances allotted me the opportunity to pry much further than I had ever ventured before.

"No, that's not how it works."

"Then—"

A woman opened his office door. If she had knocked, neither of us was paying enough attention to have noticed. One of his receptionists, this one with deep brown eyes and hair that matched their darkness, peeked her head through with another mug of what I assumed was more coffee in her timid hand that lay just inside the room.

Nox stood, resting his hands against the sturdiness of his desk as he growled, "Get out," in a volume much lower than I would have guessed, his words so venomous it didn't need to be shouted to be feared.

They landed as intended, and she scurried out, softly shutting the door. I glared at him as he lowered himself back into his chair and smoothed the lapel of his suit coat as if demeaning his receptionist was just enough for him to remember who he was and his role here.

"It's not that simple," he began, pulling his pocket square out and running the hemmed edges through his fingers. "I'm not privy to all the details on how it works. But I know very few that would carry that blue mark and find themselves in debt at all. And without a vial to scan, I'm even more inclined to say he was never a client to begin with, which means something else triggered your tattoo."

At the blankness in my stare, he continued. "Imagine casting a wide net in a sea, and you're only looking to catch pufferfish. First, you need to make sure you have a net that's designed to *only* catch pufferfish, *and* you also have to time it just right so that a pufferfish happens to swim into your net while you're there."

What?

"You've never even been near the shore, have you?" I nearly laughed at how ridiculous his analogy was.

Fierce eyes cut any laugh that would have passed my lips.

"It doesn't matter, you get the idea—you have to be looking for the right thing, and it has to be at the right time." He rolled his eyes and reached into his pocket, pulling out a thin cigar and matches. He didn't ask if I minded before he was trimming the ends and lighting it up in his office, creating a saturated smell of tobacco, coffee, and flesh. At this rate, I imagined I'd never be hungry again. "What I inject is much the same, it's meant to tap into my network of clients, and it's meant to alert you only when one of them should happen to pass away. It would be terrible business if all my clients ended up dead a week after signing, don't you think?" He took a drag, and dark billowy smoke piled out of his mouth.

I scooted back in my chair away from him and his smoke, but he didn't seem to notice.

"So, for you to get an alert..." He rubbed his freshly shaven face, the smooth tanned skin moving against his fingers. "I don't know how it could happen."

"Would it help if you knew whose skin that was?" I raised an eyebrow, dangerously choosing what information to share with him and what to withhold. He pulled the cigar away from his clamped lips mid-drag. "You can't ask how *I* know this, but his name was Osyren."

The rest of his jaw plummeted. He got up and kicked the edge of the desk, causing more papers to flutter down to the floor as he paced behind his chair.

"If you know there's been an expansion of debt collectors, evidently reporting to someone new, and I know this guy was some hunter from the kingdom named Osyren." I started picking at the indent of skin on my thumb that I had torn into last night. "Where does that leave us?"

His repetitive steps paused at the word hunter, the repeat of the word Zymir had used, one foot hovering above the carpet, but just as quickly, he proceeded with the line he was carving out with his reflective, brown leather shoes.

"It leaves *us* nowhere. It leaves me with less business, and it leaves you with less opportunity to lower your own debt." The fear I had seen in his eyes was fully converted to exasperation, and he threw his hands in the air. "Osyren was one of King Bryce's personal soldiers. The family may be gone, but those who've been in charge in their place will be looking for answers. Did anyone see you when you found his body?"

That was a loaded question, a tricky question. But I lied.

"No one. Vayne guards found him shortly after, though. They sounded an alarm."

He walked up to my chair, peering over me with a mix of adrenaline and authority.

"There's only one group that would target the king's servicemen." He lowered himself, so he was at eye level. "Only one I can think of that would have enough intel to know where to find him and knew he bore a Varaynian mark." His stare darted to that section of skin, which I took to be what he was referring to. "The deserters."

The deserters had been a sect of outer guards that, once the royal family had disappeared, took it upon themselves to disown the Sheirsan crest and abandon their post. They had made a display of it. A burning flag stood in the palace courtyard with their fellow soldiers gutted out around it like a shrine, the men and their families completely gone in the wake of their mutiny to create their faction of chaos and lawlessness. They slaughtered anyone who tried to stop their passageway north to the Icesone Mountains, where no Sheirsan official stationed there would ever be seen from again, including Tillian's father.

Freyah would tell me in disgust as, soon, more people joined them, content to journey into the unknown toward whatever was left of the settlement in the mountains. The life of those who turned their back on the kingdom spurred those unhappy to join them.

A revolting taste hit the back of my throat at the thought.

"They have a name for themselves now," he said as he stood, his expression matching the unsavory feelings I had. "The Nevari. They're who we're looking for." He leaned against his desk and set down the half-smoked cigar in a dish he revealed hidden beneath a few scattered papers.

"What's a Varaynian mark?" The question blurted itself out of me.

He pushed up the sleeve of his suit to expose a gold watch adorning his wrist and snickered.

"I've spent far too much time answering your questions as it is, love." Cold eyes matched his snarling grin. "We're done."

I blinked, as if the scene would somehow go back to the way it had been before, as if this abrupt end wasn't slamming a door on more information that I desperately craved. I felt smothered, exposed to a world one frame at a time, only seeing what I was allowed to see when I was told to see it, and the glimpse into what commanded that time and dictated my course for years, this tattoo latched onto my skin, ignited within me an insatiable desire for more.

I was on my feet, shoulders squared in front of him, hand comfortably on a hilt I knew I could pull out in the seconds it would take him to realize what I had done. I was breathing heavily, the need of newly lit embers in my core begging for any scraps of insight he would give me.

"What's a Varaynian mark? And what the fuck do you want me to do now? What do we do if these people are able to influence this wretched thing?" I threw my wrist in his face, daring his reactions by minimizing the space between us, the vivid crimson of the tattoo stuck in an elaborate star like it had been for days, eight little points, intricacy jarring the usual blotchiness. "What am I actually *doing* here?"

My breathing was rapid, and I found my cheeks damp, emotion bursting through without allowance. I wiped the warm, livid tears away with the back of my hand and tried to steady the uneven, sharp inhales collapsing on top of one another, but they refused to comply.

Hardened orbs merely watched, disengaged and uninterested.

I could feel the blush deepen on my face in sudden self-consciousness, but I didn't wish the questions back into my mouth, I let them hang in the putrid, smoky air.

Knocking interrupted from the door behind us in three quick taps. His watch stared at me.

I was so close to answers but still so far. I felt my desperately clutched hands tearing off the ledge of learning more. My legs were dangling, ready to free fall back into the pit of endless orders on a path that was never mine to choose.

In a voice much smaller than I expected, with all the energy I had left to muster, I simply asked, "What now?"

"Now we figure out who killed Osyren, and we pray that it's sufficient to keep the kingdom from sniffing around here too closely. Now," he simpered, passing me and opening the door to let me out, "you go to the Icesone Mountains."

CHAPTER 13

I left dumbfounded. Where panic should have been creeping within my chest, I found instead the flutter of excitement. Or maybe excitement wasn't quite the right word...But there was something else causing the beating of my heart to drum so loudly. It was not solely fear of what I would encounter within the mountains. There was something new in the electrical current of my veins.

My walk back to Freyah's was mostly a blur. I passed more people this time, the sun now brightly risen and beaming colorless light from behind the clouds that had thinned. Several shop owners were already flipping open signs and unlocking doors. The streets would crowd soon as more city goers made their way to work. It was a well-organized system, everyone seemingly having a place, or at least seemingly having a way to make a living to avoid going hungry. The intersecting paths contained strangers unaware of those they passed daily, all with downtrodden faces and minds far away from here.

And here I was, one of them.

Zymir was waiting outside when I reached the brown shutters of Freyah's. I knew she'd be off to her shop by this time, but both Kori and Tillian were more inclined to soak in the extra hours of sleep when the sun was still busy climbing to its peak. His hands were deep in his pockets, the collar of his gray shirt tipped up in the back behind his neck as he watched the stone ground in front of him.

I knew he heard me approaching before he bothered to lift his head.

"Did he know anything?" he asked, twinkling curiosity ablaze.

"It went great, thanks." I tossed a look at him and leaned against the house beside him. He added nothing, waiting for my answer. "He seems to think that whoever is responsible for Osyren's death was part of the Nevari."

He craned his neck toward me immediately, the gold irises tracing my face as if confused that I spoke so casually about them, confirming what I suspected as well—that he'd be familiar with the group by name.

"Hm. Why did he think that?" The slyest of twitches pulled at the corner of his mouth.

I pushed against the wall to face him, suspicion and amusement painting my words. "Did—" I replayed the flicker of his lips again in my head and couldn't stop myself from flashing a wide grin. "Did you already suspect that as well?"

Most people would have either shrugged or chuckled it off, but Zymir kept his hand utterly concealed, divulging nothing through his face, a thick wall immediately constructed.

"I wasn't sure who to suspect, but the Nevari do seem like a reasonable direction."

"Mhm." I tallied it as a win regardless, knowing he had let the tiniest of pleasantries slip through the mortar of bricks. "Well, Nox seemed to suggest Osyren's status within the capital coupled with the Varaynian mark pointed to only one group of people with enough inside knowledge and means to carry out a hit like that."

I dangled the word as bait, hoping that by being lax, he'd take it and elaborate more than Nox did. All of this would have been facts Zymir already knew: the victim's identity, the role he held in the kingdom...Zymir had been there when I sliced the swirled blue birthmark from the corpse's side.

"Indeed, that seems like a rational conclusion to me."

Come on. He noticed the furrow in my brow and tilted his head.

"What?"

The question blurted impatiently out of my mouth. "What's a Varaynian mark?"

Genuine confusion seemed to strain his sight. "The light blue birthmark you already—?"

"No, no, I know what it is, but," I struggled and shifted my weight from one foot to another, hands in the air expressively, "but what *is* it."

He blinked at me.

"I don't understand."

"What's its significance? What does it mean, what does it do?" I was reading my palms, sliding my hands over one another as my curiosity heightened my pulse.

"It's one of the five Weaver Marks from the Varayn Clan pre-Sheirsa, the people of the west." His words were academic, precise. At my pause in fidgeting, he continued, "Vayne, the coastal city. It was a name they chose to pay homage to their history and remember their roots once they merged with the other clans."

He paused, watching as I processed the words. He continued, "Not all those who carry the lineage bore the mark, but it would emerge in some, materializing to designate their particular Weaver abilities," he added, searching for what would relax the confusion knotting my face.

I heard shuffling from behind him, the sound of clanking metal and porcelain rattling around, indicating someone else had woken. Everything Zymir seemed to retell came from books I had never read, records transcribed somewhere far from the hands of most I had ever spoken to. There was never a need to learn what happened before Sheirsa or even acknowledge a before at all...Why focus on the time before peace? Sheirsan pride was strong and ran deep. It wasn't that people *chose* to look forward. It was simply never even a thought to look back.

But Kori seemed to know a bit of her own people's lore, whether she believed it or not, or knew its relevancy. The stories she was told lived beneath the surface, through generational retellings, and found a way to live on through the tales.

"So, there were five clans then?" I had a never-ending list of inquiries, one answer setting off a chain of more wonders. All of his words were foreign to me, subjects I could only guess at their meanings. *Weavers. Weaver abilities.*

He didn't nod in confirmation, as if the truth of the matter were far more complicated than my question beckoned. The rumblings from the home were louder, and I suspected purposeful to draw our presence back inside. I sighed resentfully, knowing if I didn't go in now, someone would be headed out shortly. Besides, there would be time again to catch Zymir alone to dig deeper into the depths of knowledge he carried silently around with him, without other potential ears overhearing the secrets he possessed.

Zymir started off in the other direction, away from the house.

"You're not coming in?"

He turned halfway back toward me, his broad shoulders, sharp nose, and the corner of his eye facing me. "If we're to follow this lead, I would like to get some supplies before we leave. And I think it best if I were not present when you tell the others where we'll be going."

With that, he walked off down the street, slipping effortlessly amongst the sea of bodies, the soft snow of his hair shadowed by those he passed. There was no semblance of an alternate option—with his aim to avenge whoever killed his target, there would be no question as to his trajectory.

I entered Freyah's, knowing the conversation inside would be much different.

Tillian was up, rummaging through the kitchen shelves. After shuffling and searching, he pulled out a pan, set it on the stove, and started boiling water. His curls were flattened at the back of his head, and I assumed he hadn't been up for long. The tired bags under his eyes suggested his night's sleep was about as successful as my own.

Kori seemed well rested, sitting comfortably at the table with her legs propped up on the edge of the seat across from her. She smiled at me and patted the chair beside her.

With the addition of tea leaves, a warm herbal vanilla filled the room, and a grumble squeaked out from my stomach. I could see the sly smile on his face as it did, while he continued to hold the leaves in a rounded metal orb within the pan. He poured the steaming liquid into the three mugs set out on the counter, dropping a sugar cube into one of them.

He handed me the one with sugar, knowingly, and set the other two out for Kori and himself. At the windowsill were wrapped dough pastries with a creamy fruit tart center—he snatched the plate and offered it to me before sitting and passing it to my blonde companion.

"How long have you been up?" Kori asked, crumbs falling down her chin and onto her navy leathers.

"Only a bit," I assured. "I passed Zymir on my way in."

She reached for another pastry as Tillian's soft eyes finally met mine. The gentleness in them spoke a wordless apology, as did my very favorite tea gracing me with nostalgic fumes below.

"I went to Nox's this morning," I began, diving straight into it.

I waited for the tenderness in his stare to harden at that, but it didn't, seemingly well prepared for the statement.

"How'd it go?" he asked, taking a sip of the tea and grinning. He glanced at Kori, who had remnants of the raspberry jelly center evident on the edge of her chin.

He gestured to his face and mirrored the spot where it was—Kori watched him, blushing, and then wiped it with her forefinger and licked the sticky mess off. They seemed to be in decent spirits. I wasn't sure how long they had been up or how late the conversation went on last evening once Zymir and I had left the kitchen. But it seemed to prove decent for the comfortability between the two.

I blew on the tea, wafting the steam away from me and elongating my exhale to ensure my words came out as calmly as possible.

"It went well, given the circumstances. He believed me, which was good." It was *very* good. The conversation would have been focused on a whole other matter—my lack of a vial—if it had gone the other way. I shivered at the thought.

"He explained that there were others now out extracting, but no others employed by him. And he wasn't sure why, if Osyren wasn't one of his clients, my proximity tattoo reacted to him. But he was pretty positive if something was interfering with this," I held my wrist up, the sharp lines deep red still, "then it was something I absolutely need to investigate."

Their glossy expressions told me some of what I advised went over their heads, but they stayed listening, Tillian intensely so as he waited to take another drink.

Worry began to drip into my core as I contemplated my next sentence carefully.

"He suggested if we wanted to figure out who was responsible, we would need to investigate the deserters, the Nevari."

His features froze, and he swallowed hard. Tillian never spoke of his father. I had never met him, and he never came up in conversation. It was a wound that never fully healed, even after meticulous care to avoid touching it. And now I danced a fine line around that sore.

"What does he expect you to do then? Go up there and ask them nicely if they killed some kingdom official in Vayne?" he asked, puzzled. He rolled his shoulders back and shook his head in disbelief.

"Not directly, no." In all honesty, I wasn't quite sure what I would accomplish going up there either. I'd be stepping into one of the least traversed areas in the kingdom, one where traitors, thieves, and murderers ran amuck. "But if the Nevari are now involved with soul extractions, then we could have a much larger issue on our hands. I don't think having such a bargaining tool at their disposal in the Icesone Mountains is a great idea."

At the reference to the mountains, he set down his mug and roughly cleared his throat. A storm was brewing behind his eyes, one which could bring heavy rains or thunderous roars. Kori's tea was mostly finished, and she picked off the crumbs from her chest, utterly unbothered, whether for lack of concern or ignorance, I wasn't sure.

"We go to these mountains and look around then, is it?" she asked, a hesitant smile wavering on her lips. "Your tattoo thing was affected last time they extracted someone, maybe it would lead us to who was doing it up there?"

Tillian glanced incredulously at her. "You make it sound like an easy in and out? You're not the least bit concerned—?"

"Of course I am," she cut him off. But with a simple shrug, she added, "But I have nowhere else to be."

Kori would go with us further then, which solidified our continued journey together. I was thankful. Her humor and pleasant disposition would be needed through the trek into the cold clutches of the mountains. Especially since something told me Zymir wouldn't be a beacon of warmth and conversation any time soon.

The chaos in his eyes passed, a strong wind carrying the tumultuous clouds away, leaving a confident, steady quiet in their place.

"When should we leave?" he asked, facing her but his words directed pointedly at me.

"You're...coming?" I tried to avoid the trepidation being heard in my voice, but it was inevitable. "You've done enough," I looked around the room and then at him, "by letting us stay here, I would never ask you to—"

"Then don't. You don't have to ask anything." Seriousness firmed his jaw, and in a knowing whisper, he murmured, "I have to go, Adelliah."

I preferred to travel alone, spending years on this journey with only my own survival to be occupied with. It allowed me to be precise, and it allowed me to take calculated risks because I knew the outcome of which would only befall me. I pictured him in the woods, hunger and fear replacing the fire in his stare, his presence if we were to be attacked by the unknown like we were before when Zymir ran off ahead of us. Unease quaked me, brushstrokes of uncertainty at the thought of policing so many people to ensure maximum comfort for all of them. It would be exhausting trying to lead a tip-toe example to avoid any disagreements should Tillian's hardheadedness make an appearance.

He seemed to hear that concern, and with a playful smirk, he said, "I'll play nice, I promise." He held his hands up innocently.

Another thought racked me with guilt.

"And your mother? You'd be leaving her alone." *In the same way your father did,* I finished the thought in my head and winced.

"My mother is her own person, and she's..." he trailed, forcing air out of his lungs and raising his brows, "not as alone as you may think lately. I won't tell her exactly what's going on—you're right—it would destroy her, even though she'd understand. I'll just tell her I'm going out of town for a bit with you and my new friends." Honeyed words saturated the air as he spoke playfully, replicating the tone he'd stage for her later.

With that, it was decided.

Without a doubt, a damned plan from the start, we would journey north into the Icesone Mountains in the hopes of finding answers somewhere within the snowcapped peaks and the truth amongst those who spoke only lies. I wanted to pull Tillian aside before we left, repeat the history I had learned from Zymir and Nox, and hear his thoughts on it, but in repeating the string of words that sounded illogical even to myself, I knew he'd scoff at the notion of anything worthwhile coming from whimsical interlacing notions of reality and lore.

It was agreed we would leave the next morning and use today's light to gather what we'd need for our journey. Tillian would head up to his mother's shop to prepare her for his departure and subtly find ways to gather heavier clothes for us all to don once we hit the endless, existential winter. Kori would take some of my coin to find food that would last the duration of the trip—high protein, high fat, easy-to-carry nourishment that would provide whatever energy it could to supplement any hunting once we reached an elevation where wild game became scarce. Zymir was off doing whatever it was that Zymir did to prepare for a long journey. I was almost grateful that I didn't know what exactly that entailed.

And my task was weapons. My measly daggers were adequate extensions of my hands, used readily when needed and effortlessly obscured. But it wouldn't be enough, and my fellow travelers would need blades of their own if we were to all be evenly armed in the event we needed to separate.

I was due for a new weapon anyway, I concluded. I had been incrementally adding to my arsenal for years. As blades would dull and hilts would grow too small, I'd add more to my belt, creating a tool kit of sharp edges with well-defined uses.

As we set off on our particular tasks, I knew mine would take me close to the Sunset District again. There were plenty of blacksmiths and weapon crafters within the heart of town, but their weapons were practical second and aesthetically beautiful first. And I didn't care to waste coin on the added surcharge applied for simply being from the heart of the capital.

No, I needed weapons crafted with the sole intention of slicing flesh. Efficient and capable blades for my companions to carry. I wouldn't bet their safety on faulty artisanship.

By the time I began to make my way back through town, most of the clouds had thinned out to translucent, wispy waves. Spring blossoms on the trees were still in full bloom, the fallen ones floating in the puddles from the drizzle earlier, spreading their fresh, clean smell through the city with their lovely white petals and violet centers.

The district adjacent to the Sunset District was affectionately referred to as the Widowspeak District. It was where many of the women whose husband's served for the guard lived, and it, unfortunately, took on its name when many of their husband's never returned from tasks defending the kingdom from far away foes on our borders. There were no wars, of course, no outright advances from our neighbors, but a stationing on the border usually meant a solemn, heartfelt goodbye and years of not knowing if they were to return.

Most did not.

My favorite blacksmith lived there. And despite the nature of the circumstance for my visit, I was thankful my path would lead me to her before I left.

I walked on. Evident by the dark green shutters on some of the homes here and the etched crescent moons on the doorframes, I knew I had entered the Widowspeak District. The carved silver moons proudly denoted that these were military homes, a special honor bestowed upon those who served so that their families would share in their recognition. I found the streets significantly less congested here, most people avoiding this area for its perceived somber air.

But where there is loss, there is also an innate space created for opportunity. And the women here would sooner spit in the face of those that would look at them with pity in their eyes than wallow, meeting stares head on and full of fierce resiliency. I found the fieriest of them all halfway down an unimposing block, shop set out right in front of the home, yard entirely converted front and back with the requirements for forging weapons.

I approached to see someone else already perusing the open cases and hanging wall displays of weapons sorted by type, size, and purpose. Adira's shop smelled of burned air and tortured steel, soot from the coals in the forge tickling your nose as you walked in. The weapons display area was immaculate, though, the layer of powdered soot reserved for the setup she primarily crafted from out back.

Red waves hung around her freckled face, slim figure mostly concealed by her leather apron. A white loose-fitting top crinkled in the daytime breeze around her arms as she held up a broadsword with an ease that would have you incorrectly assuming the metal she carried was light. As her sleeves flapped around in the warm wind, the chiseled, lean muscles of her shoulders and arms outlined the years of dedication to her craft.

She spotted my approach and shot me a healthy grin. The customer she spoke to was an older man, red beard and shaved head, protruding stomach, and a similar apron to hers, except his was folded down from the chest. They spoke a language not familiar to my ears, and I patiently went to a display case while they finished.

Adira had taught me a bit about blades, relaying some of the first lessons she had learned from her late husband, who had made this his sole earning before he was conscripted. She emphasized the importance of weight and maneuverability, of properly picking a weapon that matched your skillset and desired use.

The two beside me ended their conversation with the man laughing so hard he started coughing, followed by him giving her a friendly embrace before he left, bowing his head at me when our eyes crossed paths.

"What dragged you in 'ere today?" She gave me an accusatory glance, though her words were playful.

"I'm going to need a few things, honestly." I glanced around the three-walled tent and gulped at all the options, mostly indistinguishable to me. "Looks like business has been going well?" I asked and gestured to the path the man had walked off to.

She snorted and wiped her hands before walking closer. "Arnold ne'er buys anything. He just loves to talk—he's got his own shop a bit closer to downtown, comes down 'ere for the trade secrets." She winked and wiggled her nose, the rosy skin of her cheeks deepening. "Now tell me a lil' bit about what exactly you're lookin' for?"

"I have a few companions that don't have a whole lot of weapon experience..." I knew Kori didn't, and I knew Tillian's was rather limited. "Girl's about yeh big—" I held my hand up shoulder's height, "and she's already eager enough to stand her ground and fight, but..."

"But you don't think she'd want something all too up 'n close?" She tucked a loose strand of hair behind her ear.

She asked, but was already rummaging across the shop as she spoke, her question confirmation to herself. As she ducked down behind the shelves, I could hear metal on metal being adjusted around as she searched for something seemingly quite specific. When she finally stood, she lifted up a metal shaft with a spiked ball on the end.

"Hold it," she instructed.

I did as I was told, and she watched with her arms crossed and her face pensive.

It was surprisingly light, and I backed away a few steps to swing it around as I swiveled my wrist. The weight of the end wasn't so significant that it made carrying it challenging, only adding to its force as it came down. The spikes weren't huge like in some of the other morning stars I had seen in her shop before, just sharp enough that a foe without armor would be downed immediately if they got too close. The weapon provided decent reach as well, extending from arm distance to give her a foot and a half or so of clearance and avoid the intimacy that came with my blades of choice.

"The downside of 'er is that she can get stuck in armor," she warned. "Otherwise she's good to go, though I'd have your friend swing it around a few times to get used to the feel." She rested her elbows on the clear display top, eagerness alit behind her deep brown eyes. "What else?"

"Tillian needs a blade," I offered next, cringing.

Over the years, I had spoken a few times about my hot-headed friend, which she seemed to remember instantly based on the immediate groan and doubtful look cast upon her features.

"I don't know about *that*. But let's see..." She walked toward the center display area, the wall and shelves lining the back section of the tent. She snickered a few times, her gaze lingering on what was shown above and finally crouching down to rummage some more through the expanded inventory that didn't all fit on a wall or a shelf.

"How strong is he?" she asked, no tone in the careful question.

Hm. How *strong* was Tillian? I considered his arms, pictured the muscles he'd have developed from chopping wood, and fought a blush threatening my cheeks.

"I, I don't know, based on what?"

Her wide, bright eyes sparkled with mischief. "Well, answer me this, would you say he's as strong as he'd describe *himself* to be?" When she saw my apprehension, she turned back and chuckled. "Strong men don't go on about how strong they are. Trained men never reveal how well trained they are. Remember that—the man in battle who doesn't show his hand is the one you should be wary of. It's in their nature to flaunt," she sucked her teeth, "so bet if they don't, that's the one you take out first."

Adira's husband had been a high-ranking member of the official guard. He was well respected and often called to strategize when pockets of protests from disgruntled towns would flare up. She always spoke of him in gentle reverence, though she spoke of him less and less. The rest of the men who he served with, however...She had been to plenty of palace parties, donned the sultry gowns in a time before a leather apron was her daily wear, and the bite in her words when she described how other *distinguished* men acted as soon as they could leave their wives at home left a bitter warning in the back of my mouth.

"Did'ya write that one down?" she joked, jolting the reminiscing thoughts of her previous lectures from my mind.

"Oh, it's all up here," I teased, tapping the side of my head.

I didn't need to see her behind the display case to know she was rolling her eyes skeptically.

When she stood, she revealed a broad-bladed sword with a slightly curved edge.

"It's called a falchion." She held it out for me to inspect. "Without any training, it's safe to assume someone's go-to motion is goin' to be a choppin' one." She waved her imaginary sword through the air. "To maximize the effectiveness of that motion, you'd want a blade like this—even held by someone who knows nothin' about swords, this'll do damage. Plus, it's one-handed—less things can go wrong if you're wieldin' with only one hand."

I knew she added that to explain the contradiction from a previous lesson she had emphasized: Always fight with both hands on a weapon if the option is there. More force, steadier. But without experience, there was more room for error with both hands gripped on a helm, more moving pieces involved.

I made note of her points and bowed my head to signify this would work perfectly for him. I considered Zymir then, apprehensively. I knew he didn't carry a weapon, but I also knew he seemed well equipped to handle confrontation. His means of doing so, though, were unknown. I knew anything I'd return he'd most likely not use, and so I decided whatever means of fighting he evidently preferred, he would be best to continue with.

"Any returns?" she asked as I considered if I needed anything.

I set two old daggers down on the counter, smaller, thin ones I had rotated to the rear of the belt for infrequent use. It was a pattern that worked well for us both—she'd often lend me blades to test their abilities, and when I was done with them, she'd give me a new one in place of ones I had grown tired of.

"How're the classes going?"

"Well," she smiled, "I've rationed most of these out now." She put the discard blades into a pile behind her with more. "And some of the women have even started to come to the lessons. I think...the rest, they just need some time."

"Armin' women," a raspy, slurred voice came up behind me, and I followed Adira's surprised look over my shoulder. "Beren would be rolling in his grave if he knew what you've been up to."

A broad man a few heads taller than me input himself uncomfortably close to my side, the stench of alcohol flooding my nose. His clothes were tattered, but crescent moon tattoos on the back of his hands indicated he had once served the palace as a high-stationed guard, though the stains and body odor suggested that had been a long while ago. His bristled chin was sharp, and wet, wiry locks hung on his forehead.

"Get out, Gage." Adira locked an outstretched arm, pointing behind me. "*Now.*"

With the force of his body, he slammed his palms down on the counter between him and her, snickering and curling his lip up. "Disgusting, look at you, wearin' men's clothes and doin' a man's job. Beren—"

Flipping one of my discarded daggers into her grip, she wedged it down into the table between his spread fingers, causing him to jolt backward onto his heels and nearly smash into me had I not side-stepped at that moment.

"If his name comes out of your mouth one mor' time," she warned, "I will carve that tongue o' yours right out."

She meant it. Her anger wasn't hot or impulsive—it was still and cold and precise. I couldn't imagine the anguish she had endured since her husband's passing, but I did know she stayed busy and motivated to diffuse it, empowering herself through empowering others like her. She was a force in this district, an emblem not of what they had lost, but of the innate strength they possessed.

He mumbled under his breath something most foul and scurried away. I watched him depart in the direction of the Sunset District, shoulders hunched over in his defeat at his inability to spur the humiliation he intended. I wondered who his next victim would be instead.

She sucked in air and directed her gaze back at me, softness returning smoothly and effortlessly.

"And for you?" She glanced at my belt, still well filled with blades I found useful and sufficient.

When I shrugged, unsure of what else I could possibly need, she held up a single finger and walked behind the open slit of the tent.

"Oh, my mighty Adelliah, for you, I have just the thing."

CHAPTER 14

I left her shop with more weapons than usual, my companions' hanging from my hips and the weight disproportionately pulling on my sides. Every time I glanced down at the leather sheath on my right forearm, a satisfactory warmth filled my chest. Her hidden blade recommendation was better than I had ever imagined, and my mind snowballed over all the ways I could eventually utilize it.

I hadn't realized how long I had been gone until I reached Freyah's. Everyone else was already within the kitchen with bowls full of brothy stew, the earthy smell greeting me before they did. They were spooning meat and carrots into their mouths. Kori and Zymir sat opposite of one another, Tillian wedged in between. The discomfort from the night before lingered each time his gaze passed over Zymir's tanned skin, but he said nothing.

I passed off the weapons to each, giving an abridged description and helping myself to a bowl as well. Though Freyah had been the one to prepare the meal, she was the only one not present.

"Nothing for him?" Kori asked, sticking her nose up toward Zymir.

"I..." I trailed off and filled my mouth with the hot, flavorful soup. "He didn't seem like the weapons type."

She thought momentarily at that before shrugging, agreement flickering in her small grin, as if remembering his handling of the creature in the woods and coming to the same conclusion I had—it was better not to ask how he defended himself.

Zymir's silence was confirmation enough.

"We should leave first thing in the morning," Tillian said with a mouthful of food. He held a piece of parsnip between his teeth, breathing on it while he chewed, resulting in a hefting of air in and out of his mouth clumsily.

Kori groaned, and Zymir nodded his head in agreement.

"I am familiar with a path to the bottom of the mountain," the velvet voice said, his bowl barely touched. "From there, though, we will have to find a way in."

"My father told me there were periodic doorways at the base, dug into the snow that led below ground," Tillian uttered, wincing from a bite he hadn't cooled down enough. "If we can get to those, we'll be golden."

Zymir didn't respond. His gaze seemed far beyond the bowl in which he stared, but he nodded in agreement.

Morning found us quickly. Groggy eyes and occasional yawns greeted me when I woke and strolled through the rest of the house. Freyah had not come home last night, though Tillian had assured me that their conversation had gone well, evident at least by the coats he stuffed into a large bag he carried on his back.

The path out of town northbound took us past the palace.

While you could see it from any point in town, it didn't hold as much majesty until closer to, when its high walls and dazzling archways could be better appreciated. Despite not directly passing it, as we made our way north, more and more towers could be seen stabbing into the thick morning clouds. The watchtowers in front were created with the darkest of stones so that they appeared black, and the Sheirsan flag proudly fluttered in the wind between them, silver stitched crescent moons atop one another, the round edges back-to-back, mouths open up and down against the deep crimson background.

It was breathtaking, regardless of how many times I stood mesmerized by the pure grandiosity of it. The scale and power it radiated were designed to be immediate, an involuntary, innate response as you peered up the intricate columns and marveled at the looming clock tower in the center, hands stopped for the past six years on the exact time the royal family had disappeared. Silent homage, wordless hope that they would return and that the hands would be allowed to tick forward once again. Until then, a frozen reminder that emulated the lack of any real progress since. Those in the palace now were extended families, royal officers, lawmakers, and peacekeepers. But none of them made regular appearances.

I'm told in the time before they vanished, there would be weekly events in the palace courtyards—the towering doors would open, and city goers and travelers alike would be invited to see the lavish interior and pay their respects to their king and queen. The four children were often ushered away for lessons. Their attendance was rare and never spoken of.

Though magic had mostly left the land, here too were remnants of its power. Permanent glamours in the courtyard made silver fire burn relentlessly from a central pier. If the sun hadn't begun to rise just enough so that its lit fingers were already stretching across the horizon, you'd still be able to see the unnaturally silver tongues flickering in the night sky.

Kori's eyes were glued to the distant palace as we passed, Tillian and I taking turns filling her in with the minimal history that we knew. The stories of how the mighty clans met here, in those walls, and signed their declaration of unity. The stories of first King Harolde, the symbol of strategic genius and careful planning—in my mind now, I could hear Zymir's words, though, and his telling harshly ripped through the visage I had always imagined. I wasn't sure what was left when I pictured that great hall filled with clan leaders gladly surrendering their independence in pursuit of restful nights without kids stolen away in the silence. It was now painted with streaks of red, haunted by the real ramifications beyond that ideal.

Did they know when they signed?

Was it their combined idea to begin with?

Zymir's stare stayed ahead as he led us out of town, listening to us fill in the gaps to Kori, whose eyes sparkled in expected awe and imagination. His golden eyes never broke to steal a glance at the palace, and the churning pit in my core whispered silent judgment every time I found myself unable to look away, its grandeur and history still too deeply ingrained in everything I had known since I was young.

Luckily its silhouette was soon behind us, watching us leave Alaria on the same path, for the same people that had once desecrated its magnificent interior in the blood of its men.

A shiver tickled up my spine as I watched my boots carry me further away, curiosity beckoning me further into my thoughts, wondering what sort of people seized such an already hopeless moment—the family's disappearance—and used it to topple guardsmen while making a break away from Sheirsa.

I too had known moments of deep-seated despair, borderline hatred for the inequalities doled out on the kingdom's streets in the form of the wealth gaps and abandoned children. But...I couldn't imagine killing over it.

Cold and wafer-thin, I lived off scraps on the streets until Nox had found me and struck up a deal. A deal that this kingdom made possible with its harsh conditions and unforgiving realities. Alone, lost, and desperate for any semblance of warmth, whether in the form of food in my aching stomach or in the warm embrace my young body yearned for. I had only found a caricature of the former—scraps of stale bread, watery broths, discarded leftovers in the alley trash.

But through my deal with Nox, I soon became resilient and strong. There is no greater motivator than survival, no better teacher or driving force than starvation. Expending energy becomes a risk, one you must wisely calculate or gamble away your earnings.

The northern edge of Elsarah was calling in the distance. Tops of thin trees aligned across the path ahead, a solid wall of deep green pine. But in the air was a distant smell I couldn't quite place.

Zymir's nostrils flared then as well, the unusual trace of something sinister teasing our senses, though our march continued on. His body was tensed, though, as if the looming closeness to that smell and feeling were gripping his every instinct and telling him to stay away, run as fast as his legs could carry him in the other direction. But we stayed moving, Kori and Tillian carrying the rear, not speaking minus the occasional back and forth of stories of no particular variety—favorite foods, the first time Tillian ever chopped down a tree, Kori's love of the ocean—surface level words to break the uncomfortable stillness radiating off Zymir's alert back and never wavering, dead-on stare toward the horizon.

I walked between them and him. Ears alert for their words, eavesdropping despite myself, and eyes reserved as backup for Zymir, a secondary level of watch as the mouth of the dark forest opened before us. The smell thickened.

"What *is* that?" I asked at last.

I turned back just as Kori crinkled her nose in confusion. Tillian mirrored her expression.

"I'm not sure," Zymir replied, turning his head to scan back and forth from the edges of the fast-approaching woods. "It reminds me of soot or ash, but," he sniffed and rubbed the bridge between his eyes, "there's something different about it."

Tillian quickened his pace to walk up beside me, tossing over a curious glance.

"I don't smell anything," he whispered.

I waved it off as insignificant and attempted to remove it from my thoughts as well. When we finally entered the thick forest, it felt somehow different than Elsh, somehow darker and infinitely older, like the bark here was watching and judging the tiny blips in time that walked through its breadth. The air here was cooler already, despite no increase in elevation. The blanket from the lush branches up high provided its own spotted umbrella against the midday sun, allowing pockets of light through but diminishing the feel of its warmth.

It would be a weeklong trek to get to the mountain if we were fast. No one wished to tarry, the consensus seemingly being that the sooner we arrived at Icesone, the sooner we'd find ourselves back to Alaria with answers of our own.

For the first day, our aim was to walk as far into the forest as possible, as deep as our legs would carry us. We could set up camp in the dark if needed, if it allotted a head start to our destination. Kori hummed as she walked once the forest had been our surroundings for a while—her innocent perusing of the different trees and flowers instilled the delight she first had, though she kept on track and didn't bother to slow to see the finer details.

The first day proved utterly uneventful.

Dividing up tasks by four made setting up sleeping arrangements mindless and streamlined. Tillian had brought a larger tent his mother used to use, neatly organized by rods and pins, suspended up with enough space for us all beneath it. The heavy bag he carried with our coats and additional blankets would be divided tomorrow—the weight was fine for today, but he tenderly rubbed his lower back as we sat around the fire Zymir had lit.

"I can carry it tomorrow," Kori offered.

We all paused before letting gentle laughter fall out of our mouths.

"You'd topple over." Tillian smirked.

Even Zymir, the embers of the flames illuminated in the amber of his eyes, found them widening at her suggestion. "I don't think that would be the wisest division of carrying capacity," he said matter-of-factly, prompting more chuckling from Tillian and me.

He watched our continued giggles blankly and stared at the low barbs of the flames rising just slightly over the ash.

"Ay—" Kori hollered. "Come on, I'm serious!"

"Absolutely not," Tillian said, massaging the spot at the base of his spine. "We can split it up tomorrow. You can take half if it means that much to you."

Her hazel eyes relaxed, and a victorious grin turned her lips up slightly. The mood was light, if a bit forced, but the tension tonight was more due to the uncertainty of the next few days than the newness of the people around one another. No one mentioned the mountain or our destination. Casual conversation made the ambiance feel like a camping trip, a chosen weekend getaway to relax. If the rigid shoulders and strained eyes on all of us didn't give it away, I would have believed the settled front.

As the light from the flames dimmed, Kori's yawns began first.

"Tomorrow night, we'll start practicing with our weapons," I declared, knowing that even minimal comfortability wielding them could make or break the outcome of a fight should we end up in one.

There was no better use for the time before we'd sleep. It had been decided, given this path and its history, that we would take shifts watching the camp to ensure no one came up on us by surprise, providing an additional opportunity to gain confidence with their blades and, by extension, confidence in their ability to properly defend those sleeping if it was needed. As of now, the plan was if you heard someone, or *something*, you screamed and alerted everyone of the potential danger.

I would take the first watch. Curiosity kept sleep at bay, and while I knew it would soon lessen as we drew closer and be replaced with anxiety, I figured the best use of the insomnia would be allowing the others to rest up. Kori was the first to lay down, excusing herself in a half-asleep stupor.

I waited to see if Tillian would depart next, knowing he lingered apprehensively to avoid leaving me out with Zymir alone. I grew impatient waiting for him to yield, which grew into the impulsiveness that had me blurting out from complete silence. "What is a Weaver Mark?" to truly no one in particular though intended for Zymir.

Tillian cleared his throat in his amusement, blinking a couple times.

"They're the physical manifestation of magical abilities," Zymir began, much to the surprise of Tillian, who turned to look at him curiously. "They've long appeared in different clan bloodlines, with different abilities corresponding to specific lineages, though that was more general trend than rule."

The color drained from Tillian's face as he looked from Zymir to me, puzzled, as if we had started speaking in an entirely different language about secrets hidden specifically from him. Where confusion usually yielded a sharpness from him, intense interest instead held his gaze and his rigid seat.

"But magic has long been gone from the land, right?" he asked apprehensively, as if carefully navigating the words to avoid perceived ignorance.

"Certain magic has been nearly eradicated, yes," Zymir responded smoothly, "but even Sheirsa couldn't erase it all."

"What do you mean by 'erase it'?" Tillian leaned in, listening eagerly as I had been when he first started to reveal the history of the kingdom not often spoken of.

Zymir, despite usually being unaware of tensions or tones around him, stole a glance at me, locking eyes and hesitating, worry tightening around his cheeks. His wispy, satin white locks fell slightly in front of his eyes, and it wasn't until I subtly nodded that he continued, repeating the story he had told me the last time we were in the close confines of the forest. Within the arms of the trees, it felt like secrets were born and nurtured. As if spoken here, they could be absorbed into the leaves and mossy ground, forbidden words soaked up, stored safely away from unwanted ears.

"So they worked together to get rid of monsters," Tillian concluded, missing the mark I had found after being told the same story, though his face revealed much more conflict than the simplicity his sentence implied. "How does that relate to these birthmarks?"

Grimness glowered from Zymir's eyes, but whatever thought flashed there, he kept it to himself.

"The Varaynian mark on Osyren means that he was a Weaver," he explained, navigating around the question. "Which means the kingdom has Weavers employed to their ranks—"

"Assuming they knew," I interjected.

"Assuming they knew, yes," he added, trying to piece together where exactly he was going with his sentence, a drawn-out pause following. "Why would the kingdom, once adamantly against the use of magic, against the monsters that embodied it—so much so that they went to such great lengths to exterminate them—employ someone with a Weaver Mark?"

"If they knew, it would at minimum suggest a change of heart," I suggested, but both Tillian and Zymir shook their heads.

"Or a change in strategy." Tillian breathed.

Zymir and Tillian met eyes, and for a moment, there was a shared churning of gears, both piecing together thoughts to arrive at a similar conclusion.

Zymir's head bobbed in agreement, and Tillian went blank, staring into the ground as if far away.

"How powerful are these Weaver abilities?" Tillian asked.

"It depends." Zymir sat perfectly still while Tillian kept shifting uncomfortably in his seat, the weight of the conversation adding to what had already pressed down upon him all day, mentally adding strain to the physical soreness within his muscles. "It depends on how trained they are, and I'm unsure how trained Osyren was. Using the abilities requires a huge drain of energy, so the inexperienced pose a much greater risk to themselves than those they wield it against."

"If the Nevari know about this, maybe they're trying to remove the marked guards from the ranks," I said.

"That would make sense," Tillian agreed, fiddling with the edge of his tunic. "But to hit one of the high officials, to draw that much attention, you'd think Osyren would have to be pretty essential to whatever is it they're planning."

"And why take his soul..." I whispered.

I remembered my bargain with Zymir, that whoever had killed Osyren, taken the satisfaction of doing it himself away, would be his to do with as he pleased. I considered that—the degree of hatred Zymir had for him—when he showed little interest or care to much else. I wondered when our investigation finally yielded whoever dealt the throat-slitting end, whether Zymir would continue with us further or part ways.

"I think that's enough theorizing for the night," Tillian said as he stretched his arms over his head and leaned from side to side. "I'm beat. Keep the raccoons out of the tent, will ya?"

"Yeah, yeah." I smiled half-heartedly.

Tillian left, zipping up the tent quietly behind me, followed shortly by Zymir. The rest of the night went by uneventfully until it was my time to change watch shifts.

The next several nights went by much the same.

CHAPTER 15

As dread and weariness pulled at our feet on the fourth day, we found our path northward far less traversed, the worn ground of steps lessened. It was also this day that the assaulting smell returned. It slapped my face hard, a wall of unusual burnt residue lining my nostrils. I stopped immediately, head stinging as it pounded loudly against how overpowering the smell was.

Zymir, leading us as he had been, was nearly doubled over. He was leaning onto his knees, breathing heavily, raspy air forced out of his lungs.

Even Kori and Tillian could smell it, wrinkled noses prickled upward. Tillian kept turning around, trying to identify the origin or direction it was arriving from.

Up ahead came more struggled breathing and deep pained coughs. Zymir threw me a wild glance, red-lined eyes struggling as if the smell was a cloud seeping into and damaging his sight, the effects far worse on him than I.

"What *is* that?" Tillian asked, narrowing his stare at us in concern. He sniffed the tainted breeze and started off toward his left, off toward the path in the untamed forest beside us.

Zymir was on the ground now, resting, measured inhales raising his chest as he laid on his back, knees up, one hand on his stomach and the other cupping his face, attempting to minimize the airflow. I lowered my chin to him, *stay here,* I relayed despite the obvious—that he couldn't go anywhere right now.

"Stay with him," I yelled over my shoulder to Kori as I ran to catch up to Tillian.

She pulled out her metal club, pointed edges carefully above her shoulder, poised and prepared to be leveled down if needed. She had practiced every night. As soon as nightfall arrived, she was off in her own corner, practicing her swing, letting the weight feel comfortable in her hands. And while a shimmer of anxiety sparkled in her eyes, the rest of her features smoothed, calm, and prepared if the circumstances proved necessary.

I caught up to Tillian and rubbed the metal spring on my arm sheaths, the bumpy ridges of the knob for the mechanism cool to the touch. I couldn't tell how he knew which way the violent aroma drifted from. My senses were foggy and off-kilter, too occupied trying to make sense of the smell that grabbed on and wouldn't be shaken.

He pointed ahead and swallowed hard. His hand drifted to his sword and pulled it out silently, keeping it close to his side and concealed. His eyes darted to a few trees, one near me, and one closer to him. I followed his lead, speeding up ahead and hiding behind a large oak while he did the same behind an even wider, monstrously thick trunk. He gestured ahead with a tilt of his head, and we made our way further, tree after tree, him flanking the right and I on the left.

He held up his hand, straining his face as he tried to listen.

I froze. I heard it too.

Crackling, sizzling, erupting air. As if the oxygen was being sucked out of it, whistling inward, the breeze not gently swimming through the trees, but being dragged inward. The wind swept past us, pulled, fighting against the demanding onslaught against it. Footsteps, heavy and booted, followed the bustling. I could hear three sets of distinct cadences, distantly clanking metal on metal, and softer steps—was someone barefoot?

Chains, I realized grimly. Jingling and tugging in rapid succession. It sounded like someone was being dragged.

Tillian came to the same conclusion as his face heated, and he ran to the next tree, and the next, his pace urgent.

It sounded so much closer now.

I peered my head around and saw the backs of heavy, intricate jackets. Expensive, crimson leather, the color weathered and fading, the stitches on the back periodically missing but the embroidery's image still clear: Two dazzling silver moons, stacked upon one another, on each of the three men's attire.

The smell crept down my throat. I held back the cough building behind my clenched teeth. I peered back around and saw the dark black tendrils, shadows seeping up from a pit dug in front of the men, clawing their way out before dissipating into the air in defeat.

And then, the scream.

Shrill, ear-piercing violence from the pit echoed through the forest. Ricocheting off the wood, the sound was amplified and dire. I held up a finger and made a circle—Tillian understood and started circling the men, headed for the other side of the pit where the screaming had now paused, replaced by the throaty chuckles of the men who passed a bottle between them. One kicked some dirt into the pile and another spat.

I search the ground beneath me, finding a decent-sized rock and palming it. Tillian had made his way around—I followed his darting motion, the men oblivious to his light steps and zigzagging approach. When he stopped, I chucked the rock, *hard*, in the direction between us.

The men froze, cursing.

"What in the—"

"Elric, go see what that was," the tallest man ordered. He had a sword at his hip, gemstones refracting the minimal light, and the bottle was returned to him. His auburn hair was greasy and clung to his forehead.

The thinnest groaned but did as he was told, leaving the clearing and investigating where my stone had landed, only a few paces in front of Tillian. I had to time it just right or risk him taking the brunt of the assault.

The men stayed occupied by the rim of the hole, watching the lanky one who was leerily searching between trees. I darted closer, just on the edge of where they all stood. I couldn't see into the pit from here. It was dug pretty deep. But the shadowy tendrils still flapped against the ground in protest. A muffled, strained gargle spewed from within the hole, and the man barking orders rolled his eyes impatiently.

"Fine, fine," he hissed, walking into the hole. "Hold this." He passed his bottle back to the one left standing in the clearing. The man left guarding was young, and his wavy blonde locks hung over the absent-minded eyes that seemed more bored than concerned. His jacket was the least worn, though it was a size or two too large for him, his shoulders swimming in the material and the sleeves coming past his fingertips.

I picked up another rock, held my breath, and tossed it toward him.

He greedily snatched his weapon and scanned the tree line. "Who's out there?" His voice was higher pitched than I would have guessed, and a day's worth of stubble trembled on his quivering jaw.

"I can't do everything," the sloppy words came from the hole where the shadows had started to retract into. "Go see what's going on, *now*."

I waited, watching the space between the tree behind my back and the one next to it, as his footsteps revealed his approach. My dagger was in my hand, and my breathing silent. A grunt and rustling noise from across sent my motions in action. I turned, finding him exactly where I expected, a few feet around the corner of the tree.

I aimed my weight at his legs.

He toppled backward, shock and confusion creasing through his face, but caught himself before he'd fall to the ground.

I heard the other skirmish but didn't dare to sneak a glance. The soldier, regaining both his footing and composure, lowered himself and drew his sword. He positioned it low to prevent another attempt at knocking him over. I grinned wildly at him as his eyes darted around in shock.

Seizing the moment, I launched.

The adrenaline coursed through me, propelling my attack as I tried to get behind him. He slashed his sword, trying to maximize the distance between us, but I maneuvered around it. His inexperienced balance was the key to ducking beneath his swinging arm and locking it within my own. I craned his arm backward until I heard a pop.

"Drop your weapon," I growled into his ear.

He wiggled against me, prying upwards and thrashing to get out of my grip. But I held firm as he uselessly tried aiming his sword upwards so it would land on flesh.

I bent further and further until his trembling fingers released the hilt. It was just in time to see his superior's arm dropping down, blade in hand, ready to meet my skull. I hadn't heard him leave the pit. Cursing my negligence, I popped my other arm around and pressed the locking mechanism on the gauntlet, causing a blade to thrust out. I held it at the bobbing throat of the man within my arms. I stepped backward out of the way of the impending sword, locking gazes with the dark eyes that continued forward.

"Drop it, or I slit his throat," I warned, carefully stepping away and refusing to break eye contact. The blond curls beside my face smelled of cheap soap. He hadn't been out in these woods for long, but I knew of no nearby towns or taverns.

"Sir, sir—" he tried to force out, but I pivoted the blade inward, a trickle of his blood wetting my knuckles. His mouth shut in a whimper.

"Stupid boy," he growled, stepping closer still, hands clenched tightly on his weapon. The callouses and deep white lines on them told me he had more experience than both the men he traveled with. And despite the slur in his words earlier, he stood perfectly still and expertly poised.

I didn't want to kill the man shaking against me. But I weighed my options as I tried to find out how Tillian's fight was faring. The clash of metal on metal answered, the back of his favorite tunic darting around as he kept up pace with the man they called Elric. They continued, locked in a back-and-forth dance that seemed evenly matched. With the third man occupied, I only needed to focus on these two. But the younger man was proving more of a liability than an opponent.

"I mean it," I said again as more drops of slippery liquid cascaded over my fingers.

The man laughed, something dark and thick bubbling up with it. The thinning red hair complimented his faded guard uniform well, and despite the missing copper buttons and torn ends of his sleeves, the stacked moons at his breast were undeniably denoting quite a high rank. He whistled, a sharp, high pitch noise that cut briskly through the air.

I hesitated, curious and waiting. But nothing responded to it. No one came running from the depths to join him. Still, the amusement on his unworried face angered something in my core. His inability to acknowledge the possibility of an even fight had me tighten my grip on my dagger and planting my boots firmly into the earth.

The blade connected to my armband quivered. I begged it inward, to disconnect the vocal cords on the now softly praying blond. Hushed whispers leaked from his lips, but I couldn't make out the words. The leader of the group chuckled again, licking his bottom lip and snarling.

"You won't do it." He smirked and waved his sword down, causing me to awkwardly move us both back, feet weaving around feet.

I could only see Osyren, his throat torn in two.

Would my cut bleed that much?

Would my clothes stain from the young man's wounds?

Would it be quick, or would he thrash, grasping to close the waterfall of himself pouring onto the ground?

At my hesitation, with the utmost precision, the official swung the hilt of his blade around, rubies glistening as he cut the air. And with it, disemboweled the man in my hold.

I felt his body freeze, heard the bubbling moisture escaping from his mouth. I let him fall from my arms in horror. His words were mumbled but seemingly equally bewildered as he held his tumbling innards.

It was over in a moment. From his knees, he fell forward, face hitting the dirt and wide eyes empty toward the forest canopy. A puddle gathered around the removed internal organs.

More swipes and shining blasts, and I moved instinctively with it, catching them on my tinier blades. They weren't nearly as strong as his, nor as sharp. I heard Tillian yell in the distance and heard a body fall to the ground, reverberating in my direction.

Immediate panic seized my movements and forced the fear inward, further and further, until it buried itself far below the more pressing need—the desire to get over to Tillian and see whose body had crashed so heavily downward. My wrist burned. The pointed star glowed as I brought my hand up to his, meeting his blows and ducking around.

He favored his right side, I realized suddenly, his coverage lacking on his left.

I charged, trying to throw an elbow upwards to meet his nose. But he swung faster, years of experience guiding his innate rhythm. *Stop playing*, I ordered myself, *stop wasting time*. My arms burned as I pushed toward him. My movements were twice his to keep up with the sheer distance his sword allotted him. I stepped over the splatter of his official, boots sticking with muck and dirt, and with an uptick of my arm, sheathed the banded blade and slipped a loose one from my belt between my thumb and forefinger.

I threw it, sharpness between the pads on my fingers stinging as I let it twirl toward him.

Take it, take the bait, I begged.

But he didn't, merely stepping out of their reach.

"This has been fun, truly." He grinned, eyes empty and emotionless. "But I'm growing bored of you, and I have work to finish."

He barreled toward me, arms outstretched and preventing my path beyond him. My only other option would be to retreat. To turn and run and hope Zymir's senses had alleviated. Maybe between the three of us, a blow would land that could disrupt his perfect movements. But to retreat meant bringing this bloodthirsty mess toward them, risking that they too would end up like the blond who had begged for mercy within my arms.

I stayed planted and braced.

The opening on his less guarded left side beckoned me. I tried again, tossing my arm up as bait. The metal of his blade scraped against the thick leather of my gauntlet, slowing the impact but not preventing it. Pain seized in reply, but under the meeting of his sword and my skin, I tucked below, thrusting my dagger upwards into his ribs.

He retracted, stumbling slightly. And I charged, slamming into the hilt.

I guided the blade further between the bones and deeper into the vital organs beneath. He cursed and slapped me backward. The roughness of his sleeve and the force of his muscles landed across my face. With no time to recover from the blow, I grabbed for my weapon, pulling it out as darkness flowed out from the wound that he clutched. But it wouldn't be enough, not when others waited for our return, and not when I knew he'd remember my face and wait for the next opportunity to seek his revenge.

I stabbed again as his jaw hung open in shock, through those embroidered moons, tearing the silver threads and the tendons around his heart.

Red chapped lips parted as he fell, moving back and forth as if he wanted to add something, throw one last taunt. But no words came.

I turned and ran toward the thud I had heard, wasting no time as the demanding thuds of my heartbeat reminded me that I hadn't heard Tillian still. He shouldn't have been far. They were clashing near enough that their blades locking together had been heard. The moss of the forest earth held droplets from their fight, and I followed their path, holding my slashed arm tightly against my side and wincing through the stinging. New gauntlets, already ruined. Adira would be *livid*.

I found him sitting at the base of a birch, breathing heavily. We both sighed in relief, his body tensing as he turned, having expected someone else. I lowered myself next to him, scanning his body for wounds or injuries. A cut on his cheek, swollen lip, and some bruising already forming beneath his eye, but otherwise, he seemed to have fared well. A sternness shadowed the blues of his eyes, a knowing realization pulling the usually soft corners. He had been in plenty of fights when we were young, his always at-half-boiling anger spilling over more times than I could count. But this was different. We sat with our knees brushing one another and the gentle rustling of the leaves crunching in the breeze.

His stare found my tucked arm.

"Are you all right?" he asked gingerly. He reached up towards me as his face softened.

A seed of guilt that had already sprouted in my stomach, blossomed, fruiting at the worry lines pulling around the bruises on his face. He was fine after this altercation, but what about the next one? Stillness numbed over the pain from the cut as a far greater ache slithered into my chest.

"We should see what was in that hole," I said instead, realizing that whatever had caused the violent smell was gone, and the black tendrils weren't seeping out when I had passed them on the way here.

He gripped my shoulder and squeezed, causing a warmth on my cheeks that I swallowed away. We rose and went back to the hole, the distance between us narrow. There were no words to describe the tangled heap of limbs and bones at the bottom. A vaguely feminine face was all that even resembled a person. The rest was burned, tar black skin crisp and flaking. The center of her was the worst, as if pulled apart from the inside, her ribs splayed wide, and a gaping hole allowed you to see straight through.

We stood in horrified silence, the air taken out of our lungs. I searched for what to say, but I found nothing. The arms and legs were cracked backward and grayed, burnt bone stubs stuck out from the elbows and knees. It looked like a person, but yet somehow different, even beyond the damage done to the body—the proportions were too wrong. Her back was arched at an impossible angle, and if she had once had a lower jaw, it was since gone, a drop from the top line of teeth into nothingness. I gulped and stepped into the hole.

"What are you doing?" he asked, holding me back by my good arm. His fingers felt cold, as if the sight drained him of the relief we had momentarily found.

"We, I have to check..." *to make sure she isn't still alive,* was the irrational thought burying itself into my mind, but I couldn't bring myself to finish, my voice trailing off into the wind.

But he knew, and slowly released me, finger by finger lifting. There was compassion seeping through the wounds on his face, kindness despite the black and blue coverage trying to shield it.

It was much worse up close.

The bones had slivers across them, as if cuts had seeped all the way through the flesh and carved their way through. Her face wasn't burned for some reason, and light grayed skin on her face and closed eyelids made it look as if she was slumbering despite the damage done to her. I remembered the gurgles, the screams, and pity tore at me for not being faster, for not getting answers before I brought the only one who could provide them to his knees. A startling realization tingled up my back, and I thought of how the smell had first reached us when we entered the forest days ago.

Days.

Had they been burning her for that long?

Lightness swept into me, and I forgot whether I had been breathing or not, stars flying through my vision through the haziness. I could feel the vile burning the back of my throat, and my head throbbed relentlessly.

"Let's check on the others," Tillian offered, extending a hand. Not because I needed assistance, but because I could feel his eyes looking over my paled face and could sense the concern as he watched my lips tremble.

I took his rough hand in mine and let him help me out, the razor blueness of his gaze grounding me amongst the sea of grays and ash and death. We found Zymir and Kori not too far away, in the same place we had left them, Kori seated beside him with long, bored faces.

At least they were safe, and at least they had been spared from the desecrated thing in the hole and the monsters that had caused it. Whatever she was or had been, I wasn't sure, and I didn't care. The atrocities those Sheirsan military men had caused were so vile that no wrongs she had committed would ever seem worthy of her fate.

Zymir stood, golden rays of alert still flickering, darting from Tillian to me and then down to my arm, which I had nearly forgotten about. My sleeve was damp from the blood loss. The wooziness in my head condensed, and I was thankful there wasn't much in my stomach, or else I was sure it would have been forced out by now.

Kori ran up, reaching out for the damaged arm. I obliged and held it before her, her grimace telling me the severity was worse than I suspected. She ran to her bag and pulled out a spare tunic, ripping the bottom edge off and using it to tie the wound tightly.

"We need to wash this, we need to find water," she said with an unusual calmness. She gritted her teeth as she searched the expansive, endless line of trees.

Their uniformity made finding abnormalities difficult. So much so that I hardly would have noticed the movement rapidly approaching from the distance we had just left behind...

I wouldn't have noticed had it not been accompanied by a resoundingly piercing whistle. A whistle that made all the hairs on my neck stand at attention. His whistle had been answered...

But by whom?

CHAPTER 16

We readied ourselves. Zymir scanned the spaces between the trees, shoulders flexed and patiently waiting. His chin was high, nostrils slightly flared—I knew he was calculating their exact distance, the precise time they'd be before us. There was no time to tell him what we had seen in the hole: the creature burned at the bottom, the explanation for the haunting smell we had been subjected to. There was no time to tell them of the men we had fought, their blood still emptying out into the soil just far enough out of sight.

Hooves sounded in two directions, surrounding us just as we had done to the guards, but I still could see no horses. I remembered the stinging from my tattoo and glanced down nervously at my one useful arm, worried that in my haste, I had missed new coordinates demanding my next course. But there were no numbers there. There was also no familiar red star that had made itself standard for days now. The pointed edges were compacted, forming a filigree triangle, like the head of an arrow, sharp edge pointing out. It no longer stung, but it was raised, as if the ink was responding to a change in temperature.

"How many?" I dared to ask.

It felt like a game, us hovered into a circle, anxiously waiting, allowing the intimidation of their hiddenness to seep into our imagination.

When Zymir didn't reply, I watched the concentration prickle his brow and turn his lips down.

"What?"

"I'm unable to tell," he whispered, the words frustrated and clunky. "I hear the hooves, but I don't sense any approaching horses."

Tillian piped up, "And that means *what*?"

The men were opposite one another, and Tillian stood slightly ahead of me, my battered arm a sudden weighted liability that made me redden with embarrassment. Injured already, after the very first altercation. How could I embark on such a journey and let my guard down so soon? I bit off a piece of loose skin on my lip.

Zymir's mouth was pressed shut, but he forced the words, "I'm not sure," out, much to his growing exasperation.

"They're Gyrusex," the softest of voices breathed.

Kori's face was concentrated, sweat beading down the side. The word pulled something up from deep beneath buried memories, something sinister and unsavory. But I couldn't place where I had heard it before.

Zymir understood, though, light flashing in his eyes as he blinked. And stiffened.

"Adelliah, Til'," her small voice held such unwavering strength, "whatever you do, do not follow any voices you may hear." I gulped, and Tillian's wild gaze didn't argue, merely caught in the tide and obeying anything that would prevent him from being dragged deeper into the undertow. "If you see something move, swing. If you hear anything, swing."

Voices?

She was the first to step forward, arms outstretched and palms outward, deep breaths coming out even and controlled. Gusts of wind swept around the trees with a force I could feel from where I stood, the wafts pulling on the strands of loose hair, black ribbons bouncing against my face. Tillian's breath snagged beside me, and his pupils darted back and forth rapidly, but I couldn't see whatever it was they were following.

A blur of blackness passed in front of me, like an inked paintbrush set against the canvas and pulled sharply away.

*One...*I drew my dagger.

*Two...*A second blur of blackness, closer.

Three.

I dove in, shoving my screaming instincts aside as I swung at air. But the top edge of the blade caught against something, snagging it on the up slice. The movement of fading blackness halted, shimmered, and the glamour was gone, replaced by the same deep red coat the other men had been wearing. This one far from faded, with new stitching and bright clasps around the neck.

Almond eyes and thinning hair, the man in the uniform had crescent moons sewn to his jack like the previous captain did, but the stitching on his wasn't silver. It was black, stark against the burgundy fabric. As was the mark on his throat—thick dark lines etched into a symbol that reminded me of a spider. It had what appeared to be arms jutting out on all ends, three drawn upwards and three stemming down. It covered the entirety of his exposed flesh from beneath his chin to the corner of his peeking out collar bones. He was shocked as he peered down at himself, opening the opportunity I needed. I rushed him, no apprehension this time, wielding the double blade around his outstretched arms, just as Tillian moved ahead toward a dark, glittery breeze before him.

The captain reached for my arm, trying to secure it and hold my attack. But I navigated beneath the reach, turning around him and slicing the sensitive skin behind his neck. Cursing, he wiped the blood with his hand before leveling an enraged stare my way. He smirked, and with a lofty condescension, flashed his teeth. He took his sword and slipped it behind his head where my dagger had landed, pressing it enough so that when the blade came back around, it was wet and shimmery. He held it in front of his face and licked the smooth width of the blade, trailing the center up only a few inches, the liquid gathering on his tongue. I stepped back aghast, revulsion contorting my features.

I heard the tear behind my head before I felt it. A seam split in my flesh, stinging against the cool pine air.

His wound was replicated onto me.

I could feel the drops sinking beneath my collar. My mind reeled. How could I inflict damage if he could reflect it back?

I'd leave him no time. Maybe that would work. I charged again, angling my foot behind his ankle, catching him in a back step as I ran my body recklessly toward his. He stumbled, falling back onto the earth.

More darting blackness around us, and I could see Kori and Zymir locked where there were, their mouths moving, speaking something I couldn't hear to one another. The man on the ground grasped my ankle and clenched hard, causing a crunch. I slammed on his fingers with my other boot, jamming the heel down with all the force I could muster. I tore another dagger from my belt and flung it, narrowly missing only for his impeccable reflexes.

"What have you done?" he asked from the ground, his voice warping into another's.

Sweet, singsong lightness fluttered in my ears.

What have you done?

Louder, crackling within my skull. I ignored it, grabbing another blade as he tried to stabilize himself to stand. But deafening thumping scraped inside my head, disorienting my senses. Wavy lines pulsated on my hands, sharpness giving to blur, the world around me spinning violently. Or was I the one spinning? Colors flew past my eyes, reds and greens and blacks—but the sound of clashing blades disrupted the movements. The noise yanked me momentarily out. My dagger was in hand, and my body was moving. Habitual motions spurred from years of practice and discipline guided my attacks while my vision somersaulted.

But for how long? And how was Tillian managing the mental onslaught?

My bladed hand kept pace with the captain, sparking metal clinking over and over. My body ached with the effort it took to move within the haze.

And then golden eyes moved in. Tanned skin bolted behind the military guard so fast I could barely make out what was happening, the blurs blending into one another. His hands were weapons, expertly moving around the startled guard and disarming him immediately, a thud of the sword smacking into the ground. The man's eyes were wide and flaming, trying to pinpoint exactly where Zymir spun around to counterattack, but Zymir's experienced maneuvers were too disorienting.

Zymir left no opportunity for his attacks to be reflected, no weapons were drawn and no injuries appearing. That was until his bronzed hands gripped below the astonished slacked jaw of the guard and swiftly turned, dropping the dead weight of the body beside the discarded sword. The heaviness pressing upon my head alleviated, and a relieved sigh escaped me.

I lowered to rest, mental exhaustion hitting me, as Zymir followed his same calculated steps on the man still locked in battle with Tillian. Kori appeared at my side. I hadn't noticed her approach. But she reached again for my seeping arm, the tied cloth wet to the touch. Her delicate fingers unpeeled it, the fabric resisting as she lifted. She squeezed the skin between her brow and tried her best to shield her reaction when the bandage was fully removed. The flesh was inflamed, the wound deeper than I expected. The pain had been muted by the adrenaline, but as that slowed its course within my veins, it flooded back. White-hot throbbing twinged from the exposed skin, and I gripped my other hand, so that my nails dug into the fleshy part of my palm.

Zymir stood above us now, his silhouette casting shadows as he handed down the sheepskin container of water he had brought. Kori took it without glancing up, but nervousness trickled into the calm facade she had been wearing. Her hazel stare held mine as the bottle shook in her spare hand, waiting, searching for something in my gaze that I couldn't ascertain.

She undid the screw-on top with her teeth, holding it as she poured the cold contents over the open skin. It stung, and I buried my nails deeper into my palm. She ran the water over her fingertips that held my arm, and the wetness began to shimmer. The coolness deepened to a metallic chill, as if the breath of winter kissed the aching wound. The reflective, sparkling liquid didn't wash out the damage. It held itself within the split skin, a tiny glistening pond that began to seep inward, not flow out. As the water descended in, flesh filled its place, building upon itself under the delicate hold of Kori's spread fingers.

When she finally removed her hold, the wound was filled. The new flesh was pink and raw, outlined in slightly raised white skin, which would certainly scar. But it was healed.

Kori stood with her familiar, sheepish grin.

Tillian spoke the thought I was still forming in my head.

"What the fuck is going on?" He was beside Zymir, arms out wide, signaling to everything around us.

Kori threw back a laugh that felt far more casual than the downed officials and spilled blood implied. She turned over her hand and removed the thick ring on her thumb. Beneath it, half the size of a silver coin, was a swirled, blue birthmark.

"I heard you talking about them the other night—" she began.

And I pictured it, her early evenings excused as exhaustion—how many of those were strategic opportunities to listen to the nighttime conversations? How many times was she poised to overhear us? And why did it bother me so... We never spoke about matters I wouldn't have brought up with her present, but doubt boiled.

"And you never thought to mention this?" I cut in, suspicion lacing the words despite her having just healed me.

She shrugged indifferently.

"What? So, you two could lump me in with that body you found? That Sheirsan soldier?" She chuckled a bit harshly. "No, I wasn't looking to have that conversation."

Zymir's steady face held no shock. Blank. Too blank.

"Did you know?" I shot at him. He paused, blinked, lips twitching. "*Did you?*"

"I suspected," he said, the words a bit raspy. "But I never asked. I assumed if the moment presented itself, she would reveal what was needed. It was not my information to disclose, nor was it mine to pry into."

"I was expecting a thank you." Kori rose her eyebrows, shoulders held up and high.

I sucked in air and let it slide out between my clenched teeth. I was thankful, I was appreciative, yes. But why was there always information hidden from me, like staring at a puzzle with half the pieces unpainted? How was I to gauge what picture I should be forming? How could I determine which pieces to fit together? There was an exasperation with being the last to know or to understand, which seemed to be never-ending over the last few days.

"So, I was the only one who had to share all my secrets then, eh?" I said bitterly. As I watched her face taken back by the sting of the words, a bit softer, I added, "Thank you."

Confliction flashed across her freckled cheeks, as if her thoughts were being pulled in two directions. I empathized with it. Alone for years on a path not my choosing, the voices I often surrounded myself with were those of strangers, and strangers' words, as a rule, could always be discredited, held as fallacy. Because they had no bearing on my course, no significance to my actions.

But when those words and lack thereof came from those in the space between stranger and friend, with what weight should I hold them? Out of touch for so long with those existing within that space, I was unaccustomed to the careful discretion I should hold and in what capacity. The realization made me uncomfortable.

Kori sat back down. I became aware of the dirt over my clothes and the red stains. My hair was damp against my brow, my face grimy. I turned from her, too aware of my filthy state and unable to meet her stare. But she waited patiently, legs crossed in front of her, hands on her knees.

When I finally faced her, the heat from my cheeks had lessened.

"They came to Vayne the year after the royal family disappeared." She sighed. "I was with my mother, she had just made dinner." A smaller smile graced her mouth. "My mom was always helping others... She, she would heal the poor, journey to the tents of the ill, bind the cuts of the kids I'd play with in the streets. Even though it drained her, the effort to constantly weave was tiring...but she never complained about it." Her eyes were far away now, distant. "The first memory I have is her trying to show me how to do it, sticking my nubby hands into a bucket of water on the kitchen floor." She laughed. "And I'd just splash it around everywhere.

"But over time, she showed me how we use the water, shape it, *weave* its energy into something else. Generations of healers, all the women in our family." And then her voice sharpened, and her eyes darkened. "I was eating blueberries she had washed off in the sink while she cooked, and I was squishing them all over the table. When they knocked, she told me to hide in the cupboard beneath the sink. Someone had told them she was healing people in town, but they needed proof." Droplets welled at the edge of her eyelids. "Three guards came in, and they threw her onto the table—"

"Kori, you don't have to—"

"No." Her rounded cheeks seemed sunken, but her jaw stayed rigid. She swallowed. "I want you to hear this." She wiped her nose with the back of her sleeve, her voice cracking as she continued. "They couldn't find her Weaver Mark, so they ripped off her dress, and, father was off on a fishing trip, and I, I just sat there, unable to say anything or help, and they—" her lips quivered, but she continued, "—they found hers at the bottom of her back. And they, they laughed. And they made her *suffer* for all the help she had so selflessly given to those damned fools in town."

"I don't know who told Sheirsan officials, and I don't know how they knew where to find her. But when they were done taking turns humiliating her, only after her suffering, did they snap her neck." Full streams of hot tears fell over her cheeks, but she didn't bother to wipe them away. "When father returned, he wouldn't speak to me... He was so mad, so hurt, he couldn't bear to look at me...for *years.* They took her body when they left, so we couldn't bury her—we had no grave to visit. And no one even asked where she went. They had to of known...There was a posted bulletin the guards must have hung up in the center of town the very next day after it happened—it had the official kingdom letterhead on it. And you know what it said?"

My face was also damp, I realized. I could feel the wetness as I shook my head, unable to speak.

"'Sheirsa has made the streets of Vayne safe from those who wield an unholy power. We will never rest until all of our citizens can sleep safely knowing they are protected from the *Alltani.*'" She choked out a snort. "They likened her to the monstrous beasts of legend. As powerful as fae, as alluring as sirens, as deceitful of skinwalkers—my mother, setting broken bones of children."

No words I could think of seemed enough, so I stayed silent, my healed arm draped over her shoulder, her warmth radiating through her slight shaking.

"I didn't understand what they could possibly mean, but seeing those Gyrusex, Weavers of a darker nature..." She blinked and played with a strand of hair on her forehead, avoiding a direct look at any of us. "Sure, I can understand their fear, powers when weaved like that...But to draw such a hard line? To say we're all nothing but monsters?"

There was so much of our history buried, so much shame locked up in the demanded compliance of those affected.

How had I gone so long oblivious?

The paleness of Tillian's face told me he had no concept of the horrors she described, that this history was something he had never learned either. There was something deeper in the familiar, lost look on his face, something I recognized buzzing within me as well: Shame.

We all sat quietly for a while after that. The air was saturated with blood, muscles were sore, and a tiredness heavier than I had ever felt weighed on my shoulders. Kori had recovered faster than anticipated after telling us why she hid her Weaver Mark, the contagious smile she usually wore finding her once again as she effortlessly transitioned to figuring out our next course of action. I showed Zymir the carcass in the hole, which he mostly nodded at. He made no remarks regarding her state or what sort of being she had been. Thin, angry lines were the only sign of his stormy thoughts. I didn't bring Kori. I left her with Tillian, who I knew would find a way to comfort her in the wordless way his presence often did.

Zymir helped me heave the downed men around the hole, into it, creating an unmarked grave. He even assisted with the Gyrusex officials, the ones with their black Weaver Marks, who had swarmed our thoughts using their particular brand of skills to disarm and infiltrate from within. When all the bodies were in and Zymir had gone back to check on Kori, I sat at its base. I peered down at the lifeless shapes, and I felt an emptiness. The overwhelming emotional crescendo of the day broke to nothingness: a safe, dulled detachment I found myself crawling into. That numbness moved my limbs as I left the hole. No shovels to bury them, no flames to burn them in fear they would draw attention.

I had no real sense of how much time had passed until I noticed the rosy hues spreading from the sun's departure below the horizon. We managed to walk for an hour more, not to make up the ground we had lost in the unintended stop, but to create as much distance as possible before setting up camp. A looming shadow watched me as I walked. Each step away I took, I felt both relief and cowardice.

When night finally came at last, I offered to take the dreaded last watch, but Tillian was adamant he'd be the last one forced to wake to guard. Except I didn't rest in the time leading up to my shift that would follow Kori and Zymir's. I laid in the tent staring at the nothingness behind my closed eyes, feeling the breath filling my lungs and my skin against the softness of the thin blanket above, a disjointed mind in a foreign body.

When I could finally sit around the fire, sharpening my satisfied blades while I burned my silver irises into the bright, lapping tongues of the heat, I felt hollow. And all I could see were the new faces added to Osyren's, empty with cloudy, glossy orbs, waiting for me to slumber so they could haunt me with their pleas and desperation. I couldn't bear their stares, their lifelessness.

I didn't wake Tillian for the last shift.

I sat until the sun tip-toed up, its rays casting light upon my cheeks as it rose. But I felt no warmth.

CHAPTER 17

Days passed, and leaves were replaced with pine needles. The air felt crisper and light, and my lungs incrementally adjusted to the rise in elevation. It had been five days since we left Alaria. Trading shops and taverns for woodland birds and hard ground. The mountain was now visible in the distance, light blue peaks topped with ice that melded into the denseness of the clouds.

The earth crunched beneath our feet, early morning frost coating the strands of greenery in a transparent, rigid coat. This would be the last day that the midday sun would melt the chilled layer atop the moss and blades of wild grass. We weren't far, I imagined, as the howling wind carried the bitterness from the mountain down between the arms of the spruces and cedars. There was an undisturbed beauty here, unlike the harsh winters in the city, where freshly fallen snow turned to sloshy grayness and shivering bodies lined the alleys.

Eagles led our path, reflective feathers catching the sunlight and throwing it back down to the earth as they soared. I had seen one up close as we trekked toward the mountain's edge. Its feathers were dark and light shades of earthy brown overlapped into golden richness that, when their wings expanded for flight, left little room for anything other than awe.

Tillian unfolded the coats from the bags we had split them up into. Heavy black leather lined with warm dark wool wrapped around me, and I pulled the hood over my head as the ground broke into remnants of snow that made their presence permanent year-round. It was so *bright*, this snow. To call the snow *white* was lazy. It did the reality quite a disservice. The blankets of snow ahead were shards of glass, mirrors of light that contained all the other colors. The cold air in my lungs invigorated me, and the fresh undertones of running water and peppery mint from the hardy trees filled my senses.

"I *hate* this," Kori said, holding the neck of her coat close to her chin, her red nose peeking out the top.

"Well, sure." I smiled. "We can't all live on the ocean coast."

I tossed the hood back and tugged my hair tie out, letting the black waves fall down in a hearty shake of my head.

"You're crazy." She laughed, teeth slightly chattering.

"It's not even that cold yet," I warned. "Get adjusted to it now before we're up to our knees in snow."

"You're kidding…"

"She's not," Zymir said from the front, his own coat loosely hanging open. The back of his collar, rimmed in a gray wool, highlighted the natural fit his features seemed to have amongst the wintery mix. "We may want to set up camp here and make the rest of the journey tomorrow, unless we want to try and set up camp atop the banks of snow."

"We do not." Kori smiled quickly, throwing her backpack down onto the ground with little prompting. "I needed a break anyway. I think this spot is fine." She sat on her bag, crossing her boots and reclining.

She had been nothing shy of her warm, welcoming self since the harrowing tale from her childhood. I hadn't asked much else, though curiosity begged me to inquire more about her people and their gifts. But it didn't feel right to pry into such a private matter, one that had literally cost her mother her life. It had, additionally, spurred great interest into this so-called *changed* outlook of the kingdom.

The men who had attacked us, the Gyrusex, were in official uniforms, employed by the crown. But for what?

I had to keep reminding myself of the main reason for our journey, of the specific demands of my employer: To figure out if there were debt collectors here and to see what their goal was in their extracted souls. But the further into the investigation of Osyren's death we searched, the greater my own interest in his life became. How did he fit into this bloody, webbed Sheirsan history, in what place was his tale woven?

It all made little sense. Each step closer to the mountain peaks gave me hope that some of my questions would soon have answers. The tattoo on my arm hadn't bothered me at all since our run-in with the Sheirsan officials. The movement into the arrow formation somehow dissipated back to the intricate star, though I hadn't been paying enough attention to notice when exactly it had changed. I rubbed my wrist as they began to set up camp despite the lingering day providing enough light for many more hours of travel. I thought about suggesting we continue—would snowbanks really be any more difficult to sleep on than the wet, firm ground?—but with everyone seemingly fine with stopping early today, I didn't voice it.

"It looks nice like that." Tillian winked as he walked up behind me. I hadn't realized Kori and Zymir were already searching for wood dry enough to burn.

I raised a brow.

"Your hair." He coughed awkwardly. "You haven't worn it down since we were kids."

I shook my head wildly and let the long strands drape over my face. "Yeah, this isn't the best in my line of work." I chuckled before sliding my hand over my face and throwing the dark hair back behind me.

He laughed, a warm, full laugh that, for a moment, made the invisible heaviness on my shoulders lessen.

"Practice with me?" he asked, finally setting his own bag down. He cracked his head, pulling it to one side and then the next. He drew his sword, spinning it up in a cocky wave.

He had grown comfortable wielding a weapon incredibly fast—maybe too comfortable. And it made me thankful he hadn't carried one years ago when he actively sought fights and came home worse for wear more times than not. He'd sit over in a defeated hunch while Freyah ran warm water over towels, which she'd then lay over his swollen eyes and bruised ribs. I never grasped the attraction to leveling fists against skin, but it seemed to release an inner turmoil that Tillian never voiced elsewhere. His desire for the weeks of aching pains after an altercation told me enough that he didn't need to—that this soreness was easier to suffer through, the pain easier to nurse, than it was to attempt to heal the discomfort in the wound left by the absence of his father.

"You want to get beat two days in a row?"

Heat flushed to his cheeks, recalling how Kori had dueled him yesterday, leaving him square on his ass after she managed to catch him off balance. *I was exhausted from an extra long day walking*, he had said when a chuckle escaped me afterward.

He spun the blade around and shrugged. "If you're not up for it, you can just say that..." A playful smirk teased from his lips.

I merely grinned, dropped my coat, and took out a single dagger—the longest one I had, its double-edged sharpness shining in the sunlight. I waited, giving him the opportunity to size the first advance, but he lingered before me, foolishly offering me the advantage. I took it gladly. I went in, tucking my shoulder down and slipping a foot around behind him. He expected it this time, side-stepping and turning.

The sounds of metal clinking against metal sounded, and his jabs became rapid fire. If he was holding back the last few days, he, without question, wasn't now. The challenge was welcome, and the movements we made as we circled one another helped my muscles remember their learned patterns. Heavy breaths created white bursts against the cool mountainside air, and the elevation shrunk my lungs a bit more than I had realized. But still, I wasn't about to yield even in a practice fight, and especially not when my opponent was so keen on gloating.

He caught the back of my ankle, and I tumbled onto my hands, dirt scraping against my palms. I gripped the earth, feeling its tenderness moisten my fingers, and waited expectantly as he awkwardly stood, unsure of whether to extend a hand or rise to the occasion while I was downed. His hesitation was what I was waiting for, planning on, as I jolted onto my feet and chucked my shoulder into his chest, causing his body to fall in surprise. Once his back met the disturbed patch of ground we had been kicking up, I followed, flipping him onto his chest and pulling an arm up behind him.

"Valiant effort, my friend," I whispered into his ear, holding his arm firmly but not tugging on it further.

His blues glanced up at me, not with embarrassment, I realized, but with glee. And in a moment too late, I saw his hand make for my calf, pulling it off and away as his weight moved effortlessly to reposition us so that my head cradled against the soft moss and my wrists were pressed beneath his hold. His victorious ear-to-ear smile brought back the breath that had completely left my lungs.

My heart raced beneath his body. Heat bloomed in my chest.

I was still.

"Are we interrupting anything?" I heard Kori ask before I leaned my head up and saw her approaching with an arm full of branches.

Suddenly *too* aware of our positioning, his legs straddled, face inches above my own, I thrashed my body side to side to wiggle out. His gaze held mine, though, a triumphant gleam in his eyes that I couldn't deny that he had earned. But beneath the subtle gloating, a flash froze the air between us, a momentary carnal stiffening of his jaw that once he realized I saw, he blinked and jumped off.

"Practice," he rasped, smoothing off some of the up-kicked dirt from his slacks.

"Practice?" she teased, dropping the kindling as Zymir dropped his as well, his expression oblivious or otherwise uninterested. "Do I get next then?" She winked, and I chuckled as Tillian huffed and walked closer to Zymir to assist him with breaking down some of the larger branches he had carried.

I picked up my coat by the collar, the heaviness still unusual and burdensome, folding it as neatly as I could—which was truly more of a ball of fur and leather—and set it closer to the tent where it wouldn't be stepped on.

"You're not cold?" she asked, dropping the interrogation that though I knew she'd love to have, was very much not the time based on the quick shuffling away of Tillian.

The slightest of snow had started to fall. Against the low sun, the sparkles of winter glided around and teased my exposed shoulders. The snowflakes landed and then melted, a momentary glimmer of intricate patterns and mesmerizing designs. I tossed my head back, letting the flickering of reflected light direct my eyes. The softness of the occasional bite from the flakes that landed on my nose and cheeks heightened the warmth radiating from them, stilling their activation from my tussle. The blissfully cold drops provided relief and calm.

"Not even a little." I breathed, sucking in the falling frozen flakes.

A louder roar barreled through the trees, a gust of wind passionately zipping through and causing the towering trees to sway back and forth. Their tips touched one another, high branches reaching out and slipping their needles past those of their neighbors. The chill traced its edge up my back, causing an involuntary shiver through my spine. I could feel the cold and observe the way my body prickled up in tiny bumps at its touch, but I could think of no reason why I'd feel the need to don that coat again and prevent its invigoration.

Kori grimaced, watching me wide-mouthed up to the sky. Her nose was bright red, and her freckled cheeks seemed glossy and puffy.

"You're crazy," she said mostly to herself. A faint grin lingered as she walked back to see how else she could assist with setting up camp, eyes still exuding kindness despite the rest of her body's stark rigidness in response to the temperature.

"Do you think it'll snow a lot?" I asked as I trailed her, glancing toward Zymir.

He sat with his hands crossed between his knees as Tillian started the fire. Kori sat beside him, and then I beside her, as the sparks from his flint and steel jumped out.

"It's possible." Zymir sighed, cautiously watching the thick, deep blue-gray clouds that had slid down from the mountains.

Even the sun, try as it may to run from the impending blanket, found itself tucking beneath it. As flames broke free, gasping for air and crackling upwards, Kori reached behind her for her backpack, flinging it down between her legs. I shouldn't have been surprised when from the very bottom, wrapped in a spare blanket she had been carrying, she pulled out a bottle of mead. It was a nice bottle too—the top was wrapped with a golden ribbon beneath the cork and the front design was painted with gold filigree surrounding the helm of a sword, garnet gem inside. It was quite the elaborate label for such a thing, but I couldn't deny it was lovely.

"I thought tonight," she tugged on the top, causing the cork to squeak as she turned it around and around until it eventually gave way to a *pop,* "we could use the added warmth."

She set the tip on her lips and slowly poured, taking a few swallows before passing it to me. Even without the solemn ambiance set by the fast-moving sky, there was an unnamed tension rustling around beneath the cover of swishing tree limbs. Tomorrow we would reach the entrance of the Icesone Mountains, and tomorrow we would sneak into the safe haven of the Nevari. There were no expectations that we could refer to, or stories told that revealed any of the potential mysteries within. I hated going in without intel, but we didn't have any other options. The only thing I could be sure of was that it would be heavily guarded and patrolled, and no one within that mountain could be trusted.

Despite what I had uncovered about our kingdom and their bloody past, those who dwelled within were still defectors. They had still slain the innocent on their path for independence, spilling the life of those who had never bound them or caused their plight. And death, it seemed, always bore more death.

I took the bottle from her and drank a generous portion, considering it sufficient for both mine and Zymir's share. Expectedly, he took the bottle from me and held it to his mouth, feigning a drink that no one would notice he did not swallow. Tillian's sip was surprisingly brief, and when he passed it back to Kori, she looked down into its quarter-fullness and smiled wickedly before helping herself to more.

She was right. The sweetness and alcohol landed in my stomach with an oozing warmth that ebbed from my core outward. There would be more nights like this, right? I surveyed my companions, and my throat tightened at the thought of what tomorrow would bring. And almost more worrying, the nights after that. If we did survive our foolish attempt to infiltrate the Nevari and we found the information Nox was looking for, where would we all go next? I knew Tillian would return to his mother, but the prospect of journeying out on Nox's terrible commands left an ache that the mead simply couldn't subdue.

Zymir cleared his throat as he delicately searched his pockets.

When he removed his hand, thin silver bands looped down to meet at coins woven through their centers. In the seconds of silence that followed, I reached out for what he was offering to peer at the intricate etchings in the metal. It was carved to resemble someone sitting cross-legged, both arms up, one in a fist and the other in an open circle. The being had two horns coming from atop its head. The other side of the coin was smooth and blank.

When I looked up, Zymir had passed the remaining two necklaces out.

"They're for luck," he spoke with conviction and sincerity.

And somehow, even more surprising than the unexpected token from Zymir, was Tillian being the first to put it on. He slipped the long chain over his head, and the coin rested on his sternum, low and concealed beneath his tunic. He patted it with his hand over his shirt and bowed his head to Zymir, who returned the gesture.

Kori followed with amazed delight, practically squealing at how uncharacteristically considerate the gift was.

I stared at the coin once more for confirmation as I traced the symbol into my mind. I put my head through the chain and clenched as the coin fell against my skin in anticipation of the chill kiss of metal. But to my surprise, it was warm. Despite my observing it in the howling wind and the scattered snowflakes periodically landing all around us, it felt comfortable and held no residual coolness.

"Is this what you bought that day in Alaria?" I asked, the realization flooding me with an emotion I couldn't quite place.

He nodded and nonchalantly stood to throw some more wood onto the already diminished, still-hungry fire. *Luck*...I never believed in luck. And I knew for a fact neither did Tillian. But the thoughtfulness of the gift was enough that even he had donned the necklace with no second thought. Amongst the setting sun and increasing bitterness of the snow, I smiled despite myself, and despite the circumstances that contributed to the reason we were all shivering and wetting our lips with expensive mead.

I was relieved they didn't focus too intently on the engravings, though I assumed they wouldn't have recognized the emblem. I had seen that picture somewhere long ago, in a memory just out of reach. I searched and sorted, trying to place it. But only continued to come up empty as to the context that would explain the utter conviction I had when I recognized it.

Hand carved into the silver face was the depiction of Draoi, the god of magic.

CHAPTER 18

Now *this* was cold.

Everything was snow. The freezing banks that went halfway up my shins, the blurry sky, the impenetrable wall of flurries so dense that our visibility was nonexistent. Zymir no longer led. Instead, we gathered in a clump and continued onward, toward where we had seen the highest mountain before we ventured close enough for it to disappear amongst the unrecognizable sheets of snow. Each step took additional energy to pick it up through the depths and move it forward, again and again, the material on my pants growing wet and then frozen.

No one spoke. Not that any words could be heard over the screaming winds and violent whips of icy air. I had lost any measurement of time, of how long we had been walking or how long ago the morning sun was. The sky gave no hints either. Our thick furred coats insulated our cores well enough up until now, but the relentless cold continued to increase its intensity. My face felt raw, and my eyes stung, watering against the high winds.

We had to be close. We *had* to be. The steps took us higher and higher, and though we weren't anywhere near the tip of where I'd imagine the mountain to be, the entrance should be right around the mouth of the mountain range. There was no way absconders, tired from their flee, would have the energy to go much further up the ever-increasingly dramatic slope. The ground had long turned from dirt to snow, pebbles and rocks beneath the heaviness felt slick and suffocated by the continuous blizzards.

Kori started to lag further than usual and further than comfortable. We all slowed our steps, waiting for her to catch up and minimize the distance between us. But her steps were barely bringing her closer, until she stopped altogether, blued lips shaking and her entire body trembling uncontrollably, so much so you could see it despite her oversized coat. I broke toward her, the gusts pushing against my back. I stayed as upright as I could, worried if I didn't actively fight its force, I'd end up falling face first into the rigid snow.

Each step was agony. Wintery bitterness clung to my ankles, the force of lifting them unbearable. As I reached her, the blurred outlines of Zymir and Tillian also appeared beside me, lost in the furs and leather. Kori tried to speak, but the cracks in her lips tore, dots of pink popping up amongst the blue. I grabbed her wrist from deep within her sleeve, pressing my frozen index and middle fingers against it.

Her pulse was weak, but racing.

Her skin was slick to the touch, drenched in sweat as her limbs started to quiver more violently and her body swayed. Her pupils started to dart around absently, as if dizziness and confusion made it uncertain where exactly they should focus. Panic rippled through me, and I searched my companions' eyes for any indication of what we should do. I could defend her against a slimy guard or an armed foe, but against these unrelenting conditions, there was nothing I could offer. Dreaded helpless gnawed at me, talons of fear squeezed my heart.

Zymir rubbed the sticking snow on his gloves off against the front of his coat. Against the grayed haze all around us, his hair and his skin seemed muted. But those golden eyes were like beacons, radiating lights cutting through the obscurity. As they focused on Tillian and me, I almost squirmed under their intensity until he shut them tight. He exhaled slowly, opened them, and reached toward Kori—in one sweeping motion, she was cradled in his arms, a pale, twitching mess in a sea of gray fur. He bowed his head to motion forward, and against the demanding currents, he began to walk once more.

Tillian patted a gloved hand on my shoulder and raised his eyebrows as if to confirm I was okay to continue. With a sliver of a smile and a sniffle, I nodded, and we dragged ourselves further. Against Zymir's chest and absorbing his body heat, Kori's dangling body seemed to slow its convulsions, but I knew however much time we had bought wasn't much.

Ahead, a glimmer of hope appeared in the form of an odd, out-of-place tree limb. We pivoted our approach, making the intermittent views of it our goal point. As we got close, I could see that it was bare, extra branching bodies removed, and the top chiseled to a point. It appeared to be at least twice my height. Once we reached it, we noticed the burgundy ribbon tied around it, the ends flapping around in the wind. It was tied around only once, knotted, and then left there. Symbols on the wood painted in red were flaking off and hard to distinguish, but their loops and lines were indicative that something had been here, perhaps a label or a direction.

Tillian closed in to inspect it further, moving around the perimeter for any additional insights. We had to be close. This had to be a promising sign if someone had stuck this thing into the ground. But a grim shake of his head told me that there was no information to be gathered. His eyes narrowed, and he pointed to the emptiness up ahead. I squinted—another one! There was another totem in the distance.

We hurried as fast as those half frozen and mucking through snow could hurry, until we came upon the next one. It was taller and painted in black. No discernable symbols again, and no ribbon. Up ahead, but closer than the first two poles were, was another silhouette. We trudged on to find the same, but this wood was covered in green paint. The pattern continued twice more, with white paint and then blue. I couldn't make sense of them and hardly tried, the flickering hope that we were getting close gaining mass and momentum. Kori's head tucked into Zymir, and I couldn't see it, but the shadowy concern creasing his cheeks told me enough—we were running out of time.

I focused on her, the need to get her warm, instead of the numbness creeping up my arms and legs, ignoring the wooziness whispering to me to just lay down, rest for a moment.

At the last pole, the blue one, we stared at the emptiness ahead. No pole, no random hope that maybe they were directing us further. I felt my thoughts slip further away. I reached for them, blindly, wondering what exactly it was we were looking for again. It was cold, so very cold, I knew that. How long had it been this cold? Brightness from the growing snowbanks sparkled. It was so lovely.

A hand shook me, and my head dangled around its axis. Blue dazzling eyes, Tillian's eyes, squinted at me. His mouth moved, but I couldn't hear anything from them. He shook me again, and I swatted him away. The snow was so distracting, catching my vision and beckoning me to follow. The snowflakes were like stars, frozen pieces of wonder whizzing around. But instead of darkness to enshrine their beauty, these unique twinkles of light had nothing but blank whiteness as their background, forced to spin around and free fall from the heavens to land amongst more of themselves. A moment apart from the whole. A fleeting ballet where their precise shapes and edges could be seen distinctively as their own until succumbing back into the throes of homogeneity.

The blue paint here was less worn than the paint on the previous poles. I traced the patterns, trying to understand their picture. I always wanted to paint, but my clumsy hands were never good at mastering the brushstrokes. I traced the lines with my gloved thumb, and the disjointed voices around me seemed so rushed and dire. Could they not see that someone had taken the time to create color and vibrancy amongst the emptiness out here? Was that not worth our stop? I ignored them as my fingers trailed the pattern, looping into a circle then back up into another, round and round the blue swirled.

I knew this symbol. Colors smeared in front of me as I turned back to find the deeper shade of blue reflected in the concerned eyes that hadn't left my face. Mumbled sounds spilled between my lips. Did he not see it too?

I braced my weight against the wooded beam and felt into the space around me, searching, feeling. Blue, I was following blue, but not in his eyes, the other blue. The other blue I knew.

My head had never felt so heavy, it yanked on my neck and wanted to roll, but I was reaching for something.

You need to get it together, I heard. The words slammed into my skull with urgency. *You're freezing to death.*

*You are freezing to—*I shoved the voice in my head aside and blinked. The cloudiness dissipated with each opening and closing of my eyes. I went to Zymir, who was a foot behind Tillian, shoulders held tall and back straight up, despite the weight he carried in his arms. The second his stare caught mine, immediate recognition of my clear thinking softened a building tension in his clenched jaw. I grabbed not his hand, but Kori's, pulling them both toward the beam, carefully leading them by her now completely limp arm.

I ripped off her glove, grimacing at the rigidity of her hand and its paleness. I'm so sorry, I thought, moving as coherently as I could force myself, my movements frenzied. I twisted her thumb ring tenderly until it slid off. I curled my palm around the back of her hand to prop it up and then pressed it to the beam. I could feel that cloudiness building, preparing to storm my vision and clarity. Low thumps of my heart reverberated in my ears. The ground started to shake, or my knees started to give out. I couldn't tell. Nothing was happening, and blackness was hurdling toward me.

I took her hand off the beam and turned it toward me. The darkness formed a tunnel, and a sphere of light got smaller and smaller further into the distance. Blue swirls on blue swirls. I had lined them up, and sure enough, the skin on her thumb was glowing bright, electric blue. Cracks in the wood, too thin to be seen before, started pouring out light, originating from where her hand had met the wood and spreading. Vining, creeping light, all the way to the top of the beam.

The black tunnel in my mind stretched and stretched, and I peered through the pinhole at the very end. I could no longer keep the space from closing. As the light continued to slice through the air, relief brought that curtain of nothingness completely down.

CHAPTER 19

Warm heat brushed the nape of my neck, causing my eyelids to flutter open. There wasn't much light. I could tell I was laying down, and I could feel my blood loosening as it coursed. I shut my eyes again tightly. *Where was I?*

I tried to remember, pulling the fabric of memories. There was so much light. Sapphire beams seeped out, and then the ground had vanished beneath my feet. There had been the unmistakable sensation of falling. The clenched pit in your gut when the air is pulled from your lungs, and your body complies with gravity's demands. I remembered being so very confused, and so cold. I wiggled my fingers and felt quietly relieved when they responded properly.

A jolt of panic shot down my spine.

Kori.

I sat upright and felt the heaviness of my skull lingering. Too fast. I steadied myself, searched the darkness. Wetness, stone, the distinct smell of moisture and mildew. I groaned as my gaze landed on the reflective metal bars to my right. I was in a cell. A quick glance around in the minimal light confirmed my next thought: I was in a cell *alone*. My belt containing all my daggers was gone, as was my violet pouch. I wasn't sure which unsettled me more, and I jumped up to stand in a panic.

Too fast, I chastised again, wooziness blocking my sinuses and bile inching up my throat.

"They took your friends about an hour ago," a voice from beyond my cell spoke.

I hadn't realized I *wasn't* alone. And that my friends had been *taken* from this place. For what purpose?

I ran to the bars and peered out between the spaces, making note of the long hall and evidently several other cells. Most were so dark or went so far back that I couldn't tell if they were occupied or not. But the one directly my opposite had a tray in front of it that caught my attention. It had no sloppy food remnants on it, just a copper cup in the center that was toppled on its side. The offering had been drunk, and the cup hastily placed back.

"Where?"

My voice came out cracked and hoarse. I wasn't sure how long it had been since I used it last.

"Preliminary questioning," the voice replied matter-of-factly. "Standard procedure for hopeful recruits."

"*Where?*"

A wicked laugh made my skin crawl. I tried to see into the back of the cell, but enough shadows concealed who I was speaking with. The wide black stones in the cell continued down the hall. At the very end, a flickering light from a sconce indicated there was an exit somewhere in the distance, but its far dancing shadows made it difficult to pinpoint where exactly the door would be.

"You ask a lot of questions for someone who hasn't even bothered to introduce herself," the voice snickered. "Very *rude.*"

Bony fingers gripped the bars across from me. Tight, white skin was barely a layer atop the knuckles as they stared. Jagged, over-sized nails from the fingertips clenched the metal and then tapped delightfully on its surface, creating an echoing clinking. The nails were more similar to the talons of the eagles I had seen circling the forest mountains, razor-sharp and predatory.

"Do you know where they took them or not?"

A soft hiss slithered through the bars.

"Who's asking?"

"Adelliah," I spit through my teeth. "Where were they taken?"

Hunger throughout my trip must have had a greater effect on me than I had realized. My frame was smaller, and I edged my protruding hip bone to the space between the bars, but the gap was still too narrow to attempt to cram my body through. Useless. My fatigued muscles and whimpering stomach were added variables I needed to consider if I was to escape and find my companions. The moisture suggested we were deep underground, and through the vague memories of falling, I had to guess we had landed ourselves somewhere beneath the mountain toward its core.

"The room without lies, most likely. Or maybe the room without feeling. Or the room without eyes."

"Stop playing around," I growled and stuck my face between the bars.

"Or maybe the room without air." It laughed, and a slithering sound neared the space between us. "You don't need them. You could stay down here with us. We have everything we need here." Distant rattling from its cell quickened. "We don't need them."

I balked and started to pace. No windows. I could see at least a dozen sets of bars. The lock on my door was an unsophisticated one that, had my weapons been left on me, I'd have easily been able to maneuver out of. From the direction of the sconce, a heavy door handle jangled and shoved forward. I paused my shuffling thoughts to race back to squint down the hall.

"You're up!" a surprisingly jovial voice greeted me.

What *now?* Despite the chipper tone, I took an instinctive step back.

The pale, taloned hands shrank from the bars, retracting back. Even the light the man carried did little to penetrate the shadows of that cell, where silence lingered, and a mass still waited in the corner darkness. I could feel it watching me despite no evidence of actual eyes.

Precise steps of the boots approaching already suggested that this man may have previously severed Sheirsa. His steps were a careful cadence, nearly a measured march. Plentiful cheeks illuminated against the lantern in his hand as he held it up to his face and grinned. Cheerful auburn eyes pained as they met mine.

"Let's get you out of here now that you're up," he spoke quickly, sorting through a mess of keys he pulled from the pocket of his dark gray jacket. "You must be starving," he added, his eyes painfully avoiding glancing down at my body which had been more bare than usual—my top had been slightly torn at the shoulder, the fabric hanging down, and a similar gash on my side exposed my lower abdomen.

"You all landed pretty rough." He fought to fill the silence, fidgeting in the hall as the keys slipped between his fingers. "But your friends are dry and warm in Des' receiving chambers, they'll be happy to see you."

A snicker from behind him caused his body to clench.

I straightened and stepped closer, venom daring my lips and batting my lashes.

"Will I be able to wash up beforehand?" I pulled at the dirtied clothes that admittedly were already irritating my skin. "I want to make a good first impression if we're to seek refuge approval."

In the reflection of his flames, his caramel skin glowed. A puckered white line ran from his hairline over his temple and stretched beneath his jaw, a nasty scar that must've taken ages to heal.

"Of-of course," he stammered. He mumbled a curse under his breath. "I must've taken the wrong set of keys, please excuse me for just a moment. I'll be right back." Even in a rush, his perfect steps echoed until he slipped back behind the door.

The Nevari had grown in substantial enough numbers to be a whispered threat amongst those in the capital. There had to be a screening process, but surely earning good graces would get us further than hiding amongst a group we knew next to nothing about. Plan A was to gain information by pretending to blend in: a naïve young woman bent on leaving Sheirsa for whatever promises this retched group of rebels offered. I hadn't allowed myself to consider what Plan B would entail otherwise.

"Clever, girl," it hissed in a hush. "If I give you some advice, will you do me a favor?"

"You've done me no benefits thus far—"

A frustrated rustle cut me off.

"Fine, *fine,*" it said. "No favors, no advice. Stupid girl has no idea what she's stumbled into." It spoke as if directing the words at both me and another audience. "She has no grasp of the web she's fallen stuck in..." It laughed again, an unnerving, mistuned melody that felt forced.

The clunky doorknob wobbled at the end of the hall again, and I sighed thankfully that I'd soon be away from this persistent, ominous thing.

"You walk upon the souls of the dead," the slippery voice said, knobby fingers again appearing around the bars, a blackness between them. "When their strands appear, pull."

Prison cells and solitary confinement were nothing short of torture on the brain. I knew those who had been held captive for long often surrendered to bouts of insanity and illogical ramblings. That had to be why the voice sounded pained and the words nonsensical.

The door started to creak, and I found myself glued to that blackness between the talons. An urgent hiss beckoned me forward.

"*Pull,*" it instructed me again. "When it is time, pull the silly strands of this dead land. Unravel what they've fought so long to keep woven." The mass rippled, cascading darkness folded upon itself, revealing taut skin that glimmered within its confines, vaguely reminiscent of a newly deceased corpse, protruding facial bones peeking out from its top.

No bottom jaw, empty sockets of awareness that, when met with my stare, caused a tingling at the back of my skull. A vague remembrance. A sinister similarity.

"I know you." Its words slithered into my ears, disconnected words from a mouthless being who stood bare before me. "You will remember, and you will *pull.*"

"Found 'em!" The man down the hall moved quickly, holding up the second set of keys and jangling them happily.

As he reached our set of cells, the body across from me slipped back into its dark blanket before I could ask the multitude of compounding questions swarming beneath my surface.

A polite smile found my lips, and I tensed as he tried once more with the lock. This time, I was more aware of his person, the shoulder-length dark hair tied behind his neck, the shimmer of the hilt of a sword peaking over his back, the nervousness of his jittering hands. *Some guard...* I mused. If the state of my companions wasn't still unknown, I imagined I could take his sword quite swiftly. Disarm him, replace my spot in this cell with him, and continue down the corridor. But we were going with Plan A.

Play nice.

"Got it!"

The old bolt gave way and slacked. The door breathed outward, and I stepped in the gap.

"After you," I offered, gesturing for him to show me out.

A reassuring sigh left him, and he held the ornate lantern between our faces. Despite the scar, his face was youthful and proud. The richness of his skin and the fullness of his cheeks nearly distracted me from the straighter white lines beneath his chin. Three of them, a thick center line, and two thinner ones beside it, ran from the bottom of his chin, down his neck, and continued beneath the dark leather coat. I could feel him following my stare—he bowed, respectfully turning his gaze from me to the path ahead. We walked, and I tried to match my uneven gate to his steady one, failing atrociously. Hungry dethawed steps were far from careful, and I stumbled more than once as I made my legs keep up with his.

"What brings you to the Icesone Mountains?"

I used the phrase Zymir had suggested. "I'm looking for answers that have long been hidden from me." It wasn't a lie.

"Ah." I could see his knowing smile out of the corner of my sight. "Aren't we all."

"How many prisoners do you keep down here?" I asked carefully. The door we had walked through had led down an identical passageway. And then another. Three identical halls, endless metal bars, seemingly empty cells.

"Prisoners?" He snorted. "We don't keep prisoners. These are left over from the early days before King Bryce and his family disappeared. They often shipped enemies of the kingdom here."

Ironic.

"Oh?" I mused. "So, these cells are kept empty then?"

"For the most part," he said, smile dropping as he swallowed.

Well, that was interesting. I considered pressing further but didn't want to seem too concerned for their under-utilized prisons or what the creature in the cell across from me was doing there then. And, of course, I also only half-believed him, as I imagined he only half-believed me. A growing rebellion without prisoners would be a foolish one. And maybe they weren't stored down here, but that didn't mean they weren't stuffed elsewhere, strung up and waiting for torture to reveal the secrets they carried.

I gulped that thought away.

"How's Kori doing?"

An internal heat flared within me, hating that the question hadn't burst from me sooner. I blamed the grogginess, the distractions from the stranger across the cell, the seeking of intel for my oversight. But it didn't comfort the shameful wound as I recalled her frozen, still body pressed up against Zymir. Or the feel of her icy thumb against mine when I had pressed her Weaver Mark against the painted blue swirls.

"Much better. I was actually finishing up with her earlier. It's why it took me so long to come check on you."

"Finishing up?"

"The cold had caused her body to go into shock. Our healers helped her physical wounds, warming and saving the frozen flesh, but still," he tapped the side of his head with his spare hand, "the mind often needs help recovering as well." The white of his birthmarks glimmered in the depth of his eyes.

"You can...heal the mind?" I gulped. *What ailments could plague it?*

"I can help those who need mental healing, heal themselves."

When he saw my blank, exasperated stare, he blinked in embarrassment. "I apologize. I don't mean to speak in riddles. Yes, my people's mark, carried down the Sacera's family lineage, allows us certain psychic abilities. The gifts show themselves in different capacities, but mine, well, I can navigate through other's thoughts and help them lift whatever's keeping them held down."

I considered all that held *me* down, almost daring to inquire further, but chose not to pry in fear of revealing too much. A skill like that was handy. Craftily useful. A healing ability beyond the sewing of flesh I had seen Kori wield.

I paused. Mid-step amongst these cavernous prisons, I felt an odd looseness resonate through my being.

"Adelliah," I said and extended a hand.

He took it, grasped firmly, and shook with matched confidence.

"Imre." He bowed. He chuckled to himself as he continued toward a door, finally unlike the previous unremarkable ones. This one was lavish and adorned in intricate copper fastenings. "I'm glad one of us has manners," he said over his shoulder, a slight pink still on his high cheekbones.

A ferocity bit the edges of my curtsy as I playfully walked through the door he held open against his back. I sought to memorize this path, the number of doors, every excruciating detail saturating deep into my memory to recall later. Uniquely handsome and seemingly kind as Imre came off, I knew being fetched like a caged animal was the least of my concerns below the mountain. The sword he kept turned away from me was heavy and well crafted. I caught glimpses of it when the flames of the lantern caught its edges just right—courteous as he may be, he was a warrior, and a skilled one at that.

I was so busy ignoring the smell of vanilla and lavender that came as I passed in front of Imre that I barely noticed the expansive walls of pure, shimmering obsidian that opened to a table made of coals. Though fine wood-crafting outlined a dining room table larger than Freyah's entire kitchen, the center was carved out and sunken, and glowing coals pulsated in the open glass compartment.

This wasn't a simple command center where talks of rebellion came in the form of drunken shouts hurled over a shared fire—no, this was luxurious and unambiguous.

If the embers in the table didn't scream power, the obsidian walls that rose up into the mountain's core certainly did. Slick rock reflected the towers of captive flames, four pillars around the room that stopped high enough they seemed to tower over me, but still lower than the walls whose ends were nowhere in sight.

A high pitch squeal had me turning just in time to avoid being completely knocked over as Kori's arms wrapped around my waist. Zymir and Tillian trailed behind, their entrance door similar to ours on the opposite end of the wall. Her skin felt warm. It felt...alive. I didn't know how close she had teetered on the fine line between this world and the next, but the rosiness across her face and full eyes made me thankful I hadn't found out.

Until now, I hadn't allowed myself to consider what I'd do if she had been hurt.

But I was sure my focus would've shifted from getting back to Nox, to ripping the hands off of anyone that had touched her. Or any of my friends. If *anything* had happened to them, due to my bringing them here...it would be as if I had caused it myself.

I tried to focus on my relief that wasn't the case.

Tillian remained a decent distance away as Zymir silently walked up and nodded expressionlessly. Tillian's soft curls bounced against his head as he took in the magnitude around us.

"Incredible, isn't it?" Imre mused, his voice a reminder that we weren't alone. "I've been here three years, and I still have no idea how far up it goes."

Tillian's craning neck stopped, and he carefully took in the bright white birthmark so beautifully displayed against the deeply tanned skin. Imre stared back, catching his lingering glance, and smiling wide. Zymir's calculating eyes moved to the back of the room, and the subtle turn of his head had me prepared for more people before the sound of their steps reached my ears.

A man and woman walked in, both in dark leathers and red pants, boots up to their knees. The similar width of their identical green-blue eyes and full lips suggested they were brother and sister. They had swords on their backs, and though I couldn't see them, I imagined multiple other concealed weapons on their persons, based on the way they moved.

"Des is running late," the man said to Imre, his tone careful and even.

He took a seat at the table and folded his arms in front of him. He, like Imre, had a scar near his temple, several pale pink lines stark against his ebony skin suggested that his wounds were more recent.

"Sit." He glanced up lazily, scanning our awkward stances and gesturing toward the table. When we hesitated, his voice tightened. "Now."

His causal posture juxtaposed his sharp tongue. His words were like music, a rhythm granted through an accent I wasn't familiar with, as if extra air was being directed through his nose, and he spoke with a loftiness not found in Alaria. We sat, as instructed. Tillian shifted around in his seat, and Kori's tapping on the wood created a sound that crisply sliced through the warm air.

And the coals, they simmered, endless flames trickling up between the strangers across from us. Imre sat between the siblings and stared at his hands.

I wanted to ask Kori how she was feeling or inquire as to their treatment since we arrived, but I didn't want any words passed between us to be analyzed or looked too closely at. So, we sat, and waited, and observed.

The woman's forehead glistened in the heat coming off from the flames, but she didn't move to wipe it. The angles in her face were dramatic, her cheeks chiseled. She didn't bother to hide her investigative over-look as she trailed from left to right, lingering a bit too long for my liking on Tillian, so much so that he suddenly found the edge of the table incredibly fascinating, rubbing its edge with the fleshy part of his thumb. When she got to me, intrigue flashed in her sea-colored stare.

"You have unusual eyes." She leaned in closer to stare, pushing some of her braids behind her ears, until Imre blinked in surprise and elbowed her.

"Can you *not*," he warned.

Her brother's lip curled in amusement, as if the other two often were back and forth with one another. As she brought her hands up to rest her pointed chin on, I noticed the silver moon tattoos on the backs. Another traitor, another well-trained soldier gone rogue, turning years of skill and prestigious instruction into weapons used against our own people. I realized too late that I hadn't hidden the disdain from my face.

"Oh, these ol' things?" A wicked sliver of a grin graced her face. She stuck out her tongue and ran the roughness over the silvery tattooed lines, maintaining ruthless eye contact. "I can still taste the blood of those Sheirsan soldiers we slaughtered to break free of the palace..." She trailed and waited to see if I'd take the bait. "Corrupt blood tastes the *sweetest*."

Corrupt. It was laughable. No kingdom stood without difficult decisions made. And while the issues I had with this land grew as I learned more from Zymir, it never excused violence. Or death...from either side. Death for death, and these people sought to continue it further. And to what end? At what point would they be satisfied? Would the puppet officials running the kingdom be sufficient? Or would they need the spilled blood from every last man, woman, and child before they felt they could sleep safely secured in their retched mountain?

The tension was thick and hazy, exacerbated by the radiating heat from the core of the table.

"Do we know how much longer until he's done?" Imre asked.

"Have they undergone any questioning yet?" the woman asked instead, still smirking.

"Not yet. I was waiting—"

"I call dibs on this one." She flicked a pointed nail toward Tillian, and I made my face still.

She was good—observant, hungry, full of specifically selected words to try to rile.

"Sabina," a powerful voice behind us growled. The silhouette approached, heavy coat made of what looked like wolf pelts covered the shoulders, and the bottom stretched all the way down to his boots. Their hushed silence quickly followed the straightening in their chairs. "That is plenty."

He strolled to the head of the table and removed the coat, draping it over the back of the copper studded, crimson leather chair. A thick, dark beard and scarred bottom lip pursed as he glanced uninterestedly at the table. He leaned and sat the muddied boots he wore onto the table's edge. I hoped the warmth from the coals would burn his soles.

"What brings you into my mountain?"

No mincing words or small talk, then. *Good.*

His eyes were downcast, and he waved a casual hand in the air. A squirrely young man I hadn't seen scurried to the table immediately, appearing from the shadows with a goblet of sloshing red liquid. He sipped and inhaled deeply. The others at the table were rigid before their leader. Seeing the silver moons on his hands around the silver goblet made my stomach boil, and I gripped the arms of my chair to alleviate the desire to fling myself across the table.

I understood now why they had taken my weapons.

"We come seeking refuge." Zymir's smooth confidence nearly startled me. "We ask for safe passage to join you. We will do any work in exchange for admittance."

"Hm." Another elongated sip. "Are you now? And why do you wish to leave the kingdom without war?"

Zymir bowed his head low. "To loosen the shackles of peace."

Whatever stupid riddle or test that was went well over my head. Sabina and her brother nodded in approval. Frustration flickered—Zymir knew more than he had let on regarding this place. I hoped whatever else he had chosen not to disclose wouldn't cause issues later on. But I didn't dare relay my annoyance now. It could wait.

Satisfied by that answer, he waved again for the servant to pour him more wine directly from an elaborate glass decanter, its U shape thinned at the top. When his bored look finally made its way to us, I froze. The deep forest green yanked me back to Osta, in the sweaty tavern, Echo's shrill introduction repeating in my ears. *And this one...I wouldn't bother with one...*he had said when showing the man around and landing upon me. If he recognized me, he gave no indication, continuing to scan.

Why had the head of the Nevari been slumming it in a cheap, dirty tavern in the south?

"Reid, take the men to the interrogation chambers." The brother nodded, his carefully braided locks swishing beside his head. "Sabina, return her to the healing ward until he's done." He tilted his head toward Kori, who was wide-eyed and absolutely still. "Imre, you interrogate this one."

"Sir—"

"Do you question my methods, Saceran?" He set his cup down, and the emerald daggers in his eyes carved out a chasm of fear in my chest.

"No, sir." Imre bowed low, his forehead a few inches from the table.

"Good." The man stood from the head of the table and ran a hand over his strong chin, his beard peeking through his fingers. Despite the fur coat, his attire beneath it was more defined: Leather straps crossed his broad chest, no doubt connecting to dual blades behind him. There was a ferocity about his movements as he stood, muscles controlled and yet primed if needed, his own demeanor designed to intimidate and suppress.

"You offer this mountain to those in need, but then subject them to your rigorous questioning?" My hands were still white-knuckled to the chair, but I let the words come out as calm and composed as I could, with my mind reeling about what would await Tillian and Zymir. "Pickle me quite at home."

A blanket of silence submerged the room, and despite the now uncomfortable heat, the air felt frozen and cold in the distance between us.

He laughed, a condescending laugh that tussled his dark hair as he leveled his vibrant yet somber eyes at me. The dripping bravado of unrelentless power should have yielded compliance, but the voice in my chest thrashed against the idea.

I've always hated men in power. Especially self-righteous ones.

"When the fate of hundreds rests on your shoulders," he snarled, narrowing his eyes, "you make your own call. Until then, I will run this mountain as I see fit."

"And when do I get my weapons back?"

He paused just as he was about to walk out of the room through the door far in the shadows. As he turned his head away from me, I caught the remnants of dried blood around his collar. My exasperation was distracting me. I had to pull everything I could. Like the recent cut on his left palm, the sliced fabric on that forearm, and the utter control his stare demanded when he gave others his full attention.

"Unless you're here to slaughter my men or assassinate me, I can't see why you'd need those here."

A dangerous chuckle left me before I could stop it.

"Do you ever leave home without yours?"

The top of his lip curled in amusement. He couldn't have been more than a few years older than me, though he spoke with the seriousness and contemplation only earned from years of leadership. He would have been barely legal age when the royal family disappeared. What had sent him down this path of darkness and violence...

"You'll get your weapons back after they determine you aren't a threat."

"But—"

"And only after that will I permit you to enter my grounds. Until then," he flashed the whites of his teeth in a smile that would have been breathtakingly handsome if it weren't so innately terrifying, "welcome to the Icesone Mountains."

And with that, he left.

CHAPTER 20

I stood before anyone else did, and despite the lack of weapons, I contemplated charging Imre and slinging my body right over the table. I could step up, hop over the unnecessary coals, and have my arm around his neck in a moment far too fast for them to respond. They were all armed, though, and made a display of how comfortable they were poised between one another with blades aplenty and fighting skills to match. Zymir's harsh look made me hesitate, golden warnings that said *do what they say or risk ruining the whole operation.*

And so, we all complied for the time being.

There were eleven doors in this meeting room. I finally counted those shrouded in darkness and identified their frames only when the lights in the captive-flame pillars caught them ever so precisely. Kori sped up to Sabina and followed her through the door she had entered previously. And the men trailed Reid, who paused before exiting.

"Go easy on that one, will ya?" He smirked at Imre.

Imre shot him a disapproving glare that drilled into his back all the way until he exited the room.

"He's an ass." He said under his breath to me. "Don't mind him."

Was that supposed to be some sort of comfort? Because alone in the echoing great halls with this stranger about to direct me to who-knows-what was anything but reassuring.

A scowl sank into my skin as I followed him wordlessly, dragging my begrudging feet along the marble flooring. White, spindly veins stretched along the black stone in all directions. My eyes trailed their paths to keep my mind occupied and far away from wondering what sort of interrogation this would be.

Not that without my weapons, I had much say in it.

I'd never seen torture, nonetheless, been the subject of it. My grit and will were strong, sure, but for how long? I tore at the skin on my thumb, not surprised a sore had developed from my insistent bothering of it. I could hold out for a while, but how much could I even give them? I was hardly the beacon of hidden information. And though my bones had endured plenty of years of strain and my skin wore purple-blue bruises more times than I could count...I glanced at my bleeding thumb and wondered how many fingers I could stand to lose before I'd spill everything I'd ever been told.

Get it together.

I shook my head, and Imre tossed a concerned look over his shoulder.

Livestock led to slaughter...Except here I was, led by the warm-skinned, kind-eyed young man who, despite his scar, looked too polite to be carving into my skin and orchestrating a symphony of precisely drawn-out pain.

This place was a maze.

We had passed eight doors, all on the left, all unremarkable dark wood with dulled handles. Eight doors away from the main hall, the center door furthest away led to the prisons. I kept repeating it, hoping the consistency would glue it to memory.

Imre held up his hand at the ninth door on our left. I walked in past him and noted the way his shirt clung against his chest and sides—the vague outline of a leather strap, another likely concealed dagger. I added it to the count.

The room we walked into was surprisingly bright. My mental conjuring of chains and stained blood and discarded clumps of flesh were replaced by baby blue paint and a reclined chair that—if I'm being honest—looked plush and comfortable. There was no décor—only the reclined chair and a tray further away that I couldn't quite see what lay atop.

I swallowed hard.

"I can just answer your questions, you know." I turned to him and gave him an uneasy smile. A risk, but I gently set my hand on his shoulder and moved a step closer. "I'm not here to cause any problems, I swear."

I forced the softest of looks into my silvery doe eyes. I slacked my posture and shrank myself to cave in, to let the fear I usually kept buried, bubble to the surface just enough. My hand shook slightly. It was an additional touch he made note of. *Good.*

"This won't take long." He grinned, wrapping his hand around mine, squeezing it, and then removing it.

He set the warmth of his palm on my back and walked me over to the chair. I sat defeatedly, my heart flipping in my chest and a lightness fluttering in my lungs. Wings flapped the anxious air up, and my chest rose unevenly.

"Please." I looked up at him from below my lashes.

Pity trickled out of his red-brown eyes, but he reached over to unlatch the leather wrist binds beside me. He untied the first quickly, but the second snagged on itself, caught on the metal centerpieces that rubbed against the leather, refusing to comply easily.

"Please," I tried again. His body leaned over me as he fiddled with the further strap.

He stared at me, cowering beneath him, slightly shaking in fear. And I saw his pity convert to empathy with the softening of his eyes as he paused his hurried undoing of the wrist binds.

The tunic he wore was loose and hung down toward me. I held his stare in mine, captivating it with my pleas of desperation. And then I moved.

Hands not yet bound, I reached under his top and unsheathed the dagger held diagonally across the pronounced muscles of his chest. I heaved backward just as his eyes swung down in confusion. My legs were up instantly, and I hurled them outward, planting my boots squarely and shoving him away with all the strength I had left in my hungry muscles.

He stumbled backward.

I had seconds of an advantage before he'd recover.

I got up and charged, darting to the side with the aim of slamming the door behind him and locking him in. But he was *fast*. Trained balance and control made his recovery time nearly immediate. He stepped in front of me, but I ducked, whirling my back behind his.

The dagger in my hand felt cool and slightly too heavy. It had knicks and wear, but I could tell the blade was plenty sharp. I angled it toward him with a wildness that had my heart drumming in my ears.

But there was no semblance of panic in his casual stance. If anything, there was patience as he watched. He discounted any real threat I posed to him, and it made a certain rage whisper in my ear, begging me to unleash the blade into the side of his throat.

Stop that, I warned myself, picturing the spurting blood that would drench the floor.

Instead, I curved my arm around and attempted to string his elbow up with it. He let me, doubling over and again, waiting. I kicked down the backs of his knees so that he landed roughly on them. As I went to jam my fingers into the spongy parts of his neck to drop him to unconsciousness, a blanket of snow hurled into my head, disorienting my vision.

It was the first snow Alaria had seen in ages where more than a few inches had fallen. I was young and alone and cold. And I sat on the street edge kicking up sludgy grayness. There were holes in my boots, and wetness dampened the soles of my feet. But I didn't mind—I was too enamored by the snowy buildup. Adult bodies passed by but didn't bother to look. I played with the snow, burrowing the tip of my shoes into the messy, melting wetness, and then toppled it over to my other shoe. Back and forth until it had all fallen off, and I'd have to scoop up more.

A new smell tickled my nose, and it scrunched up. Spices and orange slices and vague sweetness. So many extra feet strolled by, carrying wrapped gifts and looping as many bag handles as they could slip onto their fingers. A young girl paused, her hand held by a larger body that tugged forward. She wore an emerald velvet dress with white lace around the collar and wrists. Her soft eyes watched me, merrily playing in the dirtied gray ice, and a disgusted grimace turned down her freckles and her bright pink lips. She kicked a puddle toward me with her sunflower-painted rain boots. The splash of cloudy water dampened the already melting pile, slumping it down closer to the ground. Another swipe with the side of her boot, and the snow had all but succumbed to the water. When I looked up, she was leaving, carrying a victorious smirk and an upturned chin.

I shook my head, and the mental blanket alleviated slightly. My boot was still against the backs of his knees. His hands were up, fingers splayed.

"How *dare* you..."

"If you don't stop fighting, you'll make this harder than it needs to be." He was calm, so damn calm. I snatched his hands and held them behind his back.

I shoved the helm of the blade against his head, *hard*. He groaned and flinched, as if his captive hand instinctually wanted to rub the sore spot. I drew back, still angling the helm and not the steel, and—

I was in a back alley between an overflowing garbage can and the brick wall. Wedged and curled with my knees to my chin, I was shivering, not from the cold but from the hunger. I had already torn through the trash, finding only waste and stained clothes. I rocked and rocked and shut my eyes so tight that I hoped it would steer my focus to my swollen eyelids and not my aching stomach. I could feel the ribs now, and my chest had started to cave in slightly. Headaches and painful ringing were constant.

I rocked and rocked and wondered if it wouldn't be easier to climb into the bin of discarded, used-up goods. I'd wait until they came for trash collection, and my limp body would simply fall out amongst the rest of the garbage into the incinerator somewhere outside of town. It would be warm. It would be over so much faster than this. This waiting to die. This struggle to live day in and day out. And for what?

Hunger was not a pain you could separate yourself from, like a broken wrist or sprained ankle. It starts in your core and claws its way out. It takes and takes. Hunger was a primal beast, and while you could run from it until your legs gave out, it always caught up. Hunger was in no rush.

And then there was his outstretched hand. A man. A slick, well-dressed man in a dark suit and light tie. It reminded me of spring, light green blossoming from the dark stone-gray blazer. He smiled at me. Not beyond me, but at me. I stared at his hand, a feral animal sooner to bite his dangling fingers than reach out to them.

'I can help,' he said.

I shook my head, and my knotted black locks stuck together.

'Let me help,' he tried again.

My adolescent body should have been thriving with the throes of puberty and growth. But it was a bone prison that my skin clung to. It was a jagged cage, utterly stunted. Energy focused solely on keeping my heart beating. The ghost thumps reminded me I was alive, but I didn't feel it. I watched from the eyes of a corpse that didn't realize it might as well have already passed. I could move the limbs, but it did no good when the nerves whispered the threats of the hungry beast in my core.

He had golden rings and a golden watch. I wondered if gold tasted as good as it looked.

His hand was an offering, another option. A life not crumpled and hidden from others and from myself.

I took it, and the feral part of me growled. I'd find soon that I should have bitten his hand after all.

"*STOP!*" I roared.

My voice trembled, and I had somehow let my hands drop. My voice was raw and hoarse. How long had I been screaming? Imre was standing in front of me with no anger, no fear. But still with pity. And that sympathizing look unraveled something chained within me that barred its teeth and sought only blood.

I felt him reach for me again, the invisible tendrils stretching out toward my mind. *My* memories, the ones I chose never to reflect on, now on display for others. He slithered into a private place that wasn't his to journey to, and I knew he had seen my recollections in the way he stared at me. Like an injured animal that, if it'd just stop thrashing, you could help out of its trap.

For a split second, he let his facade falter, and confusion wrinkled the skin on his forehead. I didn't know what I was doing or how I was doing it. But I focused solely on preventing any foreign invaders from ripping into my skull, pushing the air around me, a mental space building and building until there was a protective layer all around me. His pitying glace finally slipped away into something much more appetizing—

Horror.

I tried to step closer but found my limbs rigid and unresponsive. Imre was shaking his head in shock and slumped against the wall beside the thick metal door, just as it opened toward me. His shock was diluted with relief, I realized. I held my mental defenses, imagining a safer distance much further than we actually stood from one another.

"Godsdamnit, can't handle a simple—" Reid's figure stepped into the room, and his words left him.

Imre stared at him with a strain, a bead of sweat on his forehead that filled me with far too much pride. But my limbs still wouldn't move. I was entombed.

"Ah." Reid closed the door behind him, and they shared a look. He stood pensive before nodding, as if listening.

He must've called out to him. I wasn't sure the extent of Imre's abilities, but if he could thrust himself into my thoughts and relay my past, it didn't seem so farfetched that he couldn't have beckoned Reid here for assistance.

Reid was taller than Imre, not quite as stocky, with lean muscles and pronounced veins rippled through the dark skin of his arms. He had removed the top layer of his leathers, abandoned their protection, and instead donned the sleeveless tunic that must have been underneath, exposing the expansive tattoos over the tops of his arms. Tattoos, and not birthmarks, I noted. The art was on top of his skin, not amongst it. But the immovability of my body told me that though I couldn't see any, there was likely a Weaver Mark to blame hidden somewhere.

I hated to admit it, but I could see why the kingdom wasn't fond of the marks. I hadn't even known of them for long, and already they were dolling out unfair advantages and making every step of this ridiculous plan more challenging.

"Surprising." Despite the words, Reid's expression was anything but impressed.

My knees collapsed beneath me, and I was kneeling. But I thrashed in my skin, demanding my body comply.

"We're not your enemy." Reid's airy accent annoyed my ears.

Easy to say when others bent to your will as compliantly as my joints crumpled on me. Reid took another step and crossed his arms at my helplessness, snickering. I couldn't see any blood on his clothes, nor scrapes or bruises on his face. I had to assume whatever happened to Zymir and Tillian had either been cut short or incredibly brief.

"Stop fighting, little one."

I snarled, vicious and wild. I was on my knees, but I'd let no one feel superior to me, let no ounce of satisfaction come from me yielding. He drew closer, and my useless body remained a tether. As he approached, I noticed that he wore cream-colored, silk gloves. They were tight and cut off at the wrists. There were stitches similar to the tattoos on his arms—words in a language my eyes had never seen, perhaps. The thread was gold and extravagant. I found the gloves strangely juxtaposed to the depth of his skin, to the harshness of his demeanor.

He drew close, and his gloves reached for me. I knew the men were waiting for me to calm, to submit to the realities that awaited me in this room.

The silk grazed my cheek, cupping the nook behind my head. He tilted my head up to look into his swirling turquoise eyes. His gaze drilled into me, and it was a struggle to even shake my head away from him. His magic permeated deeper and deeper. I noted Imre stepping closer, my focus unable to split from its bind.

"I *am* going easy," Reid answered to a voice only he could hear.

I groaned beneath the splintering of mind and body. They were being pulled in opposite directions, magic gripping both ends with relentless fervor.

"She'll exhaust herself if she keeps fighting," Imre warned, not to me.

Strings tightened within me. I was sweating profusely, the ripped fabric of my top drenched and hugging me. My head was throbbing from the effort it took to simply kneel. It felt shameful, and disgust welled in my pores. A radiating electricity buzzed as I felt fatigue threaten my defenses. But the jolt was somehow invigorating, and I tingled against its touch. I couldn't look down at its source, but I didn't need to. I knew. I knew where it originated from and knew a glance would only reveal another layer that I couldn't have them uncovering. I used the strength of its sting to tilt my arm subtly inward so that they wouldn't notice the red on my wrist shifting, responding, energizing.

They could feel it in the air, though. The transfer of energy seeped out into the room.

The silk behind my head gripped my nape before harshly retracting. The patience in the men was gone.

"Enough," Reid said.

His arm hesitated. I held, expecting him to use the back of it to smack me for my insolence. But he offered it instead, palm up, curled fingers—a final proposal to cooperate.

This time, with few other options in my arsenal, I spat. He tensed, not in disgust but in restraint. I shivered at the thought of how much power he was suppressing.

And then I was struck with nothing but blackness.

CHAPTER 21

"You need to get Des now. Something's wrong."

Blackness. Like an unshakeable dream that swallowed me up. Still, cool ponds of the freshest water. I was weightless. Not just my body, but everything. Rid of flesh and bones, rid of the memories of hunger and loss—I was everything and nothing all at once. And gods, I felt so *free*. My time was my own, and in the promising nothingness, the dark felt like a sea of endless comfort. I felt like Tillian must have when his mother draped a warm, wet washcloth over his forehead when he was ill. This place, this absence of a place, was a peace, unlike anything I had ever known.

"Des—"

The voices seeped into this magical place, but I paid them no mind. I was in no rush. There was nothing to rush to or from, nowhere to go, and no one to be.

"There's a wall."

"A wall?"

"A wall. Someone built it here, in the center of her mind."

"And that means what, exactly?"

Was this what birds felt like when they flew? Was I flapping my wings and soaring into a horizon that blended both sky and land? I swirled and danced, and my lack of edges, my shapeless form, was carried by a current so vast I felt like I was the waves and the moon, and I was swaying myself from one end of existence to the next.

How could so much color exist in the darkness? Why had I never been told?

"Fuck if I know…"

"…So, what do we do about it?"

"I could try to wedge through a crack, but that could bring the entire wall down."

"And?"

"*And* if someone placed a mental block in her head, they probably had damn good reason to. I've—"

I was young and old and wise and dull. Was this the place of the gods? Did they traverse this realm of nothingness? Was I trekking through their domain? I knew I could still pose questions, but even as the pockets of thoughts blossomed, they soon wilted, and I wondered why I even cared in the first place.

"—tried everything, searched around this wall, but outside of her name and her recent memories, nothing goes back further than—"

Moonlight twinkled now, peeking into my safe abyss. It curled around me and promised all was well. I followed its beckon, curious where the glisten wanted to take me, what wonders it could show. Whispers of white pulled me along. Gently, oh so gently.

"Anything?"

"Almost. Keep her limbs locked, Reid. I don't want her to hurt herself."

Have you ever tasted spring? Hopeful dew droplets so plentiful and overflowing that they burst onto your tongue with the smell of lilacs and sweet evening wine and soft first kisses and—

"Here goes nothing."

—and running wildly in fields, and laughing so hard that your ribs squeal, and—

There was something else here with me. A splinter. A sharp point, prodding, pressing down onto that watery film that formed atop the droplet. The water moved around its tip, trying to maintain the grip on itself. Again, pressure. Building pressure. Suffocating pressure. The water lapped up on either side of the intensity, trying to escape.

The point punctured through, and I gasped. Everything so lovely was swirling away from me.

Stay.

Please stay.

And then an eruption. A light bulb turned on, and nothing remained in the darkness. Artificial, blinding light.

I was on a table. A hard, metallic table. There was a single bulb hanging from a dangling chain. I could hear footsteps and clinical terms that I didn't understand. I was on my back, and there was a strap against my forehead, gluing my head down. And my arms, my legs, my torso.

There was a wheel. A crank and a lever system that, as the wheel rotated, caused the table to pivot until my face was staring at the ground and my back was exposed. There was a hole in the table. I knew the skin on my back was tasting the cold air. I wasn't afraid. Or rather, any fear I may have had felt diluted, watered down so thin that my reactions were a shadow of their original emotions.

I felt the slicing of the knife. My flesh was torn, again and again. It was precise. It was methodical. Men spoke, and I felt more pressure behind me, but my eyes could only stare at that tiled floor—it was ugly and plain. The squares were tiny and light gray and lined up so tightly that they nearly overlapped.

They hit something. I could feel it, and it felt wrong. The pain poured out with a vile, ruthless vengeance. They cranked the wheel hastily, and the table was upright again. My body thrashed in anguish as the pain tried to exit through my pores. There was a calloused hand on my forehead, cooing, shushing me.

His other hand came around, and despite the blinding agony, I focused on his silver ring. It lay on his forefinger, and it had an enormous black gemstone that was cut at dramatic angles so that the light would reflect off its multiple faces. I focused on the gemstone and tried to block out the upsurge of heightened senses. The agony was at a blinding crescendo when within his ringed hand, I noticed a syringe.

Pain.

So much pain. I was begging them to stop. To make the pain stop.

His fingers crept lower and covered my eyes so I could only peek through the crevices of light between them. I felt the needle as sobs whimpered through my chattering teeth.

Please.

When I finally felt like I was back in my body and the adrenaline had calmed, I opened my eyes. There was a mixture of embarrassment and fury that swirled together so well I could barely distinguish between them. My head hurt, and I was soaked in sweat. I smelled *terrible,* and I grimaced seeing all the bodies in the room with me.

"Are you all right?" Imre asked, a semblance of genuine concern in his words as he bit his bottom lip and rubbed his hands together.

He was kneeling on the ground in the space in front of my knees. I was sitting in a chair I don't remember leveling myself into. Reid was leaning against the back wall, arms crossed and pensive. Their leader was watching me cautiously, as if determining whether or not he should slit my throat now or see if it would be more interesting to do it later. No one spoke. I felt their stares and became more aware of how repugnant I must look. It wasn't usually a concern that passed my mind, but this was different. I had traversed land and snow and been held in a seeping prison and dragged—

"Do I *look* all right?" My words were clipped. I wasn't sure if it was the frustration or some other instinct that had me feeling this inner, untamed part of myself.

The emeralds flickered, and he brought his fingers through his coarse brown hair. At last, their leader approached, and I considered spitting at him too, but my head was far too woozy and my body far too weak to continue the facade of bravado.

"You look like a mess," he said at last.

Every word from his lips held a certain weight, and his tone contained no kindness, only revulsion, as if walking closer to me had revealed spoiled milk and rot. He knew he held power, dragged out the pause simply because he could, his men waiting for orders like obedient dogs. If *anything* was revolting, it was their blind submission. It stank far worse than I with my unclean body and dirtied attire. How do you leave one oppressive ruler to serve another? Did they have a choice, or were they led to believe this would yield a different fate, one more promising than the last? They were fools, ultimately. Fools seeking direction and leadership, and here was another man, ready to take and take and take.

"Desmond Ferin," he said, introducing himself fully. He glanced down as if he had considered extending his hand but kept it at his side. "You may call me Des."

"Well, Desmond, have I passed your little tests?"

I was so exhausted. My bones wanted softness, and my stomach reminded me with an audible groan that I hadn't eaten since the last night in the forest.

Desmond's calculating eyes narrowed, and he turned to Reid, whose lip was curled at my hostility. In the light of the room, I could see the blade he wore on his back much clearer. The leader of this band of cowards still donned a Sheirsan blade—crescent moon etchings on the hilt and winding metalwork, elaborate twists that were intended to provide additional grip in your palm when held. It wasn't a blade he should still carry. Perhaps before this was done, I'd rid him of it.

"I hadn't even started before Imre—"

"It wasn't my fault she—"

"Not both at once." Desmond halfway chuckled to himself. It was an odd noise coming from such a ruthless mouth. "Reid, you haven't spoken to the others yet?"

"I have not, no." Reid's shoulders remained up and still.

Imre stood, wiping his hands and sighing as he headed toward the door. The concern in his eyes said *let's discuss this outside*, which his friend and commander immediately understood. There were several subtle movements, shifting postures, glances, or throat clearings that suggested these men had been around one another long enough to relay that which needed no words. Useful, as far as avoiding being overheard went. Granted, it didn't stop me from following as soon as that door shut with my ear pressed against the wooden door.

Moving was peculiar. On one hand, I was abysmally tired and hungry, but on the other, my body itself felt almost lighter. It responded to my desire to move faster than usual, which was especially odd since I had spent so many years training to do just that—to make my body *listen*. I attributed it to the great likelihood I had been losing muscle mass in our trek through the wilderness and mountains. But even that explanation didn't fully click in my head.

With one ear to the door, I peered around the center of the room. The far table had a crumbled wool blanket on it that I hadn't seen before. *Had I been laying on that?* There were no windows, no signs of weapons I could pocket.

This entire place was a fortress of mazes and long corridors, but meeting hall aside, it was a rather dull one. It was predictable, I supposed. Not that I knew what else I was expecting, but it felt rather underwhelming.

And, of course, I could hear nothing from the other side of the door. I dragged myself back to the chair, defeated, and slumped in, tapping my fingertips along the arms.

The spindly muscles responded, and a memory rushed me. My arm had been tingling, reacting, before I was taken out by their joint effort. *How good of warriors could they be if it took them both to down me...?* It was a foolish thought, but it pushed a bit of the humiliation out of the emotional whirlwind, allowing residual rage to effectively take its place.

I almost didn't want to look.

I was so used to keeping it hidden that the instinct had remained while my thoughts and memories were plumaged. I knew, because if I had grown careless even in such a state, the men wouldn't be outside debating if more interrogations were needed—they'd be debating what manner of death would be the swiftest.

I stole a glance. I sucked in air, and my heart plopped into my gut. The demanding lines on my arm were still in that geometric star, but the vivid crimson I was so used to seeing was gone. Not dissipated into a rosy hue as it'd sometimes do—it was completely void of its redness. And though the lines were visible, they were a subtle, shimmery silver color. As if the red had been used and used and could no longer hold its hue. I heard rattling outside the door, so I wiped the confusion from my face. But the thoughts still lingered. *How in the world did this happen...and why?* It had never changed color in all the years I bore it. It had swiveled to numbers, deepened to a mere rash, and even found new shapes as of late...But the red was a constant that had never changed.

They didn't knock before the three men sauntered back into the room, Desmond at the rear.

"You and your friends may stay. We'll take you into town tomorrow." Desmond's unamused, locked jaw suggested that this conclusion was not something he'd decided on originally.

"Town?"

"As charming as my receiving barracks are, there's hardly enough room for everyone." He was careful, avoiding numbers and narrowing his eyes at me. "Imre will take you all there tomorrow. Tonight, you are my guests. You'll join us for dinner later." A smirk flickered. "Just make sure you wash up first."

I'd have made a jab to counter him if he wasn't so accurate. The layer of filth on me was slowly consuming my mind. And oh, warm water...It sounded like exactly what my aching muscles needed.

He waited for a nod, and once provided, he turned to leave.

"This has wasted *far* more of my time than I'd have liked." His broad back was facing me, and I was glad I didn't have to see the likely disdain peppering his brow. Reid and Imre still held their heads down in a bow as he spoke. "Touch *nothing*. You may be vouched for, but if you or any of the others so much as *think* about stepping out of line, I will skewer your heads on spokes."

I was also glad he wasn't facing me because the roll of my eyes was unavoidable.

"Do I make myself clear?"

A hesitation. I bit my lip and demanded my tongue play nice.

"*Crystal.*"

"Good."

He shut the door behind him with an unnecessary snap of his wrist that caused it to slam. Imre sighed, and his shoulders immediately laxed. Reid caught it and threw him an exasperated glance before making his way out as well.

"I'll get the rest of them," he said, and left.

Imre turned to me with an apprehensive upturn of his lips. His mouth open and closed, as if he wanted to explain what had happened, provide something that would make their combined attack justified or right. But there was nothing I'd accept as an answer. My body was sore, and my mind was a certain type of exhausted I had never felt before. It had been sorted and picked through. My memories had been *seen* and then *used* somehow to make a judgment call as to whether or not we would be allowed in. Which naturally led to a bombardment of all sorts of curiosities...

To say I was suspicious was an understatement. There was no way they wouldn't have been able to deduce our real reasons for journeying here. So why pretend otherwise? Unless it was all a rouse. And of course...there was a lingering shiver of a deeper memory...of a shackled hidden place...but I couldn't remember it well enough now to even describe it. The moment my eyes opened, it was like waking from a string of dreams. And when I tried to retrace the steps back to that place, I only found the remnants of fear. No details, nothing helpful. I was simply met with an impregnable gap I couldn't see through.

Maybe a meal would help...I hoped it would. I followed Imre out of the room to a world of increased distrust as I focused solely on memorizing our paths and drawing details where I could—no vents, no opened doors, no windows. There was little that could be used. But still, those thoughts ebbed away as we finally reached a separate wing of the maze.

These halls reminded me of the tavern in Osta. Lights adorned the left of each door frame, and copper knobs felt more welcoming than the metal bars.

"The others will be the next door over." He pointed ahead to the second door on the right. "There's a connection between the two. Both have two beds—feel free to arrange yourself however you'd like. But stay in the rooms until we come for you, please."

He wasn't much taller than me, but somehow, I felt smaller after seeing what his abilities could do. But the wall I threw up in my empty stare was cold enough that he almost retracted. There would be no thank yous, if that's what he lingered for.

"About back in that room..." He tried and rubbed the back of his head through the long strands. "The questioning process is typically much quicker, but..."

'But you made things difficult,' I imagined is what he wanted to say. *Good.* With one hand on the knob, I clenched my jaw and leaned toward him, bringing my lips beside his ear. He didn't bother to move away, which I attributed to the arrogance one gains when one can stop an opponent by weaseling into their head.

"If you and your men ever violate my mind again," I hissed and pressed a finger from my spare hand on the indent of his chin, "I swear to all the gods, I will carve those marks off your skin." I trailed my finger down his chin, under, and down his neck, tracing the thickest white line until it met the top of his tunic.

When I pulled my face away, I tried not to think about the lack of anger opposite me, and I especially tried not to think about the lines of shame tightening his lips. He reached up for my hand that still hovered at the base of his tunic and wrapped it around the finger I had pressed against his caramel skin. He removed my hand, took a steady breath, and did not break the daggers I had leveled at him with my stare, soaking up the wrath I refused to hide. As he dropped his grasp, he sighed again and made his way back down the hall.

I waited until he was out of sight to enter my room.

And as I did, I beelined straight to the porcelain tub sparkling in the distance—my top priority.

CHAPTER 22

The feel of the warm water against my skin pulled a moan from my lips that felt like a prayer. The entirety of the room was unnecessarily luxurious. And while I didn't mind the copper-rimmed double mirrors or the sparkling quartz marble floor, I *did* appreciate the selection of oils and soaps on the woven shelf beside the tub. The vanilla-almond suds soothed the tired muscles as I scrubbed off the layers of filth on my skin and dirt on my scalp.

I played with the copper faucet knobs at the end of the tub with my toes. The cool touch amidst the steam felt nice, and I let my neck lean back so that the water came up to my hairline. A sea of purple-black lay behind my neck, over my shoulders and breasts. I didn't know if my hair had ever felt so clean or smelled so nice. I inhaled deep enough that the aroma loosened the tenseness in my shoulders and turned my head side to side, stretching the muscles that sang in delight.

I leaned my head further, lost in the covering warmth. Maybe I'd never get out…I could stay pruned up in this bath and let the rest of the kingdom rot for all I cared. I groaned in defeat, though, as footsteps and voices sounded in the bedroom Imre had led me to. I slipped my ears below the watery surface, drowning them out, listening to the dulled sounds and watching the Draoi coin at the base of my necklace linger upward.

Two solid knocks could be heard from the door. The heaviness of the thuds told me it was Tillian.

"I'm almost done!"

I heard a grumble and was glad the words were lost beneath in the water.

Begrudgingly, savoring the soapy silkiness of the oils, I tipped my feet back below the water, if only to submerge them in the heat one last time before dragging them onto the frigid ground. I lifted up but was unable to raise my head above the waterline sloshing at my temple. I tried again, tugging at my head, but it wouldn't move.

All right. Maybe just a muscle spasm.

I tried to turn my head left and right again, but nothing. It was like those mornings of paralysis that struck seemingly randomly. But I hadn't been sleeping… I blinked to calm myself. I hadn't been *that* restful that I'd have fallen asleep. Inhale, hold, exhale. Three times.

Even as I tried my breathing method, I knew this was different.

This wasn't the same paralysis that crippled my body—I could wiggle my hips back and forth, lift my legs, but my head refused to leave the water.

I felt my neck, running my fingers over the pressure points I had memorized, gliding the clean strands of hair through as I sought an explanation. I sniffed again, carefully searching for a poison or additive that could have struck. But I found nothing. I opened my mouth to holler for one of them to help me, happy to find that I could still pry my jaw open.

Mouth agape, a memory flooded me.

The water had chunks of ice floating in it. It was an oval basin, and water had sloshed up from the sides of the tub onto the tile floor. Tiny tiles, all cramped together.

I knew these tiles. They were the same as in that other dream, the one just out of reach, the one where—

My blood screamed as they lowered my body beneath the surface, a pair of hands at my feet, a pair guiding my shoulders. I wasn't shivering or thrashing. But the bite of ice gnawed at my skin. The clumps of ice bobbed on the surface, and my face was entirely submerged under their silhouettes.

I couldn't explain it, but it felt like it was a test of some sort.

I laid still. I counted the seconds. Waiting, drawing out time.

I found the cold quickly gave to numbness, and I refused to let my rigid limbs tremble. But my lungs groaned for air. Just a little bit longer, I told them. I edged past 120 seconds, each second feeling slower than the last, and tried to last for just a moment longer.

123, 124, 125...

I gulped.

130, 131, 132...

And when my lungs had finally had enough, I reached for the surface. But a heavy hand reached down and held me by the base of my neck. In my panic, I sought air but gulped down only water. It hit the back of my throat and stung. My lungs were on fire. I tried to lift the hand holding me. But it was firm and gave not an inch. I thrashed and thrashed, swallowing water until the world went black.

I jolted upright in the warm, sudsy tub and realized I had been screaming...again. Was I losing my mind? I panted, appreciating the air between my lips. Appreciating more that my head had been released and could move freely again.

The door flung open and slammed against the wall behind it.

"Are you okay?"

I don't know. Was I?

"I—I'm fine." I breathed.

"You yelled. I would have entered sooner, but I didn't want to just barge in..."

In that moment, I looked to see Tillian's worried stare barreling into my own. He must've washed up as well. His curls were loose and shiny, and his skin looked soft.

He averted his eyes and stared at the metallic tiles that adorned the ceiling. It was then that the realization hit me, and I was thankful for the extra soap I had used, since the majority of my body was hidden beneath their suds and bubbles. But still, his avoidance and reddened cheeks made me laugh despite myself as I looped my arm around more bubbles to cover my chest.

"*What?*" he asked at my knowing chuckle.

When I didn't answer because none came to me, he bit his lower lip in cheeky annoyance.

"What happened?"

"I...I don't know." It wasn't a lie. "Let me change, and I'll be right out. I can fill you in after."

He sighed. "Can you please *try* to avoid giving me a heart attack like that? Can we save that for when you're actually in danger?"

"And miss the chance to see you squirm and blush?"

I couldn't help myself. Watching him try not to stare back at me after realizing my unclothed state made teasing him far too easy. His face was still flushed, and he shook his head. I could see his pursed lips as he struggled not to turn back to scowl.

"Next time you want me in your bathing chambers, maybe find a less dramatic approach."

This time I felt the heat kiss my cheeks. As he walked out, he paused sideways to look back in a dangerous linger. But he merely raised his brows and cleared his throat, as if it had gone painfully dry standing there. Once the door shut, I leaped out of the tub and hastily changed, trying to make sure my own redness lessened by the time I strolled back out.

The room itself was comfortably sized. Two twin-sized beds with thick black comforters. The walls had paintings of clouds and an endless blue sky. Whoever had painted them had done an incredible job—the strokes on the clouds made them look full and light, and there were blackbirds depicted soaring between them. Intelligent birds with razor-sharp beaks and a knack for trickery. But on the walls, they simply soared, all tilted upwards to greater heights, most near the tops of the walls and the rest on the ceiling where the painting continued.

Tillian sat on the edge of one of the beds between the two with his ankles crossed.

I sat opposite.

"We're *to appear at their dinner,* whenever that may be. But until then, I managed to score this from one of the servants."

He passed me a dark gray saucer that was lined with gold around its edge and inner circle. Atop it, a square tart with a drizzle of some sort of frosting. I hesitated, but he pushed it forward again, and I took the treat.

Blueberry. My absolute favorite.

His wide smile told me he knew, too. I raised a brow.

"I saw someone pacing down the halls outside the room. I didn't leave or anything, just peeked out. When he saw me, he asked if I needed anything. I thought I'd be a smart ass, but when he actually left to fetch me a glass of water, I figured I'd see what else he could get me." He leaned against his arms, resting backward on the bed.

"Want the last half?"

"Oh, no, you finish it." He waved the offer aside nonchalantly. "I already had three, anywho."

I chuckled, took another tiny nibble, and set the saucer next to me.

Next to the bed I sat on was a wooden door painted blue with clouds like the rest of the walls, where a small knock answered my next question before I could ask it.

"Come in. She's *finally* out," he yelled over me.

I glared but was distracted immediately as Kori lunged through the door with Zymir following. She plopped beside me, and I handed her the remaining bite of the tart, which she happily finished in one bite. Zymir chose to stand and watched us closely. I wondered how he held such patience, even here where we hoped to find who had killed Osyren and taken his vengeance from him.

"What happened with Reid?" I asked, unsure of where to begin.

"Reid had only just gotten us to some sort of questioning room when he got all flustered, told us to stay put, and then left." Tillian rubbed his thumb over the blanket.

"The room had chairs and straps. But nothing visible with which to extract information."

"I doubt he'd need weapons," I mused.

Before Kori could add anything, I proceeded to retell what had happened in the room with Imre. I told them what I suspected as far as their abilities went and told them how he had gone through my memories—evidently standard procedure to determine the legitimacy of those wishing passage. They were silent for a while, considering what I had revealed. I didn't tell them about the deeper memories, about the festering sensation when I tried to follow the winding path back to what he had uncovered.

"If they know everything, why let us stay?" Tillian asked.

"Maybe Osyren's death isn't significant to them. Maybe they have no information on him," Kori offered, lowering her entire back onto the bed and kicking up her feet.

"I doubt that." Zymir studied my apprehension. "What did they see in your memories that made them choose to let us all stay without further inquiry?"

I shrugged as casually as I could. I honestly wasn't sure. And not knowing made any fleeting feelings of achievement give way to growing suspicion.

"Knowing the skills they possess, I doubt we'll have an easy time shaking them," I said, considering the best way we should proceed. "I think our best bet is to assume they know everything, and if they know why we're here, who's to say we can't come right out and ask?"

"How long do you think we have before dinner?" Tillian had a mischievous look in his eyes as he asked, completely ignoring what I'd said.

"An hour and a half." Kori grinned.

"How do you know that?"

"Sabina told me." She kicked her legs up and groaned as she spread her arms out, rubbing against the cool, heavy blanket. "*Gods,* this is comfortable."

"Did she tell you anything else?"

"I mean, she told me her brother has a red-hot temper and hates when you answer questions with questions. And she told me that the best drink pairing with venison is—"

"Let me get this straight, while we were debating which devices would be used to torture us, you two were gossiping and discussing wine pairings?"

"And tasting them." She stuck her red tongue out at him and rolled over on the bed as if she would curl up and sleep.

Tillian leaned over to slap her boot, but she scooted away and laughed.

The feline grace and stern eyes of Sabina were not ones I pegged for being warm and welcoming. Her entire demeanor screamed *stay away,* and her ability to read the relationships between us without hearing us interact made me wary. Her knowing glances had me wondering if her observation skills were even greater than Zymir's, and unlike him, she seemed quite poised to blatantly use the knowledge she extracted through it.

"Did you happen to see any Weaver Marks on her?" I asked.

"We didn't get *that* close." She winked. "But no, I didn't see any. If her brother has one, does that mean she does too?"

We turned to Zymir to answer that one.

"It's possible. There is an aspect to the marks that follows bloodline, of course. But it's not a given. She may have one, or she may not. Regardless, with her position as a foe, and a skilled one at that, means that we should assume she's quite qualified to defend Desmond if it came to that."

"Maybe if you didn't automatically assume everyone was an enemy, you'd have had a warmer welcome as well." Kori glared at us, and I couldn't tell if she was being serious or not.

"They *are* our enemies," I reminded her. "None of these people are without blood on their hands."

She stared up at the ceiling.

"You say that as if ours are clean," she said in a small voice, a careful voice.

I knew her intent, and I understood the point she was trying to make, so I didn't bother to pick apart all the reasons we were not the same as these people. But I suppose her comment landed as I glanced down at my freshly cleaned skin, imagining all the dried blood on them I had accumulated, all the blood that I fought relentlessly to forget.

"Since we have time before dinner, I think we should see what else we can find amongst these rooms. The hallway is long, but I swear I saw a wide paneled door at the very end. If we found any records, any offices, we could have a better idea of their motives." Tillian stood and made his way toward the door.

"They said to stay," Kori said, sitting upright.

"Of course, they did," he countered, "but if they have nothing to hide, why keep us in our rooms?"

She looked hesitant. Her exchange with our captors seemed significantly more positive than ours, though I wasn't sure if it was truly due to their good intentions or, more likely, due to her subtle charm and disarming personality. Without weapons, we'd have to be careful, though. Careful and ready with a good explanation if we're caught.

"You two stay." I looked to Kori and Zymir. "If anyone comes looking for us, tell them we're occupied in the respective bathrooms."

Zymir's golden stare flickered apprehensively, worriedly. But the conviction I held said, *don't worry, I know what I'm doing, trust me.* And he did, in the faintest of nods.

We left immediately, wanting to give as much space as possible between now and when they'd come fetch us later. Tillian led, sticking his head into the hall like he had prior. Both ends stretched far, but we turned toward the opposite direction than the one I had arrived from, where sure enough, there was an out-of-place door at the end. We stepped lightly, and I kept an eye behind us, ready if someone was to appear at the rear. The hall was an L shape, and the end broke at that redwood door with fancy paneling and engravings at the top. It was the preferred option over having to blindly choose to go left or right.

But naturally, it was locked.

Tillian wiggled the handle again, as if it'd change its mind and let us in. But it wouldn't budge, and I found the emptiness at my hip extra haunting. My lock-picking kit was one of the first tools I ever attached to my belt, and not having it felt foreign.

"Well," he peeked up at me from below his furrowed brow as he dismissively let go of the handle, "left or right?"

Eh. Both seemed the same—like a line of hotel doors, identical and boring. But to the left, there was a solid metal door that looked as if it led to somewhere different, whereas to the right, the hall appeared to simply lead to another L, with more options stemming from there.

"Left," I whispered.

The metal door *did* lead to something different. A winding staircase coiled up and down—mostly down, deeper and deeper beneath the mountain. I swallowed and wondered how many more *mostly empty* prison cells lay beneath our feet. Since I had already seen more of them than I cared for, we went up.

Our steps were silent and hasty. I took the lead as I found my curiosity gaining momentum the further up we went, in tune with the changing doors at each floor, more and more unusual the higher up we went. One that glistened like the obsidian in the meeting hall, one that held no grooves or even a doorknob, one that seemed made of solid glass. All locked.

'Or maybe the room without eyes' ...I remembered that *thing's* ramblings and stuffed its voice away. I wasn't sure about the nature of these halls, but its odd warnings seemed to echo in my skull despite holding fast not to listen.

When we finally hit a door four floors up that appeared relatively normal—it was a mint green color with white trim and a white enamel doorknob—we decided to give it one last try. This time it was unlocked.

Beyond the door was not a hallway but a single domed room. The top of the dome had illustrated constellations—stars and planets amidst an evening sky. I recognized some, the Hunter, the Virgin, and the Ram, finding their points based on their distance to the bright violet star that always stood at the very tip of the sky. It led in no direction other than straight up, regardless of where in Sheirsa you were, and while navigationally useless, it was a constant variable that always shown warmly upon travelers. The remaining twinkles in the ceiling I didn't know and wasn't sure where in the kingdom one would stand to see them, as I was quite familiar with the vast nighttime sky and had never come across such unusual patterns and alignments.

"This is breathtaking," I said as quietly as I could.

Tillian moved past me to the back wall, where a map was held by pins on all four corners. It looked like Sheirsa, but not. The shape was the same, but our borders were removed so that the land held no indication of ownership. It was expansive and nondescript, but there were notes written all over it in a dialect I did not know. There were arrows inwards toward Alaria, which was circled in red and crossed out in black. And in each of the corners, there were symbols, one I recognized and the rest I did not.

To the top left, the Varaynian symbol, the double-swirled blue loops. The top right was white, in the shape of a bear's head with blank orbs left out for eyes. I guessed it was a reference to the Sacera clan Imre had mentioned. Bottom left, green, a woman's head with pointed ears and fangs, and the bottom right was red, a bird of prey's head turned sideways, beak sharp and elongated, a flame in its eye. I gulped and scanned for the spidery symbol I had seen on the officers' necks from the forest, but it wasn't on the map.

Tillian stared at the top of the worn tapestry's edge—it was the entire length of the wall, stretching much higher than we were tall, stopping right as the ceiling started to slope over for its curve.

"Have you ever seen writing like this?" I asked, running a delicate finger over the fabric.

He didn't turn to me as he considered the script, an assortment of looped letters that ran both horizontally and stacked upon one another. I couldn't decipher which way it should be read, or if it was meant to be read at all.

"Sort of." He traced a symbol and tightened his jaw. "My father had a book once, with writing like this on the cover."

I hadn't even thought about his father up until this very moment. His father, whose last known stationing was in the Icesone Mountains. Guilt tried to break the dam holding back my emotions, but I stayed steady. His eyes were blank as they scanned over the map, and I knew that I needed to keep my thoughts even—this was his wound, and if he needed me to tend to it, I didn't want my misplaced guilt in the way.

"Do you remember what the book was about?"

He shook his head.

"He wouldn't read it to me. When I saw it, I had asked, but he said it wasn't for children. When I begged and begged, he told me that it was an ancient book of the dead and that it'd only give me nightmares."

Before I could react, he added, "I wouldn't overthink that," as if he knew where my thoughts were headed, "I think he just didn't want me bothering him."

Mesmerized by the tapestry, I tried to commit it to memory, remembering the lines and symbols as best as I could. Part of me wished I had allowed Zymir to come with us—if anyone knew what this all meant, it would be him. In my scan, an unsettling character amongst all the scribbles paused my process. An eight-pointed star cushioned between what I assumed were other letters or words. The lines were thin and doubled, the edges pointed like arrows, and there were smaller stars in the center. I glanced at the silvery lines on my wrist and cursed. I held up my arm to confirm, and Tillian followed the comparison with his eyes.

He reached out and gingerly traced the lines on my arm. I froze and struggled against the urge to stop him. No one had ever felt it before. A tingle went up my arm at the touch.

"It's silver. Was...was it silver before?"

"No. I don't know why, but I noticed it earlier during my bath."

"It's so intricate... Almost lovely, even."

"Maybe, when it's not scorching my skin, sure." I pulled my arm back down.

He sighed, presumably at how much the words made his skin crawl and unsettled his heart. Tillian liked a problem he could solve. Practical, solution-oriented, yet ready to haphazardly throw himself into harm's way. I knew referencing the pain was a cheap way to end the conversation I didn't want to have, and I didn't feel great doing it.

We hadn't spoken more about how much I had kept hidden from him. And as more was revealed, I felt a contradictory distance and closeness grow between us. In one respect, I had lied and hidden intimate details that though he insisted he should know, really were withheld to keep him safe and keep my happenings private... And while I didn't regret that decision, I could see the lingering mistrust there, feel him wondering if I had told him everything, or just enough. On the other hand, I had led him into this dangerous world of mine, one that was so shameful I had a hard time looking into those familiar blues of his, fearful I'd find judgment. But there was still none. And for that, I was thankful. I could work on the trust, build it back up brick by brick, so long as those eyes still held the same fondness they always had.

"Have you ever gone so long between," he paused and glanced around, "I don't know, going and getting more assignments?"

That realization hit me square in the chest, though I didn't know if it was correlated or not.

"No, I haven't. Usually a week max, but," I counted in my head, "this has been longer. And when I saw him last," there, that flicker of mistrust lingered as he listened, "he didn't put anything into the tattoo. Usually, each time I deliver vials, he siphons in this—"

Red liquid.

Could it have been dyeing the tattoo all along?

The knob behind us wiggled, and our eyes shot to the door. *Shit.*

Shit, shit, shit.

There were no tables, no closets, nowhere to hide, as Desmond strolled through the door, his face anything but kind.

CHAPTER 23

I was in Tillian's arms, mine draped over his shoulders, pulling my lips away from his. He blinked in disbelief, and it was a challenge to remove my fingertips from the curls at the nape of his neck. He must've chosen the lavender soap. I could smell it as I lingered, breathing it in, our mouths only inches apart.

"Am I interrupting something?" Desmond snarled as he leaned against the door frame.

"Obviously," I said, narrowing my eyes at him.

I moved away, though I ached with an unfamiliar sense of longing as I did.

"I'm confused." Desmond stepped forward.

Gods, did I wish I had my weapons... Tillian moved closer to me, a hair in front so that he was closer as the Nevari commander approached.

"See, I'm confused, because I thought I had made my instructions quite clear—were you not told to stay in your rooms?"

"We needed privacy," I said as suggestively as I could. Tillian looked as if it had finally clicked into place what I was doing. He nodded along, though I could practically feel his racing pulse from where I stood.

Desmond had changed. He wasn't wearing his wolf pelts and dirtied clothes. His shirt had a low cut in the collar, exposing the muscles in his chest and the silver chains hanging from his neck. Colorful lines peaked up, some sort of tattoo covered his upper body, but I couldn't make it out. His knuckles had rings I hadn't noticed before, and he had tidied his beard, so it was sharply cut beneath his chin and along his ears. And his eyes—they were practically feral, the deep green contradicting the fire in their intensity as he looked from me to Tillian and then back again.

"And the rooms weren't up to your liking?" He cocked his head condescendingly.

"Have *you* tried sharing a twin bed?" I countered, testing him, egging him on so he'd believe the lies I spun.

I could practically feel the temperature in the room raise. But I held my chin high even as he sauntered closer...and even as he slipped a knuckle beneath it and lifted it slightly so that our eyes were locked. Tillian was tensed, and his hands were balled into quivering fists. A vague tickle vibrated on my wrist, and I pushed the sensation away. *That* was the last thing I needed.

"Get out, *now.*"

It was a forest fire in his eyes—flickering, controlled rage setting the greenery ablaze. The lighting in the room only darkened his features, making his dark hair nearly pitch black and the angles of his face haunting. It wasn't cruelty I had seen before in his locked features—it was discipline, discipline forcing restraint. I wondered for a moment if my knees would give out before I could step away, out from under his stare. But I willed the strength to stay in my face, to not yield even an inch. I wouldn't give him the satisfaction.

When he finally lowered his hand, I allowed the shadow of a smile to politely grace my face as I held Tillian's hand and walked past. His responding snicker threatened to boil my patience over, but I hurried to the doorway.

"Adelliah?"

I waited and tilted my head.

"Try pushing the beds together next time." He matched the false friendly smile I had given him and nodded to excuse us.

As soon as the door shut behind us, we were running down the stairs at maximum speed. We ran until we reached our floor's door, then rocketed down the hall. Tillian hesitated for a split second, unsure which of the identical doors were ours. But I had counted, and as soon as we turned right at the locked paneled door, I led us back to our connected suite, slightly winded but relieved.

"I'm taking it went well," Kori asked wide-eyed as we stumbled into the room, out of breath.

I sat on the floor against the shut door, and Tillian paced in front of me.

"Yes and no," I said. Tillian kept moving around the room to release the tension that had built up in our confrontation.

I explained what we had seen, trying to describe it in as much detail as possible so that Zymir, who ignored Tillian's pacing, could potentially use the shreds to put together a larger picture.

"I had mentioned already that there were other clans. Your description would suggest either they were using an incredibly old map, or whoever had designed the tapestry put their emblems on to pay homage."

"Four clans, five Weaver Marks?" I asked, clarifying.

His golden eyes bobbed as he nodded.

"Those men from the forest, with the black marks, they don't have a clan of their own?"

"They do not. Gyrusex were the least tied to lineage—it would often appear randomly, even in families that had never bore marks prior. Their abilities made them incredible assassins or warriors for hire. So, while not belonging to a clan of their own, individuals often tied allegiances to different, or multiple, clans through contracts."

"That doesn't really help us any," Tillian said, pausing the line he was digging into the ground through his pacing. "Do any of those symbols mean anything to you? What about the mark on her arm?"

Zymir sighed fully and walked to get a closer look. I wiggled under his inspection, but he solemnly shook his head.

"I'm not familiar with what this could be, or if it means anything at all." Tillian finally sat himself on the bed as Zymir continued, "It could very well be an old compass design. Some had points for not only the directions, but the spots in between."

A compass. Perhaps.

"I, I don't think this matters any," I said quietly, tucking my arm behind me. "I think the bigger concern is why only Alaria was circled on that map."

And speaking that thought made it feel much more real. I had considered not looping back to that detail, fearful that they would confirm my own concerns—that whatever it meant, whatever it was they were intending, led back to the capital itself. And if the Nevari's track record was anything to go off of, whatever it was they could be organizing would be anything but discreet.

As the uncomfortable silence filled the room, each of our thoughts tumbling down different directions, I momentarily considered what would even be gained from heading back toward the capital. Regardless of how numerous they had become, it paled in comparison to the armies of the Sheirsan kingdom. Conscription had ended a few years ago once they stopped searching for the missing family, but even then, most still opted for the two years of now voluntary service once they turned sixteen. Even the civilians of Alaria would put up a fight if traitors came knocking at their doors.

And then, a knock at ours.

Three quick knocks on the suite door, and I groaned audibly. Had an hour and a half truly gone by so fast?

"Let's go. Dinner's starting in ten." It was Imre's voice, soft and calm and still vaguely chipper despite our last interaction.

Our conversation cut short, and concerned glances aside, I swallowed dreadfully at having to sit at the table around the men who had been present as my memories were ripped from my head. It felt like I was attending nude, on full display before eyes that had already picked through me. A growl threatened from the back of my throat, but I knew regardless of how I felt, I'd be ready to walk in as if it had never happened, as if those intimate moments meant nothing to me, and as if their knowing didn't shake me to my bones.

Grimly, we left, feeling vastly unprepared and immeasurably uncertain.

Things went from bad to worse rather seamlessly, it seemed. As we all followed Imre, I half considered taking him out before we'd reach the meeting hall where we'd be eating. There were four of us against his one. But damn it if the prospect of getting blood on his now pearly white outfit didn't churn my stomach. I told myself that was the only reason—it would be messy, most likely—because it was so much easier than acknowledging the faces of all the dead that still haunted me whenever I closed my eyes. They always had the same expression, too, regardless of whether their fate was caused by the unknown like Osyren or through our altercations in the forest. It was always the same, and it was always accusatory. They watched with lifeless eyes that didn't need mouths to say *you did this to me.*

This is your fault.

It was much the same expression Desmond wore once we entered the meeting room.

Sabina and Reid sat to his left side, with Imre taking the seat furthest besides Reid. Desmond stood, hands on the table, eyes trailing us as we followed suit and took the spots across from them. A wild, satisfied grin painted his face, and I found myself emulating one of my own.

Oh, what silly games he wished to play.

The tension was thick. Desmond sat. Ringed fingers curled around the ends of the arms on his chair. He slacked backward, waiting as he looked over his table from beneath his brows. His knowing glance met mine, flickered to Tillian, and then back, with a smirk as he twirled a toothpick between his lips.

"Are the rooms to your liking?" he asked, turning toward Zymir, who sat the closest to him on the right, and then Kori, who sat beside him.

Zymir nodded, and Kori blushed. At the blossoming on her cheeks, his grin grew wider.

"So." I tilted my head nonchalantly and played with the silver place setting. Burgundy, velvet napkins were folded in half, with etched silver utensils and a wide wine glass atop it. "Should we talk about Osyren before or after dinner?"

Tillian gritted his teeth and stiffened. I was the furthest away from Desmond, though it didn't feel like it as his towering stare befell me once more.

"Is she always so rude?" he asked, leaning up and resting his chin in his palm.

"After," Reid answered harshly. He looked as if I had personally offended him. His grip was taut around his knife, which I hadn't noticed until now that all the settings on *this* side of the table were without.

After it would be then. The smell of garlic and venison hit me, and I almost didn't mind waiting. My mouth salivated at the immediate recognition. Hands whizzed past me, setting down plates and pouring wine. I held up a hand to decline the offer and glared at the whirlwind of motion around me. Was this how these people spent their lives? Exorbitant luxury while those in the streets of the cities they left behind starved?

Something else twisted my stomach as I peered down at the meal before me. I pictured those cells beneath us and wondered how many people searching for safe passage were sent away, how many were forced back into the mountains, and how many were simply never allowed to leave at all? Wine sloshed around and around in a glass, cups clinked in merriment, loud chewing and chewing and chewing...

The food on my plate watched me. Meat, root vegetables, bread. The toasty kind that breaks and almost hurts the inside of your mouth. The steam was visible despite the unnecessarily warm temperature here again—it reached my nose, and I knew what it was, but it was dulled. It was gray and unappealing. Reid and Sabina joked loudly and crudely, spurring a chuckle from Kori.

After an initial pause, my companions reluctantly ate. Desmond had offered to take a bit from one of our plates if it would ease our concerns that it was poisoned, with Tillian gladly shoving the plate forward immediately. And after, it was simply dinner. Dinner around a table with wine and laughing and overflowing portions, and yet back in Alaria, civilians slept in the streets, people sold their bodies for money and stole so that they may go another day in bones too large for the skin they lived in and—

There was a silence, and I looked up to see everyone watching me. *Dammit.* I couldn't focus, wasn't hearing their words for a moment, too wrapped up in my thoughts. *Maybe the food was poisoned after all.* My mouth opened and hesitated, and somehow sensing the knot at the back of my throat, Desmond's eyes scanned my face. I could feel them, each second drawn out, and feel as his gaze tightened in acknowledgment. It was lost in a single blink, so fast I immediately doubted I saw it at all.

"Your name." He smiled. "Sabina had asked you your name."

A coarse, dry swallow, and a whispered, "Adelliah." I had forgotten she wasn't privy to my interrogation when that was revealed.

Tillian's hand drifted to my thigh beneath the table. The curve of his hand was familiar and grounding. A squeeze. A squeeze that said *I'm here. Whatever it is that's happening, I'm here.*

I blinked a few times and smelled the rosemary. Its herby aroma filtered through the momentary lack of smell. Saliva moistened my tongue, and I finally started to eat. I refused to peel my eyes off my plate in fear my lapse in focus would draw more unneeded attention or inquiry. And I could only imagine the amusement that would most likely befall the siblings' faces.

Kori dove into the silence with a conversation about the beach, asking if any of them had ever been to the west. *Thank you.* The faces around the table were enamored as she told the story about when she'd walk down to the beaches in the early mornings to try and see the moment the sun rose over the horizon—which started when she was five, she added and laughed, noting how panicked her parents were, waking at the crack of dawn to a five-year-old waddling in through the front door with sand between her toes and seashells in her hands. Another laugh, and Imre continued from there.

He spoke, telling of how he always wished to see the sea. But how he'd yet to do so. There was a lake you could barely see the other side of that he lived near when he was quite young, but no one ever went there much—the fishing was lousy, the shore covered in algae. And by the time his fascination with the water truly took hold, it had fully receded. He'd found his appetite for water only appeased when searching for rivers in the forests.

Perhaps he grew up around the Elsarah forest then. The name of his hometown he had conveniently left out.

My plate was half eaten. Chewing between stories allowed my hand and mouth to work mindlessly. And the distractions had helped me avoid my thoughts, where helplessness taunted me.

Hands reached between Tillian and me, setting down a glass of cold water, the condensation dripping down the sides and onto the table. I hadn't even noticed the lack of water poured—until I gripped the icy surface and felt the lingering wooziness in my head subside as I drank. As I brought down the empty glass save for the ice cubes curling around one another, I met the emerald eyes of whom I assumed was to thank for the only glass brought to the table. Not that those words would leave my lips.

The sound of utensils on plates slowed as dishes were finished and taken away.

My mind was solid, stabilized. I wasn't sure why I had been affected so thoroughly. But no amount of triggers could jeopardize why we'd come here in the first place.

"See," a slight snarl, Desmond's sly upturned lip back in place, "a little patience, and you end up with a meal *and* answers."

"Answers? You haven't given us any answers." Tillian's voice surprised me.

"Impolite, my guests," he said, waving a head dismissively at us and turning his head toward his...guards? Friends? I hadn't a clue. "Tell me what you'd like to know about Osyren."

"Everything." I breathed. "Everything you know."

"Everything? I know quite a lot." He spun a ring around on his finger. "I know he hunted creatures for the kingdom, and I know he took great pleasure in doing so."

I would have never been able to notice it before, but after observing his stillness so frequently, I noticed Zymir twitch at *pleasure*.

"I know he liked his women young and his alcohol old, and I know he never stopped slicing a beast until he had its heart ripped out of its chest."

I grimaced, waiting for a reaction from Zymir, but whatever ounce of emotion he had let slip from his stance prior was entirely locked in place now.

"So, Adelliah, I ask again, what would you like to know?" His eyes sparkled in a knowing way, in a way that said he knew, but wanted to make me say it.

"Did you kill him?" I reached down to the lip of my chair between my legs, lifted, and scootched the chair so it ran horizontal to the table so I could face him directly—give his arrogance my full attention.

"I did not." He clapped his hands together and stood, still rubbing them together. "See how easy that was." He looked down at me, both from the height and not.

Your glass could be a weapon.

I stiffened. The thought had been in my voice, but...but it hadn't felt like my thought.

Smash it, jab the jagged ends right into that thumping vein on his neck—see it, there, running along from his ear down to his—

"Do you have any information that could help us figure out who did?" Zymir spoke up, keeping his voice void of any indication of just how much the answer meant to him.

"I'm surprised your debt collector didn't have any answers for you." He sat back down, his face stone solid.

I struggled to find the words. The light off the coals danced in tune with the breaths Desmond took. Upward they teased as he inhaled, down they relaxed as he exhaled. Or maybe my mind was playing games of its own.

"She doesn't," Zymir replied for me. "But his soul *had* been extracted. Do we have other collectors employed here at our arsenal that could shed some light on what happened?"

We. Our. Sabina watched his confident golden eyes and nodded approvingly. Desmond carefully took the toothpick from his teeth and set it on the table.

"We had two."

The world was spinning.

"But they were not ours." He waved a hand for his glass to be refilled. Once topped off, he leaned back against his chair and stared past the end of the table into the glistening obsidian wall opposite him. "These two were patrolling our northwestern border," he tipped the glass toward the siblings, "when they found them, a man and a woman, unconscious in the snow. We brought them in for questioning, and neither would speak. There was something...unusual about them. I considered that maybe they didn't know our language, so I sent Imre in to determine their intentions. As we arranged to have his memories scanned first," his jaw grew taut, "I found the bags that they both carried."

From beneath the table, he brought my bag up and set it on the table. The empty velvet pooled up in a bunch against the hard surface. It slacked, and I was thankful I had delivered all that I had to Nox, its interior therefore less incriminating.

"Their bags were black, with silver stitching. But similar. However, theirs were far from empty. He had two vials, and she—" his stare continued beyond us, pulling up the recollection, "—she had eleven."

Eleven souls. Eleven vials.

Once I started delivering three at a time, the weight of my bag had been maxed. And not in terms of physical carrying capacity. While my clients were always—up until recently—already dead by natural causes when I arrived, it didn't mean their remains, the vials that held the last intimate parts of them, weren't heavily weighted with each step I took back until they could be delivered. The first time I had ever tried to extract three before returning, I was violently ill the entire trek home. I had stayed an extra day in the tavern in Osta, burying my bag beneath the bed so I didn't have to look at it, stuck in the fetal position until I had to force myself to fight the nausea and return. Nox had implied my reaction was a physical manifestation of my unease, that it wasn't a real ailment. But it sure *felt* real to me.

How could she have carried so many seemingly unaffected?

"Regardless, when Imre went to grab them, both were found dead in their room. Poison capsules smashed between their teeth. It wasn't until we started experimenting on the vials that we began to piece together why they may have been here and who they may have been working for. But without their memories, it's guesswork and assumptions mostly." Ungluing his stare from the wall, they pivoted to me.

"Do you still have them?" I asked softly.

"No." A tenseness stretched the table.

The color had drained from Imre's face, and Reid stared into his lap. Whatever nerve I had come close to, I didn't feel like wasting time poking around.

"Well then, what did you find out before you lost them?"

A heavy hand slammed onto the table, and the remaining glasses vibrated.

"We didn't *lose* them," Sabina snarled, a dagger palmed and rested atop the table.

"Semantics." I waved. Reid rested a warning hand on her shoulder, but she kept her position.

Desmond cleared his throat and didn't reprimand her for the outburst. From the glowering expression on Reid's face, I imagined she had only just beaten him to the words he wanted to hurl as well.

"Their clothes were branded," the commander spoke as if he'd taken a bite out of sour food. "They may not have worn the official uniforms, but they were Sheirsan sent, and Sheirsan employed. And the vials..." his nostrils flared, "the vials didn't respond to heat or cold. We emptied one in a controlled environment and found that once out of a vial, the substance simply dissipated into the air."

They had emptied one, draining it like spoiled milk. The act felt egregious.

"This leaves us nowhere," Zymir said, turning his head and thinking.

"This leaves *you* nowhere," Desmond corrected. Zymir went to speak, but the commander held up a finger to stop him. I cringed as his jaw closed tightly in response. "Though this leaves *me* with a pretty mind that knows more than she realizes about what the kingdom is doing extracting souls." A violent, too-white grin.

And those helpful, whirling hands of servants I had never bothered to look at appeared again, with a metallic neckband that snapped around me in the time it took to blink. The material felt icy and heavy and fit so snugly that my skin moved against it with every swallow.

I told you to use the glass.

CHAPTER 24

Tillian went to stand but found his body rigid in his chair along with the rest of us. Reid's steady, concentrated breath told me the effort it took to lock them in their chairs was a challenge. And I still had no idea what powers Sabina potentially wielded.

"Escort these three back," Desmond said to Sabina, who nodded. "This one stays."

Tillian thrashed, his body banging against the solid wood behind him.

"You'll go *politely*, or I'll make sure my conversation with your friend here is anything *but.*"

"Are the dramatics quite necessary?" I pursed my lips and tapped on the metal around my neck.

"We can't afford mistakes this time. Not when we have something so valuable in our grasp. And not when so many other lives depend on it."

"To what end? How do you measure the lives of those here against those still loyal to the kingdom?"

"Do you think I only act for my own interest? Do you think the fate of those in the mountains doesn't extend to those in your cities?" Desmond gestured dismissively for Sabina to escort Zymir, Tillian, and Kori out. Sabina stood, and her floor-length red dress draped down. Gold bands covered her wrists, and a slim golden chain hung low and visible for the plunging neckline. The gold sparkled against her dark skin, like the tips of the flames against the coals.

"I think men like you see what they want to see." I shrugged, my neck pinching the band.

"And I think you know only what you're shown."

I glanced beside me and nodded, conviction in my eyes as I relayed for them to leave without issue. These were gifted, armed ex-military. This wasn't the time for a move. There would be time for that, *oh* would there be time for that, but right now, it was time for them to leave.

"I'm not—"

"You are," I cut Tillian off with a serious, cold stare. *Get back to the room and figure something out.*

I ignored the cocky amusement on Desmond's face as he raised his brow, waiting, calculating our interactions, and weighing the relationships between us that he could later leverage.

Sabina curled her fingers into the men's shoulders, pointed crimson nails dipping into their skin. "Let's go," she purred and cocked her head so that Kori knew to leave as well.

Those round, hazel eyes watched me, searching for something as she began to follow. I wondered if she was regretting the trust she had wagered on these strangers, or if she was still holding out that they were pure of heart and well-intending. I almost envied her naivety, but I couldn't afford it.

Begrudging footsteps clacked against the reflective floor, sounding further and further as they departed the way we had come.

Surrounded by the two Weavers and their commander, I felt fear quake within me. But I hushed it. There wasn't time, and it'd only distract me. Fear was useless and a pitiful crutch.

"Get on with it."

A sharp buzzing sound came from the collar, and I stilled my fidgeting.

"Your navigation tattoo is acting like a conduit," Imre said, barely a whisper. "When we questioned you—"

"When you helped yourself to my memories—"

"Yes." He raised his voice and then softened it. "Yes, well, something in your system responded defensively, and that, that tattoo pulled energy out of the air before you stifled it."

"Am I waiting for some sort of question?"

"What is it?" Imre was heading this exchange evidently, and the gentleness of his eyes darkened.

"Was that not in there?" I stuck out my lower lip. "Could you not find that up here?" I pointed to my head and felt the fire rise from the coals in a rapid upward wave.

"You can make this quick," Desmond said, the flames reflecting in his eyes, "or we can make things extremely slow." The warmth in front of me tinged toward uncomfortable, and sweat beaded on my forehead. It settled as Imre shifted in his seat.

"I don't know." At their doubtful, empty stares, I repeated, "I don't know. I have no idea. I've had it for as long as I remember. And all it's ever done is sting and burn and cry out when I'm supposed to go collect. It's usually a rash, or coordinates, though it's been stuck like *this* for days."

Imre and Desmond shared a glance I couldn't interpret.

Imre filled his lungs up, as if steadying himself. "Tell me about your mother."

Blankness.

I... I paused. And searched. I pushed the files aside and sorted through memories, deeper and deeper into my head, going further back. I remembered flashes of Alaria and pushed beyond that. A familiar creeping tapped at the edge of all I could see, beckoning me closer. I pushed through time, but there was a cloud. A dense, black, swirling cloud of something sinister and raw.

My mouth was dry.

Another nod between them. Reid's trained eyes never left me in fear one flicker of movement would have me no longer complying. Complying as if there was an option. As if this wasn't another step on the path I was forced to walk, order after order, reacting to how the pieces fell before me.

"Where were you born?"

A nervousness scraped its talons down my mind, cool liquid bursting through in a chilling numbness. *Stop.* Stop asking me questions. Stop making my mind backtrack. I was stuck between now and this wall, and the wall would not budge. The wall would not let me peek over top, and my hands were too dirty and calloused from digging out the dirt in front to get beneath it. Could they not see how long I've tried to tear it down? Did they not see the nail marks carved into its impenetrable face?

At my silence, the softness I so desperately hated slacked Imre's rigid cheeks, relaxed his jaw.

"Don't you *pity* me." My fingertips were shaking, bouncing off the wood.

Another buzz from the vibrations around my neck went through to my skull.

"I don't—"

My rage cut his words short. "Don't *lie to me.*" My voice hollowed, and a strength within it snapped.

Desmond eased over to where I sat in an apprehensive, slowed gate as he knelt down, so his face was level with mine.

"Do you not see what they've done to you?" he asked, but his words flew past my ears as I imagined how his jaw would look if he got close enough for my boot to jam into it. "I don't know *what* exactly it is they're doing,

Adelliah, but we've been finding others like you. Others who the kingdom have used to try and manifest some way to get the royal family back."

"Tell me, what does *like me* mean?" A growing ferocity threatened to boil my blood to the point it'd spurt out from my skin.

He hesitated, calculating, debating his words. The fire in his eyes stared back at my own.

"You know nothing about me." The clouded wall in my mind felt so close now, I could smell the decay on it. "You decided long ago to turn and run." A flinch. "You saw a kingdom you disagreed with, so you fled. And you abandoned your post, and your city, and all those who dwelled inside of it. How long have you been hiding in your mountain?" The flames from the coals burst upwards, and Reid leaned backward in his chair to avoid the too-curious tongues.

"How *dare* you—"

"Do you know how many starve while you eat in excess here?" I found my opening, and I felt the wedge widen. I couldn't stop myself from picking at wounds. "You are a *coward*."

The heat roared against my face and singed the ends of my hair.

"Desmond!" Imre's panicked voice yelled over the wall of flames dividing them from us.

His pale skin hardly glistened as full droplets of sweat cascaded down mine. His wide grin never faltered despite the erupting rage churning in his eyes. "You don't think I know what you're doing?" The flames shot back down, hovering a hair above the coals that I knew now were truly just for show.

"Looks like peeking through the cracks wasn't enough. Break down the wall, Imre."

"Sir." Imre gulped and leaned over the table. Reid was blowing on the burnt ends of his too-close braids, a careful scowl halfway turned away.

An invisible hand brushed my forehead, and I gritted my teeth at Desmond and then at Imre. *Let them try. Let them try to get in again.* A burning whisper said *use me, use me, use me.* And I could feel the lines on my wrist pulsating with power, begging to be unleashed. The distraction had worked, and that dark, ominous cloud was further away, its impending presence delayed. I leaned into the sensation coursing through me. The tattoo pleaded for me to relinquish control, and as I felt the imploring fingers reach out for me once more, I did.

A sharp electrical current buzzed through my neck, and the smell of burnt flesh sizzled. I wanted to scream as my flesh seared, but I held it in my mouth.

"We got these," he tipped his head toward the metal buzzing at my neck, "courtesy of Sheirsan prisons. They'd use these collars to neutralize any and all forms of magic one could wield."

Magic.

"How do you," I coughed the pain out through clamped teeth, "not see your own hypocrisy?"

The green of his eyes softened into the color of a muted, grayed forest. "How do you not see I have no other choice?"

It was then that the invisible fingers scraped below the sweaty skin of my brow and plunged. And this time, they did not hesitate. They didn't search or wander—the fingers made their way straight to that impermeable wall and slipped not between the cracks, but pounded against its entire being. My mind roared in protest. It reeled back, all efforts focused on protecting itself and shielding the wall that quaked against Imre's powerful blow.

The wall shook.

My body shook with it. I was within myself, focused on the mental attack, my eyes either shut or so utterly useless I wasn't even bothering to use them.

Get out.

Another *BOOM,* and bricks started crumbling down.

I gasped for air, which centered me back in my body—my quivering, sweaty, aching body. I tried to fight again, to dive into whatever it was Imre was doing in the deepest crevices of my mind. But I couldn't.

"Imre?"

A suffocating wind gusted as bricks toppled, and my reality splintered. White, bright light blinded me—I couldn't see, and for a moment, I felt nothing: No pain, no fear, no rage.

It felt wrong.

"It's down." He breathed, winded and panting.

Cold air swept past ground that had never been traversed. Beyond the rumble, there was nothing. I waited, as I guessed we all did, for whatever was hidden to reveal itself. But the barrenness was stark and endless. And some innate part of me shrunk even smaller, oddly disappointed. I felt empty. Because I *was* empty.

"Do you see anything?" Desmond asked, his position a step away in anticipation.

Imre's far-away stare made the emptiness echo in my head.

"There's nothing here," Imre whispered. His face was blank and unreadable.

"What...what does that mean?"

"I'm not sure." Imre stole a glance my way. The unseen fingers in my mind started to retract, leaving a soothing chill behind. It lightly caressed over the fallen wall, through the catalog of memories, and as they slipped out of my head, my body deflated.

"What—" I hated how my voice involuntarily shook. "—What did you find in the others?"

There had always been an emphasis on the importance of now. Day to day, mission to mission. Reflection was for learning, for refining a task to see how it could be improved upon. And there had never been loss associated with it—because I never even considered searching further back. Did that make me...different? Did that make me *wrong?* I had never pondered the absence of memories beyond a certain point. I knew most people couldn't remember *that* far back. It had never occurred to me that my recollection distance was stunted. I wouldn't have believed that a stint was constructed if I hadn't felt its rigidity myself. A concrete wedge. *Manufactured* in my mind, if Desmond was to be believed.

Why did I feel such loss over something I never knew I was missing?

Imre corrected, "While we had others with remnants of Sheirsan experimentation, it was never so..." I tensed. "...absolute."

"Everyone else had repressed memories, important details hidden from them, or aspects of their lives forgotten from before the kingdom had intercepted them. From before, *whatever* it was that was done to them. And we still don't have a clue what it is they're trying to accomplish..." Desmond's voice was frustrated and vaguely disappointed.

But at least there was an opening there.

A window into what could help us get back on track.

"You think they're using citizens for experiments, and you think it has something to do with the family's disappearance?" There would be time to grieve this loss aching in my mind, but not now. I kept my posture hunched and small and *pathetic. Let them think they've broken me.* I ignored the softer part of me that asked: *But haven't they?*

I withheld none of the pain in my eyes as I reached out for Desmond and set a shaking palm on his shoulder.

Look at me.

He did, and despite the window straight into my soul, he peered back unafraid, unflinching.

"What did they do to me?" I let the tears form and let them appear to be held back from overflowing. *See what you want to see.*

He shook his head and stared down. I saw the loose threads of seemingly unrelated variables. A Weaver Marked, Sheirsan hunter had been killed and his soul extracted. A band of rogue rebels in a mountain believed the kingdom was experimenting on its citizens. And Nox had determined more soul collectors were out working under someone else, which Desmond himself had confirmed. But how did they relate, if they did at all...?

Nox would need answers. We all needed answers.

"The collectors you discovered, how long ago was that?"

"About a year."

"So, before Osyren." Well, they weren't to blame then. Desmond nodded slightly, curiosity peeking through his somber, grayed face.

A ripple dimpled his forehead.

"I came here thinking you were to blame for his death," a false, perfectly timed sniffle, full doe-eyes, "but maybe that's exactly what the Kingdom wanted everyone to think. If they placed blame on the Nevari, they'd be strengthening the already negative public opinion." Not that they had alerted the public at all. In fact, they had been very quiet after his death. Hidden it. But he didn't need to know that. "I'm thankful for whoever ended him, though, either way. If what you're saying is true, then the hunters may very well be supplying people for the experimentation. It's not like there are many other creatures left for them to hunt."

And I saw it then, the response I was looking for. *I'm thankful,* I lied. *Let me know to whom I should provide thanks.* At the word, his defenses slacked in acknowledgment. And even if he wasn't the one who caused it, I knew in that moment that he knew who did.

But he was a commander, and he wasn't a stupid one. So, he said nothing.

"They'll pay," he said in a hush, "very soon."

A polite smile found my face though my head started to throb. "Is this still necessary?" I pointed to my neck. The band around it was no longer buzzing, and my wrist had gone quiet.

"Yes."

"No."

Desmond's "no" followed Reid's "yes" at nearly the same time. A wordless exchange passed between the two, and then the collar was off. Whatever control mechanism they used to lock it, unlocked, and it fell into my lap with a thud. I ran my hands over the tender, blistered flesh.

"I'll walk you back to your room," Reid said, standing with a bored expression.

I followed obediently.

Words seemed inefficient as I retold what had happened. Tillian wore only anger as he held his head in his hands. I kept only the part I hadn't reconciled undisclosed—I told them of the foraging in my mind, but instead of the out-of-place shame I felt that nothing was found, I left it at *whatever they saw, they didn't tell me.*

"Interesting," Zymir said beneath his breath, causing Tillian to shoot him a vile look.

"What about them having the capabilities to interrogate us one by one with the help of assorted Sheirsan devices to aid them is interesting to you? What about them snapping that thing on her neck is *interesting* to you?" Tillian stood and faced Zymir, body cornering his against the wall.

"We learned the kingdom may be experimenting on its citizens, and we learned that there is a chance she was part of that population. You don't find that fascinating? You don't wonder to what ends they may be striving to obtain?"

Tillian stepped a hair closer, breathing unevenly. "I don't believe a word that comes from that smug, cocky bastard's mouth. What makes you think he's being honest?"

"For what purpose would he lie?" Zymir's eyes flickered to my own as if asking both of us.

"Because that's what they do. They *lie.*" Tillian threw his hands up in the air. "So, she had some repressed memories? You're telling me instead of believing that maybe she put up a metaphorical wall to protect herself, that she was kidnapped against her will, *had gods-knows-what done to her,* and then released with not only no recollection of what happened but no long-term side effects?"

Long-term side effects... Memories were getting hazy since the ordeal in the meeting hall. But I hadn't considered that possibility. I avoided painstakingly rethinking through any odd events for fear I'd panic and associate every quirk with whatever slim chance existed that it stemmed from some sort of experiment.

Zymir was careful and patient. But I knew Tillian's anger—it was fast, red hot, and destructive.

"I don't think they're lying," Kori said. She was crossed-legged on the bed, the dark blonde bangs on her forehead were parted. "After my mother died, not only were those awful signs posted everywhere, but many women went missing. I," she played with her hands and looked down, "I admit that I didn't pay a lot of attention at the time. But I remember a friend of my father's talking late one night about it. A beggar here, a widow there. It was only for a few weeks, all the disappearances. But," she sucked in air and winced as if the words were painful, "unfortunately, most of the women who had gone weren't ones anyone was searching for any time soon. I think everyone assumed they had left. Or...Just didn't care enough to investigate."

Tillian deflated slightly in the following silence. "I think we leave tonight," was all he said, still standing uncomfortably close.

I flinched as Zymir tilted his head sharply. "We have made no progress regarding Osyren."

"*Fuck* progress." Tillian waved his hands exasperatedly. "What else did you expect from them? If you two actually think there's something going on, why stay *here*?"

Zymir's golden, blank eyes hardened. And he stood straighter, a tension pulling at his temples.

"I came here to find out who killed Osyren. I'm not leaving until I have something to go off of." Icy words floated in the space between them.

Tillian snorted with frustration. "And if they start interrogating us all like that? Then what? Will you roll over for them to go through your memories too?"

I stepped toward them, hoping they'd diffuse themselves, but ready if they didn't.

Zymir closed the gap closer as he met the fiery intensity being thrown at him. "I cannot leave until I know. That is the *only reason* I am here. Leave if you'd like."

"You don't give a damn what happens to anyone else in here, do you?" Tillian was raising his voice now, all sorts of misplaced anger at this place and these people spurting through his lips. "You're fucking *selfish*."

Zymir cocked his head to the side, and his eyes radiated in the low light of the room. It was then that I remembered I never told Tillian Zymir's reason for joining us. *Stupid, stupid, stupid.*

"Til', that's enough," I warned.

"No, it isn't." He didn't bother to look back at me. "We're on a wild goose hunt with nothing to go off of. That man is dead, and unless we want to increase the chances to end up just like him, I say we leave."

"Then *leave*," Zymir let the softest of snarls escape him.

"Why can't you just *get over it*?"

And then Tillian was up against the wall. Zymir had snatched him by the collar and lifted him off his feet, pivoted, and slammed him against the wall as if he weighed nothing.

"Get over it?" Zymir's body seemed to be slightly glowing in the evening lighting. Kori hopped off the bed and walked to him, but he held up his other hand to stop her. "You're a spoiled, coddled brat," Tillian thrashed against the wall, "who doesn't know when to keep his mouth shut."

Tillian reached his hungry fists toward Zymir, but Zymir lifted him off the wall and shoved him roughly back into it again to stop him. "I can't just *get over* what Osyren did. You have no idea what that monster—"

"I don't give a shit what he did," Tillian hissed.

"Enough!" I rushed and set my hands on Zymir's flexed shoulders. "He doesn't know." Zymir refused to turn to me. "He *doesn't know!*"

"Doesn't know what?" Tillian asked. He, too, avoided my eyes, his body dangling above the ground.

"Osyren was a butcher. And his blood was *mine* to spill." I felt the ground practically shake at his conviction. "It was mine, and I will stop at nothing to slaughter every last person who took that from me."

And then Tillian, in his stupid, too-angry-to-be-thinking way, laughed. And I could do nothing to shield him from the blow that found the side of his head.

"You wouldn't understand because you've never had anything taken from you—you're a child." Zymir's knuckles rested beside himself with the blood from Tillian's nose. "My sister was ripped from our home in the middle of the night, hung up by her hands, and tortured for hours. They removed her vocal cords so she couldn't scream, and they covered her in the blood of others they slaughtered so I couldn't track her scent. They cut out her bones and sliced off her limbs, and when I finally found what was left of her—"

Zymir, always so calm and so unemotional, was trembling. The sight of it filled me with such deep fear and sorrow that it hollowed out my chest. I couldn't breathe as he described what they had done. Tillian had gone flaccid in the haunted man's grasp.

"They had burned her pieces into unrecognizable soot. I have followed the trail of those men and hunted them one by one. And he was the last. The very last I had to make feel every ounce of the pain they caused her. And instead—" the skin on his knuckles had started to dry, pieces of grayed skin dusted off in the air, "—someone came and gave him an easy, quick death. And for that, I will not stop. I will not rest until I take what is mine."

He dropped Tillian with a thud, and at least on the ground, my friend finally had enough sense to stay. And to shut up. Zymir tilted his head as he watched the depleted man left in embarrassment on the floor before turning and excusing himself to the room on the other side of the suite. Kori and I shared a look, and she followed, leaving Tillian and me in the solemn, tired air.

CHAPTER 25

I sat beside Tillian. He was crumpled and averted his eyes. I leaned against the slight chill of the wall and rested my head back. The birds on the ceiling soared, and I was tethered. The weight of my limbs felt like anchors. Tillian leaned back so that our shoulders brushed, and his gaze followed mine to the ceiling.

"I didn't mean it."

"I know."

"I didn't mean to take it out on him, he—" a quivering breath and he ran his fingers through his hair, "—he was just who was here." There was shame in the admittance.

"I know," I repeated softly.

His curls fell onto my shoulder as he slumped and rested his head against me, letting the weight hang without holding. His jagged breaths smoothed to even ones. His heart rate slowed to normal. And we simply were. For just a moment, we sat, and we weren't sitting here in the Icesone Mountains with empty questions, and we weren't defeated and exhausted—we were sitting, our bodies' pulses matching and our breaths aligning. We were at the glistening amethyst pond he had shown me in Alaria, time slipping past effortlessly.

"We should try and get some sleep," I offered.

A groan and then a yawn was confirmation enough.

We went to our separate beds. I turned away as I slipped off my tunic and pants, sliding my legs beneath the smooth satin sheets that glided between my knees. I could hear his breath change, deepen to the cadence of slumber. And as my head cradled into the pillow, I found myself quickly following.

I was barefoot in bright orange sand. It was hot and burnt the sensitive skin between my toes. Endless sand as far as I could see. I walked quickly to avoid the heat radiating off it, hopping as the surface grew warmed and warmer.

Sand all around.

But behind me, a fallen wall. Rubble stretched across the horizon. Huge shattered bricks left to crumble. With the hump of broken bricks at my back, I let my sizzling feet lead me away. Ahead, the crystal sand gave way to more of a clay-like substance. It was beneath the sand, I realized, squishing my feet back and forth to move the sand away. The clay was relieving and damp. I hurried further away from the abandoned wall toward where the surface sand was scarce.

There was light but no sun.

Until a twinkling blue star appeared to dart around in the foreground. It weaved and somersaulted and flashed in a cycle of three bright bursts before pausing and repeating. In the barrenness around me, I followed it. There was nothing else to see, nowhere else to explore. It was empty.

And so, I followed the bouncing blue beacon. Until its presence was not infinitely in front of me, but in the obtainable distance. I ran, determined to get to it. As I approached, its size grew. The blinking in threes seemed more like pulses as it stretched wider and taller. But no unease gripped me. In fact, as the glowing blue ball of light grew, a delightful sense of achievement filled me. Warmed me.

So close now. So close I could practically reach out and grab it.

But that ball was not a ball, and that light was no longer a light.

Its bright blue edges outlined a human shape, and though weariness warned me to proceed carefully, the utter absence of anything else here told me to investigate. The smell of salt tickled my nose as I stood before the silhouette—the smell of the ocean, I realized with a jolt.

And before I could think better of it, I reached out to touch it.

The shimmer rippled, and the blue light exploded. I shielded my eyes, turning away until the brightness subsided.

Osyren stood, reeking of the ocean and algae, lifeless eyes staring ahead. I reached out to him, to tap and wake him up. To force a spark back into the eyes. But as my hand grazed his still glowing body, the sound of tearing barreled into my ears. Tearing flesh, like ripping fabric yanked from the seams. His neck opened itself, but no blood pooled out—only more of the same blueness that had shielded him in the distance prior. As blue light dripped from his gash, it soon started to run out. The edges of the skin remained a luminescent blue like that of an electric jellyfish, and the remaining liquid transformed into a silvery goo that I immediately recognized.

I didn't take it, I tried to say. But there were no words in this place. I don't have it, I wanted to yell as his eyes turned down in sadness as he peered down at his own silver insides dribbling through the flaps of flesh. Instead, he reached out a closed hand toward me.

I stepped toward what he held as he dipped his head down, so it hung limp. His torso started to slack, but his arm remained rigid, held up by an invisible force.

I went to his hand, and his fingers felt like ice. I lifted them one by one to reveal what it was he offered.

A full silver vial with a Varaynian mark on the label rested in his palm.

I woke, out of breath and freezing.

But the warmth of the body behind me held my shivers. The body was atop the covers, considerate of my unclothed state beneath. But the hold was strong, and muscled arms wrapped around my front, calming the involuntary convulsing.

My cheeks were wet.

"I'm here," he whispered from behind into the curve of my ear. The touch of his lips was like the softness of petals. I craned backward toward their delicateness, and he squeezed me tighter against him. "I'm here," he promised, and our bodies snugly leaned against one another.

The smell of lavender was muted, but *his* smell, the vague smell of sweetness, like honey tea or blueberry pastries, surrounded me and beckoned me to sleep. His arms were comforting. His touch was soothing. I hovered in that gray space between waking and slumber, not wanting to move, until a startling realization blew the grayness away.

The clarity pulled me fully awake, and I gently moved my body away from the warmth despite the longing to stay.

"What are you doing?" The words came out in a yawn.

"I've been so stupid." I hurried my legs over the edge of the bed and into my pants. I slipped my top over my head.

Tillian sat up groggily and blinked a few times, adjusting to the deeper darkness in the room. "What're you talking about?"

I leaned toward the table next to the bed and pulled the copper string on the lamp. He shielded his eyes and groaned.

I had been so focused on my weapons and the lack of my bag that I hadn't even thought of what I *did* still possess. Stupid, stupid oversight that I wouldn't let cloud my thinking again.

"I think Osyren's vial is somewhere under the mountain," I said slowly while reaching into my pocket. "And Mion is going to show us where."

I hastily rummaged to the bottom and found Mion's tightly wound coils. I brought him out and watched him wake under the glow of the lamp. Ready for a command. Tillian watched with increasing awareness.

"Mion, find Osyren." I waited as the prongs elongated and the legs formed from the chaos. Sure enough, after careful unraveling and a moment to consider, Mion skittered down and waited at the bedroom door.

"Do you think that'll work if he's dead?" Tillian rubbed at his eyes.

"Only one way to find out. If there's any residual essence of life in the vials, it should be able to track it."

"And if it does find it, then what?"

I hadn't thought that far. This idea on how to find the vial was the first proactive step I'd taken. Everything else, a reaction. And I was so tired of reacting and getting nowhere except further stripped of my confidence and being no closer to answers.

"I'll follow Mi for ten minutes and turn back no matter what. If I'm not back in twenty, you wake the others." I could see him wanting to argue, but I hurried to the door. I pointed to the ornate, copper-lined clock beneath the lamp, its old face worn and yellowed—but operational. "Zymir should be able to find where I am, but," I searched around the guest suite as I spoke, trying to find something to help if things went dire but found nothing, "but…" I trailed off.

"Oh, put one of the lotions on from the bathroom, in that wicker basket they left out, it'll—"

"It'll give him a stronger smell to track," we both said at once. I wasn't sure how or why his sense of smell was so far superior to ours, but we both knew having an odor to follow would help, especially since it was less risky than leaving tissues, which I had eyed for a moment and then dismissed as an option.

I darted into the bathroom as Mion stayed at the bottom lip of the door. I hastily squirted the menthol-scented one into my palm and slathered it up the length of my arms. It felt absolutely ridiculous, but if it allowed him to find me a second sooner if things went dire, then it'd be worth the aggressive minty smell that radiated off me. The mark on my wrist was level, no raised lines, and I couldn't even make out its features in the darkness. I considered that a good sign. Maybe it, too, was sleeping.

I went to the door and looked back to Tillian, whose alertness had returned to his eyes. "Twenty minutes," he said, reaching for the clock and setting it in his lap.

"Twenty minutes," I swore, and ran out into the hall.

Mi's delicate metal steps on the thinly carpeted floor were barely discernable, but I had been following that sound for years. We twisted and turned in the halls, only illuminated by sconces at the ends. The rooms they afforded the higher technologies, but the rest of the maze, it seemed, preferred the old ways. Or Desmond simply preferred the fire.

I followed Mi down the opposite direction than the staircase we had tried exploring earlier. It led down two more halls from that fork, a left then right, and then I finally hit my first door. A heavier, metal one, like the ones down on the lower levels where the prison cells were. I couldn't map where I was in relation to those, despite the small sections I had remembered—I couldn't figure out if they all led to the same place or just others like it. I couldn't even grasp how large or small this place was to help make that call.

The door was unlocked.

I trailed the pitter patter down the winding halls, toward a slump that made the path decline further. The coiled feet sounded sharper as the soft ground gave way to stone. And the distinct smell of mildew and moisture reappeared.

I had to be in the prisons.

Maybe not the same prisons, but similar ones. Winding metal looped the base of the sconce at the beginning of the hall, where the smell arose. I considered picking up the lit beacon, wiggling it through the metal holder, but I didn't have much time, and I didn't want the light to draw attention. In and out. Follow the path and get back to the room. We could investigate whatever was found tomorrow.

The hall had no doors, no rooms I could see. But Mi continued straight ahead, certain and unwavering. I had gone through six doors now. I kept the number clear in my head. Because to get lost, would cost seconds. And should I need to hurry back, I'd need every last one.

I heard the sound of rain come from beyond the door in front of us, the seventh door. A waterfall of droplets deep below the mountain. I opened the door for Mion but saw no water. This hall was the smallest—they had all slowly decreased in length, but this one didn't have a door at the end to keep tunneling further down. There was a door to my right and a door to my left. The end of the hall was a wall.

I had reached the end of whatever wing this was.

Mi paused, spinning around on its legs, calculating. The sound of the downpour was so loud I couldn't figure out which door the noise was coming from. Or if maybe water was falling onto the ceiling above us.

Mion finally moved sideways toward the door to my right. I approached, and it climbed up my leg, then my torso, and rested on my shoulder. We must have arrived, though the ball of wiring preferred a view instead of the usual place in my pocket, it would seem. There wasn't a handle, I realized with growing irritation. I had to be drawing near my ten-minute mark—I had run as fast as I could without being too loud, but it had taken a substantial bite of my time to get here.

I searched the face of the door, scrambling my clumsy fingers over the wood. There had to be some sort of mechanism. The very way to get into this place under the mountains had been a riddle, one I hadn't so much as solved as gotten lucky at the last possible moment. Remembering the correlating colors with Kori's Weaver Mark was a disorientating guess that happened to trigger the door beneath the snow, but here, with vital seconds passing by, I couldn't find a single distinguishing mark on the door that could help me figure out how to get in.

Luck.

I had gotten lucky.

Feeling rather naïve, I reached for my neckline and held the coin of Draoi between my forefinger and thumb. *I need your help. For just a moment.* I pressed against the risen engraving, picturing the cross-legged man in my mind. And as if in reply, from the never-ending, expansive nothingness that had been unlocked in my mind, came a tingle. From the base of my skill but yet further, a ripple of acknowledgment.

Think. Come on, think!

You can collect the souls but not find them. Such a pity.

The words sounded in my head, just as they had at dinner, in my voice, but from a source not my own. I pushed the words back into the air, though they fueled my haste.

I tapped my foot along the bottom of the door, ran my hands up the sides. Nothing. Nothing but the feel of moist air seeping through the seams. A breeze was whispering from out of the door. I pressed my cheek near where the door met the wall and tried to peek into the gap, but it was too tiny to see anything. As I felt along the edge, my necklace swayed, tapping the door's face.

Until it swung closer and didn't ricochet off.

I had been tapping along the gap as my face moved slightly closer to the center of the door, and I looked down to see the chain still oscillating, but its taps had stopped because the bottom of the chain and the coin were fusing into the door itself.

Blurred lines ate the coin, concealing it inside until it swayed back out.

It was a glamour. It wasn't a door at all.

I moved my search to the front of the door near the very center and, sure enough, felt a buzz of energy in the space. I pressed with my fingertips, and the door didn't stop them—they moved through the surface.

Thank you.

Once I established the center where the border was merely show, and before I allowed fear to drain my adrenaline, I inhaled, and pushed myself through the space.

When I opened my eyes on the other side, I blinked rapidly to make sure my eyes were working properly. All the walls were falling water from so high up I couldn't see. The air was warm and smelled fresh, like a rapid current darting through rocks and down hills. The surface of the waterfall was bright, and the drops that hit my face were real—*this* was real, not a mirage, not a trick of the eyes. Water, most likely from melted snow above the mountain, cascaded down all around me. Mion pivoted around in excited circles on my shoulder.

"Okay, sure, but *where?*"

The bits of wire continued to spin, as if to say, *here ya dumbass, where I told you.*

The water was falling down quicker than I thought as I dipped my fingers beneath the flowing curtain. As I broke one of the streams, the water split, moving around my hand and creating a bigger gap.

A gap that revealed several glistening objects just behind the watery enclosure. My throat caught as I swallowed. I could feel the wetness move up my outstretched hand as I reached further in, my skin wetting up to my wrist. Further still, and up to my elbow was drenched. The jagged split in the water as it touched me broke to a window of vials. An entire collection, vial after vial and vial.

My wrist burned in reply despite the cooling touch of the interior rain. It yelled at the wrongness before me, the catalog of jarred souls stacked upon one another. I could barely breathe, and I wasn't sure if it was because of the growing horror as I scanned more shelves of vials behind the blanket of water, or because of the agony coursing through my right arm in response. The silvery mark on my arm was swirling. Removed was the eight-pointed star—now it was an angry, dense storm, unsure of what shape it wished to form. It screamed at my skin and howled in my ears as the color oozed and shifted like clouds about to erupt.

Even without having to look, I knew the other walls of water would be hiding more of the same. A library of souls hidden deep below the ground, far from the people they once inhabited. I almost wondered if I'd ever be able to find Osyren's vial, but somehow as my eyes flickered across the assortment, I knew I'd be able to tell.

His slit throat appeared in my mind, his hunched body. And his nails. The torn nails and scrapes on his hands that told the tale of his unwillingness to die. Zymir's words tried to remind me of who the corpse I had seen really was, but having only seen his lifeless shell, I struggled with the only pictures I had left—the ones from my dreams: The one that haunted me nearly every sleep of his suspended body vomiting black ooze, and the one from last night—the one reminding me of why I was here, and what I needed to retrieve.

My eyes paused on a vial that looked back at me. It was waiting. It was ready. Because it had called for me.

As I reached for it, I felt a gaze from a familiar set of lifeless orbs, as if to say *yes, here I am.*

The outside of the vial was labeled. I turned it over in my hand as I removed it from the shelf and through the gap in the waterfall. I was beginning to hate the immediate recognition of the two blue swirls. Damned Varaynian mark. I wondered how many more were labeled and what purpose they served. But I knew I was past ten minutes, and my friends would soon risk searching the halls for me.

The water behind me stopped. Immediately. No residual drops or lingering streams from up high. A breeze caressed my forehead, and the hairs on my neck stood.

"Going so soon?"

CHAPTER 26

I spun around to see Imre standing in the doorway. My mind flooded with words that could explain my whereabouts or my reasons. I felt his invisible hands lunge for my mind, and I decided then that the only way to get out of here would be through him.

I shoved forward, brushing past his outreach. The reflective white tunic he had been wearing earlier against his tan skin shone brightly in the room, even without the water to heighten the glare.

"Hey!" he yelled with dire sharpness.

I hurled past without looking as I darted around him and then under his arm as he tried to stop me. I leaped through the mirage entrance and yanked Mion from my shoulder into my pocket for safekeeping. I ran, indifferent to how loud my panicked steps were. Through each door, each hall, each tracked turn. I knew he followed closely, the sound of his chase seconds behind, and a wave of power reached out to me, hungry fingers ready to pull me back mind first.

I was leading him back to the suite. I was leading him back to my friends.

My steps and heart pulled in opposite directions. As we neared the fourth door, I swore and ducked left instead of right, down a hall I hadn't journeyed down before. We were still near the prisons, the smell of stagnant air thick. I had no goal, no preferred direction—my legs stung with urgency as I tried to put as much distance between us as they'd allow.

But he didn't let up.

He was shouting something unintelligible, but I didn't lose focus to try and decipher it. The solid, dark walls gave way to bars and cells. And I wondered if these cells would be as *mostly* empty as the others he had retrieved me from. Clanking, echoing steps here—unavoidably loud and revealing. The cells down these blocks at least *seemed* empty. The flickering lanterns reveal closed doors without locks.

I needed to buy time. I needed a distraction.

Another door, a more familiar one, a recognizable distance between them.

These *had* to be the same cells.

Down the path, a singular tray sat in arms reach of the bars behind it. And a tin can, open on top, was the only item on the tray. I heard his steps, unwavering and unrelenting, and slowed my pace.

"Okay, okay!" I yelled, turning with my hands up above my head.

A wall of assault paused inches before me. I could feel the tingling energy, the neediness crackling the controlled surface.

Imre sauntered up, puzzled but relieved.

"Let's go." He pulled a glowing chain from the pouch on his chest that, at the snap of his wrist, made the magnetic balls of the chain solidify into cuffs. "Des is going to be *furious.*"

"I couldn't sleep," I said, sidestepping incrementally. The distance between us remained, but he continued to circle me with the rigid chain firmly in his grip.

"I told them *be careful, be gentle,* and here we are, with nosy eyes on our ungrateful guests regardless." *Just a bit further.*

Maybe the softness I had seen down here before was a ploy. Because there was no kindness in his auburn eyes now. It was a show, a false flag to convince me that maybe this one would give us an inch of wiggle room. *One more step.*

"You played your part well."

His lips turned up with a sinister delight that made my throat clench. It was like looking at someone else entirely. The gentle features warped and were ragged.

"I always do." He grinned.

I walked toward him in defeat, lowering my hands so that my wrists were toward him.

As he reached for them, I launched forward, and he instinctively backed away, shoulders pressed against the metal bars behind him. The patient darkness behind him grinned, opening up to reveal bone-white talons that hungrily accepted my gift. A set of claws clamped down on his neck, and an upward slice in the blackness hollowed out a string of sharpened, pointed teeth. A smile, too wide, hovered in the nothingness. A room of teeth and claws.

He thrashed, and his eyes widened in horror, gripping the talons, trying to lift them off of his skin.

His arms were pulled between the bars, so his chest was arched, and a chilling voice like none in this world whispered, "Thank you," before pulling his limbs back harder.

I ran. I didn't turn, despite the escalating screams begging me to reconsider. I soared, and my chest burned from the air. I pushed through it. Hallways broke from prison cells to guest suites, and I knew I had only moments to reach our room.

Imre's voice lingered in my mind. But I didn't have time to consider what I'd done.

As I approached our suite, out of breath and shaking, I swung the door open wide so that it nearly caught on the interior wall of the room. I entered, ready to reveal the vial I had taken and begin to potentially process all the others stored deeper below ground, but found the room empty.

Of course. I had gone over my twenty minutes, and they left to search. I fed myself that lie as I took in the sheets on the floor, the broken lamp, the signs of struggle. I went over to the nearest bed and flipped through the pillows. I ran to the bathroom to find it as I had left it. The door between the separate rooms was hanging off its hinges, so I carefully went to see what state the adjoining room was in.

And it was so much worse.

Blood sprays were on the sheets, reflective wetness shimmering even off their black faces. My breath was chaotic. *Calm yourself.* I demanded control from my trembling limbs as I searched through what I could—but there was nothing worthwhile. The side table was knocked over, a mug of tea I imagined Kori was drinking out of had been thrown at the furthest wall, broken pieces littering the floor.

"I've had enough of your insubordination," a voice growled from behind.

I spun to face Desmond at my heels. His hand gripped my neck before I could think, and he threw me against the wall connecting the rooms. My legs kicked, and rage clanked between my teeth as he held me suspended and dangling.

I tried to yell something nasty or threaten what I could, but his fingers pressed against the sides of my throat, and stars appeared in my vision. I tore at his forearm, ripping my nails into his skin and gashing his flesh. But his hold didn't waver.

"You're making things complicated," he hissed, moving his face closer to mine as the sparks and blurriness flew. "You have no idea what you've done."

I dug my nails deeper, and he tightened his hold, lifting my body away from the wall and slamming it back again, so my head jarred into the surface. I waited for a hit, a dislocated jaw, but none came. He squeezed until the air drained from my lungs and the sparkling displays in my eyes eclipsed the sight before me. My hands fluttered down in defeat as my mind slipped away.

I woke in a cell not dissimilar from the one I started in. But I wasn't alone.

"They took the other two for questioning," Tillian said from a darkened, hunched-over shadow in the room.

My head throbbed, and I tenderly touched my neck—I wondered if his touch would bruise. Tillian stayed seated as I crawled toward him, my limbs still waking with a resentful ache.

"I'm sorry, I should've come back faster. I didn't—"

"They barged in right after you left," he said, lifting his head. His eyes were dark and empty. "They must've known we'd try to leave again."

"I saw blood."

"A bunch of men came. The two siblings and a few others separated into both rooms. I had barely put on my pants when they knocked me to the floor. The others were screaming, and I tried to get to them, but I was fucking useless. Zymir kicked down the door between the rooms, Kori was with him, to come get *me*—there were downed bodies behind him, I have no idea how he did it—but as soon as he entered, Reid incapacitated him, made his muscles into stone." His words were dragged and rigid. "Reid stilled our bodies, and they dragged us all down here."

I wished this was a terrible dream. A suffocating, immobilizing dream I could count to three and be free from.

"Desmond wasn't there?"

"No. Why?"

"He was who was waiting for me when I got back..."

His head peeked up, and he finally reached toward me, pulling me into his arms. "Are you all right?"

I nodded my head against his chest and burrowed into him. He rubbed the nape of my neck, slowly circling over the bunched-up hair. I hated this. I wanted to curl up and sob. I wanted to rock myself into a blubbering mess until I exhausted myself into nothing. But I couldn't. Not yet.

A light turned on, and the entire room was illuminated. We were in a cage, a cell in the middle of a room with stone shelves and assorted steel devices hung up on swaying hooks—tongs and pliers and varying lengthened blades. There was an operating table near us. Leather straps stuck out at each corner. It was a solid chunk of porcelain that was hoisted from ties on the ceiling. There were pulleys near one end, excess rope coiled should it need to be tipped downward and wiped clean. In the center of the room, a grated drain. A blood-stained, grated drain. The holes between the crisscrossing metal looked sticky and congealed.

I pictured the body in the forest. I imagined the horrors inflicted upon Zymir's sister. Were similar terrors delivered in this room?

Were we about to be on the receiving end of such nightmares?

The single door in the room opened, and Zymir and Kori walked in. Her head was down, and she led toward the cell, with Zymir trailing and his face a calm neutral.

"We'll be back shortly," an airy, cold voice said.

The guard escorting them was taller than Zymir. His chest was covered in plated shoulder protection and light chain mail. A broad sword's helm peaked up from his back. As he reached to unlock the cage, his soil-colored eyes darted up. "Get to the back of the cell."

I hesitated. My mind felt like glue. Tillian stood and offered me a hand, which I grabbed and used to hoist myself onto my legs. We inched to the furthest part of the cell and waited as the guard opened the door, ushering in the two with a hard hand on their backs.

His shoulder had a golden sun painted on the armor, and the hilt of his blade had the same. He strolled out of the room, whistling. As the door shut, the switch for the lights clicked off again, its location outside the room, and darkness fell upon us once more.

"How do you suppose we get out of this one?" It was Kori's voice, not shaking with fear as I expected, but strong.

"I'm open to suggestions," Tillian said. I could feel him step closer. Our arms brushed against one another.

"How did your...questioning go?" I asked, thankful I hadn't seen any wounds on them but aware that didn't mean much. I wondered if Imre had made it from the clutches of that beast in the cell.

"It didn't," she said. "They sat us in an empty room, told us Desmond would be there shortly, and then rushed out."

"Well, that's...good? That's something. I'm glad they didn't..." My voice trailed off, and I let the silence fill the sentence.

"Oh, it's not," she said, her voice dropping solemnly. "When they returned, they said Desmond was leaving and would be unable to commence the questioning until tomorrow. But..."

Distant solitary droplets echoed in the chamber.

"We overheard them yelling in the hall," Zymir picked up for her.

"And?"

"They're moving, Desmond and a few hundred men, from the sound of it—they're planning on attacking Alaria and taking the capital." Zymir's voice was annoyingly calm, and Tillian's body went rigid at the words.

"I'm sorry, *what?*" I hated the darkness. I could see their silhouettes and feel the helpless air amongst us, but I craved seeing them so I could gauge their reactions better.

"That map you and Tillian saw was not an old one like we had thought. It held their plans to cut off the snake at the head—close off the capital from all sides, choke its resources until she recedes."

"You'd need more men if your goal was preventing the influx of resources," Tillian said sharply.

There was a seemingly endless silence that ate away at us. Because while we feared for our fate trapped in this cage, the fate of so many more now dangled before us, and our own captivity seemed to pale in comparison to what would befall the innocent living within Alaria. A few hundred men couldn't possibly blockade all the roads in and out of the city. But they could go door-to-door slaughtering, painting the streets red like they had all those years ago.

"We need to warn them," the words yanked from my chest out into the charged room.

"How?" Tillian's arms were tensed, and he moved a hair away. "We're trapped in this damned cell—if we *could* get out, we'd still be without our weapons, we'd still need to escape their guards, and we're still nearly a week out from the city's perimeter."

"I know where our weapons are," Kori said with a jolt. "Sabina had mentioned them offhand earlier."

"And Imre...Imre shouldn't be a variable, at least." I could feel Tillian's quick turn toward my mumbling, but I didn't feel like elaborating.

"I can get us out of the cell." Zymir wasn't shuffling uncomfortably like the rest of us were, but despite that, on the edge of his tongue was a quiver of emotion. The gold of his eyes lit up, brightening the space between us in the room with a warm glow. I stepped back despite myself. Our eyes met, and across the distance, I remembered the look he had when we escaped Vayne—an animal backed into a corner, or a rabbit caught in a trap.

"We'll wait until the guard comes again. And when he does, follow my lead."

He blinked, and the lights in his mesmerizing eyes dimmed. Time seemed painfully slow, but we waited. I felt Tillian move in front of me, slight enough that my shoulder grazed his back. The positioning had happened seamlessly at the eerie change in Zymir's eyes, but he said nothing of it.

The lights turned on, and my eyes stung. It was the same man as before, the skin under his eyes blued from exhaustion. How long had we been stuck in this prison? An hour? Several? Drawing out time made each second scrape by.

"Back of the cell," he ordered, lazily watching us scramble as he held the lock and waited for us to comply.

He slipped the key in and turned. He chewed on the inside of his cheek as it unclicked, pulling the heavy door out and holding a hand to keep us stationed where we were.

"Just you two this time." He pointed at Tillian and me, curling his fingers and gesturing for us to walk forward. He blew a strand of golden hair up off his face as we hesitated. "I won't ask again."

I avoided side-eyeing Zymir and walked toward the open door.

His foot jutted out, catching mine just as I began to step, causing mine to tumble over his and fall toward the filthy ground. I caught myself on hands and knees, cursing and throwing a vile look his way for good measure.

"None of that," the guard barked, his hand twitching as if wanting to reach for his blade. "Get up!"

I groaned, grasping my knee and cursing. Tillian waited, leaning over to offer help standing. "*Fuck*, come on," I leaned back onto my butt and rubbed my kneecap, adding an extra whine to my voice as I added, "Gods, that hurt! Can't keep to your own corner?"

"Can you not watch where you're walking?" Zymir asked, flicking his eyes down, bored.

"All right, enough. Get up." The guard rolled his eyes and reached out to hurry us along.

Zymir's hand snatched his arm before I could blink. He bent it backward and heaved the man onto his knees. The young guard's mouth hung open, and his pupils danced wildly between us.

"Pl-pl-please," the man dribbled as Tillian took the guard's blade from its sheath. "You don't understand, we're—"

"I don't care," Tillian said, the broad sword twirled dangerously in his hands. "What're your men planning?"

"Nothing! Nothing, I swear!" The bounce in his hair seemed almost charming as his face trailed from Tillian's to Kori's to my own. "We're not *planning* anything. We're—"

"We don't have time for this," Zymir said. He pressed the man further down with his knee and, with his spare hand, clenched the back of the guard's neck. With a sharp snap of his wrist, the man fell with a thud.

"Hold on!" Tillian rushed to Zymir, brows raised and eyes wide. "We didn't say to *kill* him. That wasn't—"

"He's fine," Zymir replied, walking past all of us to exit the cage. "He'll probably have a headache from such a clumsy landing, but he's unconscious. He's fine."

The slacked body rose and fell slightly, subdued breaths confirming his claim.

The air in the room moved as if sucked up into the space around Zymir. His face paled, cheeks hollowed. The skin looked dry and flaky. He turned away from my notice, casting his gaze down.

"Put his body under the table," he said softly.

Tillian looked as if he wanted to question the order, but he obliged without issue, as if knowing that despite the lack of time for the apology that was in order for his behavior earlier, he'd at minimum follow his directive now. He took the guard's upper body, and Kori held his boots as they walked him toward the porcelain table. I couldn't move my eyes away, despite Zymir's inability to meet them.

His snow hair started to look dry and weathered, and soon strands fell to the floor. He looked up over his shoulder for a fleeting breath and, as he exhaled, craned his neck backward. The taut skin crackled pink, and grayed pieces of skin, like bark on a birch tree, peeled off. The pieces of flesh coasted down in the air but dissolved into tinier flakes before they could hit the ground.

A thump and the body had been placed. But the two stayed near the table, lingering, waiting.

More flakes of skin and hair shed from Zymir's statue until pockets of what lay underneath began appearing. Tanned skin darker than his own peeked out, and strands of dark hair grew from his scalp, spreading and growing until it landed just above his shoulders. His body continued to molt, shedding pieces of itself that disintegrated into mere twinkles in the light.

A final blink, with an inner eyelid that crossed his eye horizontally, and the golden orbs were a gentle, warm auburn. Even his chest had shed, sharpening into more rounded muscles and a slightly wider build.

The face that stared back at me hesitated to speak.

"Let's go. I'll tell them I'm moving you all to a different cell block." His stare flickered to the wall where amongst the instruments for torture were extra chains and cuffs, some for necks and some for wrists, others still in such odd assortments I couldn't make sense of them. "It would lend to our story if you followed in chains..."

"Absolutely not." Tillian was blinking fast and rubbing at his face, as if doing so would wipe away the changes he witnessed on the face looking at us. "Absolutely *not*," he repeated, leveling himself against the table as his legs wobbled. "Just what...what..."

Kori steadied him, a patient hand resting against his wobbly arms as he leaned.

"He's a shifter." Her voice didn't tremble. She wasn't afraid. Her voice held *wonder*. And watching the gleam painted over her face ignited a wonder of my own as I sought to memorize the look—Kori, who stopped so that her fingers could trace the ridges on the trees. Kori, who followed the scattered path of wildflowers. Kori, who smiled before monsters.

CHAPTER 27

I hadn't moved. Marveling at the exact replica of Imre had me torn. Torn between dwelling on how I'd left the real Imre to his fate with the creature in the darkness several floors below, and the more pressing matter: Processing that Zymir was not human. He merely wore human skin.

I immediately recalled the story of his sister with newfound understanding. His hatred toward Sheirsan hunters wasn't general—it was personal.

"There are three men approaching," he said. "They'll reach the door in six minutes if we don't leave now."

So many things were clicking into place. Cogs in an unusual machine I had felt misfiring but couldn't diagnose until now.

"Weapons next, was it?" Kori asked with a wink, aligning us back to our task at hand.

A dangerous moment. I could see it in the way Zymir's more almond-shaped eyes now creased in concern, the way his Adam's apple bobbed and sank. An animal with its leg caught in a trap, its only option to bite off its own appendage in hope the exchange would yield a better outcome.

Shifter.

Monster.

The shiver that had ran up his spine that day in Vayne—the only gap into what his walled-off mind was like—had revealed a creature cornered, desperate to be free, willing to pay whatever the cost to live. To *live*.

This wasn't the face of a monster.

This was the face of the hunted.

"Weapons." I nodded back. "I guess Mi can take it easy. Lead the way." I tipped my head toward Kori and while even the friendly skin he wore did little to help his expressionlessness—the slight uptick at his lips was more than enough to have a smile yank at my cheeks.

It felt like madness, really. To be smiling here.

But there was a profoundness that resonated in my core as I saw the recognition in him. The moment he registered that *I saw him* and that *I was not afraid.*

"Let's go." Tillian was beside me, his hand holding my bicep. A twitch of his lip, and he added, "After you," to Zymir.

We walked, following Kori and Zymir's lead. We couldn't run without drawing too much attention, so we hovered into a casual, too-eager gate. Tillian had dropped his hold on my arm but stayed close, his eyes never leaving the back of Zymir's head.

Obtaining the weapons was mindless and without issue. A simple storage closet nestled between rooms on the first floor of unimposing guest suites. The closet had cleaning equipment on the bottom shelf, some folded towels and linens, and rows of assorted bath oils. The top shelf, hardly hidden, held our weapons. Lazily settled atop one another, my velvet bag sat crumpled at the back.

As I fastened my belt, counting to make sure all six blades were present, a familiar heaviness rested on my hips. The comfortability gave me a glimmer of hope that we'd do this. *Actually, do this. Actually get out of this place.*

A droplet of optimism was more than enough to refuel me. And I sorted through our next, more challenging dilemma—*how* to get out of here.

"How much of a head start could we have if we left tonight?" I asked.

We were wandering the halls now, backtracking and absent-mindedly staying just close enough to the cells that our excuses would seem believable.

"And go back through the snow?" Kori asked, brow raised. Her hair spun as she shook her head dramatically. "We barely made it through the first time, and we had rested all night before. Now?" She snorted. "We'd have to be fast. And I mean *really* fast if we wanted to beat them anywho."

Think.

Think.

Think.

"They have to get supplies here somehow." Step after step warned me our time was fleeting. "In the winter, when the snowfall is even greater, how do they bring in extra food? There may be farmable land to the north, but that tiny stretch wouldn't be enough to feed them for long. Not if they had to carry it on foot."

"There are other marks," Zymir pondered, "that deal with ingenuity, the innovation of resources. Some with the skills to create things such as your *Mion.*" He cocked his head as he said it, unsure of what else to call it. "And this is a place where the Weaver Marked may find refuge."

"And maybe they used those abilities to help solve that problem..." I brainstormed with him, letting the idea linger. "How?"

"What would be the easiest way to traverse over snow banks, through endless forests, undiscovered by others all the while?" Zymir sounded genuinely puzzled as we looped another corner we must've already passed twice.

"There's no way." Kori chuckled dismissively, rolling her eyes. "You'd have to fly over!"

I spun my face toward Zymir, who stopped in his tracks. Kori's chin drooped as her head oscillated back and forth between Zymir and me.

"No." She laughed, waving her hand through the air. She blinked. "You can't possibly think they could *fly* over?"

"That, or tunnel?" Tillian offered sheepishly. "But these floors already go so far deep, I couldn't imagine how much further they'd have to dig to accomplish that."

I pondered both outrageous ideas. The lines between reality and possibility blurred now that creativity was amplified with abilities that could turn water into healing and thoughts into weapons.

"I wouldn't have any idea where to look," I admitted. "Or what to look for. Can you...would you be able to track something like that?" I asked Zymir, who was already shaking his head.

"No, I may have heightened senses," *or something like that...there would be time for questions later,* "but I can't track that which is handcrafted."

"Well, Mi, I guess you're back in." I tapped my fingers into my pocket, only to find eye prongs already erect and coiled legs half undone. "Eavesdropping, were we?"

Zymir stopped as we turned a corner and faced another hall that came to a fork. Uneven footsteps sounded from up ahead, and Zymir's back stiffened, his hand paused behind him to silence us. He didn't bother to turn back as an unfamiliar body strolled from across the hall in front of us. The female silhouette paused and glanced over, her hand drifting to the sword at her waist. Her pale blue eyes focused on Zymir, and then she leaned to the side to see our bodies tightly lined up behind him.

"Everything all right over there?" she called, tilting her head. Her voice was direct and strong, a full sound that matched the rigid armor covering her abdomen and the slant of her held-high chin.

Zymir sidestepped so that his body blocked ours. His clothes were the same dark gray tunic he typically preferred, sensible, not unusual, or remarkable in any way. I hoped they'd be bland enough they wouldn't yield questions. It's not like I'd had the forethought to strip Imre of the glossy white top he had been wearing down in the prisons.

"Transporting," Zymir's voice honeyed over, a perfect immolation of Imre's gentleness. "You can accompany me if you'd like?" He shrugged, and I caught the corner of his alluring smile. Though he wore Imre's lips, the mere sight of such a flirtatious smirk made me stifle the shock threatening my face.

She looked him up and down and raised the corner of her lip. "I think you're more than capable of taking care of that yourself." She tapped her forehead knowingly, and I was glad our gamble that others were familiar with his mind-altering abilities paid off. Because the last thing I had wanted was to don chains or cuffs again. My neck still ached from the blisters they had gifted me at dinner.

"Suit yourself." He winked and tossed his long dark locks over his shoulder.

She continued down her perpendicular hall, and we waited out the seconds to increase the distance between us.

"Where were you on that one?" I whispered behind him.

"I apologize." he turned slightly. "Her smell is...*unusual*...it crept up on me."

That made me uneasy. Trusting Zymir's tracking abilities was a fundamental aspect of getting out of this maze unseen. If that became unreliable, our presence would surely set off concerns sooner or late.

"All right, we need to at least try to find something *now*," I warned. "Mi, let's go!"

"We don't even know what we're looking for. I doubt it'll be able—" Tillian's tone was growing tight and impatient.

But Mion scurried out before he could conclude his sentence. Prancing and jovial, it climbed up to my shoulder in a whirlwind, tapping its spidery legs in rapid succession.

"Mi, I need you to locate..." I scanned the curious faces of my companions as they watched me attempt to determine how to best word our request, "um, something *crafted*. Something *big* and *created* just like you." It slowed its repetitions, contemplating.

I contemplated as well, trying to think of something that could carry us over the vast lands from here to Alaria...

Mion lowered its body closer to my skin, analyzing. Carry us *over* the land. It was vague and naïve, but we had nothing else to try, no other options to explore. Because if we were to get to Alaria too late...it wouldn't be worth journeying there at all—who knew in what state they'd leave the city.

Mi didn't budge from its perch. Waiting.

Perhaps I wasn't specific enough.

Perhaps with the skills Zymir spoke of, there were *several* artificial creations beneath the mountain. I imagined how precarious our journey here was—how narrowly we had avoided disaster out in the harsh elements. And then I remembered what had led our path from the forest edge to the endless winter of Icesone. I pictured the glistening golden brown wings, expertly navigating the air, diving from the sky, and swooping toward tree limbs like they were nothing.

Wings.

"Mi, we need an artificial creation with wings," I added. Zymir's lips pressed together, their ends a flicker of an upturn, and he dipped his head in agreement.

And Mi nearly leaped from my shoulder. I leaned forward, trying to catch it, fearful it'd break its tiny metalwork with a landing from up high, but it settled safely on its coils. It popped an eye prong up and down, and then blew down the hall.

We chased, trying to keep up with its speed as it soared down a hall we hadn't taken yet. In another time, I'd have loved to see a layout of this place. It's endless loops and halls and rooms—this maze, how long had it been here? Surely some of those prisons had been here long before the Family had disappeared. For how long has this place been hidden amongst the snow and ice?

At the end of a hall we faced a door painted a deep forest green, with twining filigree sketched overtop, surrounding a woman's face with fangs and pointed ears, just like the emblem on the map we had seen earlier.

The door was average width but ran from the floor all the way flush to the ceiling. Mi wasted no time, tapping its footing along the edge and circling the handle impatiently. The handle was steel, and instead of a knob, there was a cut-out hole so your fingers could curl inside to move the door. No hinges. I shook the internal mechanism to force the door open, pulling it toward me and pushing it away, but it didn't budge.

Mi darted up and down in quick succession next to my hand. I immolated its action and tugged *up* on the handle. The door rose from the ground, slipping higher into the ceiling, revealing a metal room barely large enough to fit us all. I hesitated, but Mion dove into the room as if to say *let's go, you were the one who said you were in a hurry.*

We packed in tight, shoulders all touching and bodies uncomfortably warm by proximity.

"No offense," Kori piped up, "but the sooner we figure out how this works, the better. Not that I don't like the company, but godsdamn do some of you *stink.*" She sniffed the air and squinted at me. "Why do you smell so...minty?"

I stifled a laugh and shot her a look. *I'll explain later.*

"Mi, um, what do we do?"

Mion, who had finally reperched on my shoulder, spun around once, slowly, a sarcastic move which said *looks like I have to do everything myself.*

It jumped to the dark-gray wall and climbed to the top of the room, suspending itself on the ceiling, where a series of identical round buttons rested just above our heads. It hovered past the first six buttons, lined in rows of two, scrolling across to the second set of six, landing on the last button all way at the end. Thirteen buttons total. With a dangling, loosely wrapped metal appendage, it pressed onto the button and then unclipped itself from its hold. Mi detached, landing roughly on my head, its prickling feet scratching my scalp as it hurried not onto my shoulder, but all the way into my pocket. I could feel it roll into a tight ball.

"Should that be worrying?" Tillian asked, face flushed with heat.

I parted my lips to reply as the ground trembled beneath us. Metal clanking and a woosh of steam sounded loudly above our heads. The metal sheath door slammed back down, trapping us.

With a final shudder of the room, all the concerning noises stopped.

And then the room flew up.

The world shook, and the walls vibrated. I feared they'd collapse onto us, our momentum causing me to shift all my weight into my knees and steady myself. It was *loud,* churning gears and whistling steam erupting from above our heads. I understood why Mi was curled up now. Our closet-sized room was catapulted higher and higher. Tillian had both arms out, stabilizing himself between two of the walls with wide eyes and his mouth ajar.

Kori looked positively wild. Elation radiated from her, and she didn't bother to brace herself, a sparkle in her eyes as they teared up from the force of moving higher. The ends of her hair bounced off her forehead and danced against her ears.

The eventfulness was short-lived, and the movement came to an abrupt halt that made a disorienting dizziness circle in my vision. On seasick legs, I wobbled on the no longer moving ground.

"Get me out," Tillian murmured between the hand covering his mouth. "I need out."

I reached for the handle and lifted the door, sliding it back on its track and letting him dart out ahead. He hunched over, breathing heavily through careful bursts of air to prevent his still sloshing stomach from discarding its upset contents. I averted my eyes partially for privacy and partially to avoid him seeing the suppressed giggle daring itself out my mouth.

"Oh my..." Kori was speechless, and I had barely noticed anything other than Tillian's sensitive stomach.

My vision widened, and I stumbled back a step. We were on an exposed platform carved out of the mountain's top. We weren't just at one of the peaks. We were practically in the clouds. A shimmering dome wrapped up high, evidently protecting the dark cement from the elements as snow fell onto the translucent edge and slithered downward. The ground itself was dry, the air comfortable. But all around was a dizzying array of high winds and snow slapping into the face of the dome that coveted a space between two other far-off peaks.

The horizon belonged to the dense, endless sea of stormy clouds that were engorged by full bellies of flurries. I hadn't realized how lost my sense of time was or how much I had craved the openness above the mountain's maze. I longed to feel the wind brush my cheeks, but with the elevation we were at, that gentle touch would tear into the hollows under my eyes. I wondered if it was violent enough up here that it'd rip the long strands of hair from my scalp.

I was so distracted by the air above me that I hadn't even realized Kori's head wasn't tilted up at the jagged mountain peaks. I found her turned around, facing the opposite direction than where the metal door had opened us up to.

It was then that I understood her gasp.

There were ships like none I had ever seen.

Ships, not just on land, but a mountain's height above the ground. Dozens of them lined up in neat lines. A whole fleet of ships hovering straight up despite no seas to cradle them. Masts stabbed empty in the sky, nearly grazing the protective layer shielding us above. There were no sails, and they were slimmer than the boats I'd seen docked in Vayne. They appeared to be made out of some sort of wood—the edges were expertly smooth and the surface a deep red-brown. Kori was running, indifferent to the risks, and pointed directly toward the nearest vessel. There were several different sizes of ships. The row nearest to us held the smallest and the ones further towered over those. I refused to consider just how many men could fit atop each.

I followed, waving on the other two hurriedly. If this was our way out, whatever this was, we might as well be quick about it.

"I've never seen something quite like this." Kori breathed, her palm reaching toward the finely rounded nose of the ship.

Ships on water came to a point, often adorned by carved statues for decorum. But these were rounded on both ends.

"Can you feel that?" Zymir asked, scanning the entity down its length.

At our silence, he, too, felt the ship, cautiously letting his fingers trace the smooth edge for just a second before withdrawing in a shutter.

"Well, what're you waiting for?" Kori asked, circling the ship to where the gangway was open and extended from the ship's body.

She took careful steps onto the ramp and began inspecting the inside. It wasn't expansive. There was no room to go below deck like on some of the larger models that had deep hulls. I followed her, scanning for any means of flying this thing.

"Where're the wings?" Tillian asked skeptically, the last to follow suit.

I felt Mi in my pocket, still tucked into a ball, satisfied that we'd gotten to where we were supposed to and indifferent to assisting us further.

Zymir scratched at his neck as he neared the front of the ship, deep gashes slicing through his disguise that sutured themselves back up. Maybe wearing different skin was uncomfortable. Perhaps it couldn't be sustained for long. Or maybe the prospect of soaring through the skies had him as nervous as me.

At the bow, the helm stood as it would a normal ship, wide spokes on a wheel that could direct our trajectory. Except near the very center of the wheel, at the axel where the handled spokes met, was a sharply cut gemstone. The gemstone was chiseled, so it bore eight sides for each spoke to originate from, and in this lighting, it looked like it could be green, or blue, or gray—against the wood from which it rested, the colors were muted and hard to distinguish.

"I do feel that," Kori whispered, as if only now hearing Zymir's question.

She stood next to me, inspecting the wheel, running fingertips along the creases in the wood and ducking under to observe it from the opposite side.

I slanted my head at her, and she clarified, "It feels like...it feels like something is aware we're here. I feel...like we're being watched." At Tillian's side to step to move further near the ramp, she waved a hand at him. "It feels like acknowledgment, not...not anger. It almost feels like..." She bit her lip and continued inspecting the helm.

"Like it's half asleep," Zymir finished.

Kori nodded and slipped under the wheel again, now back at helmsman position, her hands gripped on the handles. She tried moving the wheel to trigger a reaction, but the ship didn't move. She ran her forefinger along the lines of the gemstone in the center, outlining, searching.

A grumble groaned out, so subtle it was as if the wood was simply sighing at our weight. Her tracing paused, and in the center of the stone, a pinhole-sized flicker of light illuminated and then was gone.

"Do that again." Tillian breathed, his back to the edge of the ship, his hands firmly gripping the wood that came up waist high. Inch by inch, with his hands planted, he joined us at the bow.

She started at the top, traced over and then under, and met her origin point, but nothing responded this time. She slipped off her ring and tried again, the swirls on her thumb lighting up in a soft blue glow.

Another flicker in reply, stronger. It grew from the size of a pinpoint to half its width, roughly the size of my palm.

"Oh, come on." She closed her eyes and inhaled, her chest rising and holding. She sat the base of her hand at the base of the stone, cupping her hand over most of it, and then firmly set her skin flush on the surface.

The groan we had heard returned, and the ship rocked back and forth. Her eyes shot open, and they appeared far away. She nodded a few times, as if listening.

"It's awake." The dangling edges of her hair blew backward as if caught in a gust of wind, though I felt no breeze. "*Oh*, she's awake. Everyone, hold on tight. I'm going to try something."

Tillian scooted himself down the wall to sit, tucking his knees to his chest. Zymir and I stayed on either side of her, each of us with a hand on the wooden stern and a hand on her shoulder. I glanced at him, at the skin starting to flake away to reveal the pale beneath it. The ends of his hair were shortening, spots of white peeking through.

"Are you sure this is—"

"Nope!" Kori cut off Tillian with a wide grin, and streams of light jumped off the stone, circling her hand and wrapping around it.

There seemed to be nothing in this world that caused her to flinch, to hesitate. I had never met someone who embraced the unknown so fully.

She didn't bother to close her eyes as she tilted her hand back onto its heel and gazed up toward the sky.

Wood creaked and groaned, rocking back and forth. The ship leaned backward, and I planted my feet firmly to accommodate the incline. It was upright, angled toward the sky just as the metal box we'd arrived in shook violently and opened its mouth.

Someone else was here, I could see the box shiver with movement, and it was moments before they'd turn and see us making away on one of their ships.

"Kori, we—"

"Give her a second," she hushed. Her fingers wove the light strands still whirling around her hand.

I could hear it before I saw it, the sound of air flapping against the ground. Louder and louder, stronger gusts of wind smacked down beneath us. And the ship began to rise. I peeked out over the side but saw nothing, the sound a drum of wind and power.

As the angle we hovered at began to even out, I sighed in relief. But the sigh was cut short as the air in my lungs was emptied, and the ship jolted upward and forward. A star rocketing through the night, we beamed upward. Feathery strands of light jutted out the sides—I could see them now, bright, strong lines made of light green light.

CHAPTER 28

Our path was up, and fast. My eyes were glued over the side of the ship toward the body exiting the metal door. He ran, white fabric flapping in the wind, his hair pulled back from his effort.

The auburn stare met mine, and I could've sworn I felt white hands haphazardly lash out toward us, but we were too far for their tips to reach. I wasn't sure how Imre had made it out of the prison cells with that *thing*, but as we popped out of the protective barrier and braced for the elements, I memorized his patient stance, rigid and watching us until his silhouette was little more than a shadow. And then, not even that. A memory, a blip, a fading feeling I hoped I wouldn't face any time soon.

We were all hunched down, as near to the ground as we could, except Kori, who somehow managed to stand despite the tumultuous winds whipping around the ship. Between the mountain peaks we rose, dangerously high, the air exhausting itself from our lungs. I patted at her, hurried slaps to try and get her to angle the ship down. But the sweat on her brow and fierce bite on her lip told me she knew as well—that too much higher, and we'd pass out from the elevation, leaving the ship unmanned and plummeting to the frozen wasteland below.

Violent howls clawed at my ears. I couldn't feel my face, and snowflakes clung to my eyelashes, intercepting my vision with every blink. The ship shook, magical wings beating against the currents, failing to fight their gust, and weaving sharply to the left. It tipped, teetering roughly, and we braced ourselves as balance somersaulted.

Flapping pushed against our lopsidedness, fighting to even itself, but our angle continued to dip. Tillian crouched on the side that it leaned toward, horror painted brazenly as he held onto the edge. We were nearly even with the horizon, tiptoeing the line of capsizing. My chest was seizing as we wiggled in place.

Kori had one hand on the gemstone, the other one on the wheel handles, fighting the force it demanded as it heaved down. She leaned dramatically against it, throwing her entire weight into the grasp. Zymir, still on the other side of her than I, braced next to her, lending her his stability as he reached for a handle to push it back the other way.

We were going to spill out.

The mountain air blew in a rage, and we shook again, bodies scrambling to regain hold. But the angle was too dramatic, too sharp for where Tillian was wedged, and I saw his loosening grip before he realized his fingers were slipping.

I lurched toward the center mast, sliding down and landing on it with my heels, rounding down and hooking my arm around its width. Peering straight down, I spotted the jagged rocks, the sharpened points that stabbed through the dense clouds surrounding us. I extended my hand, digging my other into the mast, my nails crying in agony.

He hesitated, and I saw the moment his regrip turned to clutching air. Panic stuck his eyes, and he flopped forward, reaching toward me, but the ground was pulling us, and the wind was shaking us. And his arm met nothingness but the space between us.

I was too far.

He'll die. The voice was monotone, uninterested.

But I knew the voice was right.

Do you wish to watch him die?

I blinked back the moisture blurring my sight. A current from above slammed down, and my mind lurched to the furthest reaches, to the barrenness. I dug into the space, the endless nothing. I scoured the crevices, wishing to be there instead of here. Wishing to hurl myself into the void. And a sizzling pain answered from someone deep in there, from a place I could not see, with words I did not understand.

But as I watched Tillian's body slide out of the ship, that pain found a home in my wrist, an excruciating crescendo that I focused on, let ground me and calm my frenzy.

We had escaped the maze of the mountain, and I wouldn't let him fall.

My wrist seemed pleased, the peak of pain dampening and a tingling radiating down my hand and through my outstretched fingers.

He'll die.

You'll watch him die.

I willed his body toward mine. Against the rocking that heaved him, his body refused to slip further out. It froze, temporarily free-floating, and I demanded that his hold reach mine—there could be nothing else. There would be no other outcome I would allow. As if caught by an unseen rope, he shot up, hand gripping mine and holding firm.

Zymir was yelling, the coarse, unusual sound breaking the trance I had been in. He had both hands on the wheel beside her now, and a throaty growl was erupting from his mouth. The airship's wings tucked in and then extended fully, forming a wall against the perilous winds. We stabilized even, and then darted back down. We flew down and down and down, away from the mountain top and away from the platform of ships.

The wind against my face turned from severe to brisk, and we followed the slope of the mountain down toward the ground. So close I could see the snow banks, the outskirts on the horizon of dense trees.

For a while after we stabilized, none of us spoke.

I stayed back against the mast, Tillian beside me, our breaths calming and synching.

As we broached the forest's edge, Kori angled the ship higher, above the tree line.

"I think we should be good now," she said, removing her hand from the controlling stone.

"You think?" Tillian was resting his head back, watching the dazzling night sky.

"I think," she said, finally collapsing onto the wood and resting next to the wheel. "It's some sort of elemental. The entity tied to this ship. They weaved her essence into the wood, using its magic to give it flight." She rubbed at her eyes. "But she knows where the palace is. And that's where we're headed."

"I'm not even going to ask."

I elbowed him in the ribs, but not sharply. "Well, I am. Elemental?"

"It's an old spirit, tied to the elements. They caught them, and the Ranu marked Weavers wove them into the wood, combining their air affinity with technology that gave the energy an outlet—an outlet that allows the ships to fly." Her voice was drained, tired.

The green emblem, the Ranu clan, was their name then. I made note of that and added it to my growing catalog regarding the four clans that comprised Sheirsa.

She must've seen the grimace on my face and quickly added, "Oh, she's not mad, though. She was..." she yawned, and her cheeks rose so that her freckles caught the moonlight, "confused, I think... I think she found this fate preferable to that of other elementals."

Servitude over death. A creature of the wind, light as air, constrained to a wooden tomb.

When your options are stripped, I supposed anything was better than not existing. I ignored the queasiness the thought brought me.

"And *she* told you this?" Tillian's forehead crinkled.

Kori rolled her eyes and sank, resting entirely on the wooden ground. The effort it took to get the airship safely out of the mountain's wind tunnel left all of us deflated, and in the crisp night air, a curtain of exhaustion dropped. She grumbled out a *mhm,* and her limbs softened.

If they hadn't already left, the Nevari would be trailing us soon. With not just a few skilled warriors, but fleets worth. Imre and Reid were plenty dangerous on their own. A battalion of Weaver Marked was nothing shy of a death sentence.

They could envelop Alaria in nightmares. Burn it to ash. Make the people forget its name or their own.

A comforting aroma of pine filled my nose, and I watched the grayed treetops in the distance. One of us should keep watch. Peering around, Zymir still stood near the hilt, his shimmering white air returned and his squared shoulders alert. I didn't know what the right answer was. I knew no amount of rationale could ever scrub clean the blood stains from the kingdom's hands. A veil had been lifted only at the corner, allowing me a peek into our genocidal past, but who knew how far the fabric stretched—who knew how much it concealed?

But that much power.

That much potential destruction.

I shivered. Wielded by the ambitious, those who'd stop at nothing in pursuit of complete control…If gone unchecked, there was nothing that could stop those with such gifts from reshaping this entire world.

The kingdom didn't need that power.

Sheirsa killed ruthlessly. Unambiguously.

They eradicated.

Drained the ponds.

Burned the roots.

Stained the earth.

Even without that power.

I ignored that pensive voice in my head and leaned closer against Tillian. I shushed its words, letting them drift to that spot of nothingness. The roughness of his fingers at the back of my head pulled me back into my body, shutting that door in my mind. The spots of warmth circled, rubbing the base of my neck, burrowing past my hair to gently touch my skin. I lowered my head onto his chest, sighing. My muscles relaxed. *Actually* relaxed, not just untensed.

I lifted my head slightly, letting the tip of my nose graze the soft skin under his jaw. His arm tightened around me, tucking my body into his. I couldn't move. Breathing in the air in the crook of his neck, the barest of my skin still hovering atop his, I couldn't will myself to pull away from the touch. Instead, I tilted my head, resting comfortably against the rhythmic rise and fall of his chest.

He paused and inched away. I flinched at the coolness that immediately filled the gap between where we had touched. But the space was then filled with his palms around my chin. His fingers scrolled back to behind my ears, where he curled his fingers and drew my face to his. Our lips met and parted, and I forgot where I was for a moment.

Forgot everything I was for a moment.

There was only the taste of him, the feel of his coarse hands cupping my face, the smell of lingering sweetness.

I waited until he withdrew his lips, a pained sigh escaping them. Against the moonlight, his eyes were clearer, a lighter shade of blue like springtime. They traced my face, staring at my lips, slowly raising to meet my gaze. I wanted to plummet again, freefall into his embrace. I considered diving, listening to that ache in my core that begged me to reach up to his lips.

But I knew if I did, I wouldn't stop. I'd lose myself in their want, oblivious to everything else around us. We lingered in that tension, tasting the static between our needing mouths. The hand he held at the back of my neck curled the hair around it into a ball, as if steadying us both from moving closer. I felt his eyes flicker to my slightly arched neck, and I pressed my lips together to keep the noise I threatened to make inside me.

Boots scuffled from the front of the airship, and the spell was broken. His grasp dropped as he shot a dangerous look behind me. But he turned to lean against the mast once more, pulling me close. His heart rate began to slow to normal, a comforting thud beneath my ear.

The wings of the ship were a cadence of air softly passing through the night, opposite the beats of his heart. I'd glimpse the light green lines of energy, the point of the shimmering feathers. Tillian and I watched through the repeated, momentary window to see the sparkling wings over the side of the ship as our bodies rose in unison.

The rhythm of everything lulled us to sleep.

As soon as the sun rose, we were all awake. Its arms stretched far, and there was no hiding from their touch. Far below, the birch and cedar had already replaced the spruce and pine. Leafy green was vibrant, alive. Minus the pockets where it wasn't, of course. From the elevation, pockets of burns were carved into the forest's face. Patches of singed earth stretched as far as I could see, their rims dark. I remembered the smell of the burning creature and shuttered at the thought of what each spot of scorched forest could mean. Kori was begrudgingly awake, a hand covering her eyes and a scowl beneath it. And I wondered if Zymir had moved at all last night, his statue still overlooking the front of the ship, standing turned away from us.

A blemish in the distance, a blurry darkness that I knew meant the palace was finally in sight, be it barely. I peeked over the edge of the airship, marveling at the vastness below. Tillian strolled up beside me, his hands wrapped around the wooden lip of the side.

"What is *that?*" Kori breathed, averting her eyes from the hilt and glancing toward Tillian's hand.

I followed her stare, and the blood drained from my face. Overtop his right hand, a black ribbon of dead skin curled, tucked underneath where I wondered if it continued. He withdrew his hands and shoved them deep into his pockets, swallowing hard.

"Let me see it," she said, leaving the wheel and reaching out to him. When he turned away, she scoffed and yanked at his arm. "Oh, come on," she chided.

He shifted his weight from one foot to the other as she inspected his hand. He wiggled his fingers, rotated his wrist, just as she instructed. She stroked the thick black line, and he confirmed he still had feeling in the skin.

"It's fine," he murmured.

She looked up at him exasperated until he stopped fidgeting. "There's no nerve damage, which is good. But still," she flipped his hand over and confirmed the mark wrapped around his palm, "the skin isn't just darkened, it looks irritated and raw." She pressed on the line harder, and he flinched back, but she held onto his wrist. "It almost looks like a rope burn."

I couldn't think straight.

You'll watch him die. I had heard it. Or thought it. I didn't have the energy to confront that building mass of snowballing questions picking at the wound left by my exchange in the mountains. Whatever the Nevari had done back there, whatever it was they thought they destroyed…

I didn't need fabricated walls constructed in my mind.

I had plenty of my own.

And those walls told me to stop peeking over what was left. Whatever this was, whatever was slowly tearing into my thoughts, in my voice, whatever it was that was spreading, was a maze all its own.

And I didn't have time to risk entering it. Not when I feared I'd never find my way out.

I blinked and met the concerned crinkle in Tillian's eyes.

"What?" I asked, my mouth suddenly dry.

Kori popped her hip out. "And here I thought you had managed to get more sleep than I had." She blew a strand of hair out of her sight. "I was asking if you had any water in your bag." She pointed to my velvet pouch. "I don't know if it'll do any good, but it won't hurt to try."

I stared at the bag, having forgotten it was wrapped over my shoulder. I shook my head and rubbed my temples. Everything seemed a bit too bright, a bit too loud. Orbs of light seemed to expand around their faces, the sun's strength seemingly greater.

"You all right?" Tillian reached for my elbow, but I heaved it away.

The wind against my cheeks smoothed the heat from the sky, but not enough. The rays prickled and kissed my forehead, focusing their attention solely on me. A tongue of heat licked the back of my neck.

Tillian's chest was behind me, and his arms looped up through the space under mine.

A rope burn.

When I was young, Tillian and I had found a rope in a vendor's square in the center of town. The armor vendor had left his shop in a hurry. His space was a mess, with empty boxes discarded and bottles laying on their side. We couldn't care less about that, though. We had run straight to the substantially long rope left rolled up atop a piece of cardboard, its frayed edges cut in a hurry.

The game was his idea. He gathered it up, wrapping it around his forearm. We took it to a less traversed alley closer to his house, where we unwrapped it into a straight line in the middle of the street.

Let's see who's stronger, he had challenged, spitting in his hands before gripping his end.

At the other side, I stared down at my pale hands, the strands of rope sticking up through my fingers. *Are you ready?* He yelled, slamming the rope up so that it slapped against the stone beneath.

I gripped hard, nodding. The rope slithered from my grasp, narrowly slipping right out before I fell forward to catch the very end of it. The rope scratched my palms, and as it tugged, my flesh stung. I kept my knuckles locked in place as he grumbled, frustrated, and yanked again. It felt like ants were biting my skin, but I refused to release my fingers.

The rope slacked for a moment, Tillian's body tilted toward me. The force of my hold propelled me backward, and the gasp in my chest resonated in my fingers leaping up. He snapped the rope, and it flew out in that space I had left open as I fell all the way onto my butt. He was cheering, jumping around with his loose end of rope. And I stared at my swollen, pink palms.

"Adelliah!" Tillian was crouched in front of me, waving his cupped hand so that air would meet my breath.

I was looking at Kori. My head was resting in her lap, and I stared up at her, her eyes shut in concentration. She fluttered them open and released the rigidity in her shoulders.

"What was that?" she asked, setting the back of her hand against my damp hairline. "Has she even done that before?"

"I-I don't think so," Tillian stammered.

The dials for brightness were back to normal. And my ears relaxed at the regular volume.

"I haven't slept well," I said, slowly lifting my head. "I'm fine." I sat up and noticed Zymir standing above Kori, the first time I had seen him standing at the front of the ship. I shifted off her lap, wiggling out from between them.

Tillian reached an arm out to slow my stand, but I dipped out of reach. I didn't want to be coddled, and I didn't want to be touched.

"I said I'm fine." My words were clipped and my tone harsh. Perhaps a tad harsher than I intended, but it served its purpose, and he let me walk through toward the front of the airship.

"When will we reach the city?" I asked. The smudge of the palace was already more defined. The shape of peaks could be seen starkly against the clear sky.

Kori and Tillian shared a look that I didn't bother to comment on. We had bigger problems than my lightheadedness.

"At this rate, we should be within the perimeter by nightfall." Zymir returned to his position and gestured up ahead as he spoke. "I imagine we'll want to find a more subtle way to make our appearance."

An airship landing in the center of the capital would most likely land us with swords at our necks, and I didn't feel like finding out if they'd let us speak or cut out our windpipes before we could.

"Kori, tell the ship we'll land on the western side of the city, along the forest where we came in last time. We'll enter on foot from the Sunset District."

"That's the *safer* option?" Tillian crossed his arms.

"It's practically abandoned," I countered. "And the guards have all but given up on policing the area."

"*Practically* abandoned, meaning the people who are left are the violent ones, the ones we have to worry about."

I rolled my eyes despite myself, and he shook his head in disbelief. "Zymir and I were there the night you met Kori, and it was fine." His eyes darkened. "Do you have a better idea?"

"I don't see why we can't just land closer to the center of town. By the merchants. Go the direct route and walk into the palace." I opened my mouth to speak, but he cut me off. "We're coming with news they need to hear, will *want* to know about. I don't get why we have to tiptoe in. They're—"

"They're quick on the draw and would sooner pluck the answers they want from our corpses than be thrilled with a dazzling display of magic and showmanship." My pulse was elevated, my patience dangerously thin. There was no reason for my severity, but I didn't possess the energy to argue.

"You think Sheirsan guards would *kill* us because we landed in this thing?" He cocked his head, and the condescending tone whispered to the embers igniting within me.

"Of course, *you* don't mind the guards, you've never caught their attention." I saw a flinch from Kori, which spurred the venom in my words. "You've never been asked to move from a dead sleep behind alley trash, and you've never had to hope their needy hands don't reach for where their eyes linger. We're entering from the west, and that's the end of discussion."

Maybe I understood Tillian's angry outbursts more than I realized. Because while the hurt that flashed in his face made me queasy, I couldn't deny that it felt unusually good letting the words in my mind spill out. I never brought up the conditions I lived through when we were young—when he'd go back home, and I'd drag myself to another vacant spot next to a particularly warm building. I never wanted him to know to what extent I struggled and fought to stand on even ground with him.

But that didn't mean I'd let his privilege go unchecked. Especially not now, when he'd had years to grow and understand the intricacies of the ever-growing poverty around him.

His grumble and turn signaled that he'd accept my directive. Zymir tilted his head when I met his stare, and I dismissed his inquiry without words. Tillian would be fine, and he wouldn't ask, because asking would reveal answers he didn't want to hear. And that worked plenty fine for the both of us. It always had.

I was angry, and I knew it was misplaced. I knew it was because I had left that mark on his hand. I wasn't sure how I'd done it, but I knew the unusual wound that stained his skin was my doing. And it seemed easier to throw my uneasiness into frustration than feed the welling self-doubt that demanded answers I couldn't provide.

I should've apologized. Not made him feel guilty for questioning my opinion.

And maybe that was why when he finally made his way toward the helm, where all of us now patiently watched the palace increase in size along the horizon, he didn't push the issue. His face wasn't even residually mad. There was a certain understanding as he caught me watching him, a look that reminded me that he knew firsthand how much easier it was to diffuse the anger at the unknown into something more tangible.

I wanted to ask him if he remembered when we played in the dirty alley with the rope. Maybe whatever gap the Nevari claimed to have discovered existed prior to those memories. And maybe if I asked Tillian, the warmth would return to his cheeks as he told me about how I struggled to sit for an entire week straight from the bruise I got from landing so hard. I knew I shouldn't let the ridiculous mind games they played gnaw at me so.

But still, I didn't ask.

I couldn't.

Because if he didn't remember, and the memories were not shared but my own, then I'd be left so much more utterly hollow than I already felt. And the echoes ricocheting in my head were already so loud I feared they'd crack my skull from the inside.

We were silent as the ship shifted slightly right, and we continued toward the ominous black mark in the skyline.

CHAPTER 29

T he airship landed roughly amongst the trees lining the western edge of Alaria. Dirt swept up from the earth, clouding the air as Kori steadied the machine just in time to avoid us spilling out. The seemingly endless sun had finally departed, leaving only lingering deep orange splotches amongst the clouds.

The path toward the palace was the same Zymir and I had taken. Or at least it looked like it. The streets looked the same, the smell of unclean bodies and human waste the same, the heavy atmosphere of hopelessness the same. It clung to my lungs and saturated my clothes. The outline of the moon was up—jarring yet patient, as it waited for the lingering brightness to subside.

I ignored the discomfort on Tillian's face as he tried to avoid staring up at the lifeless bodies crumpled like used trash down a particularly gruesome alley. Starved, empty bodies stacked upon one another, a lump of them. I reached for Kori's hand, expecting it to be rattling, but found it still. I held it regardless, her chilled fingers looping firmly. I refused to avert my gaze as we passed the destitute, the haunted, sunken eyes that clattered in their sockets absent-mindedly. Avoiding them somehow felt worse. Like turning away was to deny their existence, to ignore their plight in favor of my own convenience.

As we strolled deeper into the city's arms, I kept my head high not for pride, but in acknowledgment. So that they knew I saw them. And that I wouldn't pretend they were anything other than what they were—people, like me, traveling along paths they did not choose.

A familiar bald head appeared in front of an abandoned storefront. It hung loosely, held by his knees, his arms slacked beside him. We approached, and my gut clenched at the purple bruising covering the exposed skin. In his hand, an empty bottle, snugly protected in the rigid, cold grasp.

I had to know. I paused in front of the mass, waiting, hoping I'd see a gentle rise that could allow me to continue. When the movement didn't come, I broke from the group and stood before him. Standing felt wrong, so I quickly squatted onto my heels, bringing my face in front of his. Curiosity outraced apprehension, and I lifted his head back despite Osyren's face peeking at me between blinks. He was never far, reminding me.

When his exposed neck didn't reveal a wound, I caught a sigh escaping my lips. But it was short-lived. The bruising on his head had been nothing compared to his face. Swollen eyelids eclipsed his eyes, his cheekbones shattered inward, and his lips were torn. The blood was not fully dried. Prickled wet bubbles lay atop the darker red stains, outlining his nostrils and dribbling down toward his open mouth.

"This was recent," I said, unable to stand.

"Then we should be hurrying," Tillian grumbled, kicking at the dry dirt.

A grotesque smell reached my nose and momentarily broke me from my trance—followed by the shuffling of boots scuffing the ground. A wet laugh ground against my ears.

"He ain't goin' be hollering around here anymore," a disgustingly familiar voice snapped.

I turned to find the same man who had been hassling Adira leading two other men—both thin and straggly, smiling wide with missing teeth. Except one was balding, the other had oily shaggy hair that stuck to the sides of his head. The man at the front, Gage, wore a belt similar to my own, with assorted hag-tag weapons and dented blades stuck into the leather loops. He wiped the sweat from his chin and grinned.

"No more of his ramblin' nons—"

"What did you do?" I stared at the mole beside his nose, drilling a hole into it to avoid looking into his eyes. My voice was taut, coming from somewhere much deeper within me.

"What's it any business of yours?" He tucked his fingers into his waistband and leaned back.

Liar.

They're all liars. The homeless man had been rambling, stumbling out words regarding being tricked.

And he had ran. *Ran* when he had heard that sloppy laughter and snickering.

"Hey, we were just leaving." Tillian held up his hands and gestured with his head for me to join them.

"What did you *lie* about?" I found the words escaping my lips before thinking them.

Emotion lit Gage's face, a flash of something like shock and amusement twinged his cheeks upward. "Keely tell ya somethin'?" he asked, referring to the dead man. The others behind him shared a look and flashed their teeth.

I waited, knowing this loudmouth would fill the silence for me.

"I offered him a *fair* trade," he said, bowing sarcastically and waving encouragement from behind. "A fair trade! Loaf of bread for a bottle! One for one!" The men nodded. "It's not my fault he didn't want to trade back." His upper lip twitched.

The homeless man, Keely, had been slurring. He was upset and confused and lost. Visibly unwell, perhaps sick for a long while, enough time for it to wedge into his brain.

Recognition flooded my senses, and I turned away in horror at the bottle still clutched in his hand. I sniffed, bile tickling the back of my throat. "How many times?" I asked, a calm rage stifled.

"He kept falling for it." He shrugged. "The first couple times, I thought he'd forgotten 'cause he'd actually drank too much of the *real* stuff, but he'd forget so often he was practically in a loop."

The smell coated my nostrils, and it took everything in me not to retch right then and there. *Urine.* They had been tricking the old man, his brain no longer able to hold his memories, forcing him to relive their game daily. Offer the drunk some booze cause he couldn't resist it, trade him for his food, then hand him a bottle of piss... I could hear his voice in my head.

Liars.

"And that wasn't enough?" His mole twitched as I pointed to the bludgeoned man.

His face widened into a full smile. "What can I say?" He shoved his hands into his pockets. "I got bored."

A swift breeze tumbled through my mind in wicked anticipation. My skin pebbled, and I could feel each measured beat of my heart.

Thump... A bead of sweat snaked along his temple.

Thump... He swirled his thumb around the outside of his pocket, denting the fabric.

Thump... A protruding vein vibrated as he laughed.

Thump... Thump... Thump... Thump...

My fist was in his stomach.

Rivers of red washed over my wrist, and I could feel the rough leather of my dagger in my palm. A wet gurgle came from his mouth, and I twisted my blade back and forth, watching the bubbles spill out in his spit. I wondered if Keely stuttered as he died, trying to wedge out words between his broken teeth and fractured jaw.

There was a whirlwind of movement, blurs of bright colors whizzing past me.

A heavy droplet of blood hit the top of my boot. I could feel the warmth from the inside of his chest and yanked my arm back in fluttering shock. His body collapsed in an unoriginal fold and seized for a few moments on the ground. Panic rippled through my veins, and I blinked rapidly, hoping that the stains on my hand would disappear if I just kept blinking.

The two men still standing glanced between my companions, Tillian having ran up beside me and the others a step behind. Sensing their disadvantage, they scurried off into the night. My knees wobbled, the joints loose and uneven.

Kori had a hand on my back, pressed firmly against the sporadic, panicked breaths. "Let's get that hand washed off," she whispered, gently reaching toward my pouch.

I had water in my pouch. I didn't remember confirming that my canister still contained water. But she pulled the velvet from my side confidently and pulled out the glass bottle, twisting off the top and beckoning with her fingers for me to pass her my hand. I didn't look down as she splashed the liquid over my hand. She delicately scrubbed at my knuckles, swirled the water over the webs between my fingers, ran a stream under my nails. My damp skin felt exposed and alert in the chill of the evening air tunneling through the street.

"Let's go, it's getting late," Tillian said.

His back was still turned away from me. A thick coating of disgust filmed my vision as I stole a glance down at my boot. The single, round droplet dried and left a vague outline, nearly colorless against the black.

Kori peeked at me from beneath her brows and waited for my nod to start walking down the street. She gave Zymir a pleading look, darting from him to the body, and Zymir nodded. He effortlessly dragged the body next to Keely, the weight of it slouching over onto the ground.

We continued toward the palace, words removed from the space between us. I wondered where their thoughts were, what judgments flurried in their heads. I wondered what Tillian's spring eyes would reflect when I looked at them next. I wondered if Kori's hands felt tainted simply by touching mine.

But mostly, I wondered why, as I had plunged my blade into Gage, I hadn't seen Osyren's haunted orbs.

I hadn't seen the wound beneath his chin. Or his suspended, lifeless face from my dreams.

I hadn't seen anything at all.

Our path led to the crimson cobblestones in the center of Alaria. The path toward the palace was designated in its colors, speckled bricks painted yearly in red and silver to ensure the colors stayed vibrant. The street had silver crescents painted on the towering lamps that lined both sides of the street. And up ahead, the Alarian Gate, an archway that led to the double doors of the castle's main entrance—the same ones that used to stay open for parties and visitors.

As we traversed under the arch, the impending magnitude of the castle bellowed down upon us. Pointed columns, dazzling levels of stone that stabbed the clouds, flags flapping in the wind. Even at night, it felt like the palace was watching. Despite the fact it was merely a shell of its former glory. The dining halls and ballrooms had seen no liveliness since the night King Bryce and his family had disappeared. Shadows and dust replaced fanciful gowns and polite whispers.

As we approached the three levels of stairs that led up to the public entrance, Zymir slowed his pace. His golden eyes radiated in the early darkness of night, and they flickered up to the door and then back to the red bricks beneath him.

"I can't go in." He met our gazes and shook his head. "It would be unwise for one of my kind to join you. If anyone figured out what I was, your credibility would be jeopardized."

I wanted to object, but the sincerity in his eyes halted me. If things were to go awry, if we weren't believed, or worse, were believed to be traitors, then his fate would be gruesome and drawn out. And I couldn't bear to think of the cruelty they would deliver. I hated the thought of him waiting out here, but it was the only option.

At the base of the stairs, I turned around and approached him, understanding softening the disarray my face had been holding.

"I should have given this to you sooner. I apologize," I fumbled with the tie on my bag, "but everything happened so fast, and I nearly forgot." I reached the bottom of the bag as his eyes followed my every movement. "This is yours."

I extended my closed hand over his outreached one. As I transferred the vial into his palm, he blinked in immediate recognition as it touched his skin, even without glancing down.

"How?" A shadow eclipsed his irises. "Who?"

"The night we were caught. I had gone looking for this. Call it a hunch," I rolled my shoulders dismissively, "but I found it in a collection of..." my brain glossed over all the endless shelves of vials, "several others."

He finally spared a look at the shimmering liquid captive in his hold. His grip tightened securely around it.

"I still don't know who did it...if it was one of the Nevari or Desmond himself, but I wanted to make sure I gave this to you now." *Just in case.*

He cocked his head to the side as if he had heard the thought and matched it with a blistering look of his own. There was an ingrained fear tiptoeing in my core as I felt the doors of the palace staring. There was something about this place that just felt *wrong*, even from outside the door. Maybe it was the unnecessary, exorbitant reminders of wealth, or maybe it was the knowledge I had gained, knowing now why it stood at all. Either way, its soaring walls and watchtowers made my skin crawl with dread.

"Thank you," Zymir said. The ends of his cheeks twitched and pulled up, revealing a kind smile that somehow didn't feel quite as out of place as I expected it to. It filled me both with joy for having seen it, and dread for the reason behind it. "I'll stay outside the courtyard perimeter. And I will meet you by the arch when you all are finished." He reached toward his chest and rested his palm over the outline of the coin beneath it. "Good luck."

A subtle, resounding vibration tickled my chest where my necklace sat. Nerves. Nerves heightening my senses.

I nodded, and we started up the stairs. We neared the door, and I clenched the silver knocker that had etched moons along the top and bottom. Before lowering it, I peeked behind my shoulder to see Zymir already gone. With a churning stomach, I lowered the handle and knocked it hard in three short bursts. My heart felt suspended in anticipation as we waited to be let it.

"Coming!" A cheerful male voice called from behind the door.

The door creaked on unused hinges, opening inwards toward the castle center.

"Welcome," an older gentleman greeted us, his grin darting between his bushy gray mustache and short-trimmed beard. "How can I help you?" He crossed his arms casually, the deep red fabric of his sleeves tucking into himself, revealing the emblem on his chest denoting five stacked silver moons.

"We need to speak to the council." My voice was as confident as I could feign it to be.

There was always a Sheirsan council, even before the Royal Family disappeared. A table of eight men appointed by the King himself. They continued to monitor the more serious matters pertaining to the kingdom, such as when they stopped years of conscription but raised the taxes.

"It's quite late," he murmured. "May I ask what brings you at this hour? I can request a meeting, but many are already tucked away in their chambers."

Pricking sensitivity rose the lines on my wrist, and I could feel the silver mark heating itself. I stiffened and turned my arm inward, but not before his eyes flickered at the movement.

"It's sort of a long story," I stammered, "but it's in the interest of Alaria's safety, and it's incredibly urgent. Please, I won't be long, but it'd be easier if everyone—"

"Tomorrow, we can—"

"We don't have time to wait until tomorrow."

His bushy gray brows creased with annoyance, though his face continued to play courteous host. My wrist was throbbing. I could feel the pounding in my eardrums. *Not now. Please, not now.* The pain cracked, and my fingers arched in instinctual reply. Curiosity twinkled in his eyes, and I knew it hadn't gone unnoticed.

"Please, sir," Tillian smiled, smoothing some curls back off his head. "We come bearing news of an invasion. And every second we waste is a second the enemy draws closer."

"Enemy?" His laugh was husky as his gut bobbed. "Boy, we don't have enemies." As he laxed his arms down at his sides, an unusual calm settled over his features. "Hold on," he leaned forward, squinting at Tillian, "Those eyes... I'd know those eyes anywhere."

Tillian inhaled deeply in anticipation.

"You're Marek's son." He breathed. "Same damn eyes on the both of ya."

I hadn't realized how well-known Tillian's father had been. I hadn't even considered how that may play into our favor. Tillian's back straightened at the recognition, and he held out his hand.

"Tillian, sir." His voice took on an air of propriety that I'd never heard before, and the stranger met his handshake heartily. The older man pulled in his hand, bringing him to his chest and wrapping him in a one-arm hug.

"Eluard, friend of your fathers." His cheeks flushed, and he straightened out the more casual crimson tunic the officials wore. "I'll get you all a meeting at once."

He ushered us in, arm wrapped over Tillian's shoulder. Kori looked up at me quizzically, but I shook my head. I hadn't known how high-ranking Tillian's father was. I thought he was simply a guard with bad luck stationed at the Icesone Mountains at the wrong time. If he was anything greater, they never spoke of it. And whatever front my friend was donning, it felt off. He shuddered at his father's name, hence why I'd only ever heard it once or twice. The pride in which his voice shook responding to it now was a tone I'd never heard.

It was a greasy tone that warped the features of his familiar warmth into something much colder and more calculated.

At least it had worked. The cards he'd hidden revealed themselves favorably, and that's what mattered. Or at least that's what I repeated to myself, following a rounded hall through the Sheirsan palace. There were oil paintings in ornate golden frames, some larger than the man leading us. Men with white beards, ladies with curled hair, all with patronizing smiles painted into eternity. The walls glistened against the low amber light of the chandeliers.

Something is wrong. My wrist was burning, and with every step, I focused on the sound of my boots against the marble instead of the flesh shuddering. *Something is wrong.* My mind felt vast, open and listening, memorizing each windowpane we passed and scouring for anything out of place. Kori and I trailed the men, apprehensive steps out of cadence with theirs.

"I'll get the others," the Councilman said over his shoulder.

The hall broke into a series of individual desks, each one personalized with statues or dried flowers or a cup full of pens. Each wooden station was crafted uniquely—engravings lining the legs and edges of the wood, which varied in color from onyx to snow. Personalized touches for each of the eight officials rested at their respective desks.

A tapping of metal chimed in an informal rhythm further ahead, blocked by the width of the Councilman. The noise tapped again, and I realized it was the sound of rings, rings clacking against the wood of one of the desks up ahead, impatiently filling the silence of our approach. They rolled one after another, an arrogant, impatient droll.

I hurried my legs so that I could peer beyond his arm and stared at the bottom of black leather boots crossed at the ankle atop the furthest desk in the corner. The knuckled fingers rattled against the wood, and my feet stopped moving.

"You said she'd be here *before* nightfall," the gray hair in front of me said and continued walking, widening the gap between the exposed boots and my line of sight.

I yanked Kori's elbow before she could continue. The hum of my wrist placated for a few breaths, as if knowing I needed to catch it to stay focused and alert. The boots fell from the table to the marbled floor beneath it with an echoed *thump*.

"It seems they must've tarried." Desmond smiled at me, and a ripple of fear trickled up my spine.

The Councilman waved at him dismissively and stopped when he noticed our pause. "Were you not seeking an audience?" His round eyes narrowed knowingly. "Desmond, watch them. I'll return with the others in a moment."

It felt like the air was water, and my lungs were drowning.

Eluard strolled past us, returning toward the entrance where other halls broke to the wings where the council resided. Once his back was behind us, he turned slightly with a patronizing smirk and added, "I told you. Sheirsa doesn't have enemies." His steps continued coldly behind us until they could no longer be heard.

"Tell me." Desmond played with one of his necklaces, running the chain through his fingers. "Was it the ship you struggled with, or did you simply get lost?" Kindling caught in the wild of his eyes. "I had left only hours prior, and still had an entire half a day on your arrival."

Tillian's fists were shaking, and Kori stayed a step in front of me, frozen where she had stopped when I snatched her wrist.

"Do your people know?" Tillian's words came out with a lot of flustered air. "Do they know you're here?"

"I never lied," he said, face falling stern. "I'm here early, and they're awaiting my orders, as they should be."

My fingers twitched hungrily for a blade to chuck toward his head. And my wrist, subdued only momentarily, was ablaze with energy begging to be released.

"Now, now," he cooed, "you'll need to conserve your strength. You're the star of the show tonight." The sharp line of his jaw tightened. "You're why we're all here."

Tillian's head snapped back, at first with suspicion to see if I understood the words, and then with a flood of concern when he realized I didn't.

"I knew you were a coward," I felt myself saying. "It seems all you know is betrayal. Betrayal to your kingdom and then betrayal to your friends. Why *are* you here, Desmond?" His name on my lips felt sour.

"Nonsense. I'm a man of my word." He placed his hand over his heart. "And when we discovered that wall in your mind, we knew there was only one place with the skill to have placed it. And craftsmanship at that level, well," he curled his upper lip, "it meant you were something special. Something the kingdom would trade heartily to have returned to them."

The word *returned* made my head woozy.

"But I won't spoil your evening for you." His eyes sparkled. "I've done my part by ensuring your arrival. By letting you and your friends believe an attack on Alaria was imminent, you, in turn, played *your* parts wonderfully. Rushing to save the kingdom." He laughed, and the sound ground against my skull. "How noble a bunch you are. I'll forgive the offense of you thinking escaping my mountain was that easy."

It *had* felt rather simple. We had crossed the paths of few. But I had attributed it to timing, to them preparing for their attack. I had attributed it to luck. The coin resting against my sternum felt heavy and revolting.

His voice hardened. "I *let* you leave."

I stepped toward him, my vision blurring with frenzied rage.

"Why? Why're you doing this?" I didn't let my hands drift to my belt. Not yet.

The harshness in the greens of his eyes softened. "We all have our roles to play, Adelliah. I've played mine," he crossed his hands in front of him, "and now it's time you play yours."

CHAPTER 30

"You need to get out." I reached for Kori, pulling her toward me. "You need to get out, you need to warn Zymir." I looked over my shoulder at the looming doorway all the way at the other end of the hall.

"I'm not leaving you two here," she said, shaking off my hands.

Tillian's tight lips told me he understood what I was thinking—that whatever was about to happen, whatever their plan was for luring us here, was now complicated by Desmond's presence. And he knew everything. He would've had time to share the knowledge of her Weaver Mark. Tillian's family ties would surely make his safety here more promising. And for reasons I couldn't yet deduce, they needed me, tricked all of us with the sole intention of me coming here.

Which I had done so obediently, even without knowing.

I should've known it was a trap. I should've known it was too easy. And I shouldn't have led my friends into this place with me.

I should've gone alone.

Everything would have been fine had I gone alone.

But I didn't. Maybe I was selfish, maybe I was a fool for enjoying their company. Because here I was now facing the very real prospect that my decision had led them directly into harm.

And I'd pay any cost to avoid that fate.

"Kori, *leave,*" I ordered, though it felt more like a beg.

As the dark blonde strands shook back and forth again, a panic struck up my wrist in urgency. I held her hands in mine, pleading, feeling Desmond's amusement as he watched us.

They're headed back now. There was a dark cloud shadowing the desolation in my mind. Thick, swirling clouds were crackling. A boom of thunder swelled, and lightning cut through the clouds.

My hands singed, and she pulled away in horror at the black lines left on her skin from where I had held them. She reversed on her heels, stared between us, and swallowed. And then she ran.

Her legs pushed her toward the entrance, the frantic steps loud and clumsy.

When she reached the door, she pulled with her entire body so it'd move against the heavy hinges. And as her shadow left through the gap she had opened, I was thankful she didn't look back.

Bodies piled in from the connecting halls. Men and women in various decorum, fanciful evening attire, even those already in sleepwear. They were a blur, a mess of shapes and colors.

Eluard was at the front, brows creasing as he realized we were one fewer.

"You let the small one leave?" he directed toward Desmond, who nonchalantly shrugged.

"I came here as proof of my claim regarding *her.*" He stood finally, as more people joined the room. "The others aren't my concern."

Eluard closed in toward a desk near the front of the room, one with crimson paint and piles of papers stacked on the corner. He pulled out the shelf beneath the lid and revealed a wire ring with two thick, blackened keys.

"To the gate." He breathed.

"To the gate," Desmond replied, his eyes widened and lips pursed.

"You'll follow nicely," Eluard said to me, bored. "I'd prefer you waste no energy on our way—"

"Absolutely not." I snapped my blades into my hands. "*What is going on?*" I was practically shouting. My brain hurt from the confusion and adrenaline flooding in.

"At the gate, it'll all be explained," he said matter-of-factly.

"We can't take on over a dozen men," Tillian whispered dryly to me. "We might as well—"

"No." I planted my feet firmly, my wrist sizzling in delight. "No, I'm done following orders."

The air sparked with static.

"We weren't asking, Adelliah," another man behind Eluard chimed in. "We know of your debt with the kingdom, your employment with Nox."

They knew my name, and they knew of the soul collecting. I couldn't see straight. Reality was turning sideways, and the storm clouds begged to downpour.

"Help us, and we'll pay off your debt." Eluard had walked toward a hand-woven rug at the back of the room, behind the last row of desks. He lifted the corner, pulling it back to reveal a hatch that he effortlessly unlocked and snapped open. The metal door of the latch clanked against the marble, and the open mouth gave way to descending stairs. "Clean slate, no more working with Nox."

No more working with Nox.

I had never considered what that future would look like. Not seriously, at least. I could make my own money, live my own life, settle wherever I like, or travel without preference.

"And how do you know he'd accept that?" Our work was profitable, and Nox was driven by wealth. Tallied debt or not, he'd find a way to trap me, keep me working for him indefinitely. He always had.

Eluard urged the bodies to funnel down the stairs before him. One by one, the indiscriminate faces disappeared downward, a stampede of steps echoing beneath the ground. When all who remained were myself, Tillian, Eluard, and Desmond, he finally flicked his wrist toward me and fixed his collar.

"Because we employ Nox. And subsequently, he'll do anything we tell him to." His winning smile ignited lights in my vision.

My head was spinning. Nox had been contracted by Sheirsa.

Sheirsa was responsible for providing loans to the people, using Nox as a lavishly dressed puppet. And yet I'd have no time to contemplate that reveal until I had ensured my friend's safety.

One last time.

I'd follow others' commands one last time.

And then I'd be free.

Relief washed over Tillian as I wordlessly followed toward the hatch. The light from the room peered down the steps, one by one, further from the chandeliers until the stone walls were pitch black and darkness entombed us. I let the sound of the other feet lead me, curving around the stairs that winded deeper and deeper. A loud thud from overhead told me that the hatch had been closed. Tillian squeezed my shoulder, warming it with the recognition of his body right behind mine.

The stairs opened to a room.

A carved amethyst ring stood suspended by metal feet. The circular *gate*, evidently, was as tall as the intimidating archway that led into the palace and was wider than all the people in the room lined up shoulder to shoulder. It was monstrous, a carved feat of ingenuity as I tried to organize my scrambled thoughts.

The deep violet was streaked with white veins across the reflective face. Whoever had created this, smoothed the edges so perfectly that the stone appeared wet. Glistening under the ambiance of lit candles suspended in holders periodically throughout the room, the pure magnitude made it hard to remember to breathe.

Concealed by shadows, groans whimpered from a cage at the back of the room. The bars caught the flickering light here and there, illuminating several pairs of frightened eyes and tied mouths.

"They were on trial," Eluard explained when he caught my stare glued to the bars, "for the most heinous of offenses. Murder, rape, incest... We have been holding them down here away from the other prisoners. Even amongst fellow criminals, the atrocities they committed are regarded as so vile, if we don't separate them, they'll be murdered in their cells."

Stifled cries responded accordingly. There were six pairs of shadowed eyes, hauntingly pleading through the tears wetting the gag in their mouths.

There was a metal table at the center of the room, pivoted so that it angled up and down. There was a hole cut out near the top and straps for limbs at the corners.

"What exactly am I doing here?"

Thunder roared in my skull, angry for not being allowed to diffuse.

"That mark on your wrist," his eyes shot down and sparkled in awe, "consider it a gift of sorts. A gift that allows us to break into where the Royal Family has been stuck all these years."

There were several boiling questions I had, but I sputtered out, "How?"

"We'll need you to lie on this table for your safety, and we'll tap into the navigation mechanism in order to pinpoint their exact location. Once we have the coordinates, we'll activate this portal and bring them back."

"For my *safety*?" I eyed the straps apprehensively.

"In the interest of transparency, the process of getting your tattoo to adjust to our parameters may be a bit...unpleasant. And to reduce risk to yourself and others, we need to have you secured."

Don't do it, my mind called out. I hushed my nerves aside.

One last task. One more. And I'd be free.

Tillian reached out and stopped me as I stepped toward the table.

"You don't have to do this." His words were strained. "You don't, we could leave, I could help you pay off—"

"Don't." I removed his hand, gently, bringing it instead to the side of my face against my cheek. My pulse steadied for a moment against the roughness of his touch. "This burden isn't yours to carry. And if it helps bring the family back, maybe I can actually bring about some good."

I let the tenderness fall as I released his fingertips and approached the table. I turned so that the coolness stretched along my back as different unfamiliar faces worked to strap in my ankles and wrists.

The assorted council members were interspersed amongst the room, most around the candles, hunched together with eager, famished stares.

Eluard held a syringe shaped much like my own, except the barrel of his was as thick as his hand, and its contents were already full. I peeked around his fingers as he stationed himself beside me, the leather straps now pulled tight.

I waited for the familiar crimson liquid that Nox would routinely administer, but in the gaps, I only saw silver. Silverly, billowing swirls rushing over and under themselves.

"Hold still," he ordered, bringing the needle closer to my wrist.

"Hang on, that's—" My mind vibrated as the tip of the needle met the lines screaming on my skin.

The syringe held that which my vials did. The purest essence of a person. Their soul, their being, their energy. Whatever the specifics, I had only ever withdrawn it.

And now it was being deposited in my veins.

His thumb steadily clamped onto the plunger, forcing more of the viscous liquid into my arm as I thrashed against my ties. I watched him empty the syringe until my focus went past the needle and landed on the floor. The tiled floor, where small squares clung so tightly, they nearly overlapped. I remembered this floor.

My blood was on fire. It was devouring my insides and incinerating my core as it coursed through me. I could feel it climb my spinal cord and latch into my head, curved talons ripping into the flesh.

The walls shook, and the room imploded around me, ripping me from this world and tunneling me elsewhere. The only constant variable was the screaming, permeating through time and space as I tumbled with it, listening to the disjointed terror that had left my mouth and swarmed all around me.

I warned you.

This time the voice was very much not my own. Thick and raspy, drenched with oozing power.

The agony was black, the spiraling held nothing to see. But I landed harshly, nothingness breaking to a barren wasteland of orange sand. I was in the confines of my mind, or a place similar. The pain was so disorienting I didn't know which made more sense.

Why are you here?

The voice was agitated, the words chopped out. But yet, familiar.

I was on my knees, knelt into the clay underneath, my body reacting slower than usual as I tried to stand but found myself stuck. I urged my legs to straighten, and they unfolded awkwardly, my footing causing me to sway back and forth.

In the distance, there were moving shapes speeding along the horizon where the orange ground met the sky. I peered my head upward, curious as to what the sky in this place looked like, and quickly wished I hadn't. Suspended lines of shimmering twine, like a never-ending willow tree, hung above my head. Endless strands of sparkling fish lines twinkling like stars in the sky.

Why are you here? It asked again.

I wasn't sure where I was or what I should be doing. I started walking in the opposite direction of the fallen wall—so this *was* my mind—toward the vastness where I had last seen Osyren.

My wrist had stopped burning. I glanced down to see the tattoo completely gone, my flesh bare. There was no smell here, no breeze.

Nothing made sense. I ran, because I could, and because I couldn't figure out anything better to do. I ran on newborn legs, stumbling and catching myself, kicking sand behind me as I created as much distance as I could between me and the wall. It was a hopeless reminder of the disappointment and shame I felt when they reached into my mind and came up empty-handed. I ran further and further until distant voices punctured into reality.

Voices on top of voices spoke all at once, their words unintelligible.

The sparkling strings dropped lower, a few of them hovering within arm's reach.

You don't need to run.

You are no mere guest here.

The world paused, and from the up-kicked sand and dust, I felt a body appear behind me. A presence. I turned, and everything I was went limp.

Pale muscled skin, as if carved from marble, stood before me. His arms looked as if he'd dipped them into ink, solid blackness stretching up beyond his elbows. His face was covered by a white mask with intricate black symbols painted over it. The eye holes in the mask revealed nothing of the face beneath it.

Why are you here?

"Where is here?" My words felt foreign, the voice mine but somehow more chiseled.

His broad chest was exposed, and black veins trailed from his covered forearms up over his chest and across his abdomen.

Ah. So, they told you nothing. No loss, though, they only speak in half-truths regardless.

A sudden realization clicked into place, and I stepped backward. "It was your voice," I whispered in shock. "It's been your voice I hear." In Icesone, at dinner, all the dangerous promptings, the haphazard suggestions. When my voice broke to another's, it was *this* voice.

My voice? You think those thoughts were not your own?

He reached out an arm, curling his fingers, requesting I draw nearer. I inched back.

Do you not think yourself capable of such actions? It was your hand that killed the man in the alley. You cannot hide from the parts of yourself you do not like.

The mask was mesmerizing, and I caught myself distracted by the lines and loops.

You don't remember.

"Enlighten me."

The council of your kingdom has been stealing from me for generations. Trapping souls so they could recycle their own. Using them to extend their own lives, gifting themselves presents that were not theirs to offer. But it wasn't enough.

Their mortal bodies have started to crumble.

Their flesh tires.

Once they were done trying to rid the land of monsters, they faced an eternity unopposed. But immortality is not without a price. And it seems they are willing to sacrifice even more than they already have to accomplish it.

Words seemed to escape me. The vials had gone to the highest bidders, and I had finally learned why. Because even in death, these people were still not free from their oppression and misfortune. When at long last they could rest, that spark was instead funneled elsewhere, warped, and used for another's gain. And I had enabled that transaction.

They've desecrated the order of things. They've poked holes in the woven fabric separating our worlds. And yet they are not finished, not satisfied by gutting the land and tainting its inhabitants.

There are far greater crimes happening as we speak. And if they succeeded in creating you, then they will succeed again.

I was done, and I needed out. I needed to get far away from this place and these ramblings. I turned to run, but my body refused. He stepped forward, calm and calculated. A mishmash of other voices sounded around us, overlapping tones in varied pitches.

I fought where I stood, my body a prison I needed to escape from. The shimmery strings from above beckoned to me, several strands dangling before my face, light sparkling and welcoming. I laced my fingers through the threads.

Don't!

I could feel my skin again, actually feel it. I felt my breathing, my pulse, my functions reminding me that this was my mind and my body lay tied to a table far from here.

The mask's cheeks lowered as if in disappointment. More gods damned disappointment, and my anger returned in a vicious flare that coated my throat in flames.

"Who do you think you are?" The words came out feral and wicked as the strands of light splashed into my face. And in the moment of light teasing my focus away, I remembered that creature in the prisons beneath the mountain, the creature who had told me, 'When the strands appear, pull,' and without a second thought, I snatched the lines into my palms.

I held on, tugged, pulling myself higher away. I rose from the sand and continued to pull, the seemingly only option in the endless desert of mirrors and lies.

Who am I?

The shadowy silhouette laughed, a sound that bounced within my bones and rattled my teeth.

I am Ryv.

Ryv, the God of Death.

CHAPTER 31

When I woke, I wasn't sure if I'd gone back to my body or was simply in another nightmare. There was screaming and blinding lights. The amethyst gateway was shattered, shards of purple stones littered across tile. Hands grabbed at the leather straps that had rubbed my skin raw, hastily trying to unlatch them.

Where the ring of finely crafted stone once stood, now stood others. A family, all blond and beautiful, strikingly so. There was so much commotion, so much panic.

"It's okay." I looked down at Kori's pained eyes, her fingers moving too slow with panic. "It's okay," she reassured, though it felt more to herself than to me.

Guards were rushing down the stairs, swords drawn. I smelled ash and saw soot and blood on the collage of the ground. My heart banged against my ribs. I stifled bile that backed up into my mouth. Lifting my gaze from the disaster on the floor, I couldn't hold it in. I slapped at Kori, moving her to the side as vomit gushed out of me. The cell no longer held prisoners—it held corpses.

I clamped my eyes shut.

I didn't want to look.

I didn't want to think.

Take me back, take me far from here.

I could feel the strands in my hands again, their warm glow. I had held six of the strings, their flicking ends peeking out from the heel of my hand. I remembered as I pulled, propelling myself far from that place. And I remembered when they snapped. When everything went weightless, and I floated toward the broken ends, desperate to pull them back together.

The moment they snapped, the warmth was gone, and a cold silence froze my return.

A string pulled too taut by my hands.

And I knew as I looked at those bodies, somehow knew deep in my core, that somehow, someway...I had pulled those lines of light, those connections to life, and as they had splintered and snapped, so too had I ripped their souls from their bodies, leaving crumpled husks in their place.

Returned were six bodies pulled through from a place far away. The golden locks of the royal family glistened. There was not an heir missing, all six with entitled, gleeful faces.

I wanted to burn the palace down to its foundation. Let everyone here burn with it.

"Stop it," she warned, undoing the last tie as my body fell from the table. "You've exhausted yourself already. If you use any more magic, it'll kill you. We have to go. Zymir gave me five minutes to get you out."

I tried to stop the thought that blurted itself instinctively.

Then let it kill me, I wanted to say.

Then let me pay for what I've done.

"Where's Tillian?" The weight of my body was too much for my legs, and I collapsed onto my knees. I scanned the room and couldn't see him. My breathing frenzied. Where was he? *What had they done?*

Three guards turned away from the stairs as the rest charged a man surrounded by slashing weapons. Desmond stood at that center. It was Desmond with swords cutting for his neck as he dove around one. He flipped around to sink his blade into his attacker and moved on to the next. Fire sparkled in his stare as he cut his way through the attacking guards, leveling them one by one. Bodies thudded to the ground as his hair pressed against his head in a sweaty mess, his chest drenched as he fought through the encroaching crowd.

I followed his line of sight as flames erupted around his blade.

He was headed straight for the king.

He was dizzyingly fast, a crisscross of metal screeching against metal, his flames bending to his whim as he lashed them out behind him and took his blade into one hand. The spare hand directed the red-hot stream of heat, scorching bodies who approached from behind.

"Tillian left with the council," she said. "We can figure it out later, we—"

The three guards charged us, with Kori as their target. She gulped and turned her back toward me as I knelt, immobilized by exhaustion and forced to watch her sling the morningstar around and deflect their advances. She swiped and blocked the first two men. But the third rounded to her left, darting below her arm and pushing her off balance. She fell backward and didn't catch herself in time. She stuck her weapon out in front of her and slowed the force of his sword as it made its way into her shoulder. Blood pooled immediately, staining her tunic.

The guard stood over her, arms raised to deliver an ending blow. A lick of fire wrapped toward him and slithered around his neck, burning a cut clean through. Desmond didn't bother to acknowledge his assistance as the detached head plummeted beside her.

Desmond was only a few yards from the king now, who huddled around his family, leaving the guards to their job. But more were piling in, the air a rancid mix of burned flesh and iron.

Kori was already back on her feet, hurling her weapon over her shoulder and pushing back the guards, much to their surprise. Raised, confused brows met her fierce stare as she continued to hold them off.

I stumbled, my muscles screaming in protest as I stood, picking a blade from my belt. I held the helm between my fingers and launched at one of the guards flanking her, its blade sinking into his temple. She turned and smiled from ear to ear, wiping splattered blood from her face with her sleeve. The blood soaking her top was spreading, and her efforts to fight off more bodies was expediting its release.

Desmond had been stopped, a wall of guards between him and the royals. But he continued whipping his flames over their shields, reaching for the king in desperation. Their ends soon retracted, their reach lessened. He, too, was tiring from the energy expenditure of wielding both blade and magic.

Another blur of crimson uniforms faced me. I ducked, narrowly avoided the broadsword falling toward my skull. Its tip caught my ear as liquid dripped down the side of my neck and blocked my hearing as the orifice filled.

I should've run when Kori told me to. The room was a mess of the dead and screaming steel.

More guards advanced on Kori, and she retreated toward where I hobbled, her body still standing in front of mine, defending my life with her own.

A guttural roar discharged from the open hatch above. Weapons paused, and even the groans of the dying stilled. A feral growl rippled down the stairs, and with it, a beast unlike any I had seen before. Snow-colored fur coated its arms and legs, and two swirled horns jutted from its head. Its face was a bare skull, no skin censoring it, its elongated shape animalistic, wolf-like. But this wasn't a canine, and it stood on two feet, several heads above the men as it rushed into the crowd, tearing into necks and swinging its open mouth left and right.

Its fur was drenched in sticky redness as teeth and claws made their way to Kori and me.

My body had all but abandoned me. And while wavering against the few soldiers left, it would do nothing to protect us from the claws of the beast.

The space to the stairs cleared. Men left, either gutted or actively fleeing.

The skull and horns turned toward us. No more bodies left to decimate. Kori reached for my hand and tugged it gently forward. Maybe I'd have the opportunity to ask the god of death the questions I had thought of after all.

When I stared into the skull, I found vertical pupils and golden irises within the sockets. A careful growl fell from the creature's lips as it walked closer. I let myself drift away in the familiarity of that golden gaze, and the ballad of weapons clanked once more.

The exhaustion was closing in, my energy dangerously depleted.

"It's time to go," Kori said, squeezing my hand harder.

I waited, ready to let the creature charge, to let it sweep me into its arms and let my vision fade against the sounds of squelching and agonizing groans. But a snap of air from behind me cracked open the space between us, forcing my grip to detach as my body flew limply against the table.

The King of Sheirsa had stepped forward, his family safely behind him, arm pointed at me as he barked orders that I couldn't hear to the men surrounding them. Several soldiers stormed to fill the gap between my friends and me, a wall of bodies and blades poised to divide us further. Their eyes were cold, obedient. A man not much older than I leaned down, aimed to lift me from the ground. And my limbs still wouldn't budge, the muscles numb and useless.

As they stood around me, securing their perimeter, I saw their viciousness as they took in the beast, their mouths salivating to wedge their swords beneath the fur and rip out its heart. A monster, an enemy—a friend trying to save a friend.

Kori had retreated into Zymir's arms, poised between his hunched stance as Desmond was corralled toward the stairs with them. Tears drenched my cheeks, and my throat burned. I had exhausted myself, endangered them, and they would risk their lives again if they had to break through the King's highest-ranking officials.

"Leave!"

Kori's lips were trembling, her head shaking back and forth. I could only hear the disjointed words around me, their barked orders to leave me un-harmed...But to kill the others.

"Leave! You have to leave!" I was screaming, yanking the words from my chest despite how much they burned coming out.

I met Zymir's eyes, met them in his truest form, and conveyed the thoughts I felt as best as I could in the ferocity of my glare. He lowered his chin in a silent promise and flung Kori into his arms. Desmond slipped up the steps in front of him, and they ascended toward the hatch, Kori's sobs echoing off the stone.

Pain tightened around my temples, the throbbing oozing out the last of my coherence. I couldn't even struggle or thrash as the hands of strangers retrieved me from the ground, hoisting my body over a random guard's shoulder.

I didn't know what would await me. But I did know now that my capture was secured, it made their chase for the others hold far fewer stakes.

And I hoped that would be enough. I hoped they could get away, safely, and *live.*

We are alone now, the voice whispered as darkness snuck into my sight.

We are alone.

CHAPTER 32

The smell of almonds graced my nose. I was awake in a bed larger than any I had laid in before, plush crimson blankets folded over top with a mountain of pillows behind my back and head.

There was paneling along the walls, velvet curtains pulled over the expansive windows to block out the sun, and at the end of the bed, a handsome face with concerned blue eyes and freshly washed curls. Tillian rested his hand over the comforter, pressing gently against my ankle beneath it.

"I knew if nothing else, the smell of almond cookies would wake you up." He chuckled, sliding further up toward me.

The was a soreness lingering in my head, an ache around my neck from healing blisters. Despite that, a smile found my lips.

"You know me too well." I laughed, tilting my head toward his outstretched fingers.

I struggled to remember where I was or how I'd gotten here. I searched my thoughts and found only watered sunlight, blurry glimpses into vague feelings.

"What happened?"

His skin brushed my cheek and found the back of my head.

"King Bryce and the royal family have returned," he grinned and quickly added with a sparkle of admiration, "all because of you."

Why did the words feel so wrong? Why did my insides feel so empty as he spoke?

"But the others?"

There was a crackling static that buzzed in my skull but was instantly soothed by a cooling balm, followed shortly by the pressure of his lips parting mine. He pulled back, springtime in bloom, as he scanned my face and rubbed my temple with his thumb.

"What others?"

The walls of the palace were familiar and comforting, and yet I blinked in confusion.

What others? I struggled to find an answer. But a distant breeze met a solid barricade in my mind, which yielded nothing in response. He chucked, standing from the bed, though I reached out my hand in protest. He lingered with his fingers between mine, bringing them to his lips as he kissed their tips.

"I'll be right back," he promised. "Let me go get those cookies." He winked and scurried out of the room.

I slouched back into the sea of covers, tugging them up so they sat beneath my chin and stretched. A few yawns in rapid succession escaped me, and my eyelids closed again, beckoning me to rest more.

My hands wrapped around myself, one cupping into my waist and the other resting atop my chest.

As my palm sat against the bare skin of my sternum, a shiver trailed up my arm.

I swore I used to have a necklace here.

ACKNOWLEDGMENTS

I want to take a moment to thank everyone who has helped me along this journey. Being an indie author is no easy task. It can be emotionally draining and there were plenty of times I wanted to stop.

Despite the difficulties, my friends and family have been there encouraging me every step of the way.

Thank you to my wonderful husband, Billy, for listening to my imposter-syndrome filled rants and always helping me stay the course. My coworkers, for being so eager to read my words. My fellow Instagram writers for nudging me along with motivation and empathy. My father, for mentioning my book to others far and wide. My friends new and old, for their excitement. My step mother, for telling me when I was young, that one day I would be an author. I didn't believe it at the time, but here I am.

And lastly, thank *you* for reading my debut novel. I wouldn't be here if it wasn't for you, picking up this book and journeying into this world that I have created.

Book 2 (and many others) are on their way. I look forward to sharing them with you.

About Me

I live in Michigan with my husband and our four cats. My life revolves around them, and I bring them up in nearly every conversation I can. Together, we have created a home where we enjoy hosting holidays and festivities for our incredible group of friends.

I started writing when I was in middle school. Maybe even younger. I'd get lost in books and escape to a world of a magic and possibilities. After a bad bout with technology though, I lost my first story when our family computer crashed. It wasn't until earlier 2022 that I finally started writing again.

My love of reading is what has always spurred me to write. But as many of you know, once you get older, your time becomes occupied with bills and work and cleaning and laundry... And creative pursuits therefore took a backseat.

I found the time to start reading again this year. And with it, rekindled my love of writing. It can be hard to allocate spare time to yourself, or to do things that simply bring you joy. But I urge you to take that time if you haven't.

It's worth it.

You are worth it.